PRAISE FOR MARTIN EDWARDS
The Rachel Savernake Golden Age Mysteries

MORTMAIN HALL

"[A] triumph, from its tant unnamed dying man begins to crime, through its scrupulously channels Agatha Christie."

—*Publishers Weekly*, Starred Review

GALLOWS COURT

2018 Dagger in the Library winner
2019 eDunnit Award shortlist, Best Crime Novel
2019 CWA Historical Dagger Award nominee

"Martin Edwards's *Gallows Court* seems awfully bloodthirsty for a traditionally designed mystery set in foggy old London in 1930… Fans of clean-cut heroes will be rooting for Jacob, although some of us would rather see devilish Rachel clean his clock. Either that or commit a clever, more refined murder of her own."

—*New York Times Book Review*

"Highly atmospheric, spine-tingling fun… The way that Edwards keeps deepening the creepiness of this mystery until the very end is utterly stunning."

—*Booklist*, Starred Review

"Superb—a pitch-perfect blend of Golden Age charm and sinister modern suspense, with a main character to die for. This is the book Edwards was born to write."

—Lee Child, #1 *New York Times* bestselling author

"Exceptional series launch from Edgar-winner Edwards… The labyrinthine plot is one of Edwards's best, and he does a masterly job of maintaining suspense, besides getting the reader to invest in the fate of the two main characters. Fans of Edgar Wallace's classic *Four Just Men* won't want to miss this one."

—*Publishers Weekly*, Starred Review

The Lake District Mysteries

THE DUNGEON HOUSE
The Seventh Lake District Mystery

"Readers who enjoy British procedurals will find this multi-dimensional, multigenerational case very satisfying."

—*Booklist*

THE FROZEN SHROUD
The Sixth Lake District Mystery

"Martin Edwards uses the lovely landscape of the Lake District to fine effect… Clean prose and an engaging love for the territory."

—*Chicago Tribune*

THE HANGING WOOD
The Fifth Lake District Mystery

"With an unforgettable ending, this outstanding cold case will attract Lynda La Plante and Mo Hayder fans."

—*Library Journal*, Starred Review

THE SERPENT POOL
The Fourth Lake District Mystery

"...an excellent choice for discerning readers who want an unusual and challenging puzzle mystery that will keep them guessing until the final pages. Wow!"
> —*Library Journal*, Starred Review

THE ARSENIC LABYRINTH
The Third Lake District Mystery

Shortlisted for Lakeland Book of the Year

"A beautifully crafted book."
> —Ann Cleeves, CWA Gold Dagger winner

THE CIPHER GARDEN
The Second Lake District Mystery

"Fans of the British village mystery who are very particular about setting should trek to *The Cipher Garden*."
> —*New York Times*

THE COFFIN TRAIL
The First Lake District Mystery

Shortlisted for the Theakston's Old Peculier
Prize for Best Crime Novel

"A wonderful, absorbing read: a crime deeply rooted in the past, a beautifully evoked sense of the Lake District..."
> —Peter Robinson, *New York Times* bestselling author

Other Awards

2020 CWA Diamond Dagger for a career
of sustained excellence
2019 CWA Short Story Dagger shortlist
for "Strangers in a Pub"
2018 CWA Dagger in the Library for the author
whom library users particularly admire
Poirot Award 2017
2017 CWA Short Story Dagger shortlist
for "Murder and its Motives"
Edgar Award for Best Biographical/Critical
for *The Golden Age of Murder*
2014 CWA Margery Allingham Prize for "Acknowledgments"
CWA Red Herring Award 2011
2008 CWA Short Story Dagger for "The
Bookbinder's Apprentice"
2005 CWA Short Story Dagger shortlist for "Test Drive"

Nonfiction

THE STORY OF CLASSIC CRIME IN 100 BOOKS

2018 Macavity Award winner for Best Nonfiction
2018 Anthony Award nominee for Best Critical/Nonfiction
2018 Agatha Award nominee for Best Nonfiction

"This is an exemplary reference book sure to lead readers to gems of mystery and detective fiction."
—*Publishers Weekly*, Starred Review

Also by Martin Edwards

THE GIRL THEY ALL FORGOT

A LAKE DISTRICT MYSTERY

MARTIN EDWARDS

Poisoned Pen
PRESS

Published by Poisoned Pen Press, an imprint of Sourcebooks
P.O. Box 4410, Naperville, Illinois 60567-4410
(630) 961-3900
sourcebooks.com

Originally published as *The Crooked Shore* in 2021 in
the United Kingdom by Allison & Busby.

Library of Congress Cataloging-in-Publication Data

Names: Edwards, Martin, author.
Title: The girl they all forgot / Martin Edwards.
Description: Naperville, Illinois : Poisoned Pen Press, [2022] | Series:
   Lake district mysteries ; book 8
Identifiers: LCCN 2021023666 (print) | LCCN 2021023667
(ebook) | (trade paperback) | (epub)
Subjects: GSAFD: Mystery fiction. | Suspense fiction.
Classification: LCC PR6055.D894 G57 2022 (print) | LCC PR6055.D894
   (ebook) | DDC 823/.914--dc23
LC record available at https://lccn.loc.gov/2021023666
LC ebook record available at https://lccn.loc.gov/2021023667

Printed and bound in the United States of America.
SB 10 9 8 7 6 5 4 3 2 1

For Nigel Moss, a connoisseur of detective fiction

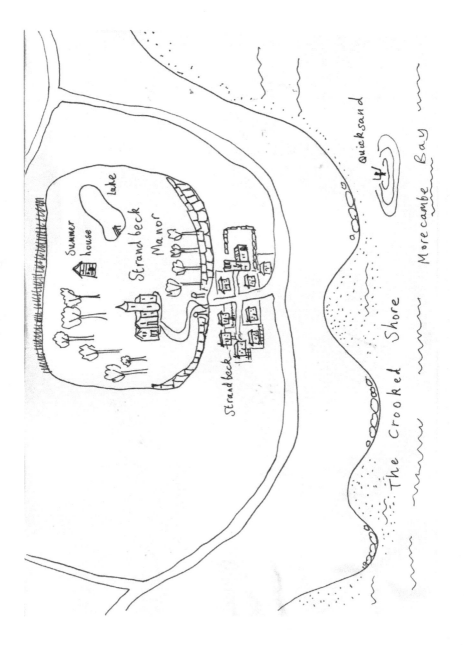

AFTERWARDS

"So you want to know why I killed Ramona Smith?"

"Yes," Hannah Scarlett said.

"You disappoint me, Detective Chief Inspector. I thought you're a mind-reader."

Hannah refused to rise to the bait. "I'd rather hear the full story from your lips."

"To satisfy your curiosity?"

"Ramona wasn't a bad woman. Selfish, yes, but many people are."

"She loved to have men eating out of her hand."

"But she wasn't cruel."

"Wasn't she?" A shake of the head. "Perhaps beneath the surface we're all capable of cruelty. Even if we don't intend it."

"Perhaps."

"You sound sceptical." A long sigh. "All right, you win. Let me explain why Ramona Smith had to die."

Chapter One

Why has a murderer come to Strandbeck?

Kingsley Melton sat on his favourite bench, gazing out over an expanse of sea and sky, shingle and sand. This stretch of coastline was jagged with tiny creeks and estuaries. People called it the Crooked Shore. Local legends warned that strangers who outstayed their welcome suffered seven years of bad luck.

Superstitious claptrap, Kingsley insisted if anyone mentioned this as he escorted them around the luxury dwellings at Strandbeck Manor. A story born of narrow-minded parochialism and misunderstood history. His heart wasn't in the denials. He loved things of the past, including the old wives' tales. Even if they did deter prospective purchasers, at least they kept the tourists away.

For Kingsley, the shoreline was a safe haven, a sanctuary from the rest of the world. The peace and quiet soothed him. He loved it best at times like these, when his brain felt scrambled. Some days he sat here for hours on end, as if hypnotised by the restless tides.

The water looked lovely, but to him it was frightening. He'd never learned to swim, and in his nightmares he often drowned.

Always he kept a safe distance from the waves. Even so, they fascinated him. The bay never stopped changing. Sandbanks appeared and disappeared; by turns the water was dappled or calm. A touch of salt seasoned the air. Listen and you might catch a curlew's mournful cry.

A skinny jogger passed the bench, loping away from the shore towards the bay. His hair was short and dark, and he wore a plain black singlet and white shorts. Without breaking stride, he glanced back over his shoulder, as if startled by the sight of Kingsley, a stoop-shouldered man in his fifties, smart in suit trousers and tie, contemplating the flicker of sunlight on the water.

Kingsley paid the jogger no heed. He was lost in dark imaginings.

———

What is Logan Prentice doing here?

Seeing Prentice again had shocked him to the core. Five minutes earlier, Kingsley had turned out of Strandbeck Lane to rejoin the coastal route leading to the Crooked Shore. A grubby blue Fiat van with a dented wing was parked by the roadside, hazard lights winking. The driver was down on his hands and knees, mending a puncture. Someone had scrawled *Wash Me!* in the dirt on the back of the van. As Kingsley drove past, the driver glanced up. He looked like a little boy lost.

It was a miracle that Kingsley didn't swerve off the road. When he parked in his usual spot a quarter of a mile away on the grassy verge above the shore, his hand were still trembling.

Logan Prentice was in Strandbeck. That slender figure, the floppy fair hair, the cherubic lips, the wide-eyed mask of inno-cence, all were unmistakeable. Kingsley had spent two years trying to scrub every last memory of Prentice from his mind. Now the past had returned to haunt him.

It didn't make sense. Kingsley associated Prentice with Sunset View, a care home perched on a hillside above Windermere, fifteen miles away. What on earth would bring him to the Crooked Shore?

Kingsley hadn't set eyes on Prentice since a drab afternoon at Sunset View, with rain streaking the double-glazed windows of the big conservatory. Prentice was playing old show songs on the piano, his hair tousled, a seductive smile plastered across his face.

"I could have danced all night," he sang.

Never mind dancing all night, most residents of Sunset View couldn't keep their eyes open for ten minutes at a time. Except for frail, little Ivy Podmore, fiddling coquettishly with her pearl necklace and smirking with adoration at the pianist serenading her. And except for Kingsley's mother. Mamma sat bolt upright in her armchair, scowling in disapproval.

Later that day, Ivy Podmore was found dead in her bed. Mamma loathed Logan Prentice and was convinced that he'd killed Ivy. Smothered her with a pillow, it was easily done. Ivy's fatal mistake had been to announce to all and sundry that she was making dear Logan her heir. The last instruction Mamma ever gave to Kingsley was that he must not let the killer get away with his crime. Within twenty-four hours, she suffered her fourth stroke and this one proved fatal.

Ivy's murder was shocking, and Logan Prentice's wickedness undeniable, but Kingsley had enough on his plate without doing the police's job for them. His mother's death had prostrated him with grief. What could he do about Prentice if everyone else thought the sun shone out of the boy's neat little backside? It wasn't his place to interfere. Anyway, he daren't push Prentice any further, for fear of provoking a cruel revenge. The people in charge ought to shoulder responsibility. Instead, they were adamant that old Ivy had passed away in her sleep. Natural causes. The care assistants were unsurprised, and the manager declared that she'd had a good innings. As for the doctor…well, whoever they were, people in charge so often let you down.

Clouds swarmed across the sky; the afternoon was chillier than expected. Kingsley scolded himself for leaving his jacket in the car. Why in heaven's name did he place his faith in the forecasters? They should be paid by results, like him. He gave a little shiver, not that he blamed the Met Office for that. It was all Logan Prentice's fault.

"I've got you under my skin," Prentice would croon.

He'd got under Kingsley's skin, all right. The man called himself an IT consultant, but he was just a computer nerd operating from a tiny rented bedsit above a Vietnamese takeaway in Ulverston. Prentice used to visit Sunset View twice a week to tinkle the ivories. He'd wormed his way into the home manager's good books after repairing her laptop. She and her carers believed he turned up to entertain the residents out of the goodness of his heart. Their gullibility made Mamma snort with cynical laughter. At one time she'd adored the young pianist, but she'd become jealous of Ivy, who was old and ugly and hopelessly senile, yet the apple of Logan Prentice's eye. The young man always made a fuss of his pet, claiming to feel sorry for her because she had no family. He talked about spreading the love and bridging the gap between the generations. The staff thought him a saint, but Mamma knew better.

"On the make, is that lad," she whispered loudly, prompting a carer in a bilious plum-coloured uniform to make furious shushing gestures. "Never mind those big puppy eyes. He's only bothered about what he can get out of her. She's so besotted, she's changed her will. Her solicitor ought to be frogmarched out of the Law Society. Absolute disgrace."

"Poor old soul." Kingsley dreaded his mother getting herself worked up.

"She's as daft as a brush." One of Mamma's favourite insults. "Acting like a teenage girl. She's eighty-two if she's a day."

And because Mamma's memory was fading fast, they repeated the same conversation twice more before he said goodbye.

———

Kingsley stared out at the bay. So often things were not as they seemed. This was true of his own life and it was equally true of the lonely coastline. From a distance, the beach appeared seductive. In reality, it was all mudflats and quicksand. The bay was a haven for birds. Redshanks, ringed plovers, curlews, you name them. They loved the mud because it teemed with life. Cockles, shrimps, lugworms, easy prey for those greedy long beaks. Natural victims. Like Ivy Podmore. Like Vesper, in a sort of way.

Kingsley ran a palm over his forehead. Throughout his life, headaches had plagued him. Over the years, the doctors had routinely dismissed his anxieties, and even Mamma's sympathy rubbed thin. She accused him of exaggerating how poorly he felt in order to gain attention, but that was unfair. His life wasn't straightforward; he'd contended with more than his fair share of bad luck and stress.

As for today, it was turning into a disaster.

He'd so looked forward to taking Tory Reece-Taylor out for lunch. At her best, she was delightful company, and the previous time they'd met, she'd been on top form. They'd kissed each other goodbye, and she'd touched his wrist and said how much she valued his kindness. But from the moment he arrived at her home in Strandbeck Manor, everything went wrong. Her greeting was perfunctory, and even before they arrived at the restaurant in Ulverston, her breath was sour with alcohol.

During the meal, Tory's mood became truculent. She picked at the pricey sea bass, complaining that the doctors wouldn't allow her red meat, and rewarded his cheerful chatter with monosyllabic grunts. He'd invested in a bottle of Chablis, and she knocked back most of it, which was par for the course, doctors or no doctors.

His confidence that she'd mellow once they returned to the Manor proved to be misplaced. Hoping to earn a few brownie points, he tipped her off about a forthcoming increase in the service charge for her flat, only to provoke a furious tirade. It was an own goal, an unforced error. He should have kept his mouth shut. Any chance of an invitation to stay for a spot of supper evaporated. Every other minute she checked her watch, making no secret of her impatience for him to be gone. Finally he surrendered to the inevitable and said he'd better make tracks.

"See you soon," he said as he was leaving her flat.

"Mmmm." Tory didn't bother to get out of her armchair, let alone give him a farewell kiss.

And then, as if this rebuff wasn't bad enough, five minutes later that bad penny Logan Prentice turned up.

———

Kingsley felt as if he were in a trance, his mind a muddle of dismay and anxiety. When he gazed out into the distance in search of inspiration, he spotted a dark figure heading straight for the sea. The jogger who had passed him a few minutes earlier. Must be. Nobody else was in sight.

Kingsley gasped.

Is he mad?

The bay was treacherous. Since time immemorial, the deceptive calm of the vast stretch of water had lured the unwary to their doom. Everyone who lived in these parts knew stories about people who were cut off by the bore and drowned. Beneath the seemingly placid surface ran hidden channels and shifting sands. The underwater landscape changed from one day to the next, wilder and less predictable than any kraken. Some folk died a few yards from dry land, caught by the currents surging up gullies between ridges of mud. The tide was ruthless. It never showed mercy or remorse, sweeping in faster than anyone could run. Even the swiftest jogger.

Kingsley got to his feet and shouted.

"Hey!"

The figure kept advancing into the bay.

"What are you doing? You need to turn round!"

Kingsley's heart pounded. His waving was frantic. A terrible memory invaded his brain.

Vesper, Vesper.

Arms outstretched as if in crucifixion, he bellowed, "Danger! You're in terrible danger!"

As he watched, the man stopped moving.

The currents were ferocious and the quicksands deadly. If your feet got stuck, you started to sink. As the mud sucked you down into its clinging depths, the liquid hardened. It was like being set in concrete. You pushed your arms and legs out to spread the weight and give yourself a little more time, but once your knees slid beneath the surface, it was time to abandon hope. When the waves crashed over you, there was no chance of escape. The more you struggled and fought, the harder the mud squeezed against your body. Trapped and helpless, you were forced to watch and wait for the incoming tide. Salt water rushed into your eyes, your nose, your mouth, filling your lungs until you could no longer breathe.

"For pity's sake, come back!"

Now he couldn't see the man. Only water.

"Help!" Kingsley screamed. "Help!"

In his distress he turned to right and left, desperate for a miracle.

But he was all alone on the Crooked Shore.

Chapter Two

"This man who walked into Morecambe Bay last week," the Police and Crime Commissioner said. "Darren Lace. Does the surname ring any bells?"

Detective Chief Inspector Hannah Scarlett considered. Kit Gleadall had breezed into her office as she tried to catch up with her admin. She was losing the battle with bureaucracy. This was her first morning back from a conference in London, where she'd presented a paper about the challenges of leading a cold case review. She was still surprised to find herself described as an expert in solving unsolved crimes. Impostor syndrome, her old failing. Would she ever free herself from its clammy, unsettling clutches?

Despite having been away for only a week, she'd found herself wading through hundreds of emails. Many had spreadsheets attached. The PCC's arrival counted as a welcome distraction. Their one and only previous meeting had intrigued her, and the way he'd parked his bulky frame on the other side of her desk meant this was more than a courtesy visit.

Gleadall was younger than the typical PCC, late forties, at a guess. Belying his rugby player's build, his movements were nimble, and he had the long, well-manicured fingers of a musician rather than a businessman. Although he'd made his money in London, he'd never lost his Carlisle accent. Fizzing with energy, he'd made no secret of his determination to break with the hands-off management methods of his late predecessor, a superannuated politician twenty years his senior. Since his election, Gleadall had hit the ground running. Running too fast for some members of Cumbria Constabulary, for sure.

Police officers hated any form of change, let alone change imposed by a rank outsider with a taste for sharp suits and a background in public relations. Like her colleagues, Hannah had feared the worst, but her initial impressions of Gleadall when he came to talk to senior officers were unexpectedly favourable. His questions about cold case work were incisive. Wonder of wonders, he even seemed to pay attention to her answers. Perhaps his heart was in the right place after all. Or did that simply demonstrate his expertise at marketing?

Her head was swimming with budget figures and the small print of internal recruitment protocols. Who was Darren Lace; why should his name mean anything to her? Preoccupied with drafting her conference paper, she'd barely glanced at reports of the Strandbeck suicide.

"Sorry, sir, my mind's a blank."

Kit Gleadall showed his white teeth. He looked like a bear with a tailor in Savile Row. "Let me give you a clue. How about Gerald Lace, known as Gerry Lace, does that sound familiar?"

Yes, in some distant recess of her memory, it did. Was he a criminal? For some reason, she associated Gerry Lace with trouble. Not for her personally; she had near-perfect recall of her own cases, especially her occasional calamities, and she was sure he didn't feature among them.

"I can't quite…" she began.

"Okay, I can see Lace's name means something to you," he said. "He was a prime suspect in connection with the murder of Ramona Smith. The disappearance of Ramona Smith, strictly speaking. Any the wiser?"

Hannah nodded. At last she had a clue as to where this was heading. "Ramona was the Bowness woman who went missing…what? Twenty years ago?"

"Twenty-one," Gleadall said. "Ramona worked in a bar in Bowness. One evening she vanished and was never seen again. Nobody has heard of her from that day to this. All the evidence suggests she's dead, but the investigation got nowhere until it was taken over by a very experienced detective. I'm told you used to work with him. Detective Inspector Ben Kind?"

Hannah hoped she wasn't blushing. How much did the PCC know? It was no secret that she'd been close to Ben Kind during his lifetime. More recently, she'd got even closer to his son Daniel. At one point she and Daniel had lived together. Not so long ago, she'd thought that one fine day, they might become a couple on a permanent basis. Now she was less sure.

Brushing thoughts of Daniel away, she said, "You've done your homework."

"Yes." Gleadall didn't preen. If he was vain, and Hannah suspected he was, at least he had the wisdom not to parade his ego. "So far, I've only skimmed the records, but it was an extraordinary case. I'm told Ben Kind was a shrewd cop."

"Correct."

"He was convinced that Gerry Lace murdered Ramona Smith, and the evidence seemed to back him up. Lace was tried for murder, but he was found not guilty, much to everyone's consternation. He was lucky in his legal team and even luckier in his jury. Nobody else was ever charged, and although the file was never officially closed, the investigation fizzled out. Not that Lace enjoyed his freedom. He and his family were given a rough time. They had a shop, which some hooligans daubed with offensive graffiti. The business went bust, and he couldn't find another job. He suffered badly from depression."

Hannah felt a prickle of dismay. "The case is coming back to me now."

"Lace protested his innocence, but you know the Lake District. Everyone knows everyone else. He was a pariah, with no chance of sinking back into grateful anonymity, the way you might in London or Leeds. In the end, he couldn't take any more. Even if you're as guilty as sin, living with suspicion must be hellish. How much worse if you did nothing wrong? You might not see the fingers pointing or hear the tongues wagging, but you know what other people are saying to themselves." Gleadall lowered his voice. "You got away with *murder*."

He paused, but Hannah didn't utter a word.

"You recall what happened?"

She took a breath. "Lace committed suicide. He left his widow a note blaming police harassment. Specifically on the part of Ben Kind."

"That's right," Gleadall said. "Remember how he died?"

Hannah's eyes widened. At last she was joining the dots.

"He drowned himself."

"Yes," Gleadall said. "He walked into the sea at Strandbeck. Twenty years on, to the day, his son followed his example. He took his own life in precisely the same way as his father. On precisely the same strip of coast."

———

Behind the wheel of his ancient Vauxhall Corsa, Kingsley Melton bumped down the looping lane that connected

Strandbeck with the rest of the world. The ancient settlement nestled under a rocky incline close to one of the narrow creeks that gave the Crooked Shore its nickname. There was only one way into Strandbeck and one way out. For him, its isolation was part of its allure. So was its misty, mysterious history.

In his mind's eye he pictured the Druids of ancient times, building their temple of stones up on Birkrigg Common. The Romans had come later to mine iron ore. Folklorists insisted that the village of Strandbeck was once much larger than the present hamlet, until the waves washed most of the buildings away. In this medieval catastrophe lay the origins of that folk tale about strangers outstaying their welcome and suffering ill fortune.

A big house had stood on the same site for centuries. Strandbeck Manor was the latest, built for a nineteenth-century entrepreneur from Manchester. Once work on the Manor was completed, he set about establishing a creek port on the Crooked Shore, a rival to Greenodd on the river Leven. He dreamed of making his fortune as a shipping magnate, but lack of capital led to his downfall. Within weeks of beginning the port's construction, he ran out of money. Only thanks to the generosity of his trustee in bankruptcy was he allowed to stay on in the Manor. While he lingered on as an embittered recluse, the new Furness Railway bypassed Strandbeck, and his vision was stolen and improved upon a few miles west at Barrow. When he could take no more, he loaded a rifle and put a bullet through his brain. Grist to the mill of those who claimed that a miasma of doom clung to the Crooked Shore.

This history of misfortune never deterred Kingsley from coming back whenever he got the chance. His love affair with this place had lasted far longer than any fleeting romantic attachment. Now he depended on Strandbeck for his bread and butter.

He worked for Greengables, the virtual property agents, and his main task was to look after the Manor and its occupants while striving to market the apartments which remained unsold.

This was his first time back at the beach since the tragedy. The drive from his bungalow in Bowness felt like a rite of passage. Watered by forty-eight hours of nonstop rain, the fields were lush and green. Nature's process of constant renewal taught a life lesson. He needed to put the past behind him. Time to make a fresh start.

Strandbeck was quiet. *As the grave* sprang to mind. No, scrub that. Think positive. People came and people went. The bay would last forever.

The emergency services had left no trace of their frantic efforts to save the jogger. Nor had the rubber-neckers who flocked to the Crooked Shore once news got round that a man had run calmly to his death in the bay. Kingsley half-expected to find the bench covered in floral tributes, in the sickly sentimental modern fashion that he found so repellent, but the only flowers were a single bunch of lilies, accompanied by a note in a round, unformed hand.

In Memory of Darren
My Love, My Life
Cruelly Taken
Rest In Peace, Darling
Jade

Jade was the woman he'd seen on television and read about in the papers. Blowsy, heavily made-up for the cameras, and vociferous. Intent on luxuriating in her fifteen minutes of fame. She was no doubt making a song and dance on social media, not that Kingsley had any truck with tweeting and all that rubbish.

It wasn't as if Jade was the dead man's widow. On the contrary, she was nothing more than an ex-girlfriend. She'd given up on their relationship before Darren Lace gave up on life.

Overhead, a gull wheeled. Kingsley caught a glimpse of white plumage out on the mudflats. A little egret was on the prowl, black bill poised for action, ready to stab its prey. Kingsley closed his eyes and inhaled the damp air, casting his mind back to his last time here, visualising the doomed jogger in his black singlet and shorts.

His spine tingled with apprehension. Was this how it felt if you were a murderer returning to the scene of your crime? Burdened by guilt, dreading exposure? Deep in his heart, he felt sure the answer was yes. There was no escape. As regards the death of Darren Lace, though, he was entirely innocent. In a so-called civilised society, the way he'd been treated after Lace's death was an outrage. Not for the first time in his life, he'd committed the cardinal error of being in the wrong place at the wrong time.

How shocking to witness a suicide, to watch a man deliberately end it all. To sit on the shore as the fellow waded into the bay until the quicksand trapped him and the salty water flooded his lungs. Kingsley still couldn't believe what he'd seen. The death of a grown man, in front of his eyes.

When the emergency services arrived in response to his garbled phone summons, he'd tried to describe what had happened. His breathless explanation made little sense. Surely it was an understandable reaction to a shattering experience? Not for the first time in his life, he'd been the sole witness to the final moments of a fellow human being. Shock and horror overwhelmed him. He felt as if he too were succumbing to the onrushing tide.

———

The rescuers did their utmost, risking their own lives, but there was never any hope of a miracle. You could survive for hours if the tide was out and you held your nerve. Quicksand was an accomplice, not a killer. You didn't die simply because you were stuck, unless you fell in headfirst or lost your footing. What finished you was the water. Once the waves came crashing in, you had no chance.

At first Kingsley felt like a hero. Waves of sympathy lapped around him, gentle and unthreatening. Because he couldn't swim, there was no way he could have saved the man single-handedly, but he was the person who had summoned help. If Fate had been kinder, everyone would have hailed him as a saviour. It was only when it emerged that he'd seen the man earlier, jogging out on to the shingle, and that he'd failed to warn him or sound an alarm, that he sensed a subtle shift in the mood.

"You *ignored* him?" a voice demanded, brimming with incredulity and scorn.

No, no, Kingsley insisted, it hadn't been like that at all. He had so much on his mind, he was miles away. He barely restrained himself from adding that he wasn't his brother's keeper. How absurd to imply that somehow he was in the wrong. If anything, he was a victim too.

The spell broken, his cheeks began to burn. How could he make people understand? When a pleasant young woman asked if he'd mind taking part in a news conference, he almost bit her hand off. A journalist offered a handsome sum for an exclusive interview, explaining that this was a priceless opportunity to set the record straight, so of course he said yes to that as well.

With hindsight, he'd blundered by talking so freely about what happened. He should have known better than to trust the media. Their only interest lay in conjuring up a story sensational enough for readers to salivate over. It wasn't enough for a man to die of his own volition. Someone else must take the blame.

A freelance reporter with an Antipodean accent wrinkled her nose, as if sniffing for a scandal.

"Tell us about your conscience, Mr. Melton. Does it trouble you?"

"Why should it?" he retorted. "I did my best."

"Really? I'm so sorry, did I misunderstand? Isn't it right that you waited until Mr. Lace was too far out to be rescued before you called for help?"

"I didn't see him!"

Her chin jutted forward, hatchet-sharp.

"You're a native of the south Lakes, you told us so. Brought up to respect the tides of Morecambe Bay. Accustomed to the hidden dangers. If you'd acted five minutes sooner, it would have made all the difference. Didn't you think to say something to Mr. Lace when he jogged right past you? Because you admitted seeing him then, didn't you?"

The newspaper interview, with his remarks set down in black and white minus the context of a friendly chat with a sympathetic reporter, made him look like a callous attention-seeker, content to watch a disturbed man lope to his death without lifting a finger to help until it was too late. The legend of the Crooked Shore gave the journalists an opportunity to ginger the story with a touch of melodrama.

As if that were not bad enough, they discovered the connection between the suicides of father and son, twenty years apart. It gave them an excuse to make a meal of Gerald Lace's acquittal of the Ramona Smith murder. What a miserable fiasco that had been. Kingsley had hoped and prayed that Ramona Smith had long been forgotten.

The interview appeared in a tabloid newspaper, previously Kingsley's favourite. The photograph of him was grotesquely unflattering. At first he'd barely recognised that gaunt, hollow-eyed man who looked as though he'd seen a ghost. His fine head of hair was his pride and joy, but on the page, in black and white, it looked faintly ridiculous and almost effeminate. He'd never buy another copy of that poisonous rag. It was an absolute disgrace.

"Call me irresponsible," Logan Prentice used to sing.

The cruel irony lay in the journalistic innuendo. It was as if Kingsley's personal irresponsibility had led to a man's death. The reporting was slanted, dripping with bias and bile. If anyone was to blame for what happened, it was Logan Prentice. Kingsley might not have seen a ghost, but he'd spotted a murderer in Strandbeck. Was it any wonder that he'd scarcely noticed Darren Lace passing, far less realised that the man was determined to die?

———

"A woman called Jade Hughes is kicking up a stink," Kit Gleadall told Hannah. "Darren Lace's ex. She left him six months ago, couldn't cope with his long-running mental health issues. Her way of dealing with grief is to blame us."

"She feels guilty about walking out on him?"

"The word she keeps using is *devastated*. According to her, everything is our fault. Darren Lace posted a note to her on the day he died, making it clear he'd never got over the way the police supposedly persecuted his father. The press scent blood. Crucifying that sad loser who sat and watched Lace wander into the bay isn't enough to occupy them. They're having a field day over the connection with his father's death." He mimicked a hoarse newspaper vendor: "*Police Condemned over Strandbeck Tragedy*, read all about it!"

Despite herself, Hannah was tempted to smile. The new PCC obviously fancied himself as a performer. To be fair, he wasn't bad.

"As for social media, the trolls are already out in force," he said ruefully. "Hashtag Gleadall Out!"

She sighed. "Yeah, the police were too incompetent to solve Ramona's murder or find where her remains are buried. We couldn't even fit up an innocent man efficiently enough to secure a conviction. Darren Lace's father was the fall guy. Now our failures have cost another life. What do you intend to do about it, Mr. Commissioner?"

"Got it in one. Cumbria Constabulary has let down two families. The victim's, as well as the suspect's. Naturally, they want a full response from the PCC."

"And?"

"I've bought myself twenty-four hours…"

Hannah couldn't help butting in. "You mightn't solve the case quite that quickly."

He laughed. "Believe it or not, even I'm not that ambitious. If I learned anything in the PR game, it's not to shoot from the hip. All the same, fast response is as vital as if one's dealing with an armed terrorist." He winced, as if remembering past embarrassments. "Actually, I've come across one or two journalists who would make rather good terrorists. I said we'd go back to them tomorrow with a definitive statement, that I wanted to familiarise myself with the details before setting out our plan of action. That's why I wanted a word with you."

"I see."

And it was true, she did see precisely what was coming. Kit Gleadall read her mind and gave a confirmatory smile.

"The murder of Ramona Smith is a cold case. Luckily for us, we have a first-rate Cold Case Review Team."

"Thanks for your confidence."

Hannah spoke through gritted teeth. She ought to be pleased, but her team had shrunk so much it was almost invisible. How could they cope with a major enquiry?

Kit Gleadall leaned forward. "Let me make one thing clear. I'm not here to take things easy. It's already clear to me that the Ramona Smith business was a debacle. Without wishing to be wise after the event, nobody comes out of it smelling of roses. We owe it to people to do a better job. Discover what really happened to Ramona. In a perfect world, find her body so that her family can have closure. As for the Lace family, there can never be a happy ending, but at least it's better if everyone *knows*."

Her stomach clenched. Now that Ben Kind was no longer alive to defend himself, he made the softest of targets.

"Is Ramona's family making a fuss as well?"

"Ramona was an only child and her parents split up when she was young. Her mother died before she did, and her father always gave the media a wide berth. Some of the original coverage hinted that Ramona pretty much got what she deserved. In this day and age it seems shocking, but things were different then."

"Perhaps not as different as we'd like to think."

Her mind had shifted into overdrive. Investigating Ramona Smith's disappearance would be one hell of a challenge. All hands to the pump. What were the chances of finding out the truth? Yes, it sounded like just the sort of case her team had been created to investigate. Trouble was, with minimal resources, the likelihood of delivering an answer to such an old mystery was negligible. At least she'd have an excuse for putting her budget forecasts to one side.

"As for Gerry Lace, his wife went on a crusade after he took his own life. She devoted herself to what she called her quest for justice. Never forgave us for the way he was treated and spent years complaining to local MPs and anyone else who would give her a hearing, demanding a public apology and compensation."

"I don't suppose there was ever much chance of that."

Gleadall nodded. "Shirley Lace died of an aneurysm at Easter. Darren was very close to her, and the bereavement probably tipped him over the edge. His sister moved away from the area years ago, and has kept out of it. Jade Hughes, Darren's ex-partner, is the one egging on the journalists. Juicy local stories are few and far between, and this one overflows with human interest. More's the pity."

Hannah took a breath. There was never a good time to introduce a note of caution, but she needed to manage his expectations. "I'll be honest with you, sir. After all this time, it's very unlikely we'll ever turn up a corpse. I realise we have to deal with the press, but we mustn't give people false hope. That will only stoke up more anger."

Gleadall sprang to his feet. His every movement was brisk, decisive. A man who knew what he wanted, she thought. Plenty of them around; what made the PCC different was the confidence he exuded in his ability to get his way.

"Yes, figuring out the truth of a crime committed more than two decades ago is a tall order. But that's the nature of cold case investigation. I've seen the stats, read the reports. Since your team was formed, you've notched up a series of impressive results. That Dungeon House business last year, for instance. Extraordinary."

Hannah nodded. There was a case she'd never forget.

"Time for history to repeat itself. Are you up for it?"

What could she say? "Yes, sir. Of course."

"Very good. See if you can succeed where Ben Kind and others failed."

Hannah couldn't let that pass. "He was the best detective I ever worked with."

"Nobody gets it right all the time. Maybe Gerry Lace was innocent, and the focus on him meant that other suspects were overlooked." He paused. "One more thing."

"Yes, sir?"

"There's a staff do here at headquarters this evening, I gather. A couple of junior officers going off on maternity leave? Thought I'd look in. Not that I want to be a party-pooper, but I said when I took on this job that it's vital for me to get to know people. Understand how things work, what makes you detectives tick. Otherwise, I can't do my job properly."

It was on the tip of Hannah's tongue to say that had never bothered his predecessor. His fatal heart attack while playing deck tennis on a yacht in the Caribbean had created the vacancy resulting in Kit Gleadall's election.

"No, sir."

"One of the leavers is a member of your team, isn't she?"

Hannah had to hand it to the PCC; he really didn't skimp on his research. "Linz Waller; it's her first baby. She's been with me since we set up the team."

"And I hear that someone else has transferred to the north east?"

"Billie Frederick, that's right, sir. Our most recent recruit, but her new partner is based in Newcastle and the travelling…"

"Okay, so you're woefully under-strength. Down to the bare bones."

"Other than admin backup, we have one sergeant, plus a consultant on a fixed term contract. Both are excellent, but even so."

Gleadall winced. "Can't make bricks without straw."

"The years of austerity," she said wryly, "have taken their toll."

"I bet." He allowed himself a smile. "We can't run complex projects on a shoestring. Looks to me as if you've been suffering death by a thousand cuts."

She pushed her hair out of her eyes. "Well…"

He was spot-on. Hannah had spent years rather than months waiting for someone in high office to break the news to her that Cumbria Constabulary could no longer afford the luxury of a unit dedicated to cold cases. A handful of high-profile successes had kept the grim reapers of Finance at bay, but eventually someone was sure to sound the death knell for her team. In the meantime, she'd been starved of resources. At least Kit Gleadall recognised the reality. His candour left her groping for words.

"I've spoken to the chief constable as well as the ACC," he said. "Don't waste precious time conjuring up a business case for new recruits. Consider it done. Two new detectives should help to ease the load in the short term. One with bags of experience, plus someone more junior. With commensurate back office support. It's not enough, but it's a start. Speak to HR tomorrow so they can get the paperwork moving."

Hannah blinked. For an insane moment she was tempted to throw her arms around the PCC and kiss him.

"Thank you…"

He silenced her with a wave of his hand. "There's a catch."

Ah, she might have known. "Oh, yes?"

"I need you to talk to Jade Hughes. An hour ago I saw her myself and gave her my personal assurance that we'd do everything in our power to find out the truth, even after so many years. I did my utmost to calm her down, but she wanted to speak to the officer in charge of the case review to reassure herself that we mean business, and aren't just fobbing her off by giving the old files a quick once-over and then declaring that nothing can be done. The media is itching to give us a bloody good kicking over this business. We need to reset the dial. Good PR will work wonders. So I agreed to her request."

Hannah said drily, "And volunteered me?"

"I'm afraid so." He looked her in the eye. "I won't pretend I found Ms. Hughes an easy woman, but we have to remember that she's suffered a grievous loss. A spot of female empathy may work wonders. Don't get me wrong, I'm not obsessed with public relations, they aren't the be-all and end-all. But we do need to build bridges with the people we serve as well as with the press."

She knew better than to fight against a fait accompli. "Understood."

"You'll see her tomorrow morning?"

"Why not?"

"Excellent. Life's too short to waste, Hannah." As if to emphasise the point, he sprang to his feet. "We need to make the most of every moment. See you tonight."

Chapter Three

Kingsley checked his watch. Time to go. He'd promised Tory that he'd arrive no later than four. Obviously, he could turn up at his office in the Manor much earlier, but he had his pride. He preferred to masquerade as a man in demand, a busy executive who spent his days dashing from one job to another. It never paid to appear underemployed, far less needy.

Tory had called him because she'd spotted an intruder in the grounds of the Manor the previous evening, just before dusk. It was probably something and nothing, she admitted, but she felt she ought to report it.

Her husky voice sounded cheerful enough, and he was glad the incident hadn't disconcerted her, given that the Manor was isolated and she was living alone. He'd been quick to offer reassurance. You'd never think it to look at her, but she had a history of serious heart trouble. The last thing he wanted was for her to suffer any acute distress.

Privately he suspected that the incident wasn't worth worrying about. The grounds to the front of the Manor were surrounded by a long stone wall, but farther back, the rear of the property was edged by rickety wood-and-wire fencing. People occasionally sneaked through a gap in the fence to save walking all the way round the perimeter. He'd seen them do it himself, and six months ago he'd given a couple of young trespassers a piece of his mind. Not that they were in the least apologetic. In fact, they'd been extremely rude.

No matter. What mattered was that Tory was in good humour. Absence evidently did make the heart grow fonder. How exciting that soon he'd be in her company again.

The Manor stood half a mile inland, at the end of a pot-holed lane; rather than walking, he drove there from the Crooked Shore. Turning up for work by car seemed more business-like, and besides, he loved to make the most of his designated parking place. A self-employed contractor in the gig economy deserved to feast on every morsel of status he could grab.

Flicking the electronic fob to open the ornate iron gates, he felt a familiar thrill. Of all the Greengables properties in his portfolio, the Manor was far and away the most prestigious and expensive. Here, he didn't simply represent management, he *was* the management.

Five years ago, the Manor had lain derelict. Ripe for bulldozing. The ground-floor windows were smashed, and patches of roof gaped open to the unforgiving elements. If the building hadn't been so remote, it would have become a vandals' playground. The grounds were wild and overgrown. The deep lake at the rear of the estate was a foul death trap, stagnant and messy with vegetation.

Since the Victorian entrepreneur's bloody demise, the Manor had endured successive incarnations as a progressive school, a care home, and a boutique hotel. After the hotel business failed, the building decayed until it became uninhabitable. The curse of the Crooked Shore hadn't lost its sting.

Salvation came in the form of a joint venture between a firm of architects and a construction company, dedicated to transforming the Manor into a dozen upmarket apartments. The renovations took much longer and cost far more than expected. Merely to transform the lake from an eyesore into an attractive, reed-fringed feature with its own wooden jetty, a natural version of an outdoor swimming pool for residents, required serious investment. The interior had to be gutted and then luxuriously fitted out from top to bottom. As a result, the developers marketed the apartments at prices high enough to make any prospective purchaser gulp. When sales weren't forthcoming, Greengables were appointed as agents, taking charge of sales of the apartments as well as day-to-day maintenance of the Manor and its grounds.

Kingsley was Greengables' local representative. His mother's death had triggered a long and debilitating period of depression, and he'd lost his zest for buying and selling antiques, the only trade he knew. A job with flexible hours, for an online, invisible employer, seemed an ideal way of feeling his way back into working life. Within a fortnight of being handed a contract, he was given sole responsibility for the Manor. In his more cynical moments, he suspected that Greengables regarded the job as a poisoned chalice. Perhaps they'd recruited him because no seasoned property specialist would tolerate the uncertainty of earnings based mainly on commission. He didn't care. Without Greengables, he'd never have met Tory.

Tory Reece-Taylor came into his life forty-eight hours after he took over at the Manor. She was the very first person he showed around the development, an exquisitely dressed woman with thick blonde hair, designer spectacles, and high heels. She explained that she lived in Rye on the Sussex coast. A year earlier, her husband had died following a long illness.

"I'm sorry," he said. "That must have come as a terrible shock."

"Not really. Winston was past his three-score-and-ten. He was twenty years older than me." Her dazzling smile dared him to stammer that she looked not a day over thirty-five. "I was his second wife. Arm candy, I suppose. His ex hated me, but I couldn't care less."

"No, of course not," he stammered. Her bluntness was invigorating but took some getting used to.

"The poor old soul was an accountant who retired early to devote more time to the real love of his life. Golf, such a bloody boring sport. They call it a good walk spoiled, one of the great understatements. Many's the time I've been tempted to bash his head in with a seven-iron and cash in on the life insurance. Poor old soul; he never dreamed what was going through my mind at golf club dinners while his chums were pawing my thighs. I reckon I earned every penny he spent on me."

Kingsley nodded, lost for words.

"In return he indulged my love of travel. The Atacama Desert, Hawaii, Machu Picchu, Goa, Dubai, Japan, you name it, we went there. Everywhere but the Algarve; they've got too many golf courses."

"How marvellous." Kingsley was a home bird. He'd never ventured farther than Rome, and he'd found the Eternal City infernally hot.

"After he died, I splashed the cash on a world cruise. Got the travel bug out of my system, at least for the time being. I'm ready to take my ease. When I got back to England, I decided to sell up in Rye. Make a new beginning."

"You've come to the perfect place!" Kingsley announced.

"You think so?"

"There's a village called Newbiggin just down the coast!"

She clapped her hand with delight, making him feel like a latter-day Oscar Wilde.

"I love the idea of living so close to the Lakes."

Kingsley frowned. "I'm honour bound to tell you that here we aren't *quite* within the boundary of the national park…"

She burst out laughing. "Oh, I knew that already. Don't worry, I'm not really a dumb blonde. And Mr. Melton…"

"Kingsley, please."

She beamed. "Kingsley, you're far too truthful to be an estate agent."

"I'm new in this job," he admitted.

Her giggle was infectious, her personality as overpowering as her lavishly applied perfume. There was something fascinatingly contradictory about her. She was an extrovert, evidently at ease in any sort of company, yet she insisted that she liked to keep herself to herself.

Her aim was to settle somewhere off the beaten track. Rye was delightful, but in summer the cobbled streets thronged with tourists. She was determined to stay close to the coast, and Strandbeck fitted the bill. The hamlet comprised a dozen houses and most of them were either intermittently occupied holiday accommodation or second homes.

The downside of the idyllic setting was a lack of local facilities. The developers' hope that, when the Manor was fully occupied, the residents would create a little community of their own, was still a long way from being fulfilled. There was no shop or post office within walking distance, and although the old Norman church survived, services were only held once a month.

Tory pooh-poohed these drawbacks.

"I won't lose any sleep over any of that. I don't like neighbours, I shop online, and I never believed in God."

Startled though he was by her directness, he found her captivating. He'd been brought up by elderly, conservative parents, and some of their prissiness had rubbed off. To be in Tory's company felt like gorging on forbidden fruit.

As they strolled around outside, she said, "This place is marvellous. Such heavenly seclusion."

Privacy was one of the Manor's selling points. The property was set in twelve acres of grounds, and you couldn't see it from the lane or the paths skirting the perimeter.

"Far from the madding crowd, eh?"

"I've had my fill of madding crowds," she said. "Mind you, once upon a time, being in a crowd saved my life."

"Really?"

Eighteen months ago, she told him, she'd collapsed while out shopping in Rye. A sudden cardiac arrest. She'd only been saved thanks to a passerby who happened to be a nurse. The woman gave her CPR while an ambulance was called. Against the odds, she'd been brought back to life.

"Good grief," Kingsley said. "What an astonishing story."

Honesty compelled him to add, "I'm afraid there's no doctor's surgery nearer than Ulverston."

Tory roared with laughter. "Don't worry. I reckon I've used up my quota of luck. Next time it will be curtains."

Appalled, he put his hand to his mouth.

"Oh, don't look so horrified. None of us knows what tomorrow may bring. My philosophy's simple. Live for the moment. If you've any sense, you'll get me to sign on the dotted line quick, before I keel over for good."

True to her word, before a taxi arrived to take her back to the station, she agreed to buy the show flat, the largest and priciest in the Manor. Not only did Kingsley earn an extravagant amount of commission for a minimal amount of effort, he was bowled over by Tory's vivacity. Thank goodness he had his own base at the Manor. There was every opportunity, every excuse, to see her regularly.

Her decision to spend so much money on an impulse amazed him. The late Winston Reece-Taylor had obviously indulged her whims, and Kingsley understood why. A woman with such verve and personality came along once in a lifetime. Easy to see why a boring number-cruncher had been swept away.

After she moved into the Manor and they became better acquainted, he discovered that she was prone to frequent mood swings. These were baffling and impossible to predict. Her outbursts of temper were savage, and her tongue cut like a knife, but on top form, she was irresistible. Night after night she featured in his dreams. He'd never experienced anything like this before. She'd changed his life.

He passed through the gates and past a clump of sycamores on either side of the winding gravel drive. As he rounded a bend, the Manor reared up in front of him. A granite fortress in the Gothic Revival style, it had steep-sloping roofs of Westmorland green slate, spindly chimney stacks, and a solitary turret by way of eccentric Victorian flourish. With a precision verging on the absurd, he parked within his designated rectangle close to his office.

The truth was, he could have left his car anywhere. Apart from Tory's electric BMW, the place was deserted. This wasn't unusual. A couple in their early seventies owned a modest-sized apartment at the rear of the first floor, although they spent most of the time away providing free childcare of their grandchildren. Otherwise, his only other sale to date had been to Fiona and Molly, a lesbian couple who ran a nail bar in Carlisle and had a sideline of investing in holiday lets. The snag was that competition for bed-nights in the south Lakes was intense, and the high rent and lack of local amenities deterred most tourists.

He was proud of his own private access to the Manor, an unmarked door at the side of the building that led into his office. It gave him a sense of belonging. This afternoon, he let himself in at the main entrance, pausing as usual to admire the magnificence of the communal hall. The lyrical sales particulars he knew off by heart. The restoration of the lobby to its former glory was calculated to take your breath away. The sweeping pan-elled staircase, reconstructed with timber of the highest quality, complemented the original newel posts, while bespoke hand-crafted sash windows combined energy efficiency with elegance in keeping with the Manor's spirit and history. Gothic stone arches, the original fireplace (now occupied by a vase of carna-tions) and a polychromatic ceramic-tiled floor produced, the glossy brochure insisted, a sympathetic yet effortless blend of the traditional and contemporary environmental consciousness.

Crossing to Tory's front door, he pressed the bell. Within moments the door was flung open. Promising, very promising. If she got stuck into the gin, she was capable of ignoring you, no matter many times you rang.

Her wide, welcoming smile displayed a lot of expensive teeth. The sweet, sensual mix of apricot and jasmine in her perfume was enough to make him swoon. The night that they'd become lovers, she'd confided her fondness for Givenchy's *L'Interdit*, and told him that the creamy fragrance possessed the thrill of the forbidden, the dangerous allure of crossing a line.

She wrapped strong arms around him. "Darling, how mar-vellous to see you!"

The vigour of her embrace winded him, but the moist touch of her lips on his cheek was exhilarating. He felt himself responding to her ardour and told himself he'd worried too much. Everything was going to be fine. Last time had just been unfortunate. Even a paragon is entitled to an occasional off day.

"Come in, come in, take the weight off your feet. Let me get you a drink, and you can tell me all about it."

Before he could utter a word, she led him into the living room and then through the glazed doors that gave on to a canopied private terrace. Outside stood a wrought-iron table and cushioned chairs. The perfect place, as he'd explained at the initial viewing, to dine alfresco and watch the setting sun.

"Earl Grey? With lemon?"

The tension in his body oozed away. "Lovely."

"How are you managing? You're even paler than usual. I've been so worried."

He was taken aback. It was unlike Tory to worry about anything. Let alone, he thought unworthily, about somebody else. A woman who had survived a sudden cardiac arrest could cope with anything, but she sounded like a nurse greeting a patient.

Since the suicide on the Crooked Shore, they'd only spoken once. After seeing him on the regional television news, she'd phoned him, agog for details of the terrible tragedy. After his mauling at the hands of the journalists, his response had been terse. The following day, he'd texted to say he was unwell. It was no exaggeration. His crippling headaches had returned, and the time it took to navigate his surgery's online booking system to secure an audience with his GP left him in the depths of despair. Alas, the appointment was a fiasco; the wretched doctor insisted it wasn't safe to give him any stronger medication. What he took was supposed to be powerful stuff, but he insisted it wasn't touching the pain. Unconvinced, she murmured about him going back to see his psychiatrist. He'd flared up and told her straight: the problem was physical, not mental, how many times did he need to repeat himself?

Thank heaven he was on the mend. As Tory poured the tea through a silver strainer, he reflected that she was on her best behaviour.

"Bearing up," he said bravely. "Now, about this intruder. What exactly did you see?"

A smile, uncharacteristically bashful, spread across her face. "Oh, it was nothing. It was getting dark, and as I was about to lock the door to the terrace and draw the curtains, I thought I caught sight of someone outside, close to the trees."

"Man or woman? Young or old?" With a professional flourish, Kingsley produced a ballpoint pen and notepad. "I'll need to write an incident report."

"Oh, please don't. It was only for a split second." She paused. "It was probably only the shadow from the trees."

The pen hovered in mid-air. He might have been a judge at the Old Bailey, about to record a damning admission.

"So you aren't certain that you did see someone?"

"Now I come to think about it, I was almost certainly mistaken. I'm so sorry, I must have panicked."

"Panicked? That's not like you, Tory. Especially since you saw this figure last night and didn't ring me until this morning."

"I wasn't thinking straight. I shouldn't have bothered you about something so trivial."

"I'm here to be bothered," he said portentously. "That's what Greengables pays me for. I've changed the gate code remotely as a precaution."

He handed her a slip of paper with the new number. Tory gave a bashful smile.

"Sorry, Kingsley. I'm such a rotten nuisance. I should have rung you back to cancel, but…well, I was hoping to see you, to make sure you were all right."

He rubbed his jaw. It crossed his mind that the call was a ruse. Tory wasn't above telling lies when it suited her, but then, everybody was economical with the truth from time to time. Including himself. All that mattered was that she wasn't bored with him. If she thought him quaint or old-fashioned or simply a bit odd, fair enough; how could he deny it, how could he pretend to be someone he wasn't? What he dreaded was losing her.

Their affair had so far been sporadic in nature, to say the least. They hadn't yet made love, unless you counted that unconsummated fiasco, which was best forgotten. All the same, their relationship was by far the most important thing in his life. It kept him going, made him feel young and desirable and *masculine*. Yet sometimes when he was talking, he caught her stifling a yawn. The thought she might care enough to invent an excuse to lure him here made his spirits soar.

"Thanks," he said. "That's very decent of you."

"Nonsense. What use are friends if we don't look after each other?"

He wanted to say they weren't just friends. In his own mind, they were lovers, without a doubt. But he bit his tongue.

Impulsively, she took his hand. "Are you really okay? You look rather frazzled."

"It's been rough," he said, opting for plucky stoicism. "But I'll live."

Tory gave a theatrical sigh. "I suppose that's more than can be said for the poor wretch who topped himself."

"I don't suppose I'll ever forget it," he said in a melancholy tone.

"What on earth drove him to such extremes?" she said, unable to disguise her habitual asperity.

"I suppose the memory of his father's suicide twenty years ago…"

She clicked her tongue in disapproval. "Even in my bleakest moments, I've always found a reason to keep going."

It suddenly occurred to Kingsley that it couldn't be easy for a woman of her age to move to a distant part of the country where she knew not a soul, after suffering the distress of bereavement. But if anyone could cope, it was Tory.

"Terrible story," Kingsley said as he drank his tea. "I suppose disturbed minds run in families."

She shot him a sharp glance. "You think so?"

"You must have heard, his father murdered a young woman, but they couldn't prove it."

"Didn't I read that the father was found not guilty?"

"You know what they say." Kingsley frowned. "No smoke without fire."

Chapter Four

"What do you reckon to Gleadall?" Les Bryant asked Hannah at the end of the afternoon. "To be honest, I don't believe in fairy godfathers. Specially not if they wear Rolexes and Savile Row suits."

"A man in a hurry, that's for sure. Beyond that, it's too soon to say. He talks a good game, but he would, wouldn't he? A PR man to his fingertips."

"Rich one, too," Les said. "Sold his business for a king's ransom when he was only forty-five. Told the newspapers he intended to fulfil his childhood dream, roaming the fells of his native county. Didn't take him long to get itchy feet, did it?"

"You've looked him up."

Les nodded. "I was curious. My contract is coming up to its expiry date. It crossed my mind I'd be surplus to requirements. Swept clean by the new broom."

A sudden panic seized Hannah. "You don't want to retire? Tell me you'll sign up for another term. We can't afford to lose your experience, even if Gleadall delivers on this promise of bringing in fresh blood."

Les allowed himself a smile, a rare treat. He'd played the

curmudgeonly Yorkshireman for so long that now it was a way of life. Hannah liked him very much. He was a good detective but above all a man she could trust.

"All right, if you twist my arm, I don't mind helping out a bit longer. It's not as if I want to spend my time fell-walking. Bad for your feet."

"Even Gleadall found you could have too much of a good thing."

"You reckon this job is just a rich man's fancy? Serve for four years and then bugger off to do something more exotic?"

Hannah spread her arms. "Your guess is as good as mine. He's not your typical public servant. My hunch is that achieving things is what turns him on. Making a difference. He's ticked all the boxes in the private sector. Now he's strutting on a bigger stage."

"The shine will wear off soon enough." It never took long for Les's inner sceptic to reassert itself. He consulted his watch. "We'd best get moving. Daren't be late for Linz's send-off."

———

"How much do you remember about the old murder case?" Tory asked. "The killing of the girl from Bowness?"

She and Kingsley had come inside from the terrace after tea and settled down next to each other on the sofa. Their arms and thighs were touching, but as yet he'd made no advances. He was learning. It was unwise to seem too eager. He must take his time.

"Mmmm." Kingsley felt the tension in his shoulders. Why rake over old coals? It was nothing to her.

"The story must have made headlines. There can't be many mysterious murders in the Lake District."

"You'd be surprised," he blurted out.

He was thinking of Logan Prentice and old Ivy Podmore, smothered to death with a pillow at Sunset View. Lately he'd found it impossible to banish Prentice from his mind.

"Really?" She leaned towards him. "I'm intrigued."

He strove for lightness. "Doesn't Sherlock Holmes have a line about that? Something about urban villainy being less sinister than the secrets lurking behind the smiling face of the countryside?"

Tory brushed this literary allusion aside. "I'm not much of a reader."

It was perfectly true. There wasn't a single magazine or book to be seen in the vast open living space. Because this was the original show flat, the carpets, curtains, and principal fittings and furniture had been included in the—suitably inflated—purchase price. On moving in, Tory had bought half a dozen Lakeland landscapes by the county's priciest watercolourists to adorn the walls, but her interest in culture and the arts was minimal.

Material possessions didn't matter to her, although a swish laptop sat on a coffee table and her home entertainment system must have cost a fortune. Yet there were no personal mementoes or knickknacks. One of the many differences between the two of them was that he loved old things and surrounding himself with clutter from the past. The main clue here to Tory's personality or tastes was a large, custom-made gin rack.

"I like a good novel myself," he said. "My father was a passionate reader with a very catholic taste. I was named after Amis senior and my sister after a Bond girl. I suppose I've inherited…"

"Cast your mind back," Tory interrupted. "You were living in the Lake District at the time of the murder, weren't you?"

He wished she wouldn't keep harping on about Ramona Smith. "Oh, yes, I've never moved away. At that time I worked in retail."

"For the family business, didn't you say? In Kendal, wasn't it?"

He felt flattered that a casual remark had lodged in her mind. When they were together, it was unusual for them to talk about their past lives, and that suited him down to the ground. All the same, there were moments when he wondered if Tory took him for granted. She often asked him to undertake little tasks for her, liaising with tradesmen or window cleaners. An ignoble thought had occurred to him. Did it suit her to keep him sweet because he worked for Greengables and with his office next door, he was at her beck and call? No, he couldn't believe she was so calculating.

"My parents owned an antique shop on Kirkland." He paused. "As I say, I had a younger sister, but she drowned when I was nine."

Tory's eyes gleamed. "How dreadful."

"My parents never got over it. Her death cast a shadow over all of us. I started working in the shop after I didn't get into university. Father died when I was twenty-five, and my mother kept the shop until ten years ago. We liked the way of life too much to give it up."

"Why did you sell up?"

"Mamma and I loved antiques but hated managing the accounts. In the end we decided to concentrate on antique fairs. Thankfully, Father owned the freehold of the shop, so we lived comfortably enough on the sale proceeds. The last of the money paid for her care home fees."

"When did you move to Bowness?"

"Actually, I've lived in the same bungalow my entire life. I was born there; it's steeped in memories. You really must come over sometime. Take a look at my treasures."

She pinched the bridge of her nose, as if working things out in her head. "So you were in Bowness all those years ago when that Smith woman went missing. It's a small town, a glorified village, really. You must have bumped into her."

"I very much doubt it." He frowned. "We kept ourselves to ourselves. Anyway, Bowness teems with tourists. In summer you can hardly move for sweaty visitors, gabbling away in every language under the sun. People come and go all the time. When the police said the woman had gone missing, a lot of folk reckoned it was a fuss about nothing. Everyone assumed she'd simply moved on."

"I suppose the trial gave rise to a big hoo-hah. What was his name, that fellow who was supposed to have done it?"

"Lace," Kingsley said. "The police believed that he'd murdered the woman and hidden her body. Rumour had it that he weighed the corpse down with a concrete slab and dumped it in the middle of Windermere. Or maybe dropped it into a ravine on one of the remote fells. When Lace got off, it caused a huge rumpus. Folk reckoned he'd committed a terrible crime and got away scot-free."

"Call that justice?" She sounded disgusted.

"Lace was tried in the court of public opinion." Kingsley shook his head. "It must be terrifying. To be hated so much."

"Don't waste your pity," Tory said. "If he attacked a young woman..."

Kingsley heaved a sigh. "True enough. And he must have done it. Why else would he drown himself? Such a terrible death, it doesn't make sense unless he was tormented by conscience. As for his son..."

"They were obviously a dysfunctional family." She stroked his hand. "I'm sorry those journalists were so horrid to you. If that man was determined to commit suicide, how could you have stopped him?"

"Precisely!"

He ached to fling his arms around her and shower her with kisses. People regarded him as an introvert, a loner, an eccentric, but he had feelings, like anyone else. Sometimes he struggled to control his emotions.

She considered him. "Nice to see you again, Kingsley. Sorry I was sharp with you last time we met."

He felt the pressure of her thigh against his and told himself not to ruin things by appearing too eager. Let alone desperate. He mustered a valiant smile.

"I won't be forgetting that afternoon in a hurry."

"I bet you won't, you poor lamb." She bent towards him and brushed his cheek with her lips. "Now, must you dash off? Surely Greengables have already extracted their pound of flesh for the day? I do hope I can persuade you to stay for a meal. I got some extra food in, just in case. Italian meatballs with pasta, your favourite!"

He wanted to hug himself with delight. Keeping his distance for a few days had worked wonders. The torment the press had inflicted on him no longer mattered. He clutched at her ringless fingers.

"Thanks, Tory, I'd love to."

———

"Linz is good fun," Bunny Cohen said, raising her voice so that she could be heard over the cacophony. "We'll miss her."

The large private function room at Effie Gray's on Lowther Street was packed to bursting. Linz and her fellow maternity leaver had chosen the music, if that's what you called the relentless rap blasting out from the speakers. Hannah had done her bit in terms of circulating before arriving at Bunny's side. She was fond of Bunny, a long-serving DC in her fifties famous for her blunt manner. Her outspokenness had probably cost her more than one promotion.

"Too right," Hannah said. "Incidentally, were you around in the days when Ramona Smith went missing?"

Bunny downed some of her vodka and lime. "Ramona Smith? Yes, I was. And not just around, I worked on the case."

"Really?"

"Yes, I spent a bit of time with Ramona's father in the days before we had proper family liaison officers. Can't pretend I liked Jimmy Smith. He insisted she'd done a runner. Refusing to face facts. Understandable, I suppose. People clutch at straws in those circumstances. Losing your only daughter must be heart-breaking, even if the two of you were at daggers drawn."

Hannah took another sip of Sauvignon. One of the perks of having bought a flat within walking distance was that she could have a drink at an office knees-up. Only one, mind. At a party, the senior officers were on show. You had to make sure you didn't make a fool of yourself, or allow anyone else to make a fool of you. Especially when so many people had their phones out, snapping selfies.

"Sounds as if you remember the case well."

"You never forget a tragedy like that. Young woman, in the prime of life. I was only on the fringe of the investigation and after a fortnight, I was pulled in to another team to work on a major fraud enquiry." Bunny peered at Hannah, searching for clues. "Why do you ask?"

"My team is taking another look at Ramona's disappearance."

"Great news." Bunny knocked back the rest of her drink. "Long overdue."

"You don't think we're wasting our time, after all these years?"

"Far from it. I used to ask myself where her body might be. Buried in woodland, under water maybe?" Her tone hardened.

"And I'd wonder what that bastard might have done to her before she died."

"That bastard?"

"The bloke who killed her. Gerald Lace."

"If he did kill her. There may be other candidates."

Bunny frowned. "Careful what you say, the walls have ears."

Hannah stared. "Sorry?"

"Don't you know?" Bunny moved closer and lowered her voice. "Ravi Thakor was in the frame at the start of the investigation. Fortunately for him, his alibi was fireproof."

"Is that right?"

Ravi Thakor owned Effie's, and over the past ten years had turned it into one of the most popular bars in the south Lakes. A wealthy businessman and local philanthropist with fingers in plenty of pies, he took inordinate care to keep on the right side of Cumbria Constabulary. A few years back Linz Waller had dated his son, and right now Hannah could see her chatting to Ravi, a tubby moon-faced man in his fifties whose natty suits were invariably complemented by a bright red waistcoat. He caught Hannah's eye and lifted his hand in greeting.

"Yeah, Ravi's always been a ladies' man." Bunny waved and Ravi Thakor responded with a nervous smirk before turning back to Linz. "As it happens, he and I once went out for a drink together. Only the once, mind, and only for a drink. This was a long time before he made his millions. If I'd known..."

Her grin was self-mocking. "Actually, no, it would never have worked. He's mad about cricket. Honestly, I ask you. Anyway, our little dalliance was years before he got involved with Ramona Smith."

"Involved how?"

"At the time she disappeared, she was working at Guido's, a bistro he used to own in Bowness. At the time he was still with

Poppy, his first wife." Bunny shook her head. "Like me, he's been married three times. The difference is that as he gets older, his wives get younger."

"So he was a suspect?"

"Yes, but he dropped lucky. Usually he spent every night at Guido's. But the night Ramona went missing, he and Poppy were out celebrating their wedding anniversary. As a matter of fact, Poppy went to the same school as me, she was a couple of years younger. Pretty girl, big boobs. She'd found out about Ramona and he reckoned he'd ended the affair with no hard feelings on either side. He swore he'd behave himself in future. Lying toad, but that's men for you. That night was his wedding anniversary and he took Poppy out for a slap-up meal at the Sharrow Bay."

Hannah nodded. The Sharrow Bay on Ullswater was one of the most renowned hotels in the Lakes. As if its location and splendour were not enough of a draw, it was said to be the birth-place of sticky toffee pudding.

"They spent the night up there and didn't get back till late the next morning. Ravi was able to account for all his movements for the following twenty-four hours. So was Poppy, for that matter." Bunny shook her head. "I was relieved to hear it. I'd hate to think I once snogged a killer."

"So they were both in the clear?"

"Yes, and when Ben Kind took charge of the investigation, he didn't take long to figure out that Gerry Lace was responsible for Ramona's disappearance. His instincts didn't often let him down."

"If we review the case, we have to do so with an open mind. No assumptions."

"I suppose you've got a point." Bunny yawned. The vodkas were taking their toll. "You know, Hannah, I reckon you've got the best job in the force. Putting right old wrongs. Miscarriages of justice, wrongful…"

"Trust me, cold case work isn't a bed of roses. Leads peter out. Witnesses and suspects turn out to have died years back. We run on a shoestring and sometimes we simply can't justify throwing any more resource at a case."

"Yeah, yeah, I get it. All the same, I can't help envying you. Not to mention Linz and Maggie Eyre."

"Even though we have to work with Les Bryant?"

Bunny laughed and they both looked across the room at Les. He'd buttonholed Linz and was no doubt regaling her with one of his innumerable anecdotes about policing in the good old days.

"Into every life a little rain must fall, eh? Les is a dinosaur, but he doesn't bother me. I suppose Linz won't mind leaving all this behind. At least until the baby starts screeching all night. Anyway, if you're looking for a maternity cover, let me know."

"You'd be interested?"

Hannah was taken aback. Bunny had spent her career on the front line and most detectives still regarded cold case work as a dismal backwater. Not proper policing. Even worse, some saw it as an easy option.

"Absolutely. I've got my years in. Last week I had a meeting with HR about taking my pension. This job gets no easier; you know the stress we're under. I'm no spring chicken."

"You look fine to me."

This was no exaggeration. Bunny's dark hair was trimmed in an immaculate bob and she didn't carry a surplus ounce. Thirty years ago, Hannah thought, she must have been stunning. Pity she'd not had better luck with men. A couple of years back, her latest marriage had broken down. That was what the recruitment advertising never mentioned. Police work wrecked relationships.

"Don't get me wrong, I'm not ready for the knacker's yard just yet. HR asked if I'd consider joining the historic sex abuse unit. They are so short-staffed they are bringing in civilians by the busload. But it's not for me. Your cold case team wasn't mentioned. I suppose it's all about funding priorities."

"You never know." Raucous laughter from a gaggle of young PCs was making the din unbearable. Hannah could hardly hear herself think. "Let's talk when we're back in the office."

Bunny's dark eyes widened. "You mean there's a chance that…?"

She broke off as the PCC joined them, a glass of orange juice in his hand. Hannah performed introductions and said, "Bunny worked on the Ramona Smith enquiry."

Kit Gleadall raised his eyebrows. "You don't waste much time, do you, Hannah?"

Bunny gave them a searching glance. "Well, if you'll excuse me, I'll be making tracks. I need to say goodbye to Linz and Jenny. Cheers, Hannah. Good to meet you, sir."

Gleadall watched her wriggle through the crowd. Admiring her neat backside, Hannah suspected.

"Bunny?"

"Short for Bryony, she once told me. Not that I've ever met anyone brave enough to call her that."

"Good officer?"

"Excellent. Wide range of experience. Feisty, but a good team player." She had to bellow to make herself heard. "I think she's tempted by the idea of cold case work."

"Stepping stone to retirement?"

"She's still got plenty of petrol in the tank."

"Like her on your team?" Hannah nodded. "What about her existing role? Will I tread on anyone's toes if I ask for her to be offered a transfer?"

Emboldened by the wine, Hannah asked, "Would that stop you, sir?"

He laughed. "My reputation goes before me, does it? The honest answer is no."

"She's discussed retirement with HR."

"So we're talking about an enlightened form of staff retention? Perfect." He clinked his glass against hers. "To the rejuvenation of the Cold Case Review Team!"

Hannah finished her drink. "I'd better say my goodbyes."

"Yes, I need to go too. Can I offer you a lift home?"

"Thanks, but I don't live far away. The walk will burn off a few calories."

He considered her. "I really don't think you need worry about that."

For a moment their eyes met.

"Thanks again for your support," she said.

"Nothing to thank me for," he said. "Mutual assistance, that's what makes the world go round. I'll see you tomorrow, before the media scrum. You can tell me how you plan to set about reopening the investigation."

Something in her expression made his eyes narrow. "Don't worry. I'm not going to breathe over your shoulder. Or leak operational material to the press in order to get a good write-up."

"Sorry, sir." She felt abashed. "I didn't mean…"

He put a hand on her arm. "No, I understand. When I was running my PR firm, I learned the black arts of spin. To be honest, I practised them, maybe more skilfully than most. That was in another life. My job here is simply to oil the wheels. You're in charge."

She detached herself and gave a brisk nod. "Thank you, sir. Good night."

"Good night, Hannah. See you tomorrow."

———

Kingsley had never enjoyed much luck with women. Over the years, he'd come to place the blame on his mother. Much as he worshipped her, Mamma had always cramped his style. Following his sister's death, he'd become an only child again. He loved being the sole focus of parental attention, but it had its downsides. In his youth, he seldom brought girls home, and when he did, they invariably failed to live up to Sybil Melton's daunting standards. If he'd made it to Aberystwyth University, everything would have been different. He'd have met a nice girl, perhaps a fellow history student, someone who shared his interest in antiques. They could have built a lasting relationship together without outside interference.

As it was, he continued to live cheek-by-jowl with his parents, and his encounters with the opposite sex were few and far between. They were also by no means conventional. Now he felt a gnawing hunger for the experiences he'd missed out on. It was never too late. Not that he hankered after an orthodox family life. Young people had mystified him even during his own youth, and he no more wanted an offspring than a smelly dog or a supercilious cat. But he yearned to share in a partnership that was loving and passionate. How wonderful to be the apple of someone's eye. Someone other than his mother, that was.

Tory excited him. An air of mystery clung to her, this exotic, widely travelled woman with more money than she knew what to do with. Outspoken as she was, she gave little away about her innermost thoughts, and this he found alluring rather than an irritant. He liked to preserve his own secrets and understood anyone who felt that certain things simply weren't meant to be talked about.

They washed the meatballs down with a bottle of Merlot,

and as they ended the meal with some coffee, Tory said, "You'd better not risk driving home. You've had so much bad luck lately, the last thing you want is to fail a breath test. Why don't you stay the night?"

It wouldn't be tactful to mention that he was probably below the legal limit for drinking and driving; she was the one who had polished off most of the wine. He smiled and said, "That's very kind, thanks, but I don't want to put you to any trouble. If the spare bed..."

"Spare bed?" She ruffled his hair. "Oh, come on, Kingsley. No need for such formality. It's not as if we're a pair of shy virgins."

The last time Tory had taken him to bed, Kingsley had felt very much like a shy virgin, but he wasn't stupid enough to dampen the mood. His spirits were soaring.

"No," he said, gazing into her eyes with what he hoped was a soulful expression, "we're not."

Chapter Five

Daylight was fading as Hannah finally escaped from Effie Gray's. She took a short cut down a cobbled yard, one of those old, fortified alleyways branching off the main street. Kendal's nickname, "the Auld Grey Town," derived from the limestone of its buildings. The yards dated from the eighteenth century, when the locals sought sanctuary from outlaws based in the badlands on either side of the Scottish border. These days the marauding Reivers were long gone, and the yards were roamed by tourists stopping off in Kendal on their way to the Lakes.

Hannah lived on the other side of the river, not far from the remnants of the medieval castle, a ruin since Tudor times. Buying a flat in the town had cut down time wasted on commuting, but she'd also wanted a private space while she decided what to do with her life. Following the break up of her relationship with a secondhand bookseller, she'd become close to Daniel Kind. For a short while she'd shared Daniel's cottage in Tarn Fold, but after the letdown of her relationship with Marc Amos, she wasn't ready to commit herself to anyone else. The snag was that, after twelve months on her own, she was nervous and doubtful about the future of their relationship.

She blamed the job, that perennial scapegoat. Day after day, she found herself so caught up in the challenges of running a team with limited resources and an overstretched budget that even when she had time off, she struggled to break free. Even when she did, it crossed her mind sometimes that the demands of police work were too easy an excuse. If she were honest with herself, there was more to it than that.

Daniel's own commitments made matters worse. She'd not seen him for six weeks. He'd spent much of the past year travelling abroad, promoting overseas editions of *The Hell Within*. His history of murder had become an international bestseller, and although she was glad for him, the book's success was two-edged. He adored meeting readers around the world and they lapped up his stories about past crimes, but his popularity reminded her of why she'd always feared that their lifestyles would prove incompatible. How could she forget that this was a man who became a famous face, a household name, before walking out on his career as a TV historian? In the wake of his partner's suicide, Daniel had battled with grief and an incoherent sense of guilt. That was why he'd fled to the Lake District. The truth was stark, and perhaps it was time for her to face it. Surely she ought to stop kidding herself? The two of them belonged to different worlds.

Police work, for all the strains and stresses, provided her with emotional refuge. Her career had veered up and down like a rollercoaster. Encouraged by Ben Kind, who had no patience with play-it-safe time-servers, she'd become a dynamic young detective, not afraid to take an occasional risk if it helped to secure justice for victims of crime. Fast-tracked for promotion to DCI, she'd seemed destined for the heights until disaster struck. A high profile trial fell through, and it suited the superior officers for her to shoulder the blame. The blow had shattered her confidence, and although technically shunting her into cold case work wasn't a demotion, it felt like a punishment. As if she could no longer be trusted to handle cases that really mattered in the here and now.

Deep down she kept the faith, still believing in herself as a detective. Marc Amos reckoned she had a confidence in her own professionalism that she lacked in her private life. In her new role she'd not only rebuilt her reputation, she'd come to relish the challenge. There was something special about heading a cold case team. Even its small size was a drawback that presented opportunities. Every now and then she grabbed the chance to get stuck into hands-on investigation—the work that had attracted her to policing in the first place and far more rewarding than measuring her life in meetings about management and money.

The evening was mild, but as she crossed the bridge over the River Kent, her mind turned to the Laces, father and son, and she shivered. How desperate must you be to take your life by walking into the sea, waiting for the waves to overwhelm you? Gerry Lace's suicide was open to interpretation. Tantamount to an admission that he was guilty of killing Ramona Smith or a cry of despair from a man wrongly accused? It all depended on your point of view.

What about Darren? How he must have suffered over the years, regardless of the rights or wrongs of the police investigation, regardless of whether his father was a murderer. And then to kill himself on the twentieth anniversary of Gerald Lace's death...

She owed it to the Laces as well as to Ramona Smith to do whatever she could to unravel the truth. Not that it would be easy. Even Ben Kind had run into a brick wall, but the passage of time was sometimes a help rather than a hindrance. Recently she'd concluded a review of an unsolved rape case in which new DNA evidence had helped to identify the culprit; he'd be tried in the autumn, with a guilty plea on the cards. Even in cases where advances in forensic science didn't assist, all was not lost. Taking a fresh look at an old file might highlight previous mistakes or new lines of enquiry. The possibilities were endless; you never knew what might happen. Whatever the doubters said, that made the work exciting.

Thank God for Kit Gleadall's willingness to expedite recruitment. Like most police officers, Hannah had harboured grave reservations about the creation of high and mighty PCCs with sweeping powers. The theory was that replacing the old police authorities with a single elected, accountable supremo would ensure that things got done instead of simply talked about by a cosy club of councillors with their snouts in the expenses trough. How it worked out in practice depended on each individual supremo. Many were minor politicians, but Gleadall had stood for election as an independent. People saw him as a breath of fresh air.

He'd made a good start. *Just as long as he behaves himself,* Hannah thought. That offer of a lift home didn't amount to crossing a line, but Hannah's instinct told her that he needed watching. A rich man, accustomed to getting his own way, with women as well as with his business activities? The moment when he'd looked into her eyes…

Striding along the footpath, she told herself not to read too much into it. To her surprise, she'd enjoyed talking to him, and not only because of his willingness to put his money where his mouth was, and give her additional and desperately needed resource. On a personal level she found him engaging. Besides, he wasn't stupid. Only a few weeks had passed since he'd narrowly won election, defeating candidates tied to the major political parties. His campaign had been ruthlessly effective. Surely he wouldn't want to risk everything by embarrassing himself with a female DCI who was perfectly capable of looking after herself?

She turned the last corner and fiddled in her bag for the front door keys. When she glanced up, her heart lurched. Her flat was on the first floor of a small, purpose-built block and the blinds were undrawn. The living room lights were shining.

———

It took a moment for her to use her common sense. Call herself a detective? A burglar wouldn't flaunt his presence. Daniel was the only other person with a key. The last she'd heard from him was a text saying that his flight from America had been delayed. Maybe he'd got back quicker than expected.

Taking the stairs two at a time, she found her front door unlocked. The flat was filled with a heady fragrance. On the living room table a dozen red roses bloomed in a Portmeirion vase. Daniel was sprawled over the sofa, his eyelids drooping. She dropped a kiss on his cheek.

"Hello, stranger. Lovely flowers, thank you."

Daniel yawned. After a transatlantic flight from west to east, he always suffered from jet lag. She could see he was fighting to stay awake.

"It was either roses or a souvenir baseball."

"You made the right choice. So what are you doing here? I assumed you'd go straight home and catch up with your sleep. Or stay with your sister if you couldn't face fending for yourself."

"Louise has swanned off to the Theatre by the Lake with her new bosom buddy."

"Oh, yes?"

Hannah was fond of Daniel's sister, but Louise Kind never had much luck with her love life. She seemed drawn to losers. Not that Hannah had much room to talk, given the ups and downs of her years with Marc Amos.

"Female, if you're wondering, an out-of-work actor. The person who saved Louise's life."

In an email, Daniel had mentioned that Louise had suffered an accident, but he'd been irritatingly vague about it. They'd planned to catch up on a video call, but her work and his promotional activities had got in the way.

"Saved her *life*? God, you told me she'd had an accident, you didn't say it was that serious. What happened?"

He groaned. "One of Louise's neighbours was poorly, so she helped out by taking the woman's golden retriever for a walk. Unfortunately, she chose to do it just after you had a freak deluge here."

"Yeah, the Met Office got excited. As much rain in one day as in a typical month, that sort of stuff."

"When the storm eased, Louise took the retriever out along the banks of the Rothay, which was in full spate. The dog jumped into the river, and when she tried to save it, she slipped on the wet grass and ended up in the water herself. The dog got out, but she was struggling. Thankfully, this other woman was out walking too. She saw what had happened and fished Louise out with no harm done. Except bruised pride and sodden clothes."

"Sounds like a narrow escape. People have drowned in the Rothay before now."

"Louise says she's lucky to have lived to tell the tale. She owes the woman a lot. And she likes her, says they've got a lot in common."

"Thank goodness she's okay." Hannah shook her head.

"Talking of new pals, my latest boyfriend moves in tomorrow, but it's nice of you to drop by."

He laughed. "I take nothing for granted."

"You think I believe that? You're a man, aren't you?" She stroked his dark hair. "So how was the last leg of your trip?"

"Fantastic." He yawned again. "I actually walked on the famous grassy knoll."

The last stop on his itinerary had been a conference in Dallas, where he'd presented a paper on the Kennedy assassination. A publisher in the States wanted him to write a whole new book about the case. As if there weren't enough.

"Exciting?"

He pulled a face. "It's no Helvellyn. Just a tiny wedge of land squeezed between a wooden fence and a highway under-pass. But there's something about seeing a place for yourself. Watching old movie reels doesn't compare. Not that I'm going to write about JFK. I told my publisher, I don't want to waste years of my life arguing with conspiracy theorists."

"What, then?"

"I've pitched a synopsis for a history of unsolved deaths. From Zoroaster to Gareth Williams."

"Gareth Williams?"

"The spy who was found padlocked in a bag."

She gestured to the huge suitcase he'd left by the door. It looked big enough to accommodate a small person.

"You're not preparing the ground for some kind of confession, I hope?"

He laughed. "Luckily, my agent and editor like the idea, so I don't need to resort to murder. Since meeting you, I've become fascinated by unsolved mysteries. While I was in the States I kept thinking back to the Dungeon House..."

"It's a year ago now."

"I can't quite put it out of my mind," he said. "Can you?"

She shook her head. Sometimes she doubted if she'd ever forget the chilling resolution of her last homicide enquiry. Since then, she'd kept busy with other forms of unfinished criminal business.

"You'll never guess," she said. "The new PCC has asked me to look at an even older murder case. A waitress disappeared without a trace from Bowness, and all the evidence pointed to murder."

"Anyone in the frame?"

"Yes, but the prime suspect was found not guilty." She hesitated. "As a matter of fact, he was arrested by your dad."

"I suppose that in those days, there weren't many major cases where he wasn't called in."

"He wasn't happy with the outcome of this one. Does the name Ramona Smith mean anything to you?" Daniel's face was blank. "The man accused of killing her was called Gerald Lace. Despite his acquittal, he never shook off the shroud of suspicion. He walked out into Morecambe Bay and drowned himself."

"Almost as good as admitting that he did it."

"Not necessarily. His family campaigned on his behalf. The widow made a huge song and dance about it, reckoned he was a victim. Now his son's former partner is leading the crusade."

"Don't tell me." Daniel's tone sharpened. "Complaints about police harassment? Big Bad Ben Kind?"

"A formal complaint was made at the time, but rejected."

"So of course their response was to complain about a whitewash?"

"More than likely. I haven't studied the details. It was a long time ago. What's brought the case back into the public eye is the recent anniversary of Gerald Lace's death. Twenty years after he committed suicide, his son jogged out from Strandbeck and did exactly the same thing."

Daniel stared. "Are you serious?"

"Unfortunately, yes." She paused. "Didn't you once write something called *History Repeats Itself?*"

"Subtitled *But Never in Quite the Same Way.* Hardly an original title, my only defence is that it was my very first book."

"Fits the bill here. This latest death has prompted the media to dig up the old story and given the journalists who don't love us a chance to put the boot in. That's why the PCC is desperate to be seen to be taking action. Every cloud, though. He's giving me two more detectives. It's still not quite..."

"So the press say that Dad got it wrong?"

His tone was biting. She cursed herself for mentioning the case before the two of them had taken time to get properly reacquainted. Preferably in bed.

"Journos will say anything to sell papers. Or paywall subscriptions. Our job is to investigate the case with an open mind; you know the drill."

"I know that after a man's death, it's easy to point the finger," Daniel snapped.

Just as you jumped to the conclusion that Gerry Lace's suicide meant he was guilty of murder, Hannah was tempted to say. She bit her tongue. Daniel wasn't usually so defensive about his father. Lack of sleep explained the tetchiness.

"Look, you must be shattered after the flight. Let me make some coffee."

Daniel shrugged, and she went into the kitchen. When she returned five minutes later with two steaming mugs, he was dead to the world.

———

Breathless and exhausted, Kingsley detached himself from Tory and rolled on to his side.

"See?" She untucked her arm. "There was no need to worry."

The last time they'd tried to make love had been a catastrophe. He'd tried to keep pace with her drinking, and afterwards he'd told himself that explained his failure. Or maybe age was catching up with him. It seemed so cruel. He'd barely begun to enjoy life after escaping from the maternal shadow. Frustrated and half-pissed, she'd uttered harsh words that he preferred to forget. But now at last they'd consummated their relationship.

"Was that good?" Right now he felt bold enough to tempt fate.

"Mmmm. Did that make you happy?"

He caressed her warm, plump breast. "Very."

"You deserve it after such a ghastly experience. How horrible it must have been, watching that man die. Right in front of your eyes."

He said nothing. Her choice of words struck him as unfortunate. Why did she have to make it sound as though she'd been administering therapy or undertaking a charitable mission? At once he rebuked himself. No need to go looking for something to be upset about. This was a moment to savour. He'd never forget it.

"Tell me this." Kingsley was conscious of her body tensing. "When you realised what was happening to him, how did you feel?"

The question shocked him, and he didn't dare to answer. He closed his eyes, but when he opened them again, the bedside light was still on, and Tory was propped up on her elbow, studying him as if he were a laboratory exhibit.

He ought to feel honoured. An attractive woman like this, someone who could pick and choose, was willing to share her bed with him. It was a privilege. Yet he felt a prickle of anxiety.

"What is it?" he murmured.

"It's such a weird story," she said softly, "what happened on the beach."

He craned his neck, trying to check the time on the alarm clock, but she was in the way and he was too tired to move.

"It's late," he said feebly. "Let's not…"

"I can't help being curious," she said. "You lived in the same place as the murdered woman. She must have been much the same age as you."

Her scrutiny was unrelenting.

"I suppose so," he admitted.

"Yet she never crossed your path?"

"Never. I told you."

"And then there was that man Lace. They accused him of the murder. He came from Bowness, as well. Did you really never come across either of them?"

"I don't remember," he groaned. "Let's go to sleep."

She gave a sigh and turned over. He dropped a bleary kiss on her freckled back, between her shoulder blades, but there was no response.

He ground his teeth. Why must she keep poking away at a sore place? His past life meant nothing to her, and he hated, he absolutely hated, being reminded of his less creditable behaviour.

How he wished she hadn't pushed him into a corner and made him lie to her about Ramona Smith.

Chapter Six

In Kingsley's dream, Logan Prentice was playing the piano. They were on a golden beach—somewhere hot and tropical, definitely not Strandbeck—and Logan was wearing sky blue speedos. His tanned, slender torso gleamed with oil. Kingsley brought him a piña cocktail from the bar and put it on top of the piano.

Logan began to sing "This Guy's in Love with You."

Kingsley wanted to join in, but the moment he opened his mouth, he caught sight of a familiar figure lumbering towards him. Mamma, waving a knitting needle like a sabre. She was furious, and he knew he was in trouble.

He woke up with a jolt and realised he was still in bed with Tory. She was curled up and snoring. A thought struck him like a thunderbolt and he seized her shoulder and shook her until her eyes opened.

"This man you saw outside last night."

"What?" she mumbled. "Go…go back to sleep."

"No, Tory, please, this is important." He was gabbling, but he didn't care. "About this intruder who was prowling the grounds. Can you tell me what he looked like?"

"What man?"

"You rang me up to report him. I know you weren't sure you'd even seen an intruder, but maybe you had. Maybe I can even tell you his name."

She rubbed the sleep from her eyes. "I don't have the foggiest what you're talking about."

He wasn't giving up. When an idea took hold of him, he was like a terrier with a bone. "Please think. Was he in his twenties? Slim, handsome, mop of fair hair?"

She peered at him. He couldn't interpret the look in her eyes. Bewilderment, yes, but something else. Surely not anxiety over being caught out? How could that make sense?

"It's the middle of the night. I was fast asleep. So should you be."

"Darling, please. Indulge me. It's…"

She poked him in the ribs. Her fingers were long and hard; it was all he could do not to yelp with shock and dismay.

"Listen to me, Kingsley. I'm not your darling and no, I won't fucking indulge you. For Chrissake, do you know what time it is?"

"Don't worry about the time. This man is trouble. No, it's worse than that; he's dangerous. He's committed murder once, to my knowledge. If he's hanging around here, you're at risk."

"Murder?" She swallowed. "You're crazy. Can't you get it into your head? I made up the intruder to give me a reason to call you."

"Are you sure?" he pressed.

"Of course I'm bloody sure." Her face reddened. "What is the matter with you? I try to show you a little human kindness after you've had a bad time, and this is how you repay me?"

"Well…"

She was in full flow, and she swatted his interruption aside.

"Waking me up in the small hours to rant about mythical tres-passers with homicidal tendencies?"

"I'm sorry." He began to gabble. "It's only just hit me. This same man was at the Crooked Shore, a few minutes before the other fellow ran into the sea. I'll let you into a secret: that's why I was so distracted that afternoon. Your intruder is someone I've met before. His name is Logan Prentice, and he's not to be trusted, he's..."

"Get this into your thick head." He flinched and averted his gaze from her angry, contorted features. Never before had he heard her speak with such savagery, using words like weapons. "There was no intruder, okay? I dreamed him up. It was just an excuse, a chance for us to be together again for one last time. More fool me, I wish I'd never bothered. I should have kept my big mouth shut and let you carry on playing with yourself in your miserable little bungalow in Bowness. Now get your scrawny arse out of my bed and piss off to the spare room."

———

How could he sleep a wink after that tirade? Impossible. Alone in the second bedroom, curled up in the foetal position, he sobbed till it hurt, whilst taking care not to make too much noise, in case Tory lost it completely and threw him out into the night.

Not for the first time in his life where Logan Prentice was concerned, he'd messed up. Tory's rage frightened him. She didn't even have the excuse of being sloshed. Yes, she'd put away most of a bottle of wine, but for her that was par for the course. And yes, perhaps it was tactless to wake her up and start firing questions at her in the small hours, but his overeagerness was no excuse for such cruelty.

Together again for one last time.

Words spoken in the heat of the moment, he told himself. She didn't mean it. Couldn't mean it. He simply wouldn't accept it.

Tory was everything to him. He'd never known a woman like her. Gorgeous, funny, sexy. For all her faults, he adored her. Not that he'd told her in so many words; he'd held back due to natural reserve coupled with an apprehension that she wouldn't take his devotion seriously. A woman like Tory could pick and choose. It was a privilege to be her lover and to share her bed.

And now she'd kicked him out of it.

———

Kingsley hauled himself out of the spare bed at half seven. After showering and getting dressed he made himself tea and toast. There was no sign of Tory, not that he expected to see her. She wasn't an early riser at the best of times. When he pressed the switch to open the blinds, it was bright outside, but he wasn't in the right frame of mind for a pleasant alfresco breakfast out on the terrace.

Smearing each slice of toast with a huge dollop of orange marmalade, he wondered how he might redeem himself. Grovelling looked like the best option. He wasn't a man to stand on his dignity, and although Tory had been beastly to him, there were extenuating circumstances. In the clear light of morning, he saw that he'd been too hasty. He'd got carried away because of his loathing for Logan Prentice. Prentice frightened him. The thought that he might be sniffing around Strandbeck Manor for some reason...

Tory was so adamant that she'd not seen an intruder that he suspected her of protesting too much. But why? Her response when he'd described Prentice suggested she was nursing a secret. Kingsley knew how it felt to have something to hide. You tended to overreact.

One last time.

No, it couldn't be. He must talk her round. Not easy with a woman who was so stubborn. But he'd never give up. He'd find a way.

As he put his crockery away neatly in the dishwasher, he heard a muffled roar from the power shower in Tory's en suite bathroom. Seized by panic, he contemplated writing a short note and making himself scarce. Anything rather than face her wrath again. But no. He must take any punishment she meted out. Faint heart never won fair lady.

When she emerged, she was wrapped in a white dressing gown. "Get any sleep?"

"Not much." He cleared his throat. "Look, I wanted to say how terribly sorry…"

"Enough!" She raised her hand. "I'm the one who should apologise. I didn't mean to be so harsh. I was having a nightmare, and when you woke me up like that, you sort of became part of it."

So intense was his relief that he felt his knees buckle. He clutched the breakfast bar to avoid falling over like a circus clown.

"Please, there's absolutely no need to apologise! I simply wanted to…"

"No." The smile had vanished. "Let's forget about mysterious intruders. I don't want to hear another word on the subject. Agreed?"

He opened his mouth to explain, but one look at her silenced him.

"You've eaten breakfast, I see. Good. I expect you need to be off. Catch up with some work. All those other Greengables properties you have under your wing."

"Well…"

"Thanks for coming round yesterday. Good to catch up."

"Yes."

There was so much he wanted to say, but he couldn't find the words. She stepped towards him and brushed his cheek with her lips.

"Now, if you'll excuse me, I've got things to do, so I'd better get dressed. Drive safely."

It was a dismissal, if not as brusque as on the afternoon of the tragedy on the Crooked Shore. She turned away from him and walked briskly out of the kitchen area.

"Take care," he said, as she disappeared from sight. "I'll be in touch."

———

Daniel was still snoring when Hannah left for work at seven, and she left him a scribbled note. She'd hauled him into bed in the spare room, thanking heaven that he'd not put on too much weight after all that wining and dining on his tour round the States.

The morning passed in a blur of activity. Kit Gleadall had waved a magic wand, casting a spell over the apparatchiks in HR as well as the force's senior officers. Bunny Cohen would join the Cold Case Review Team on a full-time basis as of Monday, along with a couple of support workers. All of a sudden, everyone in authority now agreed that bringing in another DC was an urgent priority.

"Amazing," Maggie Eyre said as Hannah gathered the team for an update in their usual briefing room. "I was convinced that the high-ups had forgotten we exist. I never knew you can actually cut through the red tape like that."

"The PCC put a rocket up their backsides," Les Bryant said. "Gleadall won't take no for an answer."

"It will be fantastic to work alongside you again," Maggie told Bunny Cohen. The older woman had looked in to say hello to her new colleagues. She'd helped Maggie learn the ropes when she was a rookie constable.

"Glad to be here." Bunny was having a quick cup of tea. "I'd better get back to my desk in a minute. There are a zillion loose ends to tie up, but I'm dying to make a start. Maybe we can finally see justice done for poor Ramona Smith."

"Maggie will give us a full briefing once she's studied the files," Hannah said. "But it's good to have someone on the team who was around at the time."

Bunny nodded. "Yes, I've never forgotten Ramona."

"How old was she?" Les asked.

"Twenty-nine. Born and bred in Bowness. Her parents were both alcoholics. Jimmy, the father, was a long-distance lorry driver. He was a hard-line socialist, and at one time he'd been a trade union activist, but he ran into trouble after he was convicted of couple of assaults. Booze-related. He earned good money when he was working, but he drank it all away, so money was short. Leila, the mum, supplemented her benefits with occasional amateur prostitution."

Maggie groaned. "What a rotten start in life."

"Yep, not a happy family. When Jimmy and Leila got drunk, they'd belt each other till they were black and blue. Jimmy walked out on them when Ramona was seven years old."

"No great loss, by the sound of it." Maggie came from a close-knit farming community. Family mattered a good deal to her.

"He moved to Coniston and had very little contact with his ex or his daughter. Ramona left school at the very first opportunity. She worked in different places around Bowness and

Windermere. Shops, bars, hotels. She changed jobs as often as some people change their knickers. Her trouble was she kept getting bored. Always after something different."

"Don't we all?" Les asked.

"Ramona and her mum lived in a rented house in the town. Not long before she went missing, her mother's liver lost the unequal struggle. Ramona's only other family in the area was Jimmy's mum. Old Mrs. Smith rented a tumbledown cottage near the coast at Bardsea. Ramona was fond of her and went over to see her most weekends. Got the local authority to send in carers, that sort of stuff."

"Did Ramona marry?" Les asked.

"No, but she was never short of a boyfriend," Bunny said. "On the contrary. Sometimes she had more than one on the go at the same time."

"Why suspect murder? People go missing all the time."

"True," Hannah said. "We shouldn't make assumptions. Let's go back to square one. Ask ourselves if she might still be alive, as well as who might have killed her."

"When was she last seen?" Les asked.

"One evening at the end of March. She finished her shift at Guido's, where she worked, and said her goodbyes. Nobody admitted seeing her after that. There were plenty of reported sightings all over the country, but they were as unreliable as usual. Not a single one was ever substantiated."

Maggie wrinkled her brow. "That can't have been the only reason everyone assumed she was dead."

"Far from it. She'd never gone missing before, and she left all her possessions at home. The few pounds in her bank account were never touched. Later on, Ben Kind and his team discovered items of evidence which indicated that she was almost certainly dead. The stumbling block was that her remains couldn't be found. Because Gerald Lace never confessed, he took the secret of what happened to her with him into Morecambe Bay."

She paused to check her watch. "Assuming he knew, of course."

Hannah said, "Thanks, Bunny. Now we'd all better get our skates on. I'm meeting Darren Lace's former partner in five minutes, then I'm off to Carlisle. There's a press conference later this afternoon. Our lords and masters want to announce that we're reopening the investigation, though we've not spoken to Ramona's father yet."

Les winced. "Unfortunate."

"You're telling me. One of the oddities of this case is that the pressure for us to take a fresh look has come as a result of Darren Lace's suicide, not from the family of the deceased."

"Is Jimmy Smith still alive?"

Everyone turned to Bunny, who spread her arms. "No idea, sorry."

Hannah turned to Les. "There's your first job, Les. To find Ramona's dad."

———

Rather than depart the Manor after leaving Tory's flat, Kingsley retreated to his office on the opposite side of the ground floor. A steel filing cabinet was crammed with brochures and other Greengables bumph, but the antique desk and chair belonged to him, not the company. They gave the room a homely touch. Eventually this office would be united with an adjoining empty suite of rooms so as to form the last flat to be sold in the Manor. Given the sluggish pace of sales, Kingsley was confident of remaining in situ for the foreseeable future.

The oak teacher's desk was strategically located in front of a window, commanding a view of the car park. He scrolled aimlessly through his inbox and waited. After half an hour Tory emerged from the building. She glanced at his Corsa and gave a sorrowful shake of the head. He hoped she'd pop over to the office for a word with him, but she jumped into her BMW and sped down the drive.

For a moment he contemplated following her, but he dared not risk provoking her into an attempt to end their relationship. It could only be an attempt, of course, because he couldn't tolerate the prospect of losing her. But he must be canny. Women were never straightforward to deal with. You had to play the long game.

His efforts to compile the usual monthly report to management were laboured. He loathed grappling with figures. In his early days with Greengables, thanks to Tory's purchase of the show flat, he'd impressed his manager, a brassy redhead whom thankfully he seldom needed to meet in person. Her name was Annabel, and each time she introduced herself as Annabel of Greengables, she screeched with laughter at her own wit, much to the bewilderment of anyone unfamiliar with the oeuvre of L. M. Montgomery.

"You're our star performer!" she'd trilled. "What would we do without you, lovely?"

In recent months, her admiration had waned. His Key Performance Indicators fell far short of the ridiculous targets she imposed, and her latest email had remarked acidly about the unacceptability of resting on laurels. Since the property market was slow everywhere, Kingsley took refuge in blaming the uncertain state of the economy. Brexit had a lot to answer for, he explained, which might be true, even though he'd voted for it.

Giving up on the report, he dug into his jacket pocket and pulled out a key. He always kept the left-hand drawer of his desk locked. Even in Strandbeck, you couldn't be too careful. He opened the drawer and took out a gun.

This was a Smith & Wesson Model 3, a .44 calibre Russian double-action revolver. Dating back a century and a half, it had been designed to the specification of the Imperial Russian Army. This little beauty was an old friend. The grips and muzzle showed signs of wear, but traces of the original blue finish remained. When you held it in your hand, you felt you were touching history. Annie Oakley, General Custer, and Teddy Roosevelt—each of them had owned a Number 3. John Wesley Hardin had shot a sheriff in Comanche, Texas, with his, a crime that Bob Dylan turned into a song. After buying this one from a fellow dealer ten years ago, Kingsley had hung on to it for his personal pleasure.

It was perfectly above board. The calibre was obsolete, so he didn't need a licence. A few killjoys had talked about changing the law so as to crack down on ownership of vintage firearms. A gun of this very model had been used in some gangland revenge killing a while ago, but in Kingsley's opinion, the type of weapon was irrelevant. Criminals determined to commit murder would continue to do so, regardless of statutory controls. Tighten the law, and the people who suffered wouldn't be drug dealers and armed robbers but ordinary, law-abiding folk who cherished history and *objets d'art*. Kingsley intended to keep his head down. Why relinquish a cherished item of personal property for which he'd paid handsomely?

Lister, the dealer who had sold it to him, had died of pneumonia a couple of winters ago. Nobody else knew anything about the Smith & Wesson. Almost nobody, at any rate. In a fit of bravado, Kingsley had once boasted to Tory about owning the gun. She'd seemed amused; perhaps she didn't believe him. Lister, notorious in the trade for sailing close to the wind, had thrown in some ammunition as part of the trade. Kingsley had never fired a weapon in his life before, but he'd risked a few practice shots one evening, out on the Crooked Shore. Just for fun, just to see what it was like. Nothing more serious than that.

Firing the Smith & Wesson made him feel powerful. It was quite thrilling. For years he'd kept the gun at home, but after joining Greengables, he transferred it to his private kingdom at the Manor. Locked in the desk drawer, it was as safe as houses.

A couple of months back, he'd done something rather silly. When he was sure the Manor was deserted, he'd taken out the gun and shot at the trunk of a sycamore. Of course, he'd missed, although not by much. The .44 was famed for its reliability. But he'd made a mistake. Even as he luxuriated in the excitement, the window cleaner's van bowled up the drive. Without so much as a by-your-leave, the inconsiderate oaf had turned up twenty-four hours before he was due. Kingsley would have given him a piece of his mind if he hadn't got a headache from the exertion of hoofing it back to his office and returning the gun to its hiding place.

He itched to show Tory the gun, to prove that there was more to him than met the eye. But he'd resisted temptation simply because he couldn't be sure how she'd react. What if she insisted that he get rid of it? Antiques and keepsakes held no appeal for her. Yes, some things were better kept under wraps.

Taking a handkerchief out of his pocket, he gave the gun a quick polish. Before he put it back in the drawer, he stroked the barrel as lovingly as if he were caressing Tory's thigh.

Chapter Seven

"Why only now?" Jade Hughes demanded. "Why does a man need to die before you people will get up off your backsides and take action?"

"The Commissioner has been very clear." Hannah was in full diplomatic mode. "Now my team is launching a fresh inquiry, we'll do everything in our power to find out what happened to Ramona Smith."

"You don't just have one death on your conscience." Jade Hughes was in no mood to listen. Given a chance to be heard by a captive audience, she was determined to make the most of it. "Darren's mother would be alive to this day if it wasn't for the police. Misery is what made her sick. Shirley gave her life to the cause. She never believed for one minute that her husband killed that girl."

"The family has suffered a good deal," Hannah said.

"You can say that again!"

"Tell me about them. I'd value your insight."

Jade was accompanied by a friend called Kylie, and Hannah by a nervous young clerical officer from Media Relations, who made a painstaking note of every word uttered. Her boss had given Hannah a long and unnecessary briefing about the vital need to risk-manage this conversation. Anything she said, any careless slip of the tongue, might be leaked, misrepresented, or relied on in future litigation as an admission of…well, the legal eagles would no doubt find some sharp hook on which to impale her.

The temptation was to become a politician, and say nothing at great length, boring Jade Hughes into submission. But Hannah's aim was to treat the conversation as an opportunity. She might just learn something.

"I met Darren three years back." Jade spoke in a broad Carlisle accent, the sort that outsiders often mistook for Geordie. "He was a mess."

"A mess?"

"Don't you know?"

Jade thrust her jaw forward like a boxer tempting an opponent to strike the first blow. Her eyebrows, nostrils, and earlobes were festooned with stainless steel; her muscular arms were covered in tattoos of mermaids with breasts almost as large as her own. She was wearing a canary-yellow T-shirt emblazoned with the slogan *Justice4Gerry*.

"You tell me."

"He was convicted of drug possession, but he was a user, not a dealer. Couple of times he overdosed on pills."

"Cries for help?"

Jade nodded. "I'm a car mechanic. We met when Darren brought his old rust bucket in for an MOT. Sorting the car was the easy bit. Getting him clean was a bloody sight harder. I kept telling him he must shape up for his mum's sake. Ever since Gerry drowned himself, Shirley only had one thing to live for. To clear his name, nothing else mattered."

"It must have been very hard."

"You're telling me. A saint, that woman. Not like Gerry, she was the first to admit that he wasn't whiter than white. Especially when it came to women. They liked him, and he liked them a damn sight too much. Shirley went to her grave believing the police hounded Gerry until he couldn't take any more. Your lot held a grudge because they couldn't nail him for crimes he never committed."

"He was lucky to have such a loyal wife."

"You never said a truer word. A lot of women would have thrown him out, but Shirley was besotted. She never forgave the police for persecuting him. Especially that detective who tried to bully him into confessing."

Hannah said nothing.

"They called him Kind," Jade said with a sneer. "What a joke. The man was heartless. He ripped the whole family apart; they were never the same again."

Hannah didn't want to discuss Ben Kind. "Shirley's campaign to clear her husband's name became her life. Was that true of Darren as well?"

"The fact his dad was a suspected murderer was a huge black cloud hanging over him every day of his life. Ever since he was a kid. He could never escape. Not like his sister."

"What about her?"

"Sandi? She was no use. Ran off to the bright lights, first chance she got."

Hannah shifted to the edge of her seat. "Didn't she believe in Gerald Lace's innocence?"

Jade's face turned crimson. "Not so fast, Chief Inspector. You're jumping to conclusions, same as that Ben Kind. I never met Sandi, but Darren told me she was a Daddy's girl. She took Gerry's death hard, but she reckoned her mum's campaign was a waste of time. She blamed Darren and her mother for talking to the police about the night Ramona Smith vanished. If they'd stuck to the original story, nobody could've pinned the murder on Gerry."

Interesting. Did Gerry Lace's daughter secretly believe that her beloved father was guilty? If so, what were her reasons? Maybe that explained the family bust-up. Hannah made a mental note that Sandi should be traced and interviewed.

"What about Sandi's relationship with Darren?"

"Chalk and cheese," Jade snapped. "She was sweet as pie if she wanted something from Gerry, but a nasty piece of work, selfish and vain. Darren was depressed that Sandi thought he was a weakling. She broke off contact with both him and their mother years ago. Didn't show up at either funeral, the bitch. Her own flesh and blood!"

"Tell me about Darren. What was he like?"

Her expression softened. "You've seen his photo, it was all over the papers. Handsome bloke, wasn't he? Fit, too, when he wasn't doping himself to the eyeballs. Competed in half-marathons. Gerry liked outdoor pursuits too; it ran in the family."

Hannah nodded. Even in the grainy photographs accompanying coverage of the Strandbeck suicide, Darren's dark good looks were unmistakeable. He took after his father. The difference was that Gerald Lace's confident grin smacked of self-regard and entitlement, while the son's cautious smile and receding chin betrayed softness and anxiety.

"Yes," Hannah said. "I didn't just mean his appearance. I'd like to know more about his personality."

"When he was in the right mood," Jade said, "he was the best company. Funny, intelligent. Because of his issues, he never held a job down for long. Kept giving himself a hard time. He was terribly insecure."

"Why do you think that was?"

"He grew up with everyone believing his dad killed a young woman. Imagine how that felt!"

"Difficult," Hannah admitted.

"You're not kidding. Kind never apologised for arresting Gerry, even though the jury threw out his case. It wouldn't have been so bad if he'd made a proper effort to find out who did kill Ramona Smith. But he couldn't be arsed. Because he thought he'd got his man, he saw no point in looking for anyone else. Let alone the girl's body. The truth is, your lot didn't only betray the Lace family, they let down the Smiths as well. Ramona's dad was never able to grieve properly. A real tragedy."

"It's more than that." Kylie decided it was time to make her presence felt. "It's a fucking disgrace."

Ignoring her, Hannah said, "Would you mind telling me why your relationship with Darren broke down?"

Jade sniffed. "Couldn't hack it anymore, could I? Fixing a car is one thing. People are different. There's no instruction manual. You can't just give them a quick respray. Darren's constant whining wore me down. Shirley was sick, and he'd lost all interest in life. There was no fun anymore, for him or me. I guessed he was back on the drugs, not that he ever admitted it. I gave him a choice. Shape up or ship out. He didn't alter his ways, so I chucked him out. He went back to his mum, and I moved back to Carlisle."

"And when Mrs. Lace died?"

"I sent him a sympathy card with a nice message, but I never heard back. Not a sodding word. Until I got his suicide note."

She sniffed again. Hannah guessed that beneath the surface belligerence lurked a decent, unhappy woman cut to the quick by the loss of a man she'd cared for. Hardly surprising that she felt a need to lash out. Just a pity that Ben Kind and her force offered such a handy target for her wrath.

"I'm sorry."

"Are you really?" Jade demanded. "Or is this just a great big scam, a phoney PR exercise? Trying to shut me up, fob me off? Hoping I'll forgive and forget? No chance of that, Detective Chief Inspector."

"No chance," confirmed Kylie.

Hannah wanted to offer reassurance, but held herself in check. Kit Gleadall wouldn't be happy if a cack-handed attempt at compassion became a hostage to fortune.

"If there's any information you can give me about Ramona Smith, perhaps something Darren or his mother mentioned to you?"

"Like what?"

"You tell me."

Jade Hughes shook her head. "All I can say is that Darren blamed himself for what happened to his father."

"He was only a boy when Ramona went missing."

"Yes, but he was the one who grassed him up, poor sod. The kid who gave his father away, who destroyed his own family without even meaning to."

———

Kingsley locked the gun safely in its drawer and left his office. He was just about to get into his car when a blue VW Passat came down the drive, making a loud, unnatural noise. Fiona Hudson waved and wound down her window. She and her wife, Molly, popped over regularly to keep an eye on the flat they let out to tourists. Fiona had pink hair and various piercings in her nose, lips, and eyebrows, all of which prejudiced Kingsley against her. Not his sort of person at all, but pleasant enough to speak to.

"Sorry to make such a fearful racket! Enough to wake the

dead, I know. The exhaust has worked loose, and I've patched it up not very successfully. I'll take it into the garage when I get chance, but we're rushed off our feet at the nail bar. It compensates for this place being so quiet."

"Any luck with bookings?"

"Thank goodness the weather forecast is fine. We have someone arriving next Wednesday for ten days."

Kingsley decided not to mention Greengables' plan to ratchet up the service charge. People were so often inclined to shoot the messenger.

He drove back to Bowness and treated himself to an early lunch at a café near the pier. A waitress offered him a menu, but he already knew what he wanted. Smoked salmon and scrambled eggs on brown toast, washed down with a latte. Just the ticket. As he swallowed his first mouthful, an idea came to him, an idea so shocking that he almost choked on a chunk of toast.

What if Logan Prentice had somehow scraped an acquaintance with Tory?

Absurd as it seemed, this idea presented a solution to the riddles nagging at him. First, his sighting of Prentice at Strandbeck on the afternoon of that wretched fellow's suicide. Suppose Prentice was on his way to the Manor? An appalling possibility, but it would explain Tory's behaviour that day. Kingsley recalled her impatience to get rid of him; it made so much more sense if she was expecting another visitor, someone she didn't want Kingsley to meet.

Second, Tory's over-the-top reaction last night, lashing out after he described Logan Prentice and suggested he might be the intruder in the Manor's grounds. If her conscience was pricking, she might opt for attack as the best form of defence.

"Everything all right, love?"

His facial expression must have alarmed the waitress, but he sent her away with an impatient flap of the hand. Jealousy knotted his stomach. If Tory and Prentice knew each other, was it conceivable that she'd taken him to her bed? Kingsley wouldn't put it past her. Her appetites were extraordinary, given her age and history of serious heart trouble. In his admittedly limited experience, he'd never known a woman make such physical demands. Did she feel the need for someone else?

He tried to eat, in the hope of taking his mind off the horrific pictures that came unbidden to his mind. Logan Prentice's lithe body wrapped around Tory's fleshy curves. It was no good. The food was sticking in his throat; he couldn't bear to get it down. He swallowed a mouthful of coffee and stumbled over to the cash till.

"Sure you're all right, sir?" The toothy waitress looked apprehensive.

He made an inarticulate noise of assent and rushed out into the fresh air, gasping for breath.

On the pavement, as impatient pedestrians jostled by, the answer struck him like a thunderclap.

Logan Prentice was planning another murder. His next victim would be Tory Reece-Taylor.

Chapter Eight

"This question is for DCI Scarlett," said a young reporter from the regional press.

Up on the makeshift podium in the Media Centre, alongside the chief constable and Siobhan, the head of Media Relations, Hannah took a sip of water and tried to compose her features into an expression of calm and competence.

"Go ahead."

The young man coughed. "After all these years, how can you possibly hope to succeed where previous investigators have failed?"

"I don't underestimate the challenge," Hannah said. "But the passage of the years sometimes works in our favour. People who once had a reason to remain silent may no longer feel obliged to preserve a confidence. Or their consciences may trouble them. Or something clicks in their mind that makes sense of a piece of evidence that previously seemed unimportant or irrelevant."

"Can you find Ramona's body?"

"I make no promises. All I can say is that my team has solved complex old crimes before. With help from you in the press and members of the public, we can do it again."

A small woman with steel-rimmed spectacles resting on a long nose almost leapt from her seat in the front row. She'd kept raising her hand ever since Siobhan first invited questions, but the chief had resolutely ignored her, and Hannah guessed that he'd recognised a scourge of authority. Suppressing a sigh, Hannah gave her a nod.

"Midge Van Beek, freelance." The woman spoke rapidly, as if determined to have her say before being frog-marched from the room by agents of oppression. "Chief Constable, isn't it time for the Cumbria Constabulary to offer a full and unqualified apology to the family of the late Darren Lace for the pain they have suffered? For repeated failures to clear the cloud of suspicion that hung over them for decades?"

The chief cleared his throat, a process which became unusually protracted. He was a grizzled veteran cop, good with people but overly fond of easy options and a quiet life. He'd announced his long-anticipated retirement shortly before the election of the PCC. Speculation was rife that, foreseeing Kit Gleadall's triumph and a future less comfortable than the past, he'd preferred to make the decision himself rather than have it snatched out of his hands. Soon he'd be able to retire to his villa in Andalusia, fitting in an occasional round of golf in between cocktails. The last thing he wanted was to mar his final weeks in post by getting embroiled in a public row. Let alone make any admission that exposed the force to claims for compensation.

Twitching in her seat, Midge Van Beek was unable to contain herself. She looked around the assembled press corps, scanning the room as if in search of a soapbox.

"In case anyone has forgotten, two men have killed themselves. They walked out into the sea…"

"You've asked a very important question." The chief spoke slowly and with great solemnity.

Hannah recognised another time-honoured technique for buying time to think. The vagueness of his expression indicated that he'd need more than a few seconds to say anything capable of shutting up Midge Van Beek.

Time to take one for the team. Hannah grabbed the microphone. "We certainly don't forget the dead, and we don't forget Ramona Smith, either. For as long as a serious crime remains unsolved, suspicion swirls around everyone involved. We owe it to those people to work night and day to bring closure. To exonerate the innocent as well as to punish the guilty."

"Thank you, Chief Inspector, thank you everyone." Siobhan, a timid young woman who was happiest when tweeting about initiatives to crack down on dog fouling, almost squeaked with relief as the time allotted for the press conference ran out. "We will of course be updating you further the moment DCI Scarlett's team has some news to report."

With that, she shepherded Hannah and the chief off the podium and into the safe haven of the green room. Kit Gleadall was waiting for them. Hannah had assumed he'd want to take his place on the podium, but he'd kept away from the limelight, watching the live feed on a large TV screen.

"Well done, Hannah," the chief constable boomed. "You certainly put that wretched woman in her place."

"Yes, congratulations." Gleadall gave a wicked smile. "Just what we wanted. You managed to say as little as possible in the most positive way imaginable. Ever thought of becoming a cabinet minister?"

"I think you should take that as a compliment," the chief said hurriedly.

"Glad to get it over with." Hannah brushed a straggly hair off her face. She'd kept postponing a trip to the hairdresser, not anticipating an appearance on TV that would give everyone in the region a chance to tut at her unkempt locks. "I find performing for the press as much fun as root-canal surgery."

"Don't undervalue yourself," Gleadall said. "You were great."

The chief was brightening already, and Hannah knew what he had in mind. With any luck, he'd be downing those tequilas in Spain before it became clear that the new investigation was getting nowhere.

"I suppose Lace was mentally disturbed, like his father before him," he said. "Nobody kills themselves as a protest against so-called police inefficiency. Hack journalists always see things in black and white, not shades of grey. Their narrative is simple. Twenty years on, we're nowhere near solving Ramona Smith's murder."

"I wouldn't call Midge Van Beek a hack," Gleadall murmured.

"The woman's a malcontent," the chief said. "Did you see the programme she made about…"

"Sorry to interrupt, but I'd better be on my way." Hannah didn't want to play piggy-in-the-middle. "The first step is to find Ramona's father and see what he can tell us. Once we've sifted through all the old statements, we'll start figuring out who else we want to talk to."

"Go for it!" Gleadall clapped Hannah on the back. "This time things will be different. You'll solve the mystery of Ramona Smith. I feel it in my bones."

Turning to leave, she glanced over her shoulder and gave him a bleak smile. "No pressure, then?"

———

Logan Prentice scared Kingsley. Until that dreadful afternoon on the Crooked Shore, Kingsley had done his utmost to forget him. Now, dodging past the swans that congregated near the ticket kiosks for lake cruises, he realised the battle was lost. Logan Prentice had taken over his mind, occupying his thoughts like an incubus, manipulative and devoid of conscience.

Leaving the crowds behind him, Kingsley took a path through the fields bordering Windermere. As the sun slid behind a sinister cloud, he found a vacant bench at Cockshott Point, a promontory jutting out into the lake below Bowness Bay. Across a narrow strip of water lay wooded Belle Isle, largest of Windermere's islands, and the only one where people lived. A Roman commander had built a villa there, and during the Civil War the island formed a Royalist stronghold. Through the trees peeped the dome of the eighteenth-century Round House, mocked by Wordsworth as a "tea canister in a shop window." Modern-day tourists marvelled at its neoclassical elegance.

For once, the lakeside scenery failed to weave its usual magic. Fear that Tory might be in mortal danger made his spine tingle. The trouble was that Logan Prentice's boyish charm was so deceptive. Kingsley had read somewhere that this was a hallmark of psychopaths and serial killers. It was so easy for a decent person to be taken in by the lies. To be seduced, literally and metaphorically. He knew that to his cost.

————

As soon as Logan Prentice started calling at Sunset View to play the piano, Mamma took a shine to him. One afternoon Kingsley arrived in the conservatory lounge just as Logan was admiring Mamma's gold and lapis lazuli solitaire ring. She introduced the two men, and they got on famously. Before long they fell into a habit of chatting with each other whenever she fell asleep over her tea and Eccles cake.

Logan was an attentive listener, blessed with a gift for making people feel special. They began to exchange confidences. Not only did Logan have the younger generation's easy familiarity with the esoteric riddles of technology, he also loved the arts. As well as playing the piano, he dabbled in amateur theatricals and was a member of a small local group based in Newby Bridge, the Newbies. He'd been given a minor role in a recent Alan Ayckbourn.

"Just small parts," he said with a roguish wink. "I'm hoping for better things. Size does matter, don't you agree?"

Kingsley chortled. His tales of life in the antiques trade enthralled Logan. The young man asked intelligent questions about how to value old jewellery and china, and was fascinated to hear about the Melton family's collection of vintage lapis lazuli, painstakingly assembled over half a century. Kingsley began to look forward to these conversations even more than the chance to spend time with Mamma. One day, he mentioned that Logan might like to pop over to the bungalow to see the treasures firsthand. Logan said that would be lovely, and they exchanged shy smiles.

Their friendship was jinxed from the moment Ivy Podmore took up residence in the home. She doted on Logan, and the amount of time she spent chattering to him soon put Mamma's nose out of joint.

Worse was a humiliating incident which concerned the disappearance of the solitaire ring. Mamma caused a rumpus by accusing Logan of pinching it. Kingsley's mortification increased tenfold when a care assistant found the ring tucked under a cushion on Mamma's favourite sofa. It might have fallen there by accident, but as the manager muttered, just loudly enough for Kingsley to hear, the attention-seeking old biddy had probably hidden it there herself. Although he'd rather die than admit it, Kingsley wouldn't have put it past her.

"Not to worry," Logan said, displaying a magnanimity that thrilled his ever-growing fan club at Sunset View. "These things happen. Anyone can make a mistake, even someone as sharp as a tack, like Sybil."

Sybil Melton wasn't mollified by his generosity. "He's a sly one," she muttered to Kingsley. "You mark my words, he'll get that old fool to give all her worldly goods next. Then her life won't be worth tuppence."

It was a horrid accusation, and Kingsley decided not to mention that he'd invited Logan to their home. At this point, Mamma was determined to return to the bungalow as soon as she'd recovered from her most recent stroke, an illusion that Kingsley dared not shatter.

The prospect of a clandestine encounter with the young pianist excited him. Even though—or perhaps because—he was a dutiful son, he'd always got a thrill out of doing things that would cause Mamma to kick him out of the house if, God forbid, she ever got wind of them. Those things usually involved women of whom Mamma disapproved. In fact, Mamma always found a reason to disapprove of women in whom Kingsley showed the slightest interest.

This was different. He had no close men friends and detested male pursuits such as playing football or going to the pub. Nor had he met anyone like Logan, a fellow sensitive, artistic, and happy to hang on his every word. How marvellous to escape the inquisitive eyes and ears of the care assistants and have a convivial get-together in private.

"This stuff must be really valuable," Logan said, when examining Mamma's display cabinet, home to her beloved collection. "Don't you find it difficult to get suitable insurance?"

"I'll let you into a secret," Kingsley said. "We don't tell the insurers their full value."

"Isn't that risky? I mean, I don't want to pry, but they must be worth a packet."

With a touch of bravado, Kingsley named a figure, and Logan's eyebrows shot up.

"Wow!"

"I suppose it is a calculated risk, but the bungalow is alarmed, and you'd never guess from the road that we have anything special inside."

"That's all right, then," Logan said.

When Kingsley invited him to play the old piano, Logan obliged with a medley of classics from the Andrew Lloyd Webber songbook. The piano, an iron-framed and walnut-veneered Art Deco antique, was badly in need of tuning, but that didn't bother Logan. As he crooned the words to "I Don't Know How to Love Him," Kingsley ruffled his hair, in a purely companionable way. For a few moments he thought something more might happen, but they were both reserved people. Logan said he really ought to be going, but he'd had a wonderful time and hoped he might visit again. Kingsley's intuition was that they had crossed a line. He hardly dared imagine what they'd find on the other side.

Forty-eight hours later, the bungalow was burgled, just before supper in Sunset View. At precisely that time, Logan was serenading Ivy Podmore with a selection from Ivor Novello while Kingsley was trying to distract Mamma with aimless chatter about the good old days in their shop on Kirkland.

Meanwhile, darkness had fallen in Bowness. The burglar alarm failed to go off, but a nosey neighbour heard someone fiddling with a key in the back door lock and scurried round to investigate. She glimpsed the burglar fleeing empty-handed, but her description was useless. She couldn't even be sure it was a man rather than a woman.

Kingsley's own house keys were safe, but he discovered that Mamma's redundant set had gone missing from the old crocodile skin handbag which was her permanent companion in Sunset View. He plucked up the courage to mention this to Logan.

"No!" Dismay was written all over Logan's handsome features. "How terribly upsetting! Surely you don't think that one of the carers could be responsible?"

This wasn't quite the reaction Kingsley had anticipated, but he supposed it was a good question.

"Well, I hate to suggest…"

"Thank God nothing was actually stolen. Of course, your dear old Mummy's so absentminded, she must have dropped the keys somewhere. Wasn't her post code written on the key ring? Anyone who picked them up would know where she lived. An opportunistic crime, I guess. Such a rotten shame." A gleam lit his lovely blue eyes. "Burglary is so…*invasive*. When you go back home, you must feel, I don't know, *defiled*."

A fortnight passed before Kingsley finally asked himself how Logan knew what was written on the key ring. The question occurred to him during Logan's third visit to the bungalow. As usual, whilst Kingsley busied himself pouring them each a glass of buck's fizz, Logan was sitting at the piano and performing his favourite Lloyd Webber number, "Any Dream Will Do."

"You didn't…mention Mamma's lapis lazuli to anyone, did you?"

Logan stopped in the middle of the chorus. He looked as if he'd been bitten by a hitherto faithful labrador.

"What? You're not suggesting I had anything to do with that?"

"Lord, no, of course not. It's just that it all seems so odd. Bowness isn't a hotbed of crime. Why would a casual thief come here? Where did he get the key? It doesn't add up."

Logan stared. "Hey, Kingsley, I'm not sure I care for your insinuations."

"Please!" Kingsley had never seen Logan's face harden or heard such an icy note in his voice. The changes made him almost unrecognisable from the kind-hearted boy who meant so much to him. "I only said..."

"I know what you're really saying." Logan stood up. "I'm just a young layabout, not good enough for the high-and-mighty Meltons. I wasn't born with a silver spoon in my gob, so the minute something goes wrong with your cosy little lives, I'm obviously to blame."

"No!" This was horrendous. Kingsley felt one of his headaches coming on. "Remember last time you were here! I care so much about you."

He moved forward and reached out to stroke Logan's silky fair hair, only to have his hand jerked away in a rapid, painful movement. Logan's cheeks were crimson with rage.

"Get your dirty paws off me, you filthy pervert!"

"What?"

Logan shoved Kingsley so hard he fell backwards on to the carpet. "I ought to have known. Your type are all the same. You'd better watch your step, Melton, otherwise people will find out what you're really like."

Heart pounding, Kingsley looked up into Logan's narrowed eyes. "Please, don't! You know how I feel about..."

"I know exactly how you feel, remember?" Logan was spitting at him. "Soft and squishy, like rotten fruit. Don't you ever dare to mess with me again. Or everyone else will know your mucky little secrets."

With that, he marched out of the sitting room. Tears streaming down his cheeks, Kingsley hauled himself to his feet. Through the bay window he caught sight of his former friend getting into the dirty Fiat van, slamming the door so loudly that a passing pedestrian almost dropped her shopping.

Half an hour later he sent Kingsley a text. As his phone pinged, Kingsley's spirits soared. Logan had come to his senses, surely. He must be ready to apologise.

Within an instant, his hopes were in shreds. Logan hadn't written a word, just sent him a photograph as an attachment. A candid shot of him on all fours, taken covertly in the bedroom of the bungalow, during his second visit here.

For Kingsley, the grinding agony of shame felt like being tortured with an electric drill.

He screamed.

When, much later, he'd recovered the power of rational thought, he knew one thing for certain. If anyone else ever clapped eyes on that vile photograph, he'd throw himself off a Windermere steamer into the deepest part of the lake.

——

There was a wooden kissing gate on the way to the shore, not that Kingsley had ever seen anyone kissing there. Squeezing through, he made his way towards the moored boats at Ferry Nab. Mamma had kept her wits right to the end, he reflected. Provoked by Logan Prentice's rapid transfer of affections to Ivy, she'd cottoned on to the selfishness and cruelty bubbling just beneath the surface affability. At least the young rogue hadn't profited from his crime as he'd hoped. Poetic justice, in Kingsley's opinion. The only problem was, he was probably still short of money and intent on finding his next victim.

Prentice was a gambler who relied on instinct rather than judgement. He'd murdered Ivy within days of her solicitor's visit to Sunset View, and her announcement in the residents' lounge that she'd changed her will. Surely he'd have been wise to allow a decent interval to elapse? Ivy was a frail old woman and it would have sense to allow matters to follow their natural course. The crime illustrated his impatience.

Kingsley watched the car ferry chug away on the short trip across the lake to Hawkshead. What game was his adversary playing? Tory Reece-Taylor was a very different kettle of fish than Ivy Podmore, and she was thirty years younger. Did Prentice plan to beg, borrow, or steal from her? It was perfectly possible that he'd dreamed up a way to soak her money, but somehow Kingsley didn't believe that would be enough for him.

Logan Prentice enjoyed making people suffer, that was the top and bottom of it. The two men had never spoken to each other again after Logan had sent his text with the compromising photo, but he'd caught Kingsley's eye at Sunset View on that last afternoon, while he was playing "I Could Have Danced All Night." There was no disguising the gloat of triumph that twisted his features when nobody else was looking. He relished humiliating Kingsley, loved to have him at his mercy. Power mattered to him; it gave him pleasure. How he must have loved pressing that pillow down over poor Ivy's mouth and nose.

Kingsley had read in a tabloid that once a psychopath tastes blood, once he's committed murder and got away with it, he finds the temptation to repeat the trick irresistible. Even if Prentice didn't need more money, he relished the sport of seduction. It gave him a thrill to charm people into making themselves vulnerable, into surrendering to his will.

For all her feistiness, Tory was susceptible. A rich woman with a weak heart. She gloried in the memory of her sudden cardiac arrest, she loved to boast about coming back from the dead. A pound to a penny, she'd regaled Prentice with the story soon after they'd met. For Kingsley, the anecdote helped to explain her philosophy of *carpe diem*. For Prentice, it would signal an opportunity. As a victim, she was no less suitable than beguiled and befuddled Ivy Podmore. More suitable, in truth, because at Strandbeck Manor there were no prying eyes, nobody to watch what Prentice was up to. Tory didn't possess a panic alarm of the kind old people (including Mamma, before she went into Sunset View) hung around their necks. If she died in her flat of a heart attack, accidental or induced, there was every chance that she'd lie there for a long time before her body was discovered.

Kingsley stopped in his tracks.

Surrounded by the beauty of the most popular part of the Lake District, he could only see one thing in his mind. A vision of Tory's prostrate corpse. Of her decaying flesh.

She must be protected, from both Logan Prentice and herself.

Kingsley squared his shoulders. Only he could save Tory's life.

Chapter Nine

"For as long as a serious crime remains unsolved, suspicion swirls around everyone involved," said the woman on the television screen.

Kingsley had put the TV on for company, as was his habit. He'd been paying even less attention than usual to the regional news until his eye was caught by a photograph of the jogger who had died at Strandbeck. The fallout from the man's death was never-ending. Now the police had vowed to look afresh at the case of Ramona Smith.

A caption on the screen named the woman as Detective Chief Inspector Hannah Scarlett. She looked pleasant, fresh-faced, surprisingly attractive, in fact, but with a determined set to her features that Kingsley found intimidating. He was surprised that this youngish woman held a post of such high rank. Probably she'd benefited from some kind of positive discrimination. It was everywhere these days. Nobody had much time for people like him. What was the phrase? Pale, male, and stale?

There was a clip of an interview with an obese, heavily pierced woman in a gaudy yellow T-shirt. Jade Hughes, denouncing those who had failed her former partner. She hoped the new cold case inquiry meant the police would put right the failures of the past. Good luck with that, Kingsley thought, as he muted the volume.

Why bother with the Ramona Smith mystery? Twenty-one years was a very long time. Hannah Scarlett should concentrate her energies on something more recent. Why not re-examine the death of Ivy Podmore? For all their platitudes about crime prevention, the police never tackled the likes of Logan Prentice.

He scrolled through the endless list of television channels. So much choice, and so little worth watching. He resorted to his store of documentaries, choosing an old history series that explored the way the past cast light on present-day social challenges. In this programme Daniel Kind and a bearded expert were discussing the psychological drivers of crime over the centuries.

"Murder for the sheer lust of killing," the expert said, stroking his beard.

"Like the Ratcliff Highway case?" Daniel suggested. "Those multiple murders in early nineteenth-century London which intrigued Thomas de Quincey?"

Lust of killing. Exactly, he might have been talking about Logan Prentice. Kingsley wondered. Greed was the obvious reason for trying to steal Mamma's lapis lazuli and worming his way into the hearts of wealthy older women, but Kingsley was sure there was more to it than that.

Logan Prentice enjoyed the thrill of persuading people to drop their guard. Once he got well and truly under their skin, they were at his mercy. Lust was the right word for his love of power, Kingsley thought. Yes, Logan Prentice was a lustful criminal.

Something clicked in his memory. He'd read an interview with Daniel Kind in a Cumbrian lifestyle magazine in which

Greengables advertised. The piece coincided with publication of the historian's latest book. He'd mentioned moving from Oxford to Cumbria and the fact that his late father had been a police officer up here.

Kingsley switched off the television and opened up his laptop. Diligent googling yielded dividends. From archived articles in local newspapers and magazines, he picked up several references to Ben Kind. He'd played a part in the hunt for Ramona Smith's killer. An article about a dinner held to mark his retirement included tributes from colleagues, including Hannah Scarlett. None of them mentioned the Ramona Smith case.

Kind senior hadn't enjoyed his leisure time for long. There was a report of his death in a hit-and-run accident one evening. He'd been knocked down on a country lane, walking home from a pub, and an appeal for witnesses hadn't borne fruit. Kingsley found no reference to anybody ever being convicted of the crime. Ironic, he thought. A senior detective's family denied justice, just like Ramona Smith's.

How had Daniel dealt with his bereavement? Did it help to explain his interest in crime? His most recent book was *The Hell Within*, and when Kingsley looked inside the online version, he saw that the book was dedicated to Hannah Scarlett.

Well, well, what a turnup.

A plan began to take shape in his mind. At the time of Ivy Podmore's death, he'd felt despairing and impotent. Things were different now. Tory needed him.

He must talk to Daniel Kind and enlist his support.

———

A collision between two lorries had turned the M6 into a car park. It took Hannah an hour and a half to escape the jam, and when she finally made it back to her flat, Daniel was nowhere to be seen. Instead she found a brief note from him. Exhausted from jet lag, he'd gone home to his cottage to get another night's rest. *See you soon,* the note said and finished with a flourish of kisses. She wished he was there to kiss her in person.

Had she upset him by mentioning his father's failure to solve the Ramona Smith case? Ben Kind had walked out on his family and moved up to Cumbria with his girlfriend. Daniel and Louise were schoolchildren at the time, and their father's desertion hit them hard. The divorce proceedings proved messy and bitter. Louise sided with her mother, but Daniel idolised his father and felt more conflicted. Sensible and objective though he was, even now he tended to take criticism of Ben personally.

It wasn't as if she'd even criticised him. Daniel knew how much she'd admired the man. No police officer solved every case. It...

Stop it. She dug her nails into her palm and told herself not to overanalyse. Daniel had just got back to England after a long and demanding trip. He was weary and needed time to himself. The note was brief, but there was nothing to fret about. No reason to listen to the still small voice whispering in her ear that their relationship was going nowhere.

She walked over to the roses and inhaled their sensual damask fragrance. After all, he'd brought her flowers.

———

Daniel was woken by the trilling of his ringtone. Rumer, "Some Lovers," a current favourite. He reached for his phone and muttered, "Yeah?"

"You're back," his sister's voice announced.

Daniel rubbed his eyes. "Yes, I'm trying to catch up on my beauty sleep."

"You need it more than most," Louise said briskly. "Good time?"

"Great, thanks." When he tried to shift position, his limbs felt as though they were set in concrete.

"I was wondering if you'd like to get together. How about dinner this evening? Stay the night if you want to have a drink and not worry about getting home. If you're not seeing Hannah, that is."

"I was with her in Kendal last night."

A momentary pause. "You sound grumpy."

"You did wake me up."

"Sorry. So how about it? Alex is dying to meet you."

"Alex?" He thought for a moment. "The woman who rescued you from the river?"

"Yes, she's wonderful. Fantastic company. You'll love her."

He yawned. "I hope you're not matchmaking?"

"No, cross my heart and hope to die. I love Hannah to bits, you know perfectly well. It's just that Alex is a bundle of fun. Not to mention stunning." Louise paused. "And she's read all your books."

"Uh-huh." He could hardly keep his eyes open. Any minute now he would be out for the count.

"She loves your writing."

"Okay, you win," he said. "What author could possibly resist?"

———

At midday, Bunny Cohen joined her new colleagues for an impromptu briefing. Les Bryant had just arrived back from

Windermere. He'd made rapid progress. Not only had he traced the whereabouts of Ramona Smith's father, he'd paid him a visit.

"Jimmy Smith is in a care home," he reported. "Not got much time left. Memory loss is only half the story. A lifetime's boozing has turned his brain to mush."

"You didn't get much sense out of him?" Hannah asked.

"The carers reckoned I was lucky, he was having a good morning. He has what they call lucid intervals." Les frowned. "If that's lucidity, I'd hate to see him on a bad day. At least his long-term memory is better than the short-term, which isn't saying much. I managed to piece a few remarks together, but it doesn't take us any forrader."

"You discussed Ramona?"

"As Bunny said, he wasn't a devoted father. Ramona was secretive, he said. Liked to keep her boyfriends dangling, puppets on a string. He took no interest, couldn't recall any names. Said she was no better than her mother. A tart, only interested in how much money she could get out of a man."

Hannah turned to Bunny. "Sound familiar?"

"You bet. A real charmer, that's Jimmy. Ramona never forgave him for deserting her. Messing men around was probably her way of taking revenge."

"Did he blacken her name as a form of cover-up?" Maggie asked. "Was there something going on between him and his daughter?"

Bunny shrugged. "He was a nasty piece of work, and I expect he gave the girl a good hiding whenever she got on his wrong side, but he was pretty much out of Ramona's life by the time she turned seven. If there was anything sexual between them, we never got wind of it."

"Okay," Hannah said, "but who knows? Maybe they met up at Grandma's cottage. What if this supposed mutual dislike was just a blind? If she tired of an abusive relationship and threatened to grass on him, Jimmy would have a strong motive to silence her. Les, can you do a bit more digging?"

"Will do."

"Thanks. Maggie's still trawling through the old files at present. She'll give us a detailed overview of the case tomorrow. As of Monday, Bunny joins us full-time, and then it's all hands to the pump. Gerald Lace is still very much in the frame, obviously, but he's dead and gone. We must consider other possibilities. Not just men, but women who might have been jealous or wanted revenge because she'd slept with their husbands."

"That'll take a while," Les said.

"Ramona wasn't a happy person," Bunny snapped. "We shouldn't judge her. Any of us, if we came from a background like that..."

"All right," Hannah interrupted. "Nobody's making judgements. Our job is to find out what happened to her. As that Van Beek woman said yesterday, we owe it to the innocent suspects as well as the victim."

"The Van Beek woman, yeah," Les said. "I saw her on the news bulletin last night. Thought it was a bit odd, actually."

"Odd?"

"A well-known TV reporter, turning up for a press conference in the far north west? Darren Lace's death is a big story, admitted, but even so..."

"What do you make of it?"

"Maybe she's taking a special interest because of a personal agenda."

"Such as?" Maggie asked.

"Turns out she is an ex-wife of our revered new PCC, Mr. Gleadall."

Hannah was taken aback. "How do you know?"

"Good old-fashioned foot-slogging detective work. Pounding the pavements, knocking on doors." Les allowed himself a sardonic smile. "Not really. Tell you the truth, I looked her up on Wikipedia."

A young woman from admin put her head round the door. "Ma'am?"

"Yes, Manjiri?"

"Message from Mr. Ravi Thakor. He saw you on television and he'd like to have a word with you. In person, if that's possible, at a time to suit you. Apparently he knew Ramona Smith."

Hannah glanced at Bunny. "So he did."

"Didn't take long to rattle his cage," Les said.

"Old sins," Bunny said. "Long shadows."

"Thanks, Manjiri," Hannah said. "Sounds like an offer I can't refuse."

———

The phone in Tarn Cottage summoned Daniel just as he finished a call on his mobile to his London publisher. He'd kept his landline because of the unpredictability of cellphone reception in Brackdale, though most of the calls he received on it were from confidence tricksters masquerading as internet service providers or H.M. Revenue and Customs.

"Daniel Kind."

"Mr. Kind, I'm sorry to bother you like this, out of the blue."

The caller paused, as if to give Daniel a chance to bang the phone down on its cradle. He was male, diffident, a local, judging by his accent. His voice was gravelly, and he sounded to be in his fifties.

"I used to enjoy watching you on television..."

"Thanks very much, Mr..."

"Melton. Kingsley Melton. I live in Bowness, and I'm an estate agent with Greengables."

"Sorry, but I'm quite happy with my present home, and I'm not looking to move."

The man said quickly, "No, no, please. That was clumsy of me. I was simply trying to establish my bona fides as a professional man. I don't want to talk about property."

"No?"

"It's like this, you see…" The man hesitated, as if he'd rehearsed this conversation only to forget his lines the moment it was time to speak. "Well, it's because you're interested in history and murder."

He paused, as if hoping to prompt a question. Daniel didn't know what to say.

"This concerns a murder committed two years ago last spring." Kingsley Melton sounded breathless, as if just he'd just run a hundred yards. "A woman was smothered, but the culprit took care to cover his tracks. Nobody even realised that a crime had been committed."

"Uh-huh."

Daniel wondered whether to hang up. Give crank callers a morsel of encouragement and they never let you go. At least this fellow wasn't a robot or scammer.

"In case you're wondering," the man said, "the victim was in her eighties and resident in a care home. The doctor and the staff convinced themselves that she died in her sleep, but a pillow was held down over her face. It was murder for money, the killer wanted to inherit under her will."

Unable to restrain himself, Daniel said, "How do you know she was murdered with a pillow?"

The answer only came after an even longer pause. "There was a witness."

In for a penny…

"Why didn't the witness come forward?" Daniel asked.

"She died."

By showing interest, Daniel had painted himself into a corner. Common courtesy dictated that there was no alternative now but to engage.

"How do you mean, she died?"

"She was also a resident in the care home." Kingsley Melton took another breath. "A stroke killed her. I'm not saying she was another murder victim. As a matter of fact, she was my mother."

Daniel couldn't think of anything to say but, "I'm sorry."

"Thank you." Kingsley Melton cleared his throat. "You may wonder why I'm calling you. It's not simply because of what happened two years ago. There's something else."

"If you have any information about a serious crime," Daniel said, "you must speak to the police, not me. That's my firm advice."

"It's not so simple, I'm afraid."

"Why not?"

"Well, for one thing, I'm afraid the murderer is going to strike again."

Daniel squeezed the receiver in his palm. "What makes you say that?"

"I know his…what's the term? *Modus operandi*, that's it. He's picked his victim. A younger woman this time. She's very well-off, but she has a history of serious ill health. A few years ago she survived a sudden cardiac arrest."

Despite himself, Daniel was intrigued. "Very worrying, Mr. Melton, but you really should talk to the police."

"I understand, but I'm anxious to speak to you first. You have experience in these matters."

"I'm a historian, not a criminologist."

"You're on good terms with DCI Scarlett of the Cold Case Team," Kingsley said quickly. "You dedicated your last book to her."

Daniel's skin prickled. "Let me give you the contact details for her office."

"No." Kingsley Melton was unexpectedly assertive. "I understand what you're saying, but I have my reasons for not wanting to go to the police. To be honest, I'm desperate to talk to you about this. An off-the-record chat; you can help me get my thinking straight. Totally informal, your choice of venue. When and wherever you want to meet."

"It's good of you to give me the opportunity," Daniel said, "and don't think I'm ungrateful, but I'm afraid the answer's no."

"Mr. Kind, I'm counting on you."

The other man's panic was unmistakeable, even at a distance. Daniel could picture the phone trembling in his hand.

"Sorry." Daniel never found it easy to say no. "I'm grateful for your confidence, but you've approached the wrong person. You can trust the police."

"But they won't trust me!" he yelped.

"What do you mean?"

"I…I have special reasons for being cautious about talking to the police. Private, personal reasons."

"I'm afraid I don't understand."

"I can't discuss it. Not on the telephone."

Daniel waited.

Finally Kingsley blurted out, "This isn't about my guilty secrets! It's about preventing a murder in the here and now. It's a matter of life and death."

———

"It's good of you to spare me a few minutes, Detective Chief Inspector."

Hannah nodded. Ravi Thakor was never less than courteous and this afternoon he was on his very best behaviour. Using her title, rather than her first name, not seeking special favours. Or at least, trying not to look as if he was seeking special favours.

"And thanks for taking the trouble to nip in here, when I was quite willing to come to Busher Walk."

They were sitting in leather armchairs in his luxurious office on the top floor of Effie Gray's, above the function room where she'd seen him the other evening. A pretty Asian girl had served them with chamomile tea and biscuits. Hannah guessed this was the most profitable club and restaurant business in town. Most senior officers would have preferred to interview him at Divisional HQ rather than see him on his home ground, where he'd feel more at ease. Hannah's approach was different. Thakor was a smart guy who wanted to get a particular message across. The more he relaxed, the better the chances of understanding what was really in his mind. Besides, his tea and biscuits were nicer.

"No problem."

He treated her to a paternal smile. Thakor made a point of supporting several police charities. In his younger days, his cash businesses had given him scope to indulge in money laundering, but a combination of natural shrewdness and crafty legal advice had kept him out of trouble. As he'd moved up in the world, he'd sold off the more questionable outposts of his business empire and concentrated his resources on Effie Gray's. He'd also indulged his passion for nineteenth-century art. A painting from his collection hung on the wall opposite his desk, a small portrait of a bright-eyed woman in a dark blue velvet cape.

Thakor followed Hannah's gaze. "Euphemia Gray herself.

She was married to Ruskin, you know, but the relationship was never consummated. He found the naked female form frightening, poor chap. With her second husband, Millais, she made up for lost time. They had eight children."

"I'm surprised she doesn't look worn out," Hannah said.

He treated her to an avuncular beam. For a long time now he'd been a pillar of the community, with everything to gain from sticking to the straight and narrow. People liked him, and even his insatiable womanising was apt to be downplayed. Just Ravi being Ravi. Hannah had met him years ago, not long after she'd first met Marc Amos. Thakor had made clear his interest in her, and she'd made it even clearer that there was nothing doing. He'd taken defeat with a good grace and since then he'd never pushed his luck with her.

"You must be rushed off your feet, so I'll cut to the chase. As I'm sure you'll discover, at the time she went missing, Ramona Smith worked for me. My then-wife and I were both interviewed at the time of the original investigation." He gave a modest cough. "For a short time Ramona and I were very close."

"I see."

She kept quiet as he told her the story, explaining what had happened with such clarity that she was sure his account was well-rehearsed. He'd first slept with Ramona within a fortnight of her starting work at Guido's. She'd recently broken up with Gerry Lace and packed in her job at the Laces' gift shop.

"If I'm honest," Thakor said in his most disarming manner, "Ramona wasn't my usual type."

"Tell me about her."

He stroked his chin. "She was modest about her appearance, and it's true that she wasn't conventionally good-looking, but she had bags of personality. Tons of energy, full of life. Good worker, bright, but easily bored. Neither of us were under the illusion that our relationship had any future. She was just looking for a good time, and frankly so was I. Look, Chief Inspector, I'm not trying to whitewash my behaviour. I was working long hours and she was…ready and willing to offer solace with no strings attached. At the time, I found that very appealing."

I bet, Hannah thought. She nibbled a marzipan biscuit.

"My first marriage was going through a rough patch," he said. "Poppy was a former model. Elegant, neurotic, high-maintenance. Ramona was her polar opposite. She loved it when I gave her presents, everything from a new bike to a spa break, but she was never demanding, never put me under pressure of any kind."

"Did you give her money?"

For the first time, Thakor looked uncomfortable. "Now and then there were cash gifts, yes. Because I knew she was hard up, and her mother had just died, so she was stuck with paying the rent on her house. I could afford to be generous, and she was very grateful."

"Never a cross word?"

"Never."

"And your wife?"

Ravi looked pensive. "Poppy was very highly strung. Gabby, who managed Guido's for me, let slip to her that I'd been with Ramona when I was supposed to have been in a business meeting. All hell broke loose. I swore to Poppy that I'd end the affair, but that wasn't enough. She insisted that I let Ramona go in every way. She told me to sack her."

"And did you?"

"You'll understand, I was in a difficult position," he said.

Hannah said nothing.

"I talked to Ramona. Explained my dilemma."

"And how did she take it?"

"Remarkably well, considering. Said she'd known it couldn't last, and she'd actually found another job. Working as a receptionist at the Bowness Grand. We came to an amicable agreement."

"Which was?"

"She'd work until the end of the week and then tell everyone she'd decided to move on. I paid her in lieu of notice."

"How much?"

The question knocked him off his stride. "Do you know, I can't remember."

"Please try."

"It was a long time ago, Chief Inspector. Ramona had a standard barmaid's contract."

Hannah returned his gaze. "But she wasn't a standard barmaid."

She was confident that, whatever the passage of time, Ravi Thakor wouldn't forget that kind of financial detail. He finished his tea, taking a few moments to consider whether there was any point in prevaricating.

"You're absolutely right." He'd chosen to revert to his easygoing, straightforward manner. "It's come back to me. I paid her six months' wages."

Hannah raised her eyebrows. "So she was entitled to six months' notice?"

"No, no, her notice period under her contract was only one week. The rest was...an ex gratia cash payment."

"Generous."

"Hush money is what you're thinking, Chief Inspector." His sheepish expression was, Hannah thought, entirely calculated. "Not at all. Ramona was good company and we'd had fun together. I simply wanted to give her a helping hand, so she could pay off her debts, make a fresh start."

"Debts?"

"Yes, she was very short of money."

"How did she run up those debts?"

"I've no idea. I didn't want to take too close an interest, if you understand. Drugs, gambling? I can't say."

"Did she do drugs? Was she a gambler?"

"Not to my knowledge." He gave a rueful smile. "The times we had together were precious, and all too short. We never talked about such things."

"Were you surprised when she went missing?"

"Astonished. She had a new job lined up, everything to live for. The Lake District was the only place she knew. She'd have been a fish out of water anywhere else. The police talked to me, of course, as her employer, and they soon found out about our relationship. Thankfully, I was able to satisfy them about my whereabouts on the night in question."

He told her about taking Poppy to Ullswater for an anniversary reconciliation.

"Your wife disliked Ramona?"

"Loathed her," Thakor said. "Understandably, you may think. And you may as well know, Poppy did have a criminal record. When she was nineteen and high as a kite, she'd attacked another model at a party. I'd describe her as volatile rather than truly violent. She even scratched me badly during a row, just before we split up for good. But she wasn't a murderer. She'd never have killed Ramona. There's no question in my mind that Lace was guilty."

"Did you know him personally?"

"No, but Ramona told me she was sick of him. He couldn't take rejection and kept pestering her even after she made it clear that their affair was over. To all intents and purposes, he was a stalker. I believe that he talked her into accompanying him to the Crooked Shore and murdered her. I only wish he'd had the decency to reveal what he did with her body."

"You were surprised when a jury acquitted him?"

"It shook my faith in English justice," Thakor said solemnly.

"What about his suicide?"

"The sign of a guilty conscience."

Thakor folded his arms. As Hannah finished her tea, he bestowed on her a beatific smile to demonstrate that his own conscience was entirely clear.

———

Logan Prentice drove down the hill towards Morecambe Bay, halting within sight of the Crooked Shore. The beach was deserted. Not a suicidal jogger to be seen. What on earth had driven that crazy idiot to end it all by walking into the quicksand and waiting to be drowned?

He lingered for a few moments before setting off for the last leg of his journey to Strandbeck Manor. Growing up, home had been a terraced house in a South Yorkshire back street. As a student he'd lived in cheap rental accommodation and since crossing the Pennines to come to the Lakes, where property was so pricey, he'd moved from one poky bedsit to another. He deserved so much better. One day soon he'd make up for lost time.

As usual, the village—if you could call a scattering of houses and a tiny church a village—was quiet. At the end of Strandbeck Lane, he stopped at the gates of the Manor and jumped out of the van to punch in the security code.

He waited. Nothing happened.

He tried again. Same result.

Dismay stabbed him. Surely Tory wasn't shutting him out?

Last weekend he'd hugged himself with delight when she gave him the code. He'd broken down her defences. Surely she'd not undergone a sudden change of heart? It wasn't impossible; she was so mercurial.

He swore loudly. A flock of birds flew off, as if in protest at his language. He vented his bitterness by kicking a stone gate pillar but only succeeded in hurting his foot. This was so fucking typical. All his life, he'd been dogged by ill luck. Every single time he thought his fortunes were about to change, Fate dealt him a low blow. One of these days…

Pulling himself together, he called Tory on his mobile.

"Darling, it's me."

"How lovely to hear your voice again, sweetheart."

"And yours, darling." Relief flooded through him. "Guess what? I'm outside the Manor. The code doesn't seem to work."

"What? Oh yes, Kingsley changed it."

Logan cursed under his breath. "Don't tell me that creepy bastard is hanging around the place again?"

"No, he's not in his office. Hang on, I'll give you the new numbers."

Yes! He clenched his fists in jubilation as the gates began to move noiselessly apart. Open sesame! Of course he'd not misjudged her—or his own ability to keep an older woman smitten. Tory was still hooked, like a fish on a line.

He drove through the gates. Each time he approached the Manor, he imagined himself as a country squire, returning to his family seat. By rights he should have been born into the landed gentry, rather than to a single mother in Sheffield. A single mother who had produced three children with the assistance of three different men. He was the youngest. Perhaps she'd lied about his parentage. Perhaps his real father was a member of Yorkshire's aristocracy, rather than a bookie from

Rotherham who had done a flit as soon as she announced her latest pregnancy. Not that she described him as a bookie. "Turf accountant" was the term she used. Logan wondered if she'd been as much of a dreamer as he was, before real life knocked the stuffing out of her.

He parked next to Tory's sleek BMW. The contrast with his van—he never washed it, on the basis that in the Lakes the next cleansing downpour wasn't far away—couldn't have been starker. But he wouldn't be poor forever. One day soon, he'd enjoy the lifestyle he deserved.

Clutching a bottle of Gordon's and box of Belgian chocolates, he waited for Tory to answer her door. She might be loaded, but she loved receiving presents. Women always did, in his experience.

"Sweetheart, what a wonderful surprise!"

"I wasn't sure you'd be in." As usual, he was economising on the truth. Tory didn't get out much. "I brought these for you, just on the off-chance."

"Oh, sweetheart, how kind!"

She clasped him to her and they kissed. Her posh perfume didn't quite mask the whiff of gin on her breath.

As he closed his eyes, his mind wandered. A question struck him.

Why had that pathetic jobsworth Kingsley Melton changed the security code?

———

Daniel was assailed by pangs of regret the moment he put down the phone. Against his better judgement, he'd agreed to meet Melton. How stupid to allow himself to be talked into something he was sure to regret. His insatiable curiosity, the yearning to discover hidden truths that had shaped his career, was to blame.

Like father, like son. A historian was a sort of detective. A detective of the past, admittedly, a detective who had never pounded the mean streets of Manchester or even Maryport. Murder, and above all the reasons why one person may feel driven to kill another human being, held an irresistible fascination for him. Since getting to know Hannah, he'd lurked in the background during several of her investigations into cold cases.

Daniel didn't know what to make of Melton's reference to guilty secrets. The man seemed to regret his words as soon as they spilled out of his mouth. He'd piqued Daniel's interest.

Like a cautious online dater arranging a first meeting, Daniel had proposed a rendezvous at a public venue. Instead of a restaurant or bar, he'd opted for his favourite secondhand bookshop in the south Lakes, a short drive from his cottage and an easy hop from Bowness for Melton. Even if their conversation proved to be a complete waste of time, he'd have a good excuse to browse the shelves and tuck into a fat slab of cake in the café.

A quick search of the Greengables website confirmed that Kingsley Melton was indeed their representative in this part of the world. Daniel clicked "Our Team" on the drop-down menu and was rewarded with a brief CV and a thumbnail photograph. Melton had clocked up many years of experience in a family retail business before moving into estate agency. In the photo, he looked haggard and hollow-eyed, as if he'd just read a damning structural survey.

The suicide at Strandbeck had received acres of coverage. After reading the newspaper reports, Daniel began to understand Kingsley Melton's reticence. The journalists had hung the man out to dry. While taking care not to libel him, they'd chosen direct quotes which conjured up a picture of a self-absorbed buffoon whose failure to act in time had cost a man's life. Daniel had enough experience with the tabloid press to suspect the truth was more complicated. Chances were that the poor devil had simply been in the wrong place at the wrong time.

———

"What have you got against Kingsley?" Tory asked in a lazy drawl.

She poured herself another gin and tonic. Logan sat beside her on the sofa, still drinking his first. In Tory's company, he paced himself. Vital to keep a clear head. What poison might Melton have dripped into her ear?

"I told you, I came across him at that care home. His mother was an old witch. I did my best with her, played all her favourite songs from the shows, but she became madly jealous whenever I paid attention to any of the other residents."

Tory ran her fingers through his silky hair. "I can understand it. Any woman would be reluctant to share you."

"Well, darling," Logan said, "now you've got me all to yourself."

"Promise?"

"Cross my heart and hope to die," he said.

"You haven't answered my question. Why do you loathe Kingsley?"

"He made trouble for me." He closed his eyes. "I didn't mean to tell you this, but he tried to touch me up. I had to tell him where to get off. Make it clear I wasn't interested. Obviously."

"Naughty Kingsley." She giggled. "I ought to be shocked, but I can't say I'm totally surprised. You're such a hunk and he's extremely repressed."

"Very." Logan said, "Though he's not as innocent as he looks."

"No?"

"When I rebuffed him, he took revenge by spreading all sorts of stories about me."

"Not casting doubt on your virility, I hope," Tory said, kissing his cheek. "Not that anybody in their right mind would believe him."

"Worse than that," Logan said mournfully. "He claimed I was on the make, only out for myself. I played the piano to the old dears out of the goodness of my heart, but he did his best to turn that against me. Claimed I was trying to chisel money out of one of the residents. Honestly, I could have sued him for slander."

"Naughty Kingsley."

"Nobody believed him, thank God," Logan said. "As it happens, I was offered money gifts, several times, but I never accepted a penny. I felt bad about saying no. It seemed ungracious, but somehow it didn't seem right to pocket their cash. For me, it was a point of principle."

"You should have said yes," she said. "It would have given the old folk pleasure."

"The manager of the home said the same, but I stood firm. I couldn't bear anyone thinking I was on the make. That's why Kingsley's slurs left such a bitter taste."

"From what he told me, that mother of his has a lot to answer for. He should have had the guts to break away, instead of frittering his life away tied to her apron strings."

He grinned. "Chained to her broomstick, more like."

Tory laughed. "I'm glad you're not jealous just because he and I…"

"I always want to tell you the truth," he said quietly, "even if it isn't easy. And if I'm absolutely honest, I am a teeny, teeny bit jealous. I mean, I know you're a free agent. A strong, independent woman."

"Yes," she murmured.

"You can do whatever you want, of course. It's just that when I think of his bony claws fumbling with your lovely body…"

He broke off to give a theatrical shudder.

"He was just a dalliance." She planted a wet kiss on the cheek. "Not young and handsome like you. Not special. Kingsley is just such a sad individual. I suppose I took pity on him."

"You're so generous," he said. "You only see the best in others."

"I'm no saint," she murmured.

He slipped his hand inside her blouse. "Luckily for me, darling."

Chapter Ten

Louise Kind was a smart lawyer, a former corporate executive now pursuing a career in academe. A pity, her brother thought, that she'd never shown much evidence of legal caution in conducting her personal life. Unsuitable men had come and gone; shortly after she'd followed Daniel's lead and moved up to the Lake District, a lover with whom she'd had a tempestuous relationship had been murdered.

She and Hannah liked each other, perhaps a case of opposites attracting, but lately, Louise had betrayed signs of impatience with their failure to settle down together. Once after a couple of drinks she'd demanded to know whether he meant to pop the question before Hannah got bored and found someone else. He never came up with a satisfactory answer. The truth was that Hannah was as wary of long-term commitment as he was of rejection.

As the crow flew, it was only a few miles from his home in Brackdale to Wordsworth country, where Louise had recently bought a cottage. By the meandering roadways of the Lake District, the drive took a good forty minutes and he spent them wishing he hadn't accepted her invitation. At her best, Louise was good company, but after spending most of the day sleeping off his jetlag, he felt in no mood for small talk with someone he'd never met. Even if that someone was a fan of his books.

He rounded the bend at Penny Rock, so called because the cost of blasting through to put in the old turnpike road had added a penny to the rates, and Grasmere came into view, a low sun shining on the water. The sight lifted his spirits. He'd dropped lucky. During his trip to the States, the weather in Cumbria had been at its foulest, but his return had coincided with forecasts of a mini-heatwave.

The Rothay curled through the centre of the village, and the road crossed the river close to the churchyard where Wordsworth and members of his family were buried. He wondered how close Louise had come to death when she'd fallen into the water. They both owed this woman Alex a debt of gratitude.

His sister's timber-framed eco-cottage was one of half a dozen perched on a rise above the lake, less than a mile from the heart of the village and the tourists who milled through narrow streets where Wordsworth, Coleridge, and de Quincey once strolled. The development was pitched at purchasers who wanted an environmentally friendly home and were prepared to pay over the odds for it. Second-home owners were barred, and car users tolerated only because public transport in the Lakes was so patchy.

The cottage had a terrace looking over to Grasmere. Louise and her saviour were sitting at a table, sipping something long and cool. As he parked, they raised their hands in greetings. He'd brought flowers for both of them, but as he approached the terrace from the gravel path he stopped in his tracks.

Louise hadn't done Alex Samaras justice. She was gorgeous.

———

"I was tempted to bring along my collection of your books," Alex Samaras said. "I'd love to get them personalised. On reflection, I decided to give you due warning. So you've got time to think up a suitable message."

Her teasing smile showed perfect white teeth, her doe eyes were large and wide. With an oval face framed by long dark-brown hair with bangs, and a tall, sinewy, androgynous figure clad in a white shirt and faded jeans, she bore a faint resemblance to Jane Birkin in her younger days. Demure yet provocative, laid-back yet mischievous.

"You do realise," Louise murmured, "the signed ones are worth much less than the rare unsigned copies?"

Alex laughed. Daniel had already discovered that when she claimed to be a fan of his writing, she wasn't merely being polite; her questions displayed a surprisingly detailed knowledge of his books. What struck him most was that she was a generous listener, absorbed in everything Louise said as well as his own attempts to explain what he loved about history.

"I insist on an inscription with a touch of mystery. *To Alex— she knows why*. Or is that too much to ask?"

"What author could possibly resist?" He turned to his sister. "So, this accident. Why on earth were you out walking a dog if the conditions were so rotten?"

Louise put on a sad face. "Seemed like a good idea at the time."

"Those words will carved on your tombstone."

"Yes, well, I've never been as frightened in my life. I was simply trying to be a kind neighbour. Wendy next door sprained her ankle and was worried sick that her dog, wasn't getting the exercise he needs. I volunteered to help out, but Max is young and full of beans, a real handful. I took him for a walk after a storm when the grass was wet through. To cut a long story short, we both finished up in the river. The difference was, I didn't mean to lose my footing, and I couldn't haul myself out. The shock was terrible and the water cold as ice. I've never known the Rothay so swollen. If not for Alex, I'd never have survived. She showed up in the nick of time."

Alex shook her head. "You're making too much of it. You'd almost reached the bank. Even if I'd not been there, You'd…"

"Pay no attention to her," Louise said. "She's far too modest. Don't be fooled by that skinny frame. One of her hobbies is martial arts."

Alex laughed. "Yes, I can look after myself, you don't want to mess with me. Put it down to a misspent youth. I adore climbing, diving, sailing…"

"I'd love to sail," Louise said wistfully.

"I promise to take you out in my dinghy one of these days. Anyway, that night, I had to make do with a gentle jog along the riverbank. I heard a loud splash. Poor Max, whooshing into the water."

"Then an even louder splash," Louise said ruefully. "That was me, losing my balance and toppling in after him. You know how grateful I am. It turned out to be my lucky day."

"Mine too. All the more so, once I found out that your brother was Daniel Kind. Incredible, I've been a fan for ages."

"How long have you lived in the Lakes?" Daniel asked.

"This time around? Less than a year. It feels like coming back home. You won't guess it from my accent, but I grew up a few miles from here. What's really spooky is that I once met your dad."

Daniel blinked. This woman was full of surprises.

"Seriously?"

"Actually, that's how I got interested in you. Your books, I mean, I don't want to sound creepy. I was living in London and needing a break from city life so I came up here. I knew the land-lord of a pub in Oxenholme, The Old Junction, from way back. He was short-handed, so I helped out behind the bar a couple of nights a week. Not for the money but for the company. That's where I met Ben; it was his local. He'd not long retired from the police force and he was at a loose end. As you do, we got chatting."

"I bet you did," Louise muttered. "Our father always had an eye for a pretty girl. That was his undoing."

"Oh, there was nothing like that." Alex giggled. "He was more than twice my age. I could tell he'd once been a good-looking fellow, but he'd started putting on weight and drinking too much. All the same, I felt sorry for him."

"How do you mean?" Daniel asked.

"He didn't seem happy." Alex paused, studying their reaction, "Obviously he missed being a policeman, all that camaraderie. He was a keen gardener, but he liked to get out of the house, said his missus didn't want him under her feet all the time. What was her name, the second wife? Cheryl, was it?"

"Cheryl, yes."

Louise's features froze into a pale mask. Ben Kind had abandoned his wife and children to come up to Cumbria with Cheryl. He'd got a divorce and remarried, and his ex-wife had broken off all contact with him. She'd never forgiven Ben for his betrayal. Neither had her daughter.

Daniel had hero-worshipped his father from afar, clinging to a fantasy that one day there would be a reconciliation, but he'd not even learned of Ben's death until after his funeral. Cheryl had seen to that.

"Sorry, that's why I didn't mention it before. I was afraid of upsetting you."

"I'm not upset." Louise's tone was muffled, and for a dreadful moment, Daniel thought she was about to cry. "I mean—it was a wretched time. Once that dreadful woman got her claws into him, we all suffered."

"I do understand," Alex said earnestly. "It's only natural, this bitterness. He confided in me, just a little bit, told me about his regrets."

Daniel felt torn. For his sister, talking about the past reopened old wounds, but he'd always wondered about his father's life after he and Cheryl moved up to Cumbria. The insights he gleaned from Hannah were precious, but mostly limited to their working relationship. He always longed to learn more.

"What did you talk about?"

"It was rather sad. He felt he'd messed up his life." She hesitated. "I'm afraid his second marriage was unhappy."

"You're dead right," he said grimly. "Cheryl was having an affair with the man she worked for."

"Ben found out," she said. "I think he was glad to have someone to talk to that he could trust. Like he said, he didn't stop being a detective just because he'd retired from the force. I don't know what would have happened if he'd lived."

"Cheryl and her boss got together after Dad died."

"Ah, that I didn't know." She sighed. "I'd seen you on the TV from time to time, and chatting with Ben prompted me to look for your books. I bought *History Repeats Itself* the day he died. I was going to ask if he'd mind sending it to you for a signature. Knowing how it hurts to lose a father you love, I hoped it might be a way of bringing the two of you back together."

"Generous of you."

His voice was raspy with emotion. Talking to this woman brought back memories. Louise was silent, staring out over Grasmere.

"I wasn't behind the bar that night," Alex murmured. "I was due to go back to London the next week, and I'd been reading a script my agent had sent. When I heard that Ben had been killed, I could hardly believe it. The landlord of The Old Junction told me he'd had been drinking heavily. It was a dark evening and I suppose his head was in a fuddle as he walked home. The accident happened on a narrow lane with no pavement. So terrible that the driver who hit him never stopped."

"Yes," Daniel said curtly.

"I'm sure it was deliberate. You can't run someone over like that and not know exactly what you've done." She shook her head. "I often wondered…if an ambulance had been called sooner, would he have survived?"

Daniel said, "If only they'd caught the bastard who did it."

"Everyone deserves justice," Alex said. "Presumably the police did what they could. But it wasn't enough. They let him down. One of their own. I was tempted to play detective myself and find out the truth. But I didn't know where to start."

For a few moments nobody spoke. Louise lifted the bottle again, but Alex put her hand over her glass.

"Better not. I don't want to get tipsy and make a bad impression."

Louise left them while she went off to make coffee, and Alex plied him with questions about his writing. Her eyes sparkled as she listened. Daniel found her enthusiasm as intoxicating as the champagne. He reminded himself that, even if she was currently resting, she was still an actor. Tonight she was simply playing another part: the admiring fan. Even so, he was only human. He couldn't help feeling flattered.

———

"You're going to kill me!" Logan panted.

Tory laughed as she climbed off him. They were on her vast leather sofa. Their lust had been so intense that they'd undressed each other before they could make it to the bedroom.

"Life in the old lady yet, eh?"

"Don't say that," he gasped. "You're not old."

Her eyes feasted on his lean, hairless chest. "Compared to you, I'm ancient."

"Don't be silly." He was getting his breath back. "I prefer women of the world."

"Nice phrase," she said. "Much kinder than cougar. Let alone wrinkly hag."

"You've got nothing to prove. Trust me, you're perfect. Experienced, passionate…"

She blew a kiss. "You're so good for my morale."

"Seriously, girls my age never satisfied me. So selfish and immature."

"Don't get the wrong idea, sweetheart. I'm no do-gooder. Believe me, I'm pretty satisfied myself."

He looked up into her eyes. "Promise?"

"Cross my heart and hope to die."

Suddenly his body stiffened, and he averted his gaze.

"Hey, Logan! What's the matter?"

"Nothing, nothing at all," he said quickly. "That was so fantastic…"

"Come on. Something's bugging you. Tell me."

He closed his eyes, and she retaliated by pulling his hair, making him flinch.

"Don't go quiet on me, sweetheart. I don't take no for an answer, you should have figured that out by now. What's wrong?"

"It's just that…"

"Go on."

"When you said *cross my heart and hope to die*, it upset me. After what happened to you."

"What are you talking about? Not the cardiac arrest?"

"Yes. Such a horrific thing. I'm afraid I might…"

She giggled. "You reckon your physical demands could finish me off?"

"It's not funny." His tone was mulish. "I can't bear to think…"

"You think too much." She put her arms around his shoulders. "What happened to me could happen to anyone, like a lightning strike. No point in stressing over it."

"Your heart stopped."

"So it did. But they brought me back to life and now I'm right as rain. A woman reborn."

She hugged him to her.

"Hey, Logan, what's this?"

A couple of tears were trickling down his cheeks.

"Sorry, darling. I know it's crazy, when you're so full of life you wear me out, but it frightens me that at any moment… I can't help thinking about it. Last night I got myself so wound up, I hardly got a wink of sleep."

She wiped his face with the flat of her hand. "You won't get much sleep tonight, either. I've not finished with you, not by a long chalk."

He mustered a smile. "You're amazing."

"I tell you this," she whispered, "what happened to me proved the truth of the old saying. What doesn't kill you makes you stronger."

"Tell me about it."

She shot him a sharp glance. "I don't like to dwell on the past."

"If I understand, it will help me not to panic about you."

"It's not much of a story. I tripped over some cobblestones in the middle of Rye, and that was enough to put me out for the count. A passing nurse gave me CPR. Without that, it would have been curtains. Another stroke of luck was that an ambulance turned up almost at once. I was whisked into intensive care. Getting back to normal didn't happen overnight. Lots of rehab, millions of pills to take, strict low-fat diet. I lost so much weight that my clothes were hanging off me—believe it or not." She cast a wry glance at her belly. "Some women would have been over the moon. Not me, I was always proud of my curves."

"Quite right too," he murmured.

"At first my confidence took a hammering. I can't have been much fun to live with. I suppose I was in denial. But then I gave myself a good talking-to. Why be bad-tempered when I ought to be deliriously happy that I'd cheated death?"

"Yes," he said. "It sounds miraculous."

"Winston could be a boring old sod, God rest his soul, but he said one thing that helped. He swore blind that, to look at me, nobody would guess anything was wrong. They wouldn't have the faintest idea I'd come back from the dead. Of course, I still take the pills regular as clockwork, the medicine cabinet is overflowing. And I've stopped eating red meat." She giggled. "But I've got back to being quite badly behaved."

"Thank God!"

"Yes, the specialist would be livid. I drink far more than I should, and I certainly don't avoid physical exertion." She patted his rump. "As you've noticed. But my philosophy is that a romp with you is worth a dozen gentle strolls along the Crooked Shore. Why live to be one hundred if you're unhappy? A girl must have her fun."

He reached for her. "And fun is just what you're going to get."

——

"Alex used to live on Santorini." Louise had returned with the coffee. Daniel thought she'd read his mind, sensed his curiosity about her new friend. "She was married to a Greek wine merchant, hence the exotic surname."

"Yes, at drama school I was just plain Alexandra Rowan. I fell in love with someone twice my age who was five years into his third marriage. Yanis told me he was ready for a change." Alex gave a wistful smile. "My mistake was to believe that meant he was ready to settle down. Really, he just wanted to get inside a different pair of knickers. I played hard to get, but that only made him more persistent."

"How long before you surrendered?" Louise asked.

Alex pretended to rack her brains. "Oh, almost a week."

The two women dissolved in laughter.

"Don't look so shocked, Daniel," Alex said. "Yanis was a well-to-do man of the world. I was dazzled, swept off my feet by the prospect of the good life. Tourists travel from all four corners of the globe to see Windermere, but for me it was nothing special. Simply because the Lake District was where I'd grown up. Santorini sounded like paradise, an island where it never rains. Or almost never. I was thrilled when Yanis told me that he lived on the edge of an extinct volcano. Within a month of meeting him, I was installed in his house on the hill at Akrotiri. From the veranda you can see the lighthouse, the cliffs of the caldera, and mile after mile of grapes."

"Sounds idyllic," he said.

"Until you get bored," Alex said. "Once Yanis divorced his wife and married me, things changed. He travelled a lot on business, leaving me on my own. I was able to sail and climb to my heart's content, but..."

"You can have too much of a good thing?"

"Exactly! Within a few months I was so fed up, I was tempted to practise my martial arts on Yanis. I persuaded him to buy a bolt-hole in London, in the hope of auditioning for shows on the West End. So I had a flat in Covent Garden, and began to pick up the threads of my career. I enjoyed myself, more than I should have done, given that my husband spent so much time overseas."

"Serves him right for not taking better care of you," Louise said. "While the cat's away…"

"Two can play at that game, though. Didn't some sleazy billionaire once say that as soon as he married his mistress, he created a vacancy? He might have been speaking for Yanis. Once the stars fell from my eyes, I knew he'd never be faithful. It was only a question of time before we parted."

"After that, you came back north?"

"Not at first. I didn't have any family left. When I came back for those few weeks, it was a sort of a trial run. The landlord and your father were the closest I had to friends. As for acting, I had a few small parts in minor productions, but my looks were out of fashion. Or maybe I didn't sleep with influential people. Whatever. In the end I gave up."

"But you've not given up on acting?" Daniel asked.

She allowed her gaze to linger on him. "Oh, no. I'm not rich enough to be completely idle. Though it's hard to find work, so thank God I'm not under financial pressure. One good thing about Yanis, he likes to settle his divorces quickly and with the minimum fuss, so he can devote himself to his latest conquest. I'm renting my cottage while I look for somewhere permanent. And that's all, folks. End of story. A woeful tale of under-achievement by comparison with the talented Kinds."

"Rubbish," Louise said. "You'll find plenty of opportunities here. That director you were chatting to at the Theatre by the Lake…"

Alex laughed. "I'm not holding my breath for an offer. Chances are, I'll be a lady of leisure for months to come, so I need to make new friends. Not that I ever expected to come across Ben Kind's daughter."

"Lucky for me you did."

"I think it was meant," Alex said dreamily. "Fate. It sounds stupid, but I've always blamed myself for your dad's death. If I'd been behind the bar that night, he wouldn't have drunk too much. I'd have made sure of that. Things might have been different…"

"I'm just glad you were in the right place at the right time when I fell into the Rothay."

Alex finished her coffee and stood up. "It's been a wonderful evening, but now I'd better make a move."

"Stay!" Louise commanded. "The night is young!"

"No." Alex shot Daniel a glance. "I'd love to, but—another time, perhaps."

After a bit of to-ing and fro-ing, Louise admitted defeat. As Alex waved a last farewell from the lane, she turned to her brother.

"Well?"

"You were spot on," he said. "She is stunning."

Louise beamed; she enjoyed being told her she was right.

"You're in luck. She's got a thing for you."

"Aren't you forgetting? I'm spoken for."

Louise's eyes were slightly unfocused. During the course of the evening, she'd had more to drink than either of her guests. "I know, I know, but…I mean, Hannah's terrific, but she's so wrapped up in the bloody job. After you went off schmoozing in the States, I invited her over and she said yes, only to cancel at the last moment because something came up with that rape trial where she was called to give evidence. It made me wonder. Is this the story of her life? Work always coming first, just as it did with Dad?"

"She's nothing like Dad."

"She learned everything she knew about policing from him. That came from her own lips and I don't think she was talking about interrogation techniques. She's obsessed with the job, same as he was."

"Two very good detectives."

"There's more to life than detecting."

Time to change the subject. "Weird that Alex actually met Dad."

Louise nodded. "She's right, it's Fate."

"How do you mean?"

"I feel a connection with Alex." Louise sounded as though the champagne was starting to talk. "She's a special person. Lovely, yes, but caring too. If I were a man, I'd fancy her like mad. Pity she's only got eyes for you."

He gritted his teeth. Louise had a unique ability to wind him up. "Hey, that's enough. Your imagination is running away with you."

"I'm not saying she's got good taste, mind you." She laughed. "She's choosy. There was a young actor at the theatre last night who was desperate to pick her up, but she gave him short shrift."

He gave a so-what shrug.

"Daniel, listen to me. Alex has got a hell of a lot going for her. Young, but not too young. Beautiful and unattached and in no need of a meal ticket. No question of her working all the hours that God sends, even if she does manage to find acting work." She stifled a hiccup. "If you ask me, Hannah needs to up her game. The competition just got stronger."

———

"I meant to ask you," Tory said. "What's the latest news about Ingrid?"

Logan squinted at the bedside alarm clock. Half past midnight. For a few seconds, he said nothing. When he spoke there was a catch in his voice.

"It's not looking good, to be honest."

She cradled him in her arms. "Sweetheart, I'm sorry. Do you want to tell me?"

He gave a hollow laugh. "If you don't mind, I won't. It's like you were saying before. Talking about this personal stuff is so difficult."

"But I talked to you."

"Yes," he said. "You did, and I'm glad."

"There you are, then. Can I do anything to help?"

His body tensed under her touch. "You do so much for me already. It's not fair to burden you with all this family upset."

"I don't mind at all."

"You're so generous," he said. "I love coming here to the Manor. When I'm spending time with you, I can forget about Ingrid, just for a little while."

"You can't forget about her," Tory said. "You don't really want to either."

He turned over to lie on his back and gaze at the high bedroom ceiling and the elaborately carved coving.

"Yes, darling," he said. "You're right, of course."

"Haven't you noticed?" She pressed her body against his. "I'm always right."

He didn't return her smile. "It's just that…oh, God, I hate to think it, let alone say it."

"What?"

His voice choked. "I think she's going to die."

Chapter Eleven

"Ramona Smith vanished into thin air one fine evening, twenty-one years ago." Maggie Eyre had the floor at a team briefing. "When last seen, she was in good spirits. No hint that she might suddenly disappear, without any warning."

A photograph on the screen showed Ramona at a Christmas party. She was wearing a paper hat and a little black dress that didn't leave much to the imagination. At first glance, Hannah thought, she was nothing special to look at. An ordinary young woman with mousy hair, a crooked nose, and a wide mouth showing dodgy teeth in a broad smile. She also had a gleam in her eyes and a firmly set jaw.

"Tell us about the last sightings," Hannah said.

She'd taken a seat at the back of the room alongside the young men and women who provided admin support to the frontline officers. She wanted everyone, even those who were simply processing data, to see the big picture. A cold case might lack the urgency of a murder in the here and now, but if people were invested in the outcome, they'd stretch themselves. They'd want to discover the truth.

Maggie glanced at her laptop screen. Hannah noticed that

her fists were clenched. Maggie was no shrinking violet, but although she hid it well, she was a nervous public speaker. That was precisely why Hannah had asked her to present the outcome of her initial review of the files. Ben Kind had taught her that you had to learn the hard way. Maggie would make a first-rate inspector one day, but first she needed to get out of her comfort zone.

"She worked as a barmaid at Guido's in Bowness, though she was due to start a new job the following week. It was a Tuesday evening, before the start of the tourist season proper, and a flu bug was going around. The weather was okay for the time of year, but business was slow. The few customers who were traced said they saw nothing unusual in Ramona's behaviour. Her shift ended at nine. She picked up her rucksack, put on her anorak, and said goodbye. They never saw her again."

"Little or no CCTV in them days," Les grumbled. "Don't suppose she owned a mobile?"

"One of those big, clunky monstrosities that were fashionable then? They'd started to become affordable, but plenty of people didn't have one. Including Ramona."

"Pity."

"She lived on her own in a rented end terrace house, ten minutes' walk from the bistro. Leila, her mother, had recently died of cancer. According to the neighbours, Leila wasn't too popular, because of the dodgy-looking men who used to call on her. As for Ramona, she had a reputation for keeping herself to herself."

"A loner?"

"Yes and no. She didn't enjoy school, or keep up with mates from that period of her life. Her teachers remembered her as bright, but someone who would rather daydream than study. Although she was quite athletic, she had no interest in team sports. The teachers thought she was like her parents. Directionless."

Les pointed to the photograph on the screen. "Looks like a party animal to me."

Maggie shook her head. "What's interesting is how few pictures of Ramona surfaced. That party is as close to the high life as she got. In Bowness, at least, she didn't have any girlfriends. Men, that was a very different story."

"What about her colleagues in Guido's?"

"Other than Ravi Thakor, who was away that evening, there was a middle-aged gay couple, two young girls, and a female manager. We'll need to look at them again, but at the time there was no reason to believe they had anything to hide."

"Did Ramona take anyone home that night?"

"As far as we can tell, she never went back home after leaving Guido's. Next day, she didn't show up for her shift. She didn't have a habit of letting her employers down. If she got bored with a job, she simply gave a week's notice and moved on. When she was sick, she'd call in. Gabby, the manager, rang her home number, but got no answer. She assumed Ramona had picked up the flu, and thought no more about it. The following day, again there was no word from her. By now, Gabby was getting pissed off, because the weekend was coming up and she was short-handed. When there was no sign of Ramona for a third day, she popped round to the house. The upstairs curtains weren't drawn and there was no sign of life. She was worried that something might be badly wrong, so she knocked on a neighbour's door. The woman who lived there said Ramona's mum used to leave a key under a plant pot in the back garden. Convenient for gentlemen callers, you see. The key was there, exactly where it should be. Gabby went into the house and found—nobody. At that point she phoned Ravi Thakor, and he said she'd better call the police."

"By which time the trail was already cold," Hannah said.

"Yes, more than sixty hours had passed since the last con-firmed sighting of Ramona. The house was searched, and all her clothes and possessions seemed to be present and cor-rect. Her savings passbook was there. The money was never touched."

"What happened to it in the end?" Les asked.

"Seven years after she went missing, her father had her declared dead. It was a pure formality. Everything she'd left went to him under the intestacy laws. Not that it gave him a motive. There wasn't much."

"What about her passport?"

"Stuffed into her knicker drawer. Over the years she'd hol-idayed in places like Torremolinos and Lanzarote. As far as anyone could tell, she hadn't taken anything other than the clothes she stood up in and the rucksack. A brand new jumper she'd just bought was still in its bag, with the receipt."

"Did she drive?"

"She'd passed her test but preferred to cycle or walk. Before you ask, the bike was found in the outside shed, and she didn't own a car. She walked to work."

"Any signs of disturbance in the house?"

"The only part that was a complete tip was her mother's old room. It looked as though Ramona hadn't been able to face touching it since Leila's death."

"Any reports of altercations the night she went missing?" Les asked. "Screams heard in the distance?"

"Nothing worthy of note. Bowness is a lively place, as we all know, but there was no evidence that Ramona had been attacked on her way home. Far less heaved into the lake."

"So why assume she'd been murdered?"

"Nobody jumped to conclusions. Far from it. The initial

inquiry was led by Desmond Loney, and he took a lot of convincing she was dead."

"Good old Desmond," Bunny said, adding disloyally, "Cumbria's Clouseau."

She rolled her eyes, and Hannah struggled to suppress a highly unprofessional burst of laughter. During his long career, Loney was a byword for his anything-for-a-quiet-life philosophy. Ben Kind used to say he raised taking the easy way out into an art form. Today, Hannah reflected, Ben was cold in his grave, and Desmond was spending his pension on Mediterranean cruises and pottering around his garden up in St Bees. Was there a moral in that?

Maggie said, "People with ordinary, relatively stable lives don't simply vanish in a puff of smoke. There must be an explanation. But Jimmy Smith was no help. He thought she'd run off with some bloke. Her grandma was senile and past caring. A few days later she went into a home for dementia sufferers, and she was dead within a month. Ramona wasn't close to her work colleagues—Ravi Thakor excepted—or even people in the same street that she'd known for twenty years."

"What about the other men she got close to?" Les asked.

"A different story. She'd had an active love life since her midteens. She liked men with money who lavished gifts on her, but she didn't want to settle down with them. One reason being that they were married."

"*All* of them?" Les asked.

"The vast majority, for sure. Naturally, that complicated the inquiry, because they weren't public-spirited enough to come rushing forward with information."

"Surprise me," Les muttered.

"To do her justice, Ramona never gossiped about her fancy men. She was good at keeping her mouth shut."

"No question of her blackmailing anyone?" Hannah asked. Ravi Thakor, she supposed, would never have considered himself a blackmail victim. He'd simply rewarded Ramona's discretion.

"Nothing came to light."

"Given that she was short of money, did she spend heavily on drugs or gambling?"

"Again, no evidence of either."

Maggie bent over her laptop and the screen filled with a montage of newspaper headlines. Bowness Woman Missing. Police Issue Fresh Appeal. Have You Seen This Woman?

"At first the case sparked a blaze of publicity. Public appeals for information, alleged sightings. Nothing came of them."

"Was suicide ruled out?"

"Not at first. She'd left no note, and there was nothing to indicate that she was so deeply troubled. Most people thought that she was at the bottom of a lake or tarn."

"There's no shortage of them round here," Les said. "Very tempting for any killer to dump her in a watery grave."

"Too right. Of course it was impossible to conduct a specific search, with nothing to go on. Desmond's investigation lost focus. Poor Ramona didn't have people rooting for her, demanding to know the truth about her fate. Things changed when Ben Kind came on the scene."

As Maggie took a breath, Hannah nodded.

"I bet."

"He'd not long moved up here from Manchester. Desmond was kicked sideways to head an investigation into a spate of robberies, and Ben was asked to look at the Ramona Smith case with a fresh pair of eyes. Straightaway he had a stroke of luck. This was found."

A green canvas rucksack, dirty and scuffed, filled the screen. "Ramona's?" Les asked.

"Yes, she'd had it for years. A constant companion when she went walking on the fells."

"Where did it turn up?"

"At Strandbeck, on the Crooked Shore."

———

For Daniel, the smell of old books was as sweet a perfume as you'd find in any rose garden. He strolled along a set of tall bookshelves in Amos Books, breathing in the heady aroma of ancient tomes on the lore of Lakeland.

"Hello, stranger," said a voice behind him. "Back from your travels at last?"

Daniel spun round and came face-to-face with the shop owner. Marc Amos was in his late thirties, amiable, and attractive to women. In his smooth, regular features there was a hint of weakness, of softness, that some people said was a clue to his character, but Daniel couldn't help liking the man. A shared bibliomania had led to their becoming friends, despite the awkwardness of Marc's having lived with Hannah for several years before she finally ditched him.

"Yes, home from the States. Great people, but I'm glad to have the chance to catch my breath. How's business?"

"As you well know, booksellers are as gloomy as farmers. We're always moaning that trade ain't what it used to be. Not that I'm complaining." He coughed. "As a matter of fact, I've got some news for you."

"Fire away."

"Leigh and I are getting married. We haven't named the day yet, but you'll be invited, for sure."

Leigh Moffat looked after catering here and at another bookshop-cum-café she and Marc ran in Sedbergh. She'd hauled Marc back onto the straight and narrow after a calamitous dalliance with a girl who worked in the shop, around the time his relationship with Hannah was falling apart. To judge by his waistline, she was already fattening him up. He must have put on a stone since Daniel first met him.

Daniel clapped him on the back. "Congratulations."

"Um—how's Hannah?"

"Rushed off her feet with work." Daniel grinned. "For a change."

"Any chance of the two of you..?"

Daniel gave a shrug. "You never know."

Marc's cheeks were tinged pink with embarrassment.

"Um—I haven't got round to telling her about Leigh and me. You know how it is."

Did he think that Hannah would torment herself with dreams about what might have been? If so, it only went to show how little he understood her. She was made of sterner stuff. Much sterner stuff than Marc, for sure.

"I'll mention it to her."

"Thanks, hugely appreciated." With that problem sorted, Marc brightened. "So what brings you here?"

"I've arranged to meet someone, and I thought I'd kill two birds with one stone. If he doesn't turn up, at least I might pick up a bargain."

Marc waved at the crammed shelves as he turned to leave. "Happy hunting!"

Daniel headed down the aisle. The shop occupied two floors in a converted water mill, with the café at the rear. The doors at the far end were flung open. They gave on to an elevated area of decking, above the rushing beck.

A man sat on his own at a table at the far end of the deck, scanning each customer who entered the café. He seemed unable to keep still, as gripped by nervous tension. The photograph on the Greengables website was almost flattering in comparison to the twitchy, gaunt reality.

Daniel strode past the counter and went out into the fresh air. The other man rose to his feet. His suit was smart and his pink tie made of silk, but somehow they didn't seem right for him. He looked born to wear a knitted cardigan and baggy corduroy trousers.

Daniel extended his hand.

"Kingsley Melton, I presume?"

———

"The Crooked Shore," Bunny said. "Where the prime suspect's son killed himself the other day."

Les peered at her. "Coincidence?"

"No chance."

"Some kids found the rucksack, hidden among bushes," Maggie said. "A breakthrough which raised as many questions as answers."

"What connections did Ramona have with the area?" Hannah asked.

"None, unless you count the ailing grandma who lived nearby." Maggie paused. "Does everyone know the Crooked Shore?"

Les, Yorkshire born and bred, was the only one to shake his head.

A view of Strandbeck at high tide came up on the scene. The photograph had been taken on a summer's day, with the water shimmering under the sun.

"Beautiful, isn't it?" Maggie sighed. "Notice how quiet it

looks. Off the beaten track, you see. The Crooked Shore isn't far from Ulverston, but it's also near Barrow-in-Furness, not exactly a tourist honeypot. Most people drive straight past on the main road, without knowing Strandbeck is there. Though it's close to one notable sight. Birkrigg Common."

"Never heard of it," Les said.

"There's an ancient stone circle. Much less well-known than Castlerigg or Long Meg and her Daughters, but a place of worship dating back to the Bronze Age. To this day, Druids venerate it."

"Get a lot of Druids round here, do you?"

"More than you'd think," Bunny said. "My first husband was interested in paganism for a time. He reckoned it was all about getting close to nature with a bunch of naked women."

"Isn't it?" Les wore his usual poker face.

Bunny scowled. "There's a reason why he's an ex."

"A week after that discovery," Maggie said, "there was another find. The anorak turned up at Birkrigg Common. Like the rucksack, it had been stuffed under a bush. Crucially, it bore tiny smears of blood."

A navy blue anorak appeared on the screen. Maggie zoomed in so that everyone could see a scattering of bloodstains.

"Ramona's blood was a match. But some of the blood belonged to a person unknown."

"Well, well," Les said.

"Ben Kind was convinced that Ramona was dead and her body had been disposed of. For starters, he focused on two prime suspects, her most recent lovers. Ravi Thakor was one, Gerald Lace the other. Each man claimed to have a cast-iron alibi for the night of Ramona's disappearance. They were persuaded to agree to DNA testing. This resulted in one match with the blood smears. The man in question was Gerald Lace."

Chapter Twelve

"This prehistoric site..." Les said. "I'm guessing they didn't dig it up to see if they could find what was left of Ramona Smith?"

"Too right," Maggie said. "Where would you start? You can't turn an ancient and historic beauty spot into a ploughed field without a hell of a good reason. Without a corpse, it's never easy to make a murder charge stick."

"It's hard enough when you do have a body," Les grumbled.

"Tell us more about Gerald Lace," Hannah said.

"He and his wife Shirley co-owned a gift shop, a couple of streets away from Guido's. Flogging souvenirs for tourists, watercolours of the Langdales, Beatrix Potter memorabilia, and all the rest. On the surface, the Laces were an attractive couple with a young son and a daughter, but both parents had health problems. Shirley suffered badly from fibromyalgia, and Gerald from depression. It didn't help that he had a habit of misbehaving with other women. Some time before Ramona's disappearance, he took an overdose of sleeping pills, but Shirley found him and his stomach was pumped. He recovered and went back to his bad old ways."

Maggie scanned her notes. "Ramona worked behind the

counter for the Laces for a few weeks prior to taking the job at Guido's. Lace and Ramona launched into a steamy affair. But they were soon caught out."

"By the wife?" Bunny asked.

"Worse than that. If it had been left to Mrs. Lace, she'd have kept her mouth shut and nobody outside would be any the wiser. But one day a cousin of hers who didn't care for Lace called in at the shop. She wanted to see how Shirley was. The CLOSED sign was in the window, but that didn't deter her. She went round the back, heard suspicious noises, peeked through a window, and saw Lace and Ramona were...well, I leave it to your imagination. After giving them a piece of her mind, she went straight round to the Laces' house and broke the news to Shirley."

"What happened?"

"Ramona walked out on her job and started at Guido's. Shirley was distraught, but even though it wasn't the first time her husband had strayed, she was prepared to forgive and forget. She simply couldn't envisage life without him."

"More fool her," Bunny said.

"Ramona's heart wasn't broken. Plenty more fish in the sea, as far as she was concerned. The problem was that Lace became obsessed with her. No way was he willing to give her up. As soon as he'd made his peace with Shirley, he pestered Ramona to resume their affair. Showered her with expensive presents, clothes and jewellery. After a few weeks, she agreed to carry on where they'd left off. Even though by now she was sleeping with Ravi Thakor."

"Complicated," Les said.

"You bet. What happened after that is the heart of the case. When we first appealed for information about Ramona's whereabouts, the cousin came forward and told us about the affair. She loathed Lace and suspected he was still up to his old tricks.

Lace was already a person of interest because another woman had accused him of rape. She'd worked at the gift shop, and they'd had a brief relationship."

"What happened?"

"Lace said the complaint was malicious, a reprisal because he'd dumped her. As soon as the woman realised that she risked having her own sexual history pored over in court, she withdrew the allegation. Claimed it had all been a misunderstanding."

Bunny shook her head. "Good old British justice, eh?"

"All this happened just before Lace took his overdose. The bottom line was that Lace had a clean criminal record. Early in the inquiry he was questioned, but he claimed his relationship with Ramona was over. He said she'd told him that she'd fallen for Thakor in a big way."

"Very different from what Thakor told me," Hannah said.

"And from what he told the police at the time. At first, though, there was no evidence to link Lace with the disappearance. Shirley gave him an alibi for the night in question, said they'd been together all the time. They'd had a meal with the children, watched television, and finally gone up to bed about midnight. It was only when the rucksack and anorak were discovered that Ben turned up the heat. Lace was interviewed again and so was Shirley. The breakthrough came thanks to their son."

"The son who killed himself at Strandbeck?" Les asked.

"Yes, it was Darren Lace who gave the game away."

———

"I can't tell you how much I appreciate your time and trouble," Kingsley said as he put the tray down on the table. From his pocket he produced an oblong of card bearing Greengables' logo. "Here, let me give you my contact details."

He was so eager to please, he might have been trying to sell a house. "This is a long story, but I'll try to keep it short."

Daniel inhaled the aroma of his coffee and homemade chocolate fudge cake. Once he got back home, he'd burn off the calories with a long walk on Priest Ridge.

"Please, go ahead."

Kingsley glanced around, like a secret agent in a black-and-white spy movie. There weren't many potential eavesdroppers. A young couple with Australian accents only had eyes for each other, while two elderly fell walkers were gorging on large chunks of lemon meringue pie with the concentration of men who had spent lavishly on their desserts and meant to get value for money if it killed them.

Leaning over the table, Kingsley said, "This is about a man called Logan Prentice. I met him just over two years ago. He's in his mid-twenties and very plausible. He runs a small business from a bedsit, specialising in computer and laptop repairs. In his spare time he does a bit of acting and plays the piano in clubs and bars. He used to call in at Sunset View, my mother's care home, to entertain the residents. He made a point of befriending elderly people with money. An old woman called Ivy Podmore took a shine to him. She had no family, and she told people at the home that she'd changed her will in his favour."

"Uh-huh."

"One afternoon, when my mother was going upstairs for a lie-down, she passed Ivy's room, which was next to hers on the second floor. The door was open and she saw Prentice bending over Ivy, who was in her bed. He was holding her pillow. At first my mother thought he was straightening it."

"Did she raise an alarm?"

Kingsley sighed. "She'd already suffered three strokes. Thankfully, her mind wasn't affected, but she was tired and frail, and just went to bed for a nap. Afterwards, she berated herself. When she got up and went downstairs for supper, Ivy was nowhere to be seen. One of the care assistants went to her room and found her dead. The doctor was called in and said she'd passed away in her sleep. My mother refused to believe it."

"Why not?"

"She didn't trust Prentice an inch. Physically weak as she was, she was still on the ball. You couldn't say the same for Ivy, who was showing signs of dementia. Easily influenced, an obvious target for a predator like Prentice. She'd been fine that afternoon, and there was nothing to suggest she was about to die. My mother was morally certain that she'd seen Prentice, ready to smother Ivy."

There was a long pause while Daniel digested this.

"You said on the phone that she witnessed a murder."

Kingsley bit his lip. "Well, yes. In a manner of speaking."

"But she didn't actually see him do anything to harm Ivy Podmore?"

"No," Kingsley admitted. "But why would he be there if he wasn't trying to harm her?"

"Let me play devil's advocate," Daniel said. "Perhaps he was simply concerned for her and took too much on himself."

Kingsley made a scornful noise loud enough to cause one of the fell walkers to glance irritably in their direction.

"To look at him, you'd think butter wouldn't melt in his mouth. Pure facade. Deep down, he's utterly selfish and amoral."

"Did your mother tell anyone in authority what she'd seen?"

"She told me."

"With all due respect, that's not the same."

"She made me swear to take the matter up. Unfortunately, she suffered another stroke almost at once, and it proved fatal. Of course, I passed on the information she'd given me."

"Who did you talk to?"

"The manager of the home. A waste of my breath. She pooh-poohed any suggestion of foul play. All that mattered to her was protecting the good name of Sunset View. Like her care assistants, she was starry-eyed about Prentice. It's so easy to fall under his spell."

"What about the doctor who examined Ivy Podmore?"

"As far as he was concerned, Ivy had had a good innings, and there was no need for an inquest. My mother hadn't actually seen her being murdered."

"Did Logan Prentice know you'd accused him?"

"Oh, yes. The manager told me that Prentice flatly denied having been inside Ivy's room, and she'd have believed him if he told her the moon is made of green cheese. Besides, I won't pretend my mother was popular at Sunset View. Simply because she took no nonsense, they regarded her as a stirrer. A malicious old crone who was still making ructions from beyond the grave."

Bitterness gave his words a scything edge. Whatever the truth, Daniel thought the man was speaking from the heart.

"As for me, I was just a gullible mummy's boy who was flailing around and making wild accusations because I was demented with grief. The manager actually warned me not to repeat a word of what I'd said, in case Prentice sued me for defamation of character."

"So what did you do?" Daniel asked gently.

"What could I do? I'd lost the person I cared most about in the world. I was in a mess and nobody was listening. Besides, the manager was right. I wouldn't put it past Prentice to sue me for every last penny." Kingsley's hands were shaking. "He's utterly merciless."

———

"Ingrid is so young," Logan Prentice said. "So lovely. So talented. I'm prejudiced, of course, but she has so much to look forward to, the rest of her life ahead of her. And now this diagnosis. I still can't quite believe it. What she's going through…it just seems bloody unfair."

Tory reached out to brush a bit of fluff off his shirt. They were sitting on the terrace at the rear of her flat, looking out towards the timber summer-house and beyond it, the lake. A heron relaxing by the edge of the water pondered its next move.

"Life is bloody unfair, sweetheart. What matters is what we do about it."

"You're right," he said. "You're so shrewd, Tory."

"It's because I'm so venerable," she murmured. "Call it the wisdom of age."

"I told you last night, you're not old," he said fiercely. "I've never met anyone so…so vibrant."

She patted his hand. "Who needs pills when there's Logan to keep me young? You boost my morale."

"And you're brilliant at boosting mine." He bent towards her and dropped a kiss on her cheek. "Whenever I'm in a foul mood, you make me feel there's light at the end of the tunnel. Honestly, I've never known anyone like you. You ought to be prescribed on the National Health."

She giggled. "Flattery will get you everywhere. I still don't know why you bother with me. Such a good-looking boy. You can pick and choose."

"I've chosen," he said. "What I find baffling me is why an elegant woman of the world is mucking around with a computer geek like me."

"What I see is a young man with bags of get-up-and-go," she said. "The world's at your feet."

"I wish." He hung his head. "Let's face it, I've achieved nothing in my life."

"Rubbish. You're your own boss, you run a business."

"My heart isn't in it. I only ever meant it to be a way of paying the rent until I could make a living as a pianist. But I was kidding myself. Yes, I can entertain a group of old biddies in a care home or a party of drunks in a pub, but I'd never get a regular gig in a hotel. Let alone on a cruise ship. So I'm stuck with repairing computers and gaming machines."

"Don't knock it. If I'd not seen your card in the shop window, I'd never have asked you to fix my laptop."

"Thank God you did. You've changed my life." He bowed his head. "Sorry if I seem twitchy. The truth is, I'm a mass of insecurities."

The heron flew over the trees and out of sight.

"You're bound to feel miserable, with Ingrid so poorly. I'm sure everything will work out."

He gave a sour smile. "Yeah, miracles do happen."

"Believe me, they do."

"You think so?"

"I know so. Ask the medical profession. I ought to be pushing up the daisies. Not lapping up the sun with a young Adonis by my side."

He closed his eyes. "Thank God you pulled through. I simply don't know what I'd do without you."

She drew his hand to her lips and kissed his fingers one by one. "Listen, Logan, I've got a proposition to make. Why don't you move in with me?"

His eyes widened. "You're not serious!"

"Never been more so. Why waste your money on rent? Two can live as cheap as one. Not that we have to stint ourselves. I realise now, the flat's ridiculously large for a single person on their own."

"That's wonderful, darling. So generous. But really, I can't let you…"

"Don't be silly." She gestured at their surroundings. "Life is for living, nobody knows better than me. What's the point of having money unless you make the most of it? For Christ's sake, don't let male pride come between us."

"I…I don't know what to say."

"Just say yes."

He clutched hold of her. "You're incredible."

"Glad you understand that, sweetheart. You can give notice to your landlord and shift your things over the weekend. All right? Do we have a deal?"

"Yes," he said happily. "We have a deal."

———

"Darren blamed himself for the rest of his life for betraying his father," Maggie said. "That's clear from the note he sent to Jade Hughes, and it explains why he chose the anniversary of Gerry Lace's death to walk into Morecambe Bay. But all he did was confide in another boy at his school. Said he was worried sick about his dad, because he'd been out late the night Ramona went missing. The date stuck in his mind, because he'd been suffering from a toothache, and his mum had been under the weather as well. They'd not been able to get to sleep and they'd kept each other company. Gerry had rushed off in his car during the evening and didn't arrive back home until after midnight. His face was scratched, and he seemed groggy and in a vile temper. He went straight to bed without a word. When the hue and cry was raised about Ramona, and Gerry was interviewed, Darren was scared stiff. He told his friend that his mum and his sister refused to believe his dad could do anyone any harm, and he felt the same. They'd all sworn to the alibi."

"Naturally, the school friend shared the secret?" Les said.

"Told his parents, and they contacted us. Ben gave the Laces a hard time, and Shirley broke down and admitted lying to protect her husband. Simply to avoid any misunderstanding, she said. Lace had no choice but to haul up the white flag and tell the truth. Or at least his version of it."

"Which was?"

"When Ramona gave into his pleas, they agreed that he'd pick her up after she left Guido's. They headed off to the Crooked Shore for some late night hanky-panky."

"Why go there?"

"Ramona's idea, according to him. Only half an hour away, but much quieter than Windermere. What's more, it was the spot where they'd first consummated the affair."

"Very romantic," Les grunted.

"Exactly what Lace said when they parked the car," Maggie said. "That's when things began to go wrong. Ramona told him in no uncertain terms that he shouldn't get his hopes up. This was a special treat because it was going to be their last time together. She'd found someone else, and it was serious. She and Lace were finished."

Les shook his head. "I'm guessing he didn't take rejection with good grace?"

"Spot on. He said they both went *'a bit crazy.'*"

"Meaning?"

"He screamed at her, and she slapped his face, and when he lifted his hand to ward off another blow, she caught his cheek with her fingernail. Hence the scratch. Something and nothing, he said it healed within days. He grabbed her by the hair, only for a moment, or so he said. When he let her go, she yanked something out of her rucksack; he wasn't sure what it was, maybe a stone. Things moved so fast, he said everything was a blur. She hit him on the side of the head and he saw stars."

"She knocked him out?" Les rocked back in his chair, barely able to contain his disbelief.

"So he claimed."

"With a stone she'd allegedly been carrying in her rucksack?"

"He did say he might have been mistaken. Whatever, nothing was ever found at the scene."

"I'm not surprised Ben Kind didn't believe him."

"It's perfectly possible Ramona struck him during a quarrel, as well as scratching his cheek. She was younger and fitter. Lace didn't know how long he was unconscious, though he guessed it was only a few minutes. When he came round, he threw up. Ramona was nowhere to be seen. At first he thought she'd stolen his car and scuttled off home. But it was just where he'd left it. So he drove himself back to Bowness and got back in one piece."

"Didn't go to A&E, then?"

"No."

"Suspicious in itself."

"According to Gerry, a good night's sleep worked wonders. He said he suffered from a headache for several days, but it had worn off by the time he was first questioned. Shirley backed up his story."

"Just like she supported him in the original lie that they spent the whole evening together."

"Yes."

"What was his story regarding the bloodstained anorak?"

"Ramona still had it on when they tussled. He might have grazed her in the course of defending himself, hence the presence of her blood as well as his."

"Did he admit taking the anorak off her?"

"No."

"So how did the anorak finish up under some bushes, in a different place from the rucksack?"

"That, he couldn't explain."

"Stating the obvious," Les said, "you don't need a corpse for a murder conviction. This man's blood was on the victim's clothing. He'd lied about his whereabouts. He finally admitted having been with her that night. She'd told him it was over between them. There wasn't a trace of her. Bang to rights, surely?"

"Ben Kind drew the obvious conclusion," Maggie said. "The CPS agreed that the evidence justified charging Gerry Lace with Ramona's murder. If the good old British public had managed to get hold of him, he'd have been lynched. Luckily for him, he was defended by Edgar Priestley."

"Never heard of him."

"Edgar used to be a byword on this side of the Pennines," Bunny explained. "A shit-hot defence lawyer who represented all the leading villains from Carlisle to Chester."

Hannah nodded. "He was famous for bamboozling juries. One closing speech from Edgar, and they'd entertain a reasonable doubt about whether the Earth goes round the sun, let alone whether his client was guilty as charged."

"Priestley came up with an alternative explanation for Ramona's fate," Maggie said.

"Oh, yeah?" Les said. "Reckoned she was alive and well and hiding in a cave?"

"He was too smart to rely on that argument. He knew as well as anyone that it wasn't likely to save Lace from a life sentence. So he maintained that *if* she was dead, it was because she'd been killed by someone else."

"Yeah, well, he would say that, wouldn't he?"

Maggie checked her notes. "Ramona had told several people, over a period of time, about a woman friend of hers. Her name was Vee, and she lived in Grange-over-Sands."

"Thought you said she didn't have any women friends?" Les objected.

"Vee cropped up more than once during the initial investigation. Once or twice Ramona used her as an excuse to turn down invitations, saying that she'd agreed to go out clubbing with her chum Vee. Jimmy Smith didn't know the first thing about Vee. He'd never heard of her, let alone met her. Nobody else had even set eyes on her. They couldn't provide us with any information about her. Strange, given that Ramona had mentioned her to both Gerald Lace and Ravi Thakur."

"Was Vee traced?" Hannah asked.

"Never. Talk about a mystery woman. Exhaustive enquiries were made in Grange, but they turned up nothing."

"So maybe she didn't exist?" Bunny suggested. "Just an alibi? A convenient excuse?"

"Edgar Priestley had a different theory," Maggie said. "His case was that Vee wasn't another woman after all. Why would Ramona make her up? She was a bit long in the tooth for an imaginary friend. No, Priestley reckoned that Vee was a man."

Chapter Thirteen

"You describe Logan Prentice as a predator," Daniel said. "What's your evidence?"

Kingsley's face turned the colour of beetroot. "I'll be honest with you, Mr. Kind. What I'm about to say won't put me in a good light. In fact, I'm utterly mortified about what I'm going to tell you. I'm ashamed of myself."

He paused, as if hoping for words of encouragement. Daniel composed his features into a bland mask.

"I've agonised about how much to tell you, but everything I've read about you suggests you're a good egg, that you won't abuse my confidence. Besides, I don't know what else to do. A life is at stake. When I made a simple mistake at Strandbeck, a man died."

"You're not responsible for that."

"You're right, Mr. Kind, but some people don't agree. I couldn't live with myself if there was another tragedy. So I've decided to make a clean breast of things."

Daniel drank some coffee. He'd resolved not to make any promises. Was this strange man about to incriminate himself?

Kingsley lowered his voice to a whisper. "You see, I was taken in by Logan Prentice. I was as credulous as Ivy Podmore. I forgot he was an actor. My mother had a valuable collection of lapis lazuli and I mentioned this to Prentice. We became friendly, and I invited him over to our bungalow in Bowness. One day, while he and I were at Sunset View, the house was burgled. The intruder was interrupted and nothing was stolen, but he hadn't needed to break in. He had a key. Prentice had taken it from my mother's handbag."

"Could you prove that?"

"Of course not, otherwise I'd have had the police down on him like a ton of bricks!" Kingsley's voice rose. "Sorry, I don't mean to get carried away. It's just that…it was very upsetting. I'd trusted him, and he'd betrayed me."

Daniel savoured his coffee cake. "If you're right, this young man may be deceitful, but why do you describe him as ruthless?"

Kingsley Melton's Adam's apple bobbed. "I confronted him about the burglary. He went berserk."

"Any innocent man would."

"He was guilty!" Kingsley hissed.

He closed his eyes. Daniel waited for him to continue.

"Sorry, I mustn't let my emotions carry me away. It's an old fault, my mother used to chastise me for it. I realise you can't simply take me at my word. That's why I need to be straight with you, however painful it is. The truth is that Prentice threatened me."

"What kind of threat?"

Kingsley's eyes remained shut. His voice was barely audible. "You see, when he and I were alone together, I behaved foolishly. At the time I was an emotional wreck. I knew my mother was never coming home again, and it was hellish to see her in terminal decline. Prentice feigned sympathy. He became a shoulder to lean on, so to speak. I was fond of him, and I was stupid enough to believe that he was fond of me. Forgive me if I don't go into sordid details, but I'm afraid I said and did one or two things that were, let's say, open to misinterpretation."

He opened his eyes to watch for a reaction.

Daniel said, "I see."

"I was at my lowest ebb. I couldn't run the risk of Prentice shaming me, and he left me in no doubt that if it suited him, he'd destroy my life, as casually as some cruel boys pull wings off flies. So after my mother's death, I crept away with my grief and pretty much went into hiding at home in Bowness."

"Did he try to prise money out of you?"

"No," Kingsley said. "The man's a coward. He isn't comfortable with a victim who knows his little games. He prefers to catch people unawares."

"What about Ivy Podmore's money?"

Kingsley shifted in his chair. "That was a puzzle, I must admit. A year after the murder, I was getting back on my feet. I'd promised my mother that I'd try to make sure justice was done for Ivy. As a starting point, I contacted the Probate Registry and got hold of a copy of Ivy's last will and testament."

"And?"

"The will was six years old, made long before she went into Sunset View. All her estate was divided between various charities and other good causes."

"In other words, Prentice had no motive for murder?"

"Yes, I was so astonished that I got in touch with the solicitors. I'm afraid I rather embellished the truth. Pretended to be a distant relative of Ivy's, over on holiday from Canada, wanting to know about her last days."

Daniel conjured up a mental picture of Kingsley Melton playing the awkwardest of amateur sleuths.

"The lawyers were guarded, as you'd expect, but I gathered

that they didn't consider she was in a fit state to make a new will during the last twelve months of her life. Apparently, she kept getting extravagant fancies and then changing her mind. Giving everything to Logan Prentice wasn't the first. Previously, she'd decided to bequeath her worldly goods to a homeless man she'd met on a bus. The solicitors humoured her, but the new wills were never prepared, let alone signed and witnessed. There was no point because they wouldn't stand up in court if they were challenged. Ivy gave people to understand that she'd made Prentice her heir, and I'm sure Prentice was deceived, like the rest of us. He must have thought he was quids in."

"So you think he killed her in the mistaken belief he was due to inherit?"

"Exactly!"

"Why bother, why not wait for her to die of natural causes? Why risk arousing suspicion?"

"Prentice is a chancer," Kingsley said. "And he's cruel. My bet is that it gave him pleasure. Having power over life and death. The mark of a psychopath."

Kingsley sounded like a true crime devotee. Daniel bit off another mouthful of fudge cake, almost more than he could chew. A good excuse for keeping quiet, letting the man talk.

"I saw Prentice again for the first time, almost a fortnight ago." Kingsley paused. "This was at Strandbeck, on the afternoon that jogger committed suicide. Have you studied the reports of that incident?"

"I've glanced at them."

"Then you'll understand why I'm so nervous about putting my head above the parapet. I couldn't tell the press or the police that the reason I was so distracted was that I'd just spotted Logan Prentice. Are you familiar with the Crooked Shore?"

"No. I'm a relative newcomer to this part of the world."

The ghost of a smile flitted across Kingsley's face. "I'm sure you'll have realised by now that to some of us locals in Cumbria, a person is still a newcomer after they've lived here for thirty years."

He explained his role at the Manor, his brief sighting of Prentice, and how he'd become acquainted with Tory Reece-Taylor.

"Since she moved into the Manor, Ms. Reece-Taylor and I have become...um, very close." Colour came to Kingsley's cheeks again. "She's a marvellous woman, like nobody I've ever met before, far less been in a...well, an intimate relationship... anyhow, you see, that business with Prentice was a complete aberration."

Kingsley scanned Daniel's expression. What was he looking for? Daniel wondered.

Clearing his throat, the older man continued. "Tory takes pride in boasting that she's as tough as old boots. Like me, she's a private person, but I sense she's had her share of knocks over the years. A while back she had a cardiac arrest. One of her favourite sayings is that she loves coming back from the dead."

"So she might easily suffer another, fatal attack?"

"Precisely!"

"What makes you think she's at risk from Prentice?"

Kingsley told him about his most recent visit to Strandbeck Manor. "My guess is that Prentice laid low after Ivy Podmore's death. Even though he got away with his crime, I suppose he was reluctant to draw any more attention to himself. To be thwarted over Ivy's will must have made him angry. And even more determined."

"You think he's bided his time, waiting to find another suitable victim?"

"Absolutely. And now he's chanced upon Tory and ingratiated himself. A rich woman with a dicky heart. The perfect victim."

"Ms. Reece-Taylor sounds much better equipped than Ivy Podmore to look after herself."

Kingsley frowned. "You think I'm making a mountain out of a molehill?"

"Your concern for her well-being does you a lot of credit." Daniel chose his words with care. "She obviously means a great deal to you. Prentice sounds like a man on the make, but you can't be sure he's contemplating anything sinister."

Kingsley swallowed hard. "What you're saying is that you don't think the police will pay any attention to me."

"I can't speak on their behalf, Mr. Melton. But let's face it. There's no evidence that a crime is about to be committed. Only supposition."

"Don't forget Prentice's track record. He killed Ivy Podmore."

"There's no proof he did her any harm. Even his alleged motive doesn't stack up."

"He didn't know she was incapable of making a valid will!"

"Even so."

"The police could speak to him."

"What do you expect them to say?"

"They could warn him off. Put the wind up him." Kingsley drummed his fingers on the table. "He's a coward. If his card was marked, he'd leave Tory alone."

"To pick on someone else, you mean?"

"Perhaps."

"If he's such a rogue, surely it's a certainty."

"All I want is for Tory to be safe." The drumming intensified. "Would you...I mean, you're a friend of DCI Scarlett. Might you have a word in her ear? She specialises in cold case work, and the death of Ivy Podmore surely qualifies as..."

"Why not approach the police yourself?"

"As I said on the phone, I have my reasons."

Daniel could restrain his curiosity no longer. "Is that because you witnessed the suicide at Strandbeck. Or is something else holding you back? Something you've not mentioned?"

The drumming stopped and Kingsley sprang to his feet. For a tall and ungainly man, his movements were surprisingly quick. Too quick, because his elbow caught the handle of his coffee cup and knocked it over. The drink spilled over the table and onto the deck.

"Sorry, Mr. Kind." In his efforts to get the words out, he was jabbering. "Tory is in danger. I hoped to persuade you that preventing a crime is infinitely preferable to solving one when it's too late. Obviously, I was mistaken."

Daniel stood up to offer his hand, but Kingsley Melton was already hurrying away.

——

"So Vee was a code name for a married lover?" Hannah said.

Maggie nodded. "If Gerry Lace's brief was right."

"Ravi Thakor?" Hannah considered. "Vee as in Ra-Vee?"

"Ingenious," Les said.

"Thakor claimed that she'd mentioned Vee to him," Maggie said.

"But do we believe him?" Les said.

Maggie considered. "Good question."

"Was there any evidence to support the barrister's theory?" Hannah asked.

"None that I've discovered," Maggie said.

"Wily devil, old Edgar." Bunny sounded almost nostalgic.

"Tell us what happened at the trial," Hannah said. "Did Gerry Lace give evidence?"

"Yes," Maggie said. "A high-risk tactic, but it paid off. Edgar

Priestley said his client was determined to tell the world what actually happened. Truth was stranger than fiction, and Lace's testimony proved it."

"Attack is the best form of defence," Les muttered.

"Gerry Lace's version of events was far-fetched, but he stuck to his guns in the witness box. The cross-examination was gruelling. At one point he was reduced to tears. If anything, Counsel for the prosecution went in too hard. He looked like a bully."

"So Lace got away with it?"

"Yes, if you assume he killed Ramona. In his closing speech, Priestley suggested that she'd arranged to meet Vee at the Crooked Shore. She persuaded Gerry Lace to take her there, and then humiliated him. Probably it was revenge for the way he'd treated her. Not even Priestley claimed that his client was a saint. But he insisted that Ramona herself was as hard as nails."

Bunny nodded. "Some truth in that, perhaps. Not that it justifies killing her."

"No. According to Priestley, it was possible that she knocked Gerry out and was then picked up by Vee. Then something went wrong. She was in a foul temper, and the two of them quarrelled. Vee killed her, maybe by mistake, and disposed of the body."

"Crime of passion?" Hannah asked.

"Your guess is as good as mine. The jury was out for ages, but eventually they found Gerry not guilty."

Les puffed out his cheeks and exhaled. "Juries, eh? Bloody hell."

"Suppose Vee planned it all along?" Hannah was thinking aloud. "An elaborate plan to kill two birds with one stone. Getting rid of Ramona and making Gerald Lace the scapegoat. The anorak and the rucksack were hidden to incriminate Lace."

"Any bright ideas about Vee's identity?" Les asked. "Other than Thakor?"

Maggie shook her head. "There was no shortage of men in Ramona's past, and all her known associates were interviewed. Nothing seemed to fit. Gerry Lace was the obvious culprit, but Priestley's whole point was that the killer was someone we *hadn't* cottoned on to."

"And the jury bought that?" Les sighed.

Maggie shrugged. "You know the score. It isn't for the accused to prove his innocence. Priestley was a past master at feeding the media with juicy titbits. His line was that no woman in Cumbria was safe because the police had taken their eyes off the ball. They were too busy persecuting an innocent man."

Les groaned. "I don't bloody well believe it. On second thoughts, perhaps I do. That's defence lawyers for you."

"After the verdict was delivered, Gerald Lace made the usual speech outside the courtroom entrance. Thanking the jury, his legal team, and his family, and asking for privacy and the chance to get on with his life in peace, blah, blah, blah. Then he pushed his luck too far, said that he was leaving court without a stain on his character. Someone threw an egg at him and shouted that he ought to say where he'd hidden the poor girl's body. Ben Kind was interviewed and it was obvious he was livid."

Hannah nodded. "When I worked with him, he hated talking about the case, but he told me about that interview. He admitted he shouldn't have talked to the media when he was still feeling raw. It wasn't his finest hour."

"I remember," Bunny said. "Although the file was being kept open, he made it clear that there were no new lines of enquiry for the police to follow. That threw fuel on the flames. You didn't need to be a mind-reader to see he thought Lace had got away with murder."

"Don't blame him," Les said. "He can't have been alone."

"Far from alone," Maggie said. "There was a lot of unpleasantness. Graffiti painted on the Laces' house and car, branding him a murderer. Customers boycotted the shop, and it closed down. The family suffered, Lace's wife and kids most of all. He struggled to find work and ended up on benefits."

"Not a happy ending," Hannah said.

"Not for anyone," Maggie said. "Shirley made a nuisance of herself, complaining to all and sundry that her husband was a victim of police failures in general and Ben Kind's prejudice in particular. And then Nadine Bosman, the woman who had accused Gerry Lace of rape, confided in one of her friends about it. She claimed that he'd attacked her in the storeroom of the shop. Word got round, and a group of local vigilantes beat Lace up. At that point he made another unsuccessful attempt at taking his own life."

Bunny groaned. "One disaster after another."

"After such a lapse of time, there was obviously no evidence to substantiate Nadine's allegation. Interestingly, she knew Ramona. They'd been to the same school. She said she warned Ramona to be careful of Gerald Lace, but Ramona said she could look after herself."

"And it didn't stop her sleeping with Lace?" Les asked.

"No, but Lace's beating sent his long-suffering wife into orbit. According to her, the police had blackened the poor fellow's name so that he was easy prey for any malicious attention-seeker. And then the worst happened."

"Gerald Lace committed suicide," Hannah said softly.

"Yes, the note he left for Shirley protested his innocence and said he'd chosen to die in the place where his life effectively came to an end."

"Strandbeck," Hannah said.

"Exactly. He accused Cumbria Constabulary in general and

Ben Kind in particular of tormenting him. His widow didn't give up on her crusade. She continued to pester us and the media, desperate to clear her dead husband's name. A gutsy woman, Shirley, but fanatical. It ruined her life and her son's as well. Darren inherited his father's depressive streak, and twenty years to the day after Gerald Lace died, his son went back to the Crooked Shore."

Maggie sat down, switched off her laptop, and finished her water in a long gulp.

"What a nightmare," Bunny said.

Hannah stood up. "It's a human tragedy. For everyone concerned. Whichever way you look, in this case there are only losers. Thanks, Maggie, that was brilliant."

Les leaned back in his chair and looked at her. "So what now, boss?"

"Our task is simple, isn't it?" Hannah spoke with more assurance than she felt. "Starting first thing on Monday, we start putting right the wrongs of the past."

One of the secretaries put her head round the door with a note for Hannah. She took a brief glance and allowed herself a brief smile.

"On second thoughts, why wait until Monday? A Mrs. Clarke has turned up in reception and wants to see me urgently."

"Mrs. Clarke?" Maggie said.

"Mrs. Nadine Clarke. Formerly known as Ms. Nadine Bosman."

Chapter Fourteen

Nadine Clarke was a small, plump woman in her early fifties with curly brown hair going grey, rimless spectacles, and a strong Lancashire accent. She explained she'd seen Hannah on the regional news, talking about Ramona Smith.

"Does my name mean anything to you, love?"

"You made a complaint against Gerald Lace, a year or so before Ramona disappeared."

Nadine nodded. "Thought you'd do your homework. You look the type."

Hannah wasn't sure if this was a compliment. She exchanged a glance with Maggie. "DS Eyre has just given my team a detailed briefing on the case. You said that Gerald Lace assaulted you, but shortly afterwards, you withdrew the allegation, and he was never charged."

"That's right, love." Nadine compressed her lips into a tight line. "Not a day has gone by since then when I haven't regretted it. Or blamed myself for what it led to."

Her voice was steady but her knuckles were white. Hannah waited.

"I was in two minds about speaking to you, but if you're

taking an in-depth look at the whole case, sooner or later you'd come knocking at my door. I'd rather get it over with."

Hannah said gently, "I'm grateful for any help you can give us."

"Since Gerry Lace killed himself, some folk have treated him like some sort of martyr. Trust me, he wasn't. I'm sorry his son died, but I can't bear the thought of the man who tried to rape me having his reputation whitewashed. It's bad enough that he got away with killing Ramona."

"What would you like to tell us, Mrs. Clarke?"

The woman sucked in her cheeks. "You'd never believe it now, but in my younger days I was quite something."

Delving into a capacious handbag, she fished out a photograph. It showed a young woman with frizzy blonde hair and a deep tan, lazing on a beach and winking at the cameraman. She was wearing a tiny swimsuit and sucking an orange lollipop. The picture was crumpled and blurred, but there was no disguising her prettiness. Nadine Bosman, half a lifetime ago.

"Never believe it was me, would you? The ravages of old age, Chief Inspector." She smoothed down an errant curl. "I enjoyed myself in those days, far too much. Loads of boyfriends, not a care in the world. Then I went to work for Gerry and Shirley Lace."

"Tell me about them."

"Shirley didn't show her face much in the shop. Always having a fit of the vapours about something, that woman. Very intense, not my cup of tea at all. I don't mean to be unkind, but she enjoyed her ill-health. It was the kids I felt sorry for."

"And her husband?"

"Gerry was good company. Nice-looking fellow, liked to crack a joke. A decent boss, turned a blind eye if you came in late after a night on the town. I heard he had a reputation as a Casanova, but that didn't put me off when he started flirting with me. One thing led to another, you know how it is."

"Uh-huh."

Nadine coloured. "He was quite a smoothie, older than the lads I'd knocked around with. Seemed more mature. Generous, too. Every now and then he could turn moody. Once he told me he'd always suffered from insomnia, he took pills to calm his nerves. I told him the insomnia didn't bother me. I wasn't intending him to go to sleep when we were together. Call me irresponsible if you like, but I just wanted some fun. I didn't want to marry him or wreck his marriage, and he was good in bed. But very demanding."

"Oh, yes?"

"Yes. Before long, he was expecting me to do things that made me uncomfortable. To cut a long story short, I dumped him. I handed in my notice, but he said he wouldn't accept it. He begged me to give him a second chance, he simply couldn't bear rejection. When I said no..."

After a long pause, Hannah said, "He attacked you?"

Nadine took a breath. "At the back of the shop, there was a big storeroom. There was an airbed, that's where... Anyway, he pushed me down onto it and started ripping off my clothes. When I fought back, he twisted my arm and slapped both my cheeks. Then he put his hand around my throat. I was scared stiff. I'd never seen him like that. He was like a wild animal."

"But he didn't go through with it?"

"No." Nadine gave a wry smile. "Another minute and he'd have choked the life out of me, but I was saved by the bell, quite literally. Someone rang the shop doorbell and wouldn't stop ringing. It was lunchtime and the shop was closed, but he'd forgotten that a delivery was due. A consignment of tea towels with maps of the Lake District. Thank God for souvenirs. Without them..."

"What happened?"

"He pulled himself together and got dressed. Went into the shop and spoke to the driver. You'd never guess what had been going on a few moments before. It gave me the chance to get away. Some of my undies were torn but I managed to tidy myself up and walk out through the shop. There was nothing he could do to stop me. He asked where I was going and I simply said home. For good. The delivery driver was watching, Gerry couldn't utter a squeak of protest."

"When did you report the attack?"

"That's where I messed up," she said. "I was so shocked by what had happened. This bloke I thought was quite nice, acting like a monster. I was terribly upset, and didn't utter a word to anyone. I was renting a bedsit in Windermere, and I stayed there for two whole days. When I plucked up the nerve to ring the shop to ask for my wages in lieu, Shirley answered. She was furious, told me she'd had to get out of her sick bed to help because I'd flounced out. So I told her what had happened, and she called me a lying bitch. I slammed the phone down on her and went to the police."

"How did that go?"

"Awful," Nadine said. "I felt like I was the criminal. Talk about the third degree, when I told them I'd been having an affair with Gerald Lace, they pretty much lost interest. Obviously, by then there was no physical evidence of what had happened. I'd chucked the torn clothes in the bin. They spoke to him, but Shirley stuck in her oar."

"She was in denial?"

Nadine snorted. "She was in denial her whole life. I feel sorry for her in some ways, but when people make out she was some kind of angel for standing by her man, it makes my blood boil. She said I'd made the story up as a way of getting money out of them. Told the police about some of the lads I'd been involved with. Two of them had seen the inside of a prison cell. She even accused me of topping up my wages from the till."

"Did you steal from the shop?"

Nadine averted her eyes. "No, but who would believe me? When I was eighteen, I had a job in a café. The staff used to help themselves to all sorts, but I was found out. I only nicked a tenner, but the case went to court, and the magistrate fined me. I didn't even realise Shirley had heard about that, but Bowness is a small place, and I was never any good at keeping secrets."

"You withdrew your complaint about Gerald Lace?"

"I was up against it, I felt I had no choice. The Laces played dirty. There was no proof of what happened, it was my word against theirs. And the delivery driver's. He said I looked fine when I walked out of the shop. The idiot didn't even notice the marks on my cheeks. Maybe Gerry bribed him, I've no idea. So I said it was all a misunderstanding. I'd lashed out at him because I was heartbroken that he'd finished me. The police were happy to close the book on it. They let me off with a stern talking-to."

"When did you tell Ramona about the attack?"

"I heard on the grapevine that she'd started at the shop. I didn't know her well. She kept herself to herself, at least as far as other girls were concerned. Maybe she didn't fancy any competition. She was a strange one. Bright enough, but content to drift from one dead end job to another. I'd been the same, but the attack changed me. Woke me up. I was sick of retail, so I started working in a library, and that's where I met Kevin, my husband."

"What did you say to her?"

"I told her to watch herself with Gerry Lace. He might seem as nice as pie, but there was another side to him."

"And how did she react?"

"She asked a few questions, and at first I thought I was getting through to her, but in the end she laughed it off. More or less said to my face that if I'd handled things better, he'd never have laid a finger on me. Not a word of thanks, she wasn't the type. So I gave up and got on with my life."

"You talked to the police after she went missing."

"When the news came out, my first thought was that Gerald Lace had lost control again. She'd probably taunted him, I'm afraid she was the sort who would do that. If things had got out of hand…"

"Public-spirited of you to come forward."

Nadine Clarke scanned Hannah's face, as if suspecting sarcasm. Satisfied with what she saw, she gave a brisk nod.

"I felt it was my duty. Kevin and I are Christians. Born-again, you might say, though we prefer the word evangelical. I hoped against hope that Ramona might be found safe and well. For all her faults, she didn't deserve to be murdered. It's not that I still wanted revenge on Gerald Lace, I didn't speak up to get him into trouble."

"You'd forgiven him?"

"Yes," she said defiantly. "But I hadn't forgotten that time in the storeroom. I'll remember it till the day I die." She paused. "I hated that man, but perhaps I ought to be grateful. What he did to me was terrible, but without that, I'd never have started again. I'd never have seen the light."

Chapter Fifteen

Daniel whistled. "Quite a view."

He and Hannah were approaching the top of Hoad Hill on a bright, clear Saturday afternoon. Whichever way you looked, the vistas were magnificent. To the north lay the Coniston Fells and the Langdales. Turn your head a fraction and you saw the Leven estuary with its tiny island and the railway viaduct over the river. Morecambe Bay spread out beyond the coastline and, in the far distance, Daniel's sharp eyes spotted the faint outlines of Blackpool Tower. Below the hill, a short stretch of water connected the bay with the town where they'd parked. This was Ulverston Canal, said to be the widest, deepest, and straightest in the world.

Daniel had picked up Hannah in Kendal that morning before heading out to the peninsulas of south Cumbria. They'd stopped for a snack in a colourfully painted café tucked away in the maze of Ulverston's cobbled streets. The place was called Another Fine Mess, a nod to the town's most famous son, the skinny half of Laurel and Hardy.

Over a veggie Caesar salad, Hannah had given Daniel an outline of his father's ill-fated attempt to solve the puzzle of

Ramona Smith's disappearance and of Darren Lace's death on the Crooked Shore. He hadn't mentioned his encounter with Kingsley Melton.

On the warmest day of summer so far, the chance to put on their sun hats and shorts and get out in the fresh air was too good to miss. Everyone else had obviously had the same idea; following the path up, they'd seen almost as many people as they'd seen sheep. There was barely a breath of breeze, even on this exposed hilltop. They meant to go on to the Crooked Shore and Birkrigg Common, but first Daniel had persuaded her to make this climb.

Their goal was an eccentric landmark that caught his attention each time he drove past on the A590, heading to the west coast. A mile and a half inland, on the crest of the hill, it looked like a lighthouse that had got hopelessly lost.

Hannah lifted her dark glasses. Standing on tiptoe in her trainers, she peered up at the Sir John Barrow Monument. Painted white and made of limestone, it towered above her, one hundred feet high.

"Now that's what I call an erection," she murmured.

Daniel laughed. "This is a copy of the third Eddystone Lighthouse, now rebuilt at Plymouth Hoe. The monument was put up to commemorate an intrepid geographer and explorer who was born in Ulverston. The spoilsports of Trinity House insisted they couldn't put a light in. Why people thought it was appropriate to pay tribute to Sir John's geographical expertise by plonking a fake lighthouse on top of a hill remains a mystery."

"You're such a mine of information." She gave a mocking grin. "And not all of it is useless."

"Last night I read up on the history of the area. 'Lancashire North of the Sands' they called these parts, before the county boundaries were shifted around. The story is in a quaint old book I picked up yesterday when I went over to Marc's."

"How is he?"

Her tone was casual. Too casual? Daniel threw her a covert glance. He was as sure as he could be that she was over Marc, but you never knew. At times he found Hannah's cool demeanour as tricky to read as Sanskrit.

"Fine."

Some time back, she'd got pregnant by Marc, only to have a miscarriage. She'd never said much about it, but the loss of the unplanned baby had hurt her badly. He had no doubt that she still grieved in private for a child she'd never see or get to know. An idea leapt into his mind. Was Leigh expecting, was that why Marc was finally taking the plunge? If so, how would Hannah react? She wasn't the jealous type, and the decision to split up with Marc had been hers, but it would be only human to feel a pang of regret for what might have been. What would be the right moment to break the news about the impending nuptials?

"Good."

She shrugged, as if to shake her former lover out of her thoughts. Even on a lovely Saturday afternoon when she wasn't on duty, her mood was pensive. He could tell her mind was roaming. Since his return from America, she'd seemed distant, more like a passing acquaintance than a lover. His fault for going away for so long. Or maybe her quietness was due to her absorption in this latest cold case. A major enquiry put extra strain on her because she took such a hands-on role. With so much mental and physical energy committed to an investigation, there wasn't much room to spare for fun. Or even him.

He squeezed her hand as they contemplated the panorama. "Are those the Yorkshire Dales in the distance?"

"Could be." She returned the pressure of his hand. "Good idea of yours to come here, do the touristy things. Call myself a local? I've never actually climbed the Hoad before."

Daniel pointed towards the estuary and its outcrop of rock, overgrown with brambles. "In olden days, a pathway ran across the water by way of Chapel Island. The route connected the priory at Conishead with Cartmel Sands. The old ruin there now is a folly, built to enhance the view in the nineteenth century. The Augustinian black canons built the original chapel on the island as a refuge and a place for travellers to pray."

"Darren Lace could have done with a few prayers." Hannah sighed. "The sands are so beautiful. You'd never guess they are treacherous."

"A dreadful way to die. How appalling to feel such despair that you decide the only way out is to sink into the mud and wait to be drowned."

"Yes, his father had a lot to answer for. Even if Gerald Lace didn't kill Ramona Smith, his lies were self-destructive. They certainly destroyed his family. The mother squandered the rest of her life on a hopeless mission to clear his name. The daughter fled at the first opportunity. The son never forgave himself for having told another kid about his dad's false alibi. I only hope we can find out what happened to Ramona."

"After all this time, it's a big ask."

She smiled. "You're telling me."

"What's your current thinking?"

"A betting man would say your dad was right, and Lace was responsible for her death."

"But?"

"We start from ground zero. No assumptions. Ben was only human. He made his share of mistakes."

"As Louise has often reminded me." He groaned. "This isn't the first time you've had to review one of his investigations."

Hannah shrugged, a brisk movement of bony shoulders under her white T-shirt. Her figure was supple, almost boyish.

Daniel thought she'd lost weight while he'd been away. She had a habit of skipping meals when she was on her own and working long hours.

"Ben stuck to his principles, come what may."

"What you mean is," Daniel said, "sometimes he'd cut off his nose to spite his face."

"He hated time-servers who carved out careers by dodging real responsibility. That's why he used to upset the top brass."

"I guess he didn't always play by their rules. At home or at work."

"The rules are there for a reason. Senior police officers need to choose their words carefully. But he was the best detective I ever worked with. There's a reason why he was always given the toughest cases."

They began the descent in silence. Halfway down, Daniel said, "By the way, Marc asked me to pass on some news."

"Oh, yeah?"

"He and Leigh are getting married."

Her confident stride faltered, but only for a moment.

"About time, I suppose," he said.

"I must call into the café one of these days," she said. "I ought to wish Leigh luck. She'll need it."

———

"You must let me help," Tory said.

Logan shook his head. "You've done so much for me already. I can't keep accepting your charity."

They were strolling arm-in-arm along Strandbeck Lane. That morning Logan had filled the van and transported his possessions from the bedsit in Ulverston to his new home in the Manor. After a picnic lunch in the summer house, they'd gone for a walk along the Crooked Shore.

Tory stopped by the low wall of the old churchyard. "It's not charity. If Ingrid is sick and in desperate need of cash to fund her treatment, it's only common sense. The cost of health care in the States is appalling."

"Something's sure to turn up."

"You weren't saying that yesterday, sweetheart. Don't you see you can't let your sister's life depend on luck, you can't let her just slip away?"

She gestured towards the lichen-encrusted gravestones.

He said, "It's not a question of pride. It's about right and wrong. Imagine what bloody Kingsley Melton would say if he got wind of it. As far as he's concerned, I'm just a man on the make. When he hears I've moved in with you, he'll go berserk. If he finds you've paid for Ingrid's treatment, he'll accuse me of exploiting you for my own gain. I can take it, it's happened before, but I can't bear you being dragged into his vendetta against me."

Tory entered the code to open the gates. "I don't give a toss what Kingsley says. It's none of his business."

"Even though you and he…"

"I told you. There's no need to be jealous."

"I'm not jealous, it's just that…"

"Listen." She looked into his eyes. "I felt sorry for Kingsley. Especially after the press crucified him. That's all there was to it. He doesn't own me. No-one does."

Logan watched as the gates admitted them. "Yes, you're a strong woman, only a fool would doubt it. But there will always be a sliver of doubt in the back of your mind, won't there? It's human nature. Young man with no money meets an attractive older lady and they launch into a passionate relationship. He confides in her about a personal calamity, she offers financial help. Looks suspicious, doesn't it? Anyone who didn't know the two of us would be cynical. People always want to believe the worst."

She put her hands on her hips. "Listen to me, sweetheart. What other people think doesn't bother me. Never has. I stand on my own two feet, make my own decisions. And now I've decided that you and me are all that matters."

———

It was a short drive from Hoad Hill to Strandbeck. The coastal lane was a narrow ribbon, looping off the main road and along the edge of the peninsula. Daniel turned off on to Strandbeck Lane and finally came to a halt in front of the tall gates barring the way to the Manor.

A large sign bearing the ubiquitous Greengables logo waxed lyrical about the exclusive dwellings on sale. *Intimate development. Meticulously restored to its former splendour. Quality bespoke homes. Highly individual living spaces. Effortless blend of traditional and contemporary.*

Tory Reece-Taylor's home ground. There wasn't a soul in sight. Ulverston was four miles away, but the bustle of the market town seemed to belong to a different world.

"Tempted to move in?" Hannah's tone was sardonic.

Until now, she hadn't spoken during the journey, responding to a couple of Daniel's throwaway remarks with a noncommittal *mmmmm*. Brooding over Marc, wondering if Leigh was going to have his baby? Or just thinking about work?

"Just nosey."

He executed a three-point turn and headed back towards the coast, where they got out of the car.

"So this is the Crooked Shore," he said. "A landscape of legends."

"You sound like a documentary presenter."

"I used to present documentaries, remember."

"So you did. Not that I often watched them, I'm afraid."

Not like Alex Samaras, he couldn't help thinking.

"You didn't miss much."

"Well, modesty's the best policy. I suppose that book you bought discusses this place?"

"A whole chapter is devoted to the medieval Manor of Muchland."

"Never heard of it."

"Strandbeck was part of Muchland. Lost villages abound on this stretch of coast. At one time Strandbeck was far more significant than it is today. The tides washed the old settlements away, so the story goes. That's probably the truth behind the folk tale that strangers who outstay their welcome here are doomed to seven years of misfortune."

"We'd better not hang around too long, then."

Fifty yards further along was a wooden bench. The quiet of the shoreline made a contrast with the stream of walkers on Hoad Hill. Despite the sun, there was nobody in sight.

"This must be where whatshisname was sitting," Hannah said quietly, "when Darren Lace ran into the sea. Imagine ignoring that."

"Kingsley Melton," Daniel said.

"That's the fellow." She threw him a glance. "Well remembered."

He didn't reply. Last night he'd lost sleep, mulling over everything Kingsley had told him, wondering how much to relate to Hannah, and whether it would make any difference, whatever he decided. In the small hours, he'd made up his mind to pick the right moment and tell her about meeting Kingsley.

They passed a metal sign on which garish yellow triangles accompanied bleak words of warning. *Beware quicksand. Beware uneven surface. Beware fast moving tides. Beware deep channels. Beware sudden drop.*

Just in case anyone had failed to get the message, a hazard notice on the lower half of the sign emphasised the risk of being cut off. Safety instructions were accompanied by a map of the shoreline and emergency phone information.

"One thing is for certain," Daniel said, "Darren knew what he was doing when he ran out into the bay."

Hannah gestured towards the water shimmering in the sunshine. "On a day like today, you're reminded of what makes life worth living. How wretched must someone be for such a gorgeous sight to lose all meaning?"

Daniel nodded. He had firsthand experience of the damage and pain inflicted by mental illness. While he was living in Oxford, his partner, Aimee, had taken her own life. Leaving academe and coming up to the Lake District had been his way of fleeing the bitter memories. Yet every historian knew that it's impossible to escape from the past.

He took a breath. "Let's get on."

They followed the line of the shingle shore for ten minutes before heading inland and up a rise. A narrow hedged path skirted Sea Wood. Once upon a time, oak timbers from here had been floated out at high tide to shipbuilders at Ulverston. Daniel had planned their route on a map over lunch, but no cartographer could capture the stillness of the air or the smell of the vegetation. He caught a whiff of wild garlic long before he spotted its white flowers among the trees.

Rather than take one of the trails through the woodland, they carried on and came out into the open. They kept walking until they could see a series of stones, none of them as much as three feet in height and set at irregular intervals in the ground.

They had reached the Druids' Circle.

———

At home in Bowness, Kingsley Melton wasn't out in the fresh air, making the most of the sunshine. The sizeable rectangle of garden was private, bounded by horse chestnut trees, conifers, and a waney lap fence, but he seldom ventured into it. Once upon a time the garden had been his father's pride and joy. After the large pond was filled in and grassed over, his father had made a half-hearted attempt at building a rockery. Now it was no more than a jumble of stones and weeds. Creeping ivy and ground elder had choked off the other plants and the bumpy lawn was a mass of dandelions; he only did the bare minimum of mowing. A timber shed was rotting away under the shade of the trees; for years he'd meant to give it a lick of creosote, but he'd never got round to it.

Closeted in his study, he tapped away on his laptop keyboard, putting the finishing touches to his report for Annabel of Greengables. On returning home from his unsatisfactory encounter with Daniel Kind at the bookshop, he'd glanced at his inbox, only to have his misery compounded by an email from Annabel. She'd told him to meet her on Monday to discuss sales performance.

Pressure he could do without. She enjoyed flexing her managerial muscles, but he couldn't wave a magic wand and conjure up buyers out of thin air. In his report he hadn't gilded the lily. There was no sign yet of an upturn. Why not launch a more effective advertising campaign or consider dropping the exorbitant asking prices? Admittedly, there had been a five percent reduction in January intended to boost sales, but that small price cut hadn't sufficed. The company was too obsessed with profit.

You couldn't buck the market. Strandbeck Manor was a destination for discerning buyers, and there weren't many around at present. The publicity surrounding Darren Lace's death wouldn't help. Press reports had salivated over the melancholy legend of the Crooked Shore. Deeply unfortunate, but no cause for panic.

He toyed with the idea of driving over to the Manor. Perhaps bump into Tory, accidentally on purpose, and rekindle things between them? She blew hot and cold, that was her nature. With any luck, she'd welcome him with open arms and apologise for treating him with such casual brutality. Not that she'd meant to hurt him, he was sure. The trouble was she had a sharp tongue. Just like Mamma.

The conversation with Daniel had bruised him. The historian was pleasant enough, but he failed to appreciate the gravity of the threat to Tory. The police would be even less interested in what he had to say. They'd regard him as a crank or a malicious stirrer, in just the same way that people used to mock poor Mamma whenever she complained about selfish motorists parking on double yellow lines or dog owners not picking up their animals' mess.

Kingsley's late father often remarked that if you wanted something doing, you'd better do it yourself. Wise words. Kingsley was the one who loved Tory, he was responsible. His first challenge was to make her understand that her life was in jeopardy.

A confrontation in person wouldn't work. What if she'd been on the gin, and was in the mood for an argument? Better to have a quiet chat on the phone and start mending fences.

No time like the present. He dialled her number.

"Tory, it's me. Kingsley."

A pause at the other end. "Hello, Kingsley."

"Thought I'd give you a ring, see how you are."

"Fine, thanks."

"About the other night…"

"Forget it. Ancient history."

"You don't mind…?"

"Look, Kingsley, it's nice of you to ring, but I am rather busy."

He managed to restrain himself from expressing ironic surprise. What could she be busy with on this sunny Saturday afternoon? Let's face it, she never put herself out; she was a lady of leisure.

"I thought we could have a chat. If not now, then maybe tomorrow or…"

"What is there to chat about?"

"Well…Logan Prentice, for one thing."

"What about him?"

Her tetchiness was a bad sign, yet there was nothing for it but to press on. "I know he seems plausible, but take it from me, he's a wrong 'un."

"He's a dear friend of mine. You mind your own business."

"Seriously, Tory, that young man is very bad news."

"You're jealous."

"You know how much I care about you. Not like Prentice. He only sucks up to rich people so he can get something out of them."

A long pause. "That's deeply hurtful."

"Please, Tory, listen to me."

"No, you listen," she retorted. "You're hopelessly wrong about Logan. If you care for me as much as you say, then you'll allow me to choose my own friends and not waste my time with your pathetic attempts to smear them."

"You don't understand!" He found himself bleating in dismay. "He's a charlatan. A confidence trickster. He loves to control people, to mess with their minds so they give him what he wants."

"Kingsley, that's disgusting."

"It certainly is." He warmed to his theme. "You can't trust a word he says, he…"

"Don't pretend to misunderstand me. I'm appalled that you can be so offensive."

She sounded as cold as a Snow Queen, yet he detected a defensive note. An unpleasant thought occurred to him. What if Prentice were actually there, in her flat?

He lowered his voice. "Is he with you? Don't worry if you can't speak freely. What he's doing to you is called coercive control. I've read about it in the papers. Don't worry, I can ring you back another time, we'll have a proper heart to heart, and…"

"Stop right there," Tory said. "I've heard quite enough."

"Please, dearest, I'm only…"

"Shut up! I've been extremely patient with you, Kingsley. Silly of me because you've read too much into my attempts to be friendly. But you've gone too far. Not content with stalking me, you're slandering a decent young man who has troubles of his own to contend with. You really don't know me at all if you imagine I'd be willing to let anyone control me. Not you, not Logan, not anyone ever."

"Honestly, I'm…"

"Shut up!" She was spitting words into the phone. "You don't seem capable of taking a polite hint, so let me spell it out for you in words of one syllable. I never want to hear from you again. Or see you again, come to that. If any problems crop up with the flat, I'll email your head office. Understood?"

There was a brief silence. Kingsley imagined her playing to a gallery of one in her living room; he pictured Logan Prentice applauding as she took a bow. She was performing for him, a puppet dancing to his tune.

"I warn you, Tory." Yes, he was whining, but what choice did he have? "Prentice is dangerous. He's killed one old woman. Now he's preying on you."

"An old woman, am I?"

"No, no, that's not what I meant!"

"The only old woman is you."

He gulped. "Tory, I can't stand by while he ruins your life."

"How dare you." Her voice was shaking with anger. "I don't want to hear another word of this childish nonsense. If you contact me again, I'll tell Greengables you're harassing me. You're a pathetic creep. And if you're stupid enough to show up on my doorstep, I'll call the police."

She ended the call, and Kingsley squeezed the phone so hard that it hurt his hand. In the privacy of his study, he wailed with dismay like an animal suffering a mortal wound.

Chapter Sixteen

"People were buried here in ancient times," Daniel said. "This was a place of ritual and mystery. Ceremonial artifacts have been discovered. A funeral urn. A century ago, they excavated cremated human remains."

Lost in thought, Hannah didn't reply.

Birkrigg Common wasn't as deserted as the Crooked Shore. Half a dozen people of various ages were walking their dogs and a bunch of Lycra clad cyclists had set about a picnic.

The stone boulders were mostly half-hidden by turf, but if you looked closely, you saw that the Druids' Circle actually comprised two circles. The inner ring, eight or nine metres in diameter, comprised a dozen low stones. Prehistory wasn't Daniel's speciality, but he knew that double circles were rare. There were more than twelve hundred stone rings across the country, but only about thirty were concentric. Birkrigg lacked the scale and majesty of Stonehenge, but its origins were intriguing and its surroundings spectacular. You didn't need to queue or pay an arm and a leg for a ticket. Nor were there busloads of sightseers to disrupt the atmosphere or traffic rumbling on a nearby dual carriageway.

"Magical, isn't it?" he said. "Even if the sceptics are right, and the circle has nothing to do with Druids or their temples."

He pointed to Chapel Island. "Look over there. Perhaps the ring was built in alignment with the pathway through the grass, the island and that tallest peak in the distance, on the other side of the bay. When they buried people…"

His voice faded away as he noticed Hannah's brow furrow. She looked as if she would much rather dig into her memories than uncover the secrets of Neolithic or Bronze Age graves. When finally she spoke, he realised that the last thing on her mind was an ancient funeral rite. She'd been worrying at something he'd said, a terrier with a bone.

"Did I mention Kingsley Melton by name? I don't recall that. I suppose you looked up the reports of what happened on the Crooked Shore?"

"It's more complicated than you may think."

"With you, it often is."

"Kingsley Melton phoned me. He wanted to talk about murder. A crime of the past and another that is planned for the future. Or so he believes."

Hannah blinked. "Good God."

"He sounded persistent and not entirely crazy, so I agreed to meet up with him."

"And?"

"We arranged a rendezvous at the bookshop; that's how I happened to bump into Marc. Melton and I had coffee and cake together. He gave me his card. Here you are."

She took the card and said, "You're not planning to stay in touch, then?"

"He's a man with a bee in his bonnet. The story he told me is bizarre."

She waved towards the acres of grass and scrubland ahead of

them. "We said at lunch we'd go for a walk round here. Tell me everything. There's plenty of time, even for the most verbose academic."

"Ouch."

"Stop ratcheting up the suspense. I don't need to be tantalised. Get on with it."

As they made a circuit of the Common, passing tumuli, cairns, and barrows as well as chunks of limestone pavement, Daniel recounted his conversation in the café. Hannah didn't interrupt or ask questions, preferring to digest the story.

"So you see," Daniel concluded, "he was desperate for you to know about the alleged murder at Sunset View, and above all about Prentice's supposedly nefarious designs on this Reece-Taylor woman. What you make of his concerns is up to you."

"Before we come on to that," she said, "what do you make of him?"

They'd reached the summit. The heat was burning their skin. Luckily, they'd put on plenty of sun cream at lunchtime. Daniel pulled his floppy white hat further down over his forehead before replying.

"He's a misfit who spent his life under mummy's thumb. She sounds like a tyrant. I wouldn't put it past her to have smothered poor Ivy Podmore herself, just to get her own back. Melton is the sort who fastens on to stronger individuals. He almost begs to be mistreated. When his mother was ailing, he formed a bond with a pretty young man, only to be done a bad turn. I wouldn't be surprised if Prentice did give some petty criminal a tip-off about the hoard of lapis lazuli."

"But?"

"Melton has latched on to this woman, and he's started to obsess about her. She's given him a morsel of encouragement, but probably regarded it as a no-strings shag. He's looking for something special. If only to convince himself he's not a repressed homosexual—Mummy would never have approved of that. He loathes Prentice and he's jealous. So is Prentice planning to kill Tory Reece-Taylor? I'd say Melton is letting his imagination run away with him."

They stopped by the white trig point at the top of the hill and admired the views. Black Combe in the west, the peaks of Lakeland and Ingleborough, the Hoad Monument, the River Leven, and the coastal village of Bardsea. To say nothing of the magnificent bay and those endless deadly sands.

"Did he strike you as someone who might take the law into his own hands?"

"Just because he hates Prentice, doesn't mean he'd dare to confront him."

"Worms occasionally turn."

"So what's your take?"

She gave a wry smile. "Hard to quarrel with your assessment when all I've got to go on is your report. Melton raised questions about Ivy Podmore's death at the time and got nowhere, probably because there was nowhere to get to. As for Tory Reece-Taylor, she's much younger than Ivy Podmore. Killing her wouldn't be the same as finishing off a senile old woman in a care home."

"She's vulnerable, though. No close relatives, Melton says, nobody to kick up a rumpus if she dies."

"You mentioned she survived a cardiac arrest."

"Yes, she boasts about how much she loves coming back from the dead, but next time she's unlikely to be so fortunate."

"If her death looked suspicious, Prentice would be the prime suspect, assuming he'd sweet-talked his way into her will. And if he wasn't a beneficiary in line for the lion's share of the loot, what would be the point of getting rid of her? It makes more sense for him to soak her while she's alive, if she's stupid enough to shower her toy boy with largesse."

"Can't argue with that."

They walked down the slope without a word. The uneven ground was thick with ferns and bracken. Her expression was sombre, and he tried to lighten the mood.

"Another story from years ago. A travelling circus came to this neighbourhood, and when their elephant died, the circus folk are supposed to have dragged it up the hill and buried it on the Common."

She frowned. "Makes you wonder who else is buried here."

"So is Louise's saviour very glamorous, then?" Hannah asked.

They'd dined at a French restaurant in Kendal and the waiter was serving coffee. Because it was Saturday evening, the place was packed, but they had secured a quiet booth at the back of the ground floor. Daniel had parked at Hannah's flat, where they'd showered and changed out of their walking gear. By tacit agreement they hadn't talked about Ramona Smith or Kingsley Melton during their meal. He'd regaled her with anecdotes about his time in the States as well as the story of Louise's rescue from the Rothay.

He raised his eyebrows. "Intuition or inspired deduction?"

"The latter, of course. Apart from saying that she's done a bit of acting and is pleasant company, you've avoided discussing her."

"Alex Samaras is very lovely." He grinned. "More importantly, she's read all my books."

"God, that's more than I've done."

"Yes, very disappointing. Alex, on the other hand, professes to be my biggest fan."

"An actress with a love of history?"

The note of scepticism irked him. "Why not? She's no air-head, that's for sure. Though the reason she came across the books is that she used to know my father."

"Seriously?" She frowned. "He never mentioned her."

"This was after he retired from the force, just before he died."

"Ah."

He told her the story. "I didn't realise Dad had figured out that Cheryl was sleeping with her boss."

"Once a detective, always a detective."

"I don't suppose their marriage would have lasted much longer. Maybe he'd have got in touch…"

"Don't." Hannah said. "I know it hurt that you never got a chance to see him again. Or say goodbye. But it's past, gone. Punishing yourself is pointless."

"Of course you're right." He mustered a smile. "Anyway, Alex is delightful, and I can see why Louise has cottoned on to her. Before you ask, she's single. Her ex-husband is Greek, and they lived on Santorini before they split up. Now she's trying to revive her acting career. Won't be easy. Writing is a tough game, but acting is even tougher."

"So she has plenty of time on her hands."

"Unlike me," he said quickly. "After all this gallivanting, my agent is nagging me to sit down and get stuck into the next book."

"What about the research?"

He shifted in his chair. "I've not made any travel plans. After so much time away, I want to get my bearings again. Back at home."

"Do you really think of the Lakes as home?"

"Well…yes. I live here, don't I? Why do you ask?"

"It's just that your work takes you all over the world. Before you left you were talking about buying a studio flat in London."

"That was before I saw the prices. A lot for a *pied-à-terre*."

"You can afford it. Your publishers are in London, the literary and TV agent. Most of the television studios…"

"I'm not going back to TV work," he said. "Been there, done that. I'd rather write."

"Even so, the Lakes can't compare as a literary hub."

"It worked for Wordsworth and Southey and…"

"You know what I mean."

"Anyone would think you're trying to get rid of me." His tone was breezy, but he was studying her. Not that she ever gave much away. Was she getting bored with him? "Not met someone charming yourself, have you? This Kit Gleadall, for instance?"

"You know perfectly well, I never mix business with pleasure."

She was right. This, he was sure, explained why her involvement with his father had never progressed beyond close friendship. All the same, her asperity suggested that he'd touched a nerve.

He took a sip of coffee. In America, he'd got into the habit of spending the end of a day alone in expensive hotel rooms with all the atmosphere and personality of luxuriously furnished prison cells. He'd watch old films on television and think about Hannah. The two of them cared so much about their work and devoted so much time and energy to it that weeks and months slipped by with astonishing speed. They'd eased into a routine of seeing each other frequently and sleeping together from time to time, but not making a fuss if other commitments meant they couldn't get together for a while. Public appearances took him around Britain as well as much further afield, and although she usually worked within the county boundaries, she'd never be a nine-to-fiver. What troubled him was the prospect of their relationship becoming a fall-back, a comfort zone.

"Hannah…"

"Yes?"

"Whilst I've been in the States, I've done some thinking. About you and me. And the future."

She looked across the table. Their eyes met.

"Today's been fun," she said.

"Yes, it has."

"You know, we've always been honest with each other."

"Uh-huh." He couldn't guess what was coming.

"I love days like today. Spending time with you. But I'm not in the mood for deep, meaningful conversation. Specially not after a couple of glasses of wine." She drew a breath. "Are you wondering whether I'm upset that Marc's getting married?"

"Well…"

"Leigh is welcome to him. She can cope with his occasional hissy-fits. They work together, so there's not a constant tension between her job and his. Me, I'm a senior police officer. Right now, that's good enough for me. Ask Louise. The days when working women felt afraid of being left on the shelf are gone."

He winced. "I didn't mean…"

"Listen to me, Daniel." She leaned across the table. "You're a high achiever. Always have been, always will be. You've so much drive, it's easy to kid yourself that life should be measured in milestones. Don't worry, I'm a big girl, I can look after myself. I won't turn into some kind of raving bunny-boiler if you hook up with your pretty actress, or anyone else for that matter."

He stared at her, unable to imagine anyone less like a bunny-boiler.

"Why are you talking this way? I don't want to hook up with anyone else."

The lights were low, but even if she'd been illuminated by a searchlight, he couldn't have interpreted the quizzical look on her face.

Chapter Seventeen

At two in the morning, Hannah was alone in her bed and wide awake. If invited, Daniel would have come back to the flat like a shot, she was sure, but she'd not given him the chance. She'd said the exercise and the fresh air had tired her out, and she was desperate for a good night's sleep. It was a feeble excuse, and he was bound to see through it, but she hadn't felt in the mood to take him to her bed.

Now it was too late, she'd changed her mind. She'd made a mistake thanks to her determination to parade her independence. Why bother, given that Daniel was more enlightened than the overwhelming majority of men she'd met, certainly much more than his father? Was she trying to create a protective shield because she was afraid of being hurt again? And was her unhappiness about Marc's habitual infidelity causing her to doubt Daniel? She had no idea what he got up to on his travels, and she didn't want to find out. He was an attractive man; it was inevitable that other women would be tempted. He'd be less than human if he wasn't tempted too.

The time had come to be honest, ruthlessly honest. In the privacy of her bedroom she could admit to herself that she wasn't as dismayed by Kit Gleadall's evident interest in her as she pretended. His confidence appealed to her, and so did his intelligence. She liked men who were good at what they did.

It was no use; she was as wide awake as ever. Might as well get up.

She padded into the kitchen and poured herself a glass of water. Something tempted her to go into the spare room, which she used as an office. She switched on her laptop and googled Alex Samaras.

There wasn't much to be found. To avoid confusion with other actors with similar names, she was known professionally as Allie Samaras, formerly Alexandra Rowan. She'd appeared in a handful of minor productions in London and the south east. Half a dozen photographs of her were online. In every single one she looked beautiful. At least Daniel hadn't pretended otherwise. Even so, Hannah's heart lurched.

And then there was the woman's suggestion that the police had let Ben Kind and his family down by failing to trace the driver responsible for his death. Was this unfair? Chances were that the driver had been drunk and panicked. Hannah hadn't been involved in the inquiry, but she'd heard there was simply nothing for the investigating officers to go on. It happened, but it wasn't good. Was there any mileage in treating his death as a sort of cold case? Should she try to do some digging, to see if by some miracle she could find some evidence to bring the perpetrator to justice, at last?

The thought had never crossed her mind before. Was she trying to compete with Alex Samaras? Were they really rivals?

The regular tick-tock of the clock on the wall sounded unnaturally loud in the silence. And something else was bothering her, an insistent voice nagging away inside her head, no matter how hard she strove to silence it. This had been going on for weeks now. She couldn't keep hiding from the truth, couldn't keep the voice quiet any longer.

I want a baby. A baby who survives this time, a child of my own. Before it's too late.

———

"Would you carry out your threat?" Logan Prentice asked. "I mean, to report Kingsley to the police?"

He and Tory were spending their Sunday afternoon sunbathing by the lake in the grounds of Strandbeck Manor. They had the place to themselves. Tory was lying on a lounger next to the jetty, showing lots of flesh in her pink bikini. Logan, wearing tiny blue speedos, was applying suntan lotion to his face.

"Only as a last resort," she said.

"He's not well," Logan said, "Yes, he's a crazy fantasist, but bringing in the cops might tip him over the edge."

"Considering what he's accused you of, you're very merciful. In your shoes, I'd be out for blood."

"What I don't like," he said, "is the thought of him lurking around here like the Phantom of the Opera. Spying on us, making a nuisance of himself."

"He'd better not try."

"Kingsley's weak but stubborn. He won't let you go without a fight. Why not ask Greengables if he can be transferred elsewhere?"

"Not a bad idea," she said. "There must be other properties for him to market. Not that he's had much joy selling flats in the Manor."

"Who wouldn't want to live here?" Logan's wave encompassed the expanse of lawn, the well-tended rose-beds and shrubbery, the lake with its lily pads and the oaks and copper beeches. "Not another human being in sight, and the only sound is the humming of the bees. We might be sole owners. Lord and Lady Strandbeck."

She touched his knee. "Happy?"

"This is the life. I could get used to *la dolce vita*."

"You will get used to it." A faraway look came into her eyes. "When I was young, I dreamed that one day I'd have it all."

"And now you do."

She exhaled. "I fancy a gin and tonic."

"Perfect." He stood up. "Let me wait on you."

"If only we had a butler. Kingsley did have his uses. My mistake was fraternising with the servant class. I gave him the wrong idea about staff relations."

Logan sniggered. "Every Paradise has its serpent."

"Yes, but the time has come for him to slither away. I hate anyone messing me about. I won't stand for it."

"I'd better behave myself, then."

"No," she said, reaching out and pulling him back down beside her. "I don't want you to behave yourself."

———

"Anyone at home?"

Louise had wandered into the grounds of Tarn Cottage and was standing in the shadow of a damson tree. This secluded sanctuary was Daniel's retreat. There was a barn, a bothy, and a tarn. In the middle distance loomed a fell with its very own coffin trail. He was stripped to the waist, hacking at the brambles sprawling over the circuitous paths of the garden. Out of reach of his desk, his laptop, his phone. He was working off his frustration about the way his day with Hannah had fizzled out. After so long apart, he'd hoped—and assumed—they would spend the night together. When would he learn never to make assumptions where she was concerned? And why, after so long apart, was she so determined to keep him at arm's length? To teach him a lesson? And if so, what did he need to learn?

"Hello. Didn't expect to see you."

"Spur of the moment decision. When I rang the doorbell and there was no answer, I assumed you must be with Hannah."

"I saw her yesterday," he said shortly.

"Oh, yes? Everything all right between the two of you?"

"Fine." He found himself snapping at her. "Absolutely fine."

Louise folded her arms. "Methinks he doth protest too much. Anyway, I've brought you a visitor with a special request."

"A visitor?"

Louise raised her voice. "Alex? Come on, he's out at the back."

Alex Samaras walked through the gate in the trellis separating the path at the side of the cottage from the garden. In her orange ruched crop top, shorts, and trainers, she looked about eighteen.

"Lovely to see you again, Daniel." She considered him with undisguised interest. "I've come to beg a favour."

"Well," he said, "you can always ask."

"I called round at Louise's with a bag of your first editions. I hoped she might persuade you to inscribe them to me sometime when it was convenient. Next thing I knew she was insisting that we call on you. Sorry to interrupt your labours."

"Any excuse for a break," he said, "I'm the world's worst gardener. I've already been stung by a bee, nicked by the spikes of the monkey puzzle, and tripped into a patch of nettles. I wouldn't mind, but the place looks more of a jungle than when I started."

Alex looked round. "Such a lovely spot. So unusual."

"The cipher garden," Louise said.

"Cipher garden?"

"Long story," Daniel said. "Louise can tell you while I go inside and wash my hands. Then I can put on the kettle and get the books signed. Sorry I can't offer lavish refreshments. If I'd known..."

Alex laughed, a musical sound that serenaded him back into the cottage.

———

"We need to talk about Ingrid," Tory said as she finished her gin.

"She sees the specialist tomorrow," Logan said. "I keep hoping against hope for better news."

"Sweetheart, she's desperately sick." He winced. "Sorry, but we have to face facts. Whatever the prognosis, it sounds as if she definitely needs this new treatment. And she isn't going to be able to pay for it by public subscription."

"Crowdfunding." His smartphone had rolled under the lounger. Retrieving it, he brought up a site called *For the Love of Ingrid*. "We hoped for better. Social media is a powerful tool, and American people are naturally open-handed, but perhaps we expected too much. The cost is so high. The medical bills are spiralling out of control."

"That's why you must let me help."

"We've been through this before. Darling, I can't tell you how much I appreciate your kindness. My gratitude is beyond words. But the amount of money is so huge, and for a person you've never even met."

"She's your sister. She's—what, twenty-nine? So very young. I've got the money, she has the need. You owe it to her to allow me to pay those bills."

He touched his phone and a photograph of a young woman appeared on the screen. Her blonde hair was tied in a ponytail and she bore a resemblance to Logan. The fair complexion, the blue eyes, the high cheekbones.

"Looks so fit, doesn't she?" He groaned. "Hard to believe this was taken only a couple of years ago."

Tory caught hold of his wrist. "You didn't answer my question."

He shaded his eyes against the sun. "Imagine how Kingsley Melton would react if he found out. He'd probably subject me to a citizen's arrest for fraud."

"We've been through this time and again. Forget about Kingsley. He's history."

"You make it very hard to say no."

"Then don't."

He thought for a minute. "Tell you what. Let's wait and see if Ingrid gets more encouraging news tomorrow. We can talk to the specialist. If things are looking up, all well and good. If not, maybe the time has come for me to bury me pride and thank you for your incredible generosity."

She nodded. "I knew you'd see sense."

"It would be amazing if you could save her."

"Nothing would give me greater pleasure, sweetheart," Tory said. "I got another chance of life. I'd love to give your sister the same opportunity to start again."

————

Hannah took advantage of the sun to walk up Beast Banks to the Serpentine Woods on the edge of Kendal. There were plenty of families around, but she told herself to stop fantasising about what might have been. Her family-that-never-was with Marc Amos, or her family-that-might-never-be with Daniel.

After a snack lunch, and a leisurely stroll along the banks of the

Kent, she resorted to her drug of choice when the future became too difficult and depressing to contemplate, and walked to Divisional HQ. She stuffed copies of the statements of the main witnesses interviewed during the Ramona Smith investigation into a briefcase. She'd study them in detail to see if there were any small points that Maggie hadn't covered in her admirable precis which might spark fresh ideas about the fate of Ramona Smith.

Back in the flat, she struggled to concentrate. After wrestling with her conscience for half an hour, she dialled Daniel's number. Might as well apologise, and see if they could make a fresh start.

No answer. He'd switched off.

She tried to guess what he might be doing. Off on a hike over the fells? Catching up with Louise? Trying his luck with Alex Samaras?

He'd made an effort last night. It wasn't even impossible that he'd intended to propose, yet she'd rebuffed him in an offhand manner and for no good reason. Simply because she'd begun to doubt they had a future as a couple, and she didn't want them to get any further entangled just because neither of them was brutal enough to bring their relationship to a halt.

Against her will, she found herself thinking about Kit Gleadall.

No, don't go there, she thought. Haven't I made enough mistakes in my life already?

———

Louise and Alex ending up staying for a meal at Tarn Cottage. Daniel dug three pizzas out of the freezer, and they dined in the cipher garden, with its tracks that wound back on themselves, false turnings, and dead ends.

As they ate, he told Alex how he'd uncovered the story of the garden.

"Quite the detective," she said.

"Like father, like son," Louise said darkly.

"If only Ben could see you now, Daniel." Alex shook her head. "So this is a garden designed as a sort of symbol of death?"

"I'm afraid so. In olden days there was a vogue for gardens with a message. They celebrated religious beliefs or mystical revelations. This one was created by a man whose mind was in turmoil. Who wanted to conjure up a living symbol of spiritual anarchy."

Alex shuddered. "Spooky."

"Very," Louise said. "I'm surprised you haven't given it a total makeover."

"Put decking all over the place?" Daniel was amused. "I'm a historian. We can't hide from the past."

"You're so right." Alex grinned. "That's a line you use more than once in your books, isn't it?"

"Hey, you weren't fibbing when you told me you're a fan," Louise said. "Stop pandering to his ego. He'll become even more unbearable."

"Oh, I'm not totally starry-eyed. Everyone has their faults. Can you cope with choppy waters, Daniel? Ever sailed in a dinghy?"

"Never," he admitted.

"There's nothing better," Alex said dreamily. "Tell you what I'd like to do. Take the pair of you on a trip in my dinghy."

"Fantastic," Louise said. "Are you game, Daniel?"

"Love to."

"Which lake?" Louise asked.

Alex spread her arms. "Spoilt for choice, aren't we? I have a soft spot for Crummock Water."

"That's a long trek from here. Why not Grasmere or Coniston?"

"I love the serenity of the quieter lakes. Far away from the tourists."

"Fair enough," Louise said. "Crummock Water is fabulous."

Daniel said, "Just make sure you wear a life jacket, Louise. Can't expect Alex to make a habit of rescuing you from the watery deep."

Chapter Eighteen

Kingsley arrived early for his meeting with Annabel. She'd proposed coffee in one of the grand hotels overlooking Windermere. The morning was warm and he walked there from his bungalow, briefcase in hand, the last quarter's statistics fixed in his mind. Since his disastrous phone conversation with Tory, he'd taken refuge in work. Poring over the figures, depressing as they were, was preferable to imagining the woman he adored as the plaything of a handsome young murderer.

At the hotel, he found himself a table with a small settee on each side. The bay window afforded a splendid view of the boats chugging across the lake. Apart from a deaf couple who kept raising their voices in a fruitless attempt to make themselves heard, the lounge was quiet. Not a bad place for a business meeting, he thought; no danger of industrial espionage on behalf of rival property agents. He ordered coffee for two and arranged his paperwork on the table surface, determined not to give Annabel the opportunity to cavil about his lack of preparation. At their last one-to-one she'd moaned that he didn't have the facts at his fingertips. This time he'd mastered his brief like a QC embarking on a High Court trial.

"Kingsley, there you are!"

Annabel's loud Geordie screech was unmistakable. A tall, broad-shouldered woman with a cloud of red hair and lipstick and nails to match was sashaying towards him. She wore a black business suit and carried a matching leather folder. The folder's slimness was a good sign; there couldn't be much to talk about.

"Good to see you again!"

He jumped to his feet. She was the touchy-feely type, something he privately deplored. Whenever they met she presented her powdered cheeks for kissing, and he knew better than to demur. Perhaps she'd decided to become more professional, because this morning she contented herself with a handshake. Her grip was surprisingly strong.

"Perfect timing," he said suavely. "The coffee is on its way."

"Oh Kingsley, aren't you well-organised!"

He felt a pinprick of irritation at her habit of addressing people by name at every opportunity, as if to remind herself who they were, but he supposed everyone was entitled to a verbal tic. A white-jacketed waiter fussed around as they small-talked. Remembering that her children were supposed to be doing brilliantly at Sedbergh School, he dutifully enquired after their progress. It seemed to him that she boasted of their achievements on autopilot, while casting a sly glance at the spreadsheets on the table. A faint smile crossed her lips. She must be delighted that he'd heeded her strictures.

"Now," she said, putting down her cup, "we'd better get down to brass tacks."

"Absolutely." He was like a puppy, panting for praise. "Your time is money. I took care to put everything in order, so that I don't waste ten minutes trying to remember what all the figures represent."

"I'm so glad you've taken that on board, Kingsley," she said.

"Efficiency is key in this day and age. Appreciating the facts of business life will stand you in good stead."

"I'm sure." He leaned against the back of the settee. "Now, where would you like to start?"

"I think we can keep this short, Kingsley."

"Good, good." He stretched luxuriantly.

"I'm afraid this won't be welcome news, Kingsley, but we've decided that it's time for us to move on."

"Move on?"

"Part company," she said. "Terminate your contract."

He gaped. "I'm sorry?"

Annabel clicked her tongue. It never took much to rub off the veneer of her bonhomie. "For goodness sake. What part of *terminate your contract* don't you understand? It's over, done, we've come to the end of the road."

"You're sacking me?"

"Well, Kingsley, sacking is an antiquated word that we prefer not to use in virtual commerce. Don't forget, you're an independent self-managed contractor, not a member of our employee cohort. But, yes, you've got the nub of it. This is a results-oriented business, and I'm afraid your performance has fallen below our required standards for far too long."

"It's…it's just a rough patch," he stammered. "The market conditions…"

"Are a damn sight better than you're prepared to admit. This is the Lake District. A world heritage site, not some urban ghetto."

He opened his mouth, itching to point out that technically Strandbeck fell outside the national park, but she wagged a finger to silence him.

"No more excuses. Your patch is the worst performing in the county. I've given you plenty of latitude, too much really, because that's my way. I'm as soft as butter, I never shoot from the hip. But the figures speak for themselves. And, as if they weren't bad enough, there's been this God-awful publicity about the suicide at Strandbeck."

"The jogger?" His temples were pounding.

"Yes, that poor devil." She closed her eyes for a moment, as if uttering a silent prayer for the dear departed. "What on earth were you playing at? I wouldn't mind, but you should have been at your desk, drumming up business. No wonder we're failing to sell properties if you spend your days gawping at a patch of quicksand."

"I don't have fixed hours," he protested. "We agreed on flexible working."

"The clue is in the word *working*. Not daydreaming on a beach while some poor sod drowns himself right in front of your eyes. Honestly, Kingsley, I feel very disappointed, and to tell you the truth, personally let down."

Kingsley felt light-headed; the hotel lounge was spinning around him.

"I'm sorry," he said, although *aghast* would have been nearer the mark, "I've put in a lot of spadework, picked up several tangible leads, I'm sure one or two will come through. It's only a question of time. Things always seem darkest before the dawn."

The red hair shook. "Too late for that, Kingsley. The decision is made. You're entitled to a month's notice under clause nine of our standard terms. Your replacement moves into the Strandbeck office a week from today, and we'll need your laptop and files back at headquarters by Friday at the latest. You'll be paid the balance in lieu, including accrued holiday pay. Payroll is up to speed, all the ducks are in a row."

"Never mind the bloody ducks!" He was almost shouting.

The grey heads of the deaf couple swivelled in their direction; even they could hear his anguish. "I love that place, the Manor."

"Then it's a pity you haven't persuaded more people to invest in a luxury flat there," she retorted.

His head was throbbing. There was no arguing with this… this termagant. He felt seized by an urge to put his hands around her neck and squeeze the last drop of jargon out of her, but it was impossible in a public space. He must play for time, for a little human sympathy.

"Sorry, Annabel, I…I didn't mean to raise my voice. This has just come as—well, a dreadful blow. I'm heartbroken, truly. Please, you have to give me another chance. I'll do anything, I'm begging you…"

"Kingsley, Kingsley." Eyes glinting with satisfaction at the speed and abjectness of his surrender, she adjusted her tone to more-in-sorrow-than-in-anger. "Didn't I make myself clear? It's the end of the chapter. Time for you to pursue other projects. To spend more time with your family."

"I don't have a family," he said in a low voice.

"Whatever. It's no bad thing to be footloose and fancy free. No ties, no responsibilities, no bloody school fees to pay."

"I'm not…"

"Chin up!" She clapped him on the shoulder. "If you take my advice, you'll consider resuming your career in the antiques trade. The gig economy isn't for everyone. Selling upmarket properties is very different from flogging vintage snuff boxes."

She opened her black folder and slid out two letters and a ballpoint pen bearing the Greengables insignia. "I need to give you this and ask you to sign a copy for our records."

Hands shaking, Kingsley did as he was told.

She snatched the signed copy from him and stuffed it back into the folder.

"Thank you, Kingsley. And don't look so woebegone. Remember the Greengables philosophy. *Every challenge is an opportunity*. You hit the nail on the head a moment ago. It's always darkest before the dawn."

———

"Ma'am, something for you."

Maggie Eyre's eyes shone as she marched into Hannah's office. She flourished a file of papers.

"Solved the case already?"

Maggie smiled. "Well, one step at a time. This is quite a turn-up."

Hannah took the file from her and extracted a typed statement on yellowing paper. The witness's name leaped off the page.

Kingsley Melton.

"The man who sat and watched as Darren Lace jogged to his death into Morecambe Bay."

Maggie nodded. "When Ramona Smith went missing, her house was searched. As I mentioned at the briefing, her mum's room was a tip. Ramona hadn't thrown anything out, probably the bereavement was still too raw. Lucky for us, because her mother's diaries made interesting reading."

Hannah pursed her lips. "Her mother, the occasional prostitute?"

"On and off for over twenty years, yes. Very helpfully, she'd kept details of her clients' names during all that time, along with how much they paid her."

"For blackmailing purposes?" Hannah winced. "It's a wonder she wasn't murdered, never mind Ramona."

"There was no suggestion that she ever made difficulties for any of her clients. She just liked to keep records. Juicy details about her bedmates are in short supply, but we can make educated guesses from the varying amounts paid about how... exotic each client's tastes were."

"So the clients who could be traced were questioned?"

"Exactly."

"And Kingsley Melton?"

"He was one of her last clients and visited her half a dozen times over the space of eighteen months. His last visit was about a year before she died."

"Not a regular, then?"

"As I say, the woman wasn't a professional. She didn't hang around on street corners, and she only worked when cash was particularly short. I suppose she got her business through word of mouth. Local recommendations."

"Like all good tradespeople, huh? And Kingsley spent heavily with her?"

Maggie's nod was accompanied by a disapproving frown.

"So what did he say when he was interviewed?"

"Next to nothing." Maggie gave the witness statement a sour look. "He sounds self-pitying, borderline indignant. As if we were breaching his human rights by asking him what he got up to. He flatly denied ever meeting Ramona and maintained he was completely unaware of her existence. If he's to be believed, his only involvement was a few transactions with her mother."

Hannah made a quick calculation. "He must have been roughly the same age as Ramona. Bowness isn't exactly Beijing. How likely is it that he never bumped into her?"

"Vanishingly unlikely, I'd say."

"Me too."

"It's weird that Ramona's anorak and rucksack were found

near the Crooked Shore, and Melton was there when Darren Lace killed himself."

"Very."

"Surely not a complete coincidence?"

"Coincidences happen," Hannah said. "But maybe there's more to it than that."

———

"So," Hannah said, having gathered her team for a briefing, "according to Kingsley Melton's statement, he was alibied for the evening when Ramona Smith went missing. By his mother."

"For what that's worth," Les said. "Only son, apple of her eye? You can bet she'd lie through her teeth to keep him out of trouble."

"How much do we know about him?" Bunny asked.

Maggie said, "He attracted attention through his odd behaviour the day Darren Lace died. Not lifting a finger to call for help until it was too late. The officers dealing with the case wondered if he knew Lace and there was bad blood between them."

"Is that likely?"

"He lives in Bowness, where the Laces had their shop, but the family moved to Penrith when their business collapsed. There's no reason to believe that Melton knew or recognised Gerry's son."

"What took him to the Crooked Shore that particular day?"

"He works for an online estate agency, Greengables, and he has an office at their flagship development, which just happens to be Strandbeck Manor."

"In other words, a stone's throw from the Crooked Shore," Hannah said. "So although it's curious that Melton was hanging around the area where Gerald Lace took Ramona, he did have a plausible reason to be in the vicinity."

"He said he often spends time there, looking out at Morecambe Bay," Maggie said. "That's not so strange; it's a lovely spot."

"One thing that is strange about Kingsley Melton," Hannah said, "is that he's convinced that murder is about to be committed at Strandbeck Manor."

Every face turned towards her.

"Anticipating our interest in him, he sent me a personal message. Daniel Kind told me about it over the weekend."

She gave a concise summary of Kingsley's allegations against Logan Prentice.

"Terrific," Les said as they digested the news, "so we're not only looking for someone who committed murder twenty-one years ago, we're supposed to prevent another killing in the here and now."

"If Kingsley Melton is to be believed," Hannah said.

"What did Daniel make of him?"

"A sad loser, basically. Melton doesn't seem to have had satisfactory relationships with women. Perhaps the fault of this domineering mother of his, who knows? He seems to have had a brief crush on Prentice. In Daniel's opinion, Melton genuinely believes that Prentice is a rogue, but maybe his judgement is warped by mixed-up emotions."

"The press slaughtered him for not doing more to save Darren Lace," Bunny said.

"He's besotted with this Reece-Taylor woman and jealous of Prentice. She obviously prefers to spend her time with a toy boy."

"Who can blame her?" Bunny asked.

"I asked Maggie to check on the alleged murder at Sunset View. An incident record was kept, thank goodness."

"Wonders never cease," Les muttered.

"Don't get too excited," Maggie said. "The investigation was cursory. Not surprising in the circumstances. The doctor was satisfied that Ivy Podmore died of natural causes. The care home manager said the Meltons were stirring up trouble for the sake of it. Mother and son loathed Prentice. Ivy hadn't actually made a new will. So there was no motive for murder."

"Not necessarily," Hannah said. "If Prentice was fooled into believing that he was her heir."

"Yes, but the sole witness to the supposed murder was dead."

"So there's no mileage in reviewing Ivy's death as a cold case?" Les said.

"We can't justify it," Hannah said. "Not with zero forensic evidence. We'd need a new witness to come out of the wood-work. A care assistant, maybe. The longest of long shots."

Maggie's brow creased. "I don't suppose we can tip Ms. Reece-Taylor off about Prentice, just in case?"

"With nothing to go on but Kingsley's instinct?"

"Hell hath no fury like an estate agent scorned," Bunny said.

"We could dig deeper into Prentice's background, fish around for anything of interest, but I can't justify diverting our resources. Suppose he is a young man on the make, having his wicked way with an older woman who enjoys spoiling him. So what?"

"If he's that dishy," Bunny said, "I might not say no myself."

"I ran a quick check on Prentice," Maggie said. "He doesn't have a criminal record."

"Like so many other criminals," Les grumbled.

"Logically," Hannah said, "we need to concentrate on Kingsley Melton. When he was talking to Daniel, he referred to guilty secrets and now we know why. He paid Ramona Smith's mother for sex. Yet he claimed he'd never met the daughter who lived in the same house."

"To be fair," Bunny said. "He probably made sure he called when Ramona was out."

"Even so." Hannah waved the business card that Daniel had given to her. "I have Melton's details. Let's see if after all these years he still sticks to his story."

"Hey," Bunny said, "you don't think he might be the mysterious Vee?"

"Good question," Hannah said. "Let's ask him."

———

Kingsley needed air. He stumbled through the revolving doors at the front of the hotel and made his way blindly along the pavement, not knowing or caring where his feet might take him. Was this how a boxer felt, when punches from a bloodthirsty opponent kept raining down and one lacked the strength to defend oneself, let alone hit back?

The persecution he'd suffered at the hands of the media after the jogger's demise had been brutal enough. The savagery of Tory's rebuff hurt a hundred times more. Now this crippling blow. Annabel had stripped him of his livelihood and self-respect, and as if that were not enough, she'd robbed him of his office at the Manor, and the chance to keep within touching distance of the woman he worshipped.

His headache was raging and he fumbled inside his jacket pocket for a couple of pills. Emergency rations. He flung the small capsules down his throat and swallowed hard.

Instinct took him along Rayrigg Road, his feet guided by a subconscious yearning for the lovely and familiar. One of his favourite ways of spending a fine day on his own was to make the circuit of Queen Adelaide's Hill and Millerground and admire the magnificence of Windermere from one of the finest vantage points in Cumbria. He pushed through a kissing gate and plodded up the stony path.

At the top of the drumlin, he looked out towards the far side of the lake. The views never failed to take his breath away. Crinkle Crags, Harrison Stickle, Pavey Ark, Loughrigg, their evocative names etched in his brain since childhood. His father, a keen walker who had a nodding acquaintance with Alfred Wainwright, the guru of the Lake District fells, had never convinced Kingsley of the joy of slogging up steep slopes in all weathers, but for all that he relished his native landscape. When life became almost too painful to bear, he took solace from the rugged grandeur of the rocky horizon.

He breathed in the aroma of grass and vegetation, feeling a light breeze ruffle his hair. Sheep contemplated him with vague indifference. This picturesque spot reeked of history. The hill, like the city in Australia, took its name from a queen who came here to visit; her boat had landed just below this hill, and she came ashore at Millerground. During the last world war, soldiers in the Home Guard had patrolled the lake in motor boats with mounted machine guns, guarding the flying boat factory and no doubt praying that Hitler would choose some other target.

Kingsley wasn't a churchgoer or a religious man in the conventional sense, but he nourished a vague and incoherent faith that good shall prevail. One day the meek really ought to inherit the earth. This conviction had kept him going through so many rough times, experiences that—he reminded himself—would have destroyed a frailer spirit. The death of his sister, his academic failures, the loss of his father, the betrayal by Logan Prentice, Mamma's strokes.

A weaker soul, Gerald Lace or his son for instance, might abandon hope in the face of overwhelming adversity and put an end to it all. Not Kingsley Melton. People thought he was a pushover, but they were wrong. No matter how many times Fate knocked him to the floor, he picked himself up and battled on. Often down, but never out.

The pills were working their magic. His headache had cleared. As he walked down by Wynlass Beck, his steps had a spring unimaginable even half an hour earlier. It wasn't just his medication. Nature's healing powers were at work. The sunlight warmed his cheeks and brow. Two plump, white-throated dippers were paddling in the stream, and he spotted the delicate yellow blooms of a patch of rare balsam, known as touch-me-not.

Touch-me-not. It was a splendid motto; he must adopt it. He threw back his shoulders and lengthened his stride. Logan Prentice, Annabel Wheeldon, even Tory Reece-Taylor, let them do their worse. Bruised and battered he might be, but he wouldn't break.

———

"I'm truly sorry," Tory said as Logan switched off the laptop. They were sitting next to each other. Outside the sun blazed, but the living room had a chill of melancholy.

He wouldn't meet her eyes. When he spoke, his voice was muffled.

"She's so brave. It's so...unjust."

He buried his face in his hands and she hugged him to her. "There's always hope, sweetheart," she said. "This new treatment the doctor talked about."

"You heard what he said." They'd listened on his laptop, not daring to interrupt. The video link hadn't worked, but the specialist, a native New Yorker by the sound of him, had sounded downcast during the five minutes he'd granted them. "It's experimental, unproven. And the cost..."

"You mustn't give up hope!" Tory nuzzled his neck. "Ingrid is depending on you. Don't worry about the cost."

"How can I not?"

"I told you I'm willing to pay."

He pulled away from her. "No, I can't let you do that!"

"Hey." She seized hold of her wrist. Her grip surprised him with its strength. "You promised that if the news wasn't good, You'd let me help. This isn't about you, it's about your sister. She's dying. I want her to have the gift of life."

———

Kingsley had turned his phone to silent prior to the calamitous encounter with Annabel, and he only remembered to switch it back on as he arrived home at the bungalow. There was a message on his voicemail from an unknown number. He listened.

The call was from Cumbria Constabulary. Some young female flunkey had left her number and asked him to ring back. She wanted to know if she could make an appointment for him to see Detective Chief Inspector Hannah Scarlett. DCI Scarlett was willing to visit Kingsley at his home, if that was convenient. Was he free tomorrow?

Had he misjudged Daniel Kind's reaction to their conversations at Amos Books? The historian had come up trumps after all. Despite his apparent doubts, he must have passed the information on to his friend. At last Kingsley was getting somewhere. On television, Hannah Scarlett had struck him as highly sympathetic. A civilised chat with her was a very different proposition from trying to persuade a sceptical underling to take him seriously.

He dialled the number given by the girl. He tried to prise some information out of her about the purpose of the meeting, but she sounded junior; if she knew what had passed between Daniel and Hannah Scarlett, she wasn't admitting it. He fixed the meeting for half past ten.

Energy surged through him. His luck was beginning to turn.

Time to return to Strandbeck Manor.

———

"It will take time," Logan said. "Years, I suppose, but I'll pay you back. My luck will turn soon. I'll get the cash together. Every penny."

"You won't," Tory said. "This is between me and Ingrid. Nothing to do with you."

"You'd never have heard of her if I hadn't mentioned..."

"True, but irrelevant." She kissed him long and hard. "Don't kick up a fuss, sweetheart, it won't make any difference. My mind is made up. I've never been a do-gooder. For once in my life, I'm going to do something for someone else."

He caught his breath. "You're amazing."

"I know," she said.

———

Daniel had just come off the phone with his publisher when Louise called. She was on sabbatical, and although she was supposed to be writing a chapter in an academic book, she looked for any excuse to avoid getting down to it. He couldn't blame her since he knew the feeling.

"About this boat trip," she said.

"What boat trip?"

A theatrical groan. "Don't tell me you've forgotten."

"You mean with Alex Samaras?"

"Who else?"

"What about it?"

"Let's do it sooner rather than later. I know you said you've got a lot of work on, but she's definitely interested, Daniel. Trust me, I can see the signs. You're lucky. She's very desirable."

It was his turn to groan. "You've forgotten, I'm not in the market."

"On the way back to Grasmere, she asked me about Hannah. Said she didn't want to tread on anyone's toes."

"What did you say?"

"I said I didn't know how things were between the two of you. Which is the honest truth."

"And what did she say?"

"Just that she didn't want to spoil things. Either interfere with your life, or mess up her friendship with me. She's afraid you think she's a shallow fangirl. A failed actor, not bright enough or serious enough for a leading historian."

"I hope you told her that I couldn't care less about reputations, mine or anyone else's. She's got tons of charm, and I enjoy her company. But that's as far as it goes."

A heavy sigh. "All right. You're making a mistake, but it wouldn't be the first time. Just tell me you'll join us on the boat trip."

He grinned at the phone. One thing about Louise, she never gave up a lost cause.

"All right. I'll go on the boat trip."

———

Kingsley parked his Corsa in his usual spot close to the Crooked Shore, but instead of ambling towards Morecambe Bay, he lifted his briefcase out of the boot and headed up to Strandbeck

Lane. Events had conspired against him for too long. His hopes for a reversal of fortune depended on subtlety, even a degree of low cunning. If he drove up to the Manor, there was a risk that Tory would spot him before the time was ripe, and that would never do.

At the gates of the Manor, he took the right hand footpath, following the line of the boundary wall until it gave way to a wooden fence. After two or three minutes he reached the point where the fence was broken. This allowed access to the Manor grounds and the route favoured by trespassers taking a short-cut. Repairing the most recent damage to the fence had been on Kingsley's to-do list for months. Thank goodness for his inertia. *Everything happens for a reason*, he told himself, and some-times things don't happen for a reason as well.

The great advantage of this gap in the Manor's security was that Tory had no view of it from her flat. She wouldn't be able to see him unless she happened to be strolling nearby.

Seeing no sign of human life in the grounds, Kingsley squeezed through the gap. He made his way through a clump of trees and shrubs into the wild garden, in other words the outer part of the estate that the outside contractors weren't paid to maintain. They worked here every Monday, and he'd timed his arrival in Strandbeck to coincide with when they knocked off. Predictably, they'd already left for the day. The lawn was freshly mown, and he inhaled the smell of the grass as he strolled across towards the far side of the building.

He let himself into his office. Everything had gone to plan, nobody had seen him. The Manor had four CCTV cameras, but only two of them were functional at present, and keeping out of their fields of view proved to be a doddle. Upgrading the security was one more task Kingsley hadn't got round to. Never mind, not his problem now. Let his wretched successor sort it out.

Through the front window he saw Tory's car. Logan Prentice had parked his dirty old van right next to it. Unless he and Tory had gone out for a walk, they must be inside her flat.

Kingsley opened first one desk drawer and then the other. After stashing a few personal possessions into his briefcase, he contemplated the antique gun and the ammunition.

He picked up the Smith & Wesson and cradled it in his hands. On impulse, he loaded the bullets. Not that he was intending to shoot anyone, obviously, but you couldn't be too careful. He gave the gun an affectionate pat and put it back in its hiding place. Merely to know it was there, should he ever need to make a point, gave him comfort and confidence.

During the Manor's redesign, his office and cloakroom had been separated from three other rooms, which remained vacant and locked. Eventually they would be joined together to constitute the last flat to be sold. Kingsley fished the key to the dividing door from his desk and entered the empty suite. Passing through the main room, he opened a walk-in cupboard at the far end. The air was stale and the dust so thick that he sneezed. In the confined space, the noise he made sounded to him like a grenade exploding.

He shut his eyes, fearing he'd given the game away. The back of the cupboard also formed the rear of a cupboard in Tory's bedroom. If she were there now, she must surely have heard him.

Nothing happened.

Breathing a sigh of relief, he reminded himself to take the utmost care. The slightest slip could lead to catastrophe. Given Tory's recent form, if she discovered him keeping tabs on her, she would show no mercy. At the very least, she'd be on the blower to the appalling Annabel, who would no doubt take great delight in marching him out of his office, changing the locks, and beefing up the camera surveillance.

He found some tissues in the cloakroom and gave the inside of the cupboard a quick wipe before settling back inside. Soundproofing in the renovated Manor was good, but the wall separating the two cupboards was a weak point. The builders had saved time and effort where they thought they could get away with it. More than once Kingsley had crouched inside the cupboard, listening to the clatter of coat hangers and Tory's tuneless humming. It excited him to picture her, blissfully unaware of his presence a few inches away.

After ten minutes he heard movements next door. Then voices, muffled yet discernible.

"Take it off," Logan said.

A coquettish giggle. "Shall I?"

"Yes."

He listened for several minutes, until he could bear no more. He crept out of the cupboard and dragged himself to the cloakroom, where he splashed cold water over his face.

What was happening to Tory horrified him. It was as if Prentice had cast a spell over the woman and made her his slave. He was robbing her of every last shred of dignity. She was helpless. At his mercy.

Kingsley fled from the office and hurried back the way he had come. At least he needn't worry that Tory was watching. When he arrived at the Corsa, his head was buzzing. For once he had no wish to linger on his bench by the Crooked Shore.

His mission was clear. Like a knight in shining armour, he needed to rescue the woman he loved. With any luck, Hannah Scarlett would help. Come what may, he must act quickly, before it was too late.

Chapter Nineteen

"Kingsley Melton? I'm DCI Scarlett and this is DC Bunny Cohen." Hannah paused as he gaped at the two women standing outside the front door of his bungalow. "You remember our appointment for this morning? May we come in?"

Kingsley was startled to see that Hannah Scarlett wasn't alone. He'd envisaged a private conversation. The detective constable was roughly his own age, with a sharp edge to her nose and chin. She scrutinised him as if he were a scrap of forensic evidence in a polythene bag. Cynicism radiated from her like a cheap perfume; he scented a hard-nosed feminist who believed men were never to be trusted.

"Well, yes," he stammered. "Of course. Follow me."

He led them down the hallway and into the sitting room at the back of the bungalow. He'd dusted so scrupulously even Mamma would have had to give his housework grudging approval. For all his efforts to tidy up, he was conscious that a stranger might think his house cluttered. Claustrophobic, even. His parents had often brought home treasures from the shop and he'd filled every remaining nook and cranny with antiques that caught his eye. He'd kept the original furniture, of course;

he shared Mamma's belief that Art Deco never went out of fashion. The leatherette upholstery showed its age, inevitably, but for all the cracks it was hard-wearing and comfortable enough, even if the bolshy-looking constable made a point of wincing as she sat down.

"Can I offer you a cuppa?" Important to be hospitable, he needed the police on his side. "Yorkshire tea, if that's all right with you. No trouble, the kettle's only just come to the boil."

"Thank you." Hannah put her leather briefcase down on the freshly hoovered floral carpet. "Milk and no sugar for both of us."

"Can I tempt you with a Viennese whirl?" He chuckled at their bafflement. "My favourite type of biscuit."

"Nothing to eat, thanks. Tea will be fine."

While he fussed around, he was conscious of the two women weighing up their surroundings, admiring the antiques. Easy to guess that they were forming opinions about him. No doubt they'd judge him to be respectable but rather a fuddy-duddy; he was well aware that was how he often came across to other people.

"It's good of you to see us," Hannah said as he poured the tea. "I'm sure you're very busy."

"I'm fortunate to be able to organise my own schedule," he said. "I could never have coped with being an employee, condemned to the treadmill, nine-to-five."

"Yet you work for an estate agency?"

"As an independent contractor, not a member of the permanent staff. At least I'm with them for the time being."

"You're leaving the job?"

It had crossed his mind that the police might check his bona fides, and he didn't want them to think that Greengables were giving him the sack. It was almost the truth to claim that the decision was his. He'd yearned to be free of the tyranny of the spreadsheets and regular reports ever since he'd moved into Strandbeck Manor. It did no harm to put a positive spin on his impending departure.

"I'm ready for a change. To be honest, I find their nitpicking tiresome. I long to regain my independence. I'm planning to go back to dealing in antiques, being my own boss. Answerable only to myself, not a bunch of jumped-up accounts clerks. Our family had an antiques shop in Kendal. We ate, breathed, and slept antiques. You've probably gathered!"

With a little laugh, he indicated their surroundings. The cabinet of lapis lazuli. The porcelain dolls' faces that used to terrify his young sister, even more than the collection of dead hawk-moths housed in a glass display drawer. The grumpy constable was mesmerised by the tropical birds in his bamboo-edged taxidermy case.

"Victorian," he told her. "Wonderful how they have retained their colours. The toucan makes such a cheerful centrepiece."

The Cohen woman's eyes were out on stalks. Anyone would think she'd never seen a stuffed bird before. Hannah Scarlett, to give her credit, didn't seem fazed by his love of curiosities. She had clear eyes and good skin, and seemed quite relaxed. Calm, unthreatening, not in the least judgemental.

She was savouring her tea. DC Cohen hadn't touched hers; surely she didn't think he was trying to poison them? Her distrustful expression struck him as rude. Anyone would imagine that he wasn't a law-abiding citizen. She was still a public servant. He paid his taxes, which paid her wages. Not to mention funding her gold-plated pension.

"You asked Daniel Kind to pass on some information to me," Hannah said. "You've made a serious accusation. I'm not clear why you didn't speak to us directly?"

He settled back in his chair. An easy question; he'd prepared for it, and the only challenge was not to reel off his answer without pausing for breath.

"I raised my concerns about the death of Ivy Podmore at the time and nobody took me seriously. I was asked for evidence which I didn't possess and which it wasn't my job to provide. Frankly, I hoped people in authority would find proof of the crime, but nothing happened."

Hannah inclined her head. She wasn't trying to argue or pick holes in what he said. Encouraging.

"When I became aware that Prentice was taking an unhealthy interest in Ms. Reece-Taylor, naturally I was concerned. Knowing his past and knowing that she is vulnerable. A wealthy woman with a history of serious heart trouble. Sudden cardiac arrest. He's less than half her age, without a penny to his name."

DC Cohen piped up. "Perhaps she takes a maternal interest in him."

"I doubt it," Kingsley retorted. "For a start, Tory isn't in the least maternal. She once told me that she was never interested in having children. No, she's a passionate woman. Not to put too fine a point on it, she has a considerable…well, appetite, if you follow."

"We follow," Hannah said.

"I'm the first to admit that Prentice is a handsome fellow with a deceptively charming manner. Animal lust I can understand, as a man of the world. But what are his motives? That's the question."

"Mr. Prentice doesn't have a criminal record."

"He's clever," Kingsley said. "Cunning, deceitful, sly. He has a confidence trickster's ability to win your sympathy, then turn it to his own advantage. Anyway, I knew that if I approached the police myself, you'd quiz me like this and point out that there was little or nothing to go on. The likelihood was that I'd be fobbed off with a cynical subordinate and get absolutely nowhere."

He couldn't resist throwing a meaningful glance at DC Cohen, the epitome of the cynical subordinate. She looked out through the window. Disapproval tightened her lips as she considered the garden, with its apology for a rockery, rusty wrought-iron outdoor furniture, and crumbling old shed.

Hurriedly, he said, "There was another consideration. You'll be aware that recently I had the misfortune to witness a suicide at Strandbeck. The press mauled me. Like a lynch mob, even though I was entirely innocent. My only crime was raising the alarm, notifying the emergency authorities that a man was in danger!" His voice trembled at the injustice he'd suffered. "Perhaps you can understand why I was reluctant to expose myself to any further risk of trial by media. However, I was troubled by my conscience, as well as my fears for Ms. Reece-Taylor. Quite apart from my personal fondness for her, there was a question of public duty. I simply couldn't turn a blind eye."

Again Hannah gave a slight nod. So far, he told himself, so good.

"Which is why you decided to confide in Daniel Kind?"

"Exactly. I was aware that he was acquainted with you personally, Detective Chief Inspector, and given his expertise in crime, I was also interested to hear his own views."

"We'd like to hear what you have to say in your own words."

"Fine." He swallowed some tea and settled back in his chair. "Are you sitting comfortably, to coin a phrase? Then I'll begin."

He recounted the events at Sunset View, mentioning his short-lived friendship with Logan Prentice, shorn of any embarrassing admissions. Since agreeing to this appointment, he'd given anxious consideration about how to skate on thin ice, and was rather pleased with the deftness of his footwork. How bitterly he regretted being so candid with Daniel Kind, even though he'd tried to avoid humiliating himself. Nothing he was saying now was actually untrue. Yes, his version of events was a tad selective. But then, all narratives were personal and subjective, weren't they?

"It was a murder for money," he said. "When it turned out that Prentice wasn't going to inherit a penny, he must have been mortified. I'm sure it hasn't stopped him sniffing around for other prospective victims, but he was too canny to use precisely the same *modus operandi*. If he became a fixture in care homes, sucking up to old ladies with pots of cash at every opportunity, people would notice and draw their own conclusions."

Hannah said, "You think he'd taken fright, even though your allegation was disregarded?"

"Definitely." Kingsley was getting into his stride. "He's neither stupid nor rash. Believe me, Prentice is crafty as well as a danger to the people he befriends for gain. Such as Tory Reece-Taylor."

"Tell me about her," Hannah said. "And her involvement with Logan Prentice."

DC Cohen shifted position, giving a heavy sigh as she did so. Kingsley was irritated by her manner. The chair really wasn't that uncomfortable, you just needed to get used to it.

"May I use your bathroom, please?" she asked.

"Of course." Kingsley pointed to the door. "Through there, then first on the right."

As she left the room, he launched into the second episode of his story. Hannah Scarlett cupped her chin in her hand, giving him her full attention in a manner he found gratifying. A pleasant woman, not in the least hard-bitten or scornful. The girl next door type. There weren't enough of them around. If he'd been a few years younger, he'd have loved to get to know her better. Today, his energies were concentrated on making her understand the threat Tory faced.

"I realise that this must seem like supposition," he said as DC Cohen rejoined them, "but if you knew Prentice, what I'm saying would make perfect sense. He's taking advantage of a much older woman."

The constable frowned, and he turned to Hannah in the hope of a more satisfactory response.

"A woman," he continued in a solemn tone, "who has already been clinically dead. It's a miracle she's still with us, let alone in such—um, excellent shape. As she puts it, she loves coming back from the dead, but her medical history puts her at extreme risk. We have a duty of care to protect her from Logan Prentice."

"I was wondering," Hannah said mildly, "what you propose we should do."

"If you could speak to Tory. The sooner, the better. Please forgive me, I don't wish to be presumptuous, but I'm sure she would be more receptive if you spoke to her personally, rather than delegating to a junior officer."

"And what do you suggest I tell her?"

He dug a hand into his trouser pocket and pulled out a piece of paper bearing his spidery scrawl.

"Here are her details. Address, landline and mobile numbers, email. Explain the risk she's running, persuade her to be on her guard. No need to mention my name."

"Even if we do talk to Ms. Reece-Taylor," Hannah said, taking the paper from him, "surely she will guess that you're behind it? You've already warned her about Logan Prentice, and she sent you off, as you put it, with a flea in your ear. Won't she simply assume that you're stirring up trouble because you're jealous that she's rejected you for him?"

"She hasn't rejected me," he said tartly. "Perhaps I didn't make myself clear. We had a little argument, as I said. A tiff, something and nothing. She can be very touchy."

"Ah, I see."

"I'm sure you can handle her," he said. "And that she'll pay heed to words of advice from a senior detective."

"What if she resents our interference? If she asks us for evidence of Prentice's criminal behaviour?"

"Check him out," Kingsley said.

"As I say, we've already established that he doesn't have a criminal record."

"A leopard doesn't change his spots. You just need to dig a bit deeper."

"If he's as cunning as you suggest, he will have covered his tracks. Suppose Ms. Reece-Taylor tells Prentice that we've talked to her, and he accuses us of police harassment?"

"That would be an outrage!"

"Stranger things have happened."

"Crime prevention is better than cure." This was a snappy phrase he'd come up with last night, and he was proud of it. "Far better that she's guided by someone in authority. She's putting her head in the sand, even when she ought to know better. The simple truth is that she doesn't want to admit she'd been gulled by a young crook. She needs saving from herself. I feel responsible for her well-being, but I need help. Above all, Tory needs help."

He leaned back in his chair, satisfied that he'd made a compelling case without getting swept away by emotion. An eminent silk would have been proud.

Hannah finished her tea. "You'll understand that there are strict limits to what we can and should do, Mr. Melton. I make no promises."

He nodded, recognising the official disclaimer for what it

was. She had to watch her back, so did everyone in authority in this day and age.

"All I can say is that we're grateful to you for drawing this matter to our attention, and we will consider very carefully all the information you've passed to us."

"I'm sure you'll appreciate the urgency," he said. "Tory's medical history does mean that she's extremely susceptible to..."

"We understand the points you've made."

Hannah and her constable stood up. Disappointment stabbed him. Whilst he'd been talking, he'd thought her empathetic, quite different from all the others who ignored what he said about Prentice. All of a sudden, he was unsure of her. Listening patiently wasn't enough. She must take action, he was depending on her.

"You will keep in touch? Make sure to let me know when you've decided what to do."

"Actually, Mr. Melton, whilst we're here, there's something I wanted to ask you."

"Yes?"

Her expression gave nothing away, but he noticed a subtle change of tone. He scanned her face for clues, but found nothing. Yet the atmosphere had changed, as if he'd opened a window and a cold gust of wind had blown through the room and rattled the teacups.

"As you've gathered, my team has been tasked with looking into the disappearance and possible murder of Ramona Smith twenty-one years ago."

He sniffed, like an animal scenting danger.

"We've taken a look at the old files and come across the statement you gave at the time."

For a horrid moment he was afraid he was going to be sick. The statement, of course! He'd striven to banish it from his mind. At the time, his brief encounter with the police had been alarming, but nothing had come of their inquisition. There was no follow-up interview. It was buried in the past. Dead and gone. Why on earth did they keep hold of such things for so many years? It was absurd. Disgraceful.

The eyes of both women bored into him. He felt the blood drain from his face, as if sucked out by a vampire. When he spoke, his voice was a croak.

"Yes?"

"You knew Ramona Smith's mother. You were a client of hers."

He sucked air into his lungs. "We were...acquaintances."

"You paid her for sexual services," Hannah said. "In the privacy of her home."

She didn't sound cold and condemning. A straw to clutch at, even if she didn't sound sympathetic, either. He kept his eyes away from the older woman, who had taken a dislike to him from the moment she'd stepped across the threshold.

"It was—a very long time ago."

Hannah waited. Was she expecting some incriminating admission? If so, she'd be disappointed.

"I only visited her half a dozen times, if that. I was young, immature; it was a time in my life when I felt very much alone." A good line, he thought. "Before long, I moved on. I've never... behaved like that since. To be perfectly honest, I'd forgotten all about it."

"We wondered whether, on reflection, there was anything you wanted to add to your statement."

The clicking of his brain was almost audible. "I answered each question as best I could. I told the police everything."

"We brought a copy of the statement to refresh your memory."

Hannah unzipped a side pocket of the briefcase, taking out a sheet of paper in a plastic wallet.

He scanned the typed lines. At least he'd not compromised himself. Apart from admitting to an intermittent sexual relationship with the dead mother of the missing woman.

It could be worse, he told himself.

He handed the statement back to her. "Yes, that's about the size of it. There's nothing more to say."

"You're quite sure you never met Ramona?"

"I made that clear. It was her mother that…"

"Was your friend?"

He glared, but couldn't detect any hint of mockery in her voice or expression.

"It was a business relationship, nothing more. I was going through a difficult time."

"Why was it difficult?"

The room was warm and stuffy. He dabbed at his brow with a handkerchief. "I was a young man. Youngish, anyway. I'd never had much luck with the opposite sex. If…if you must know, I was a virgin."

There. He'd said it. These two women had wrung the confession out of him. What were they thinking? Their faces gave nothing away.

"I suppose Leila was…an outlet." He risked a note of sarcasm. "We didn't discuss our respective families."

"Ramona lived in the same house. There must have been signs of her presence."

"I don't recall."

"Did Leila not mention her?"

His shoulders crumpled. "The purpose of my visits wasn't to discuss Leila's relatives."

The two women waited.

"I...I suppose she may have said something about a daughter. In passing. Obviously, she was alone in the house each time I called. I simply can't remember anymore. You'll have to take my word for it."

Bunny said, "Did you know anyone called Vee?"

The question caught him off balance. He screwed up his face in a parody of brain-racking.

"Vee?"

"Yes."

"I've no idea what you're talking about."

Hannah said, "Ramona had a friend called Vee."

"I told you." He stared at the carpet, his voice choking. "I didn't know Leila Smith's daughter. Or anyone called Vee, for that matter."

"Bowness is a small town, Mr. Melton. You lived here all your life and so did she. Do you insist that you never bumped into Ramona, not even casually?"

He tried to gather his strength. "Well..."

"Yes?"

"I've no recollection of meeting her."

"So you may have met her and simply forgotten about it?"

He could barely muster a shrug. The women said nothing. Mustering what was left of his dignity, he said, "I've told you. I have nothing to add."

The detectives exchanged glances. "Sure about that, Mr. Melton?" Hannah asked.

"How many times do I have to repeat myself?" There was a note of rising hysteria in his voice.

"You wouldn't be Vee, by any chance?"

He jerked his head. "What?"

"It wasn't a nickname? A term of endearment that Ramona used for you? Was it short for something?"

"Have you gone mad?" He didn't need to feign bewilderment. "I've no idea what you're talking about. What can Vee be short for?"

"You tell me."

"Valerie, Vanessa, Vincent?" He spread his arms. "I had a sister who died when she was young. Her name was Vesper, but we never called her Vee."

Hannah's eyes bored into him; she might have been an undertaker, measuring a corpse for a shroud. Her silence was a wall that he wasn't able to scale.

"This is absolutely ridiculous!" he shouted. "I invite you into my home in all good faith, trying to do my civic duty and help you to stop a murderer in his tracks, and what happens? You subject me to an inquisition. Make me feel as though I've committed a crime."

"Very well, Mr. Melton," Hannah said. "Thanks for seeing us. We'll consider everything you've told us. In the meantime, perhaps you could rack your own brains. See if you can tell us anything about Ramona. Or Vee. If you do, please let us know at once."

The two women walked into the hallway. "Don't bother to see us to the door," Bunny said. "You look upset. We can find our own way out."

———

"Well?" Hannah asked as they strapped themselves into the car.

"Oh, my God!" Bunny cast her eyes upwards. "What a piece of work!"

"I'm guessing you didn't take to him?"

"Pervy bloke with a fetish for stuffed birds, what's not to like? I mean, seriously, I got the heebie-jeebies just sitting on that nasty old chair. Sitting room? More like the set for one of those old Hammer horror movies. I wouldn't put it past him to have stuffed those birds himself!"

Hannah grinned. "His treasures would fetch a few bob on *Antiques Roadshow*."

"Fusty old garbage. Give me Ikea any day. And what about the wasteland that passes for his back garden? See how it spooked him out when I was looking through the window? I'd love to get a search warrant."

"No chance of that," Hannah said. "We don't have a scrap of evidence that he's done anything wrong."

"For all we know, what's left of Ramona Smith is in his garden shed, a victim of his do-it-yourself taxidermy."

"You don't think she's buried under the rockery?"

"Maybe I give him credit for too much imagination."

"Apart from that, you reckon he's a decent upstanding individual?"

"Ugh!" Bunny gave a theatrical shudder. "Him and his Viennese whirls. They're probably laced with weed-killer. When I went to the loo, I took a peek inside his medicine cabinet. It's full to bursting with all sorts of drugs."

"Arsenic?" Hannah kept a straight face. "Strychnine? Cyanide?"

"Prescription pills, mainly," Bunny admitted. "Loads of anti-depressants. Painkillers. Enough to kill a horse."

"He's on the edge," Hannah said. "Beneath the surface, under that desperate bonhomie, there's a sad and inadequate man, struggling to put a brave face on things."

Bunny allowed herself a rueful smile. "That's why you're a DCI and I'm a DC. I find it difficult to control my feelings. Let alone my big mouth. I'm not as compassionate as you. Honestly, he made my skin crawl."

"Dunno about compassionate," Hannah said. "Part of me feels sorry for Kingsley Melton, part of me doesn't trust him one inch. One thing is for sure. He's genuinely afraid that Prentice means to murder Tory Reece-Taylor."

Chapter Twenty

"I want to know everything about you," Tory said.

This is the life, Logan was thinking. Lounging in the sun at one's country estate, the coastline a stone's throw away. A glass of bubbly at your feet, and a semi-naked woman by your side. Why must she spoil their bliss with pointless questions?

"There's not much to tell."

He took another sip of prosecco. They'd picnicked in front of the summer house, undisturbed except for scampering squirrels and the squeal of gulls. He closed his eyes, but Tory didn't pick up on the signal that he'd ended the conversation.

"You're too modest, sweetheart. Honestly, you've got so much going for you. I don't just mean your looks. You're smart. Not just about fixing computers, either. You act, you play the piano…"

"Not very well."

"There you go, running yourself down again." She sighed. "Not like Winston. He had a fraction of your talent, God rest his soul, but he was so full of himself. Thought he knew it all."

"You and he were together a long time."

"Oh, he looked after me in his fashion, made sure I had

everything money could buy. It was worth putting up with his boring friends and their endless conversations about golf."

"Is that why you married him? The money?"

"You make me sound like a gold-digger, sweetheart." She yawned. "He pestered me for ages before I said yes. But the years passed, I'm not complaining. I had all the money I'd wished for; I could please myself. He bought me expensive clothes, luxury holidays. It was fine, but every now and then, I asked myself the old question."

"What old question?"

"*Is this it?*"

"What about children?"

"He had two from his first marriage. A miserable pair who resented me from day one. Kids are trouble. I never wanted them."

"What did you want?"

"I've never really been sure," she said lazily. "Until now. I've discovered that you're what I want, Logan Prentice. Believe me, there's no escape."

She made a grab for him and they rolled around together for several minutes. He enjoyed her passion, it was remarkable for someone her age. And it had taken her mind off the inquisition.

Except that after another mouthful of prosecco, she started up again.

"Go on, then. I want to hear all about you."

He rolled on to his stomach and told himself not to become irritated. "Honestly, there's not much to say. We grew up in Sheffield, Ingrid and me. Our father died when I was a baby. I really can't remember him at all."

This was the backstory he'd devised for himself. The truth was messier, somehow less convincing.

She ran her fingers down his spine. "I'm sorry."

"We never had much money, we just scraped along. Ingrid left home when she was seventeen. She wanted to act, she dreamed of Hollywood long before she emigrated. Pity it never worked out."

"If the specialist is right, this time next year she'll be firing on all cylinders. Maybe sooner, given that she's young." She paused. "Go on, I'm interested."

He sighed. "Mum died the week I started at uni. Car crash. From then on, I had to make my own way in life. Like Ingrid, I used to dream big. I'd be a movie star or a top jazz musician. But reality got in the way. Look at me now, understudying ham actors with the Newbies and thumping out "Auld Lang Syne" on New Year's Eve in an Ulverston pub."

"I'm going to buy a piano," she said. "I'd love you to play for me."

"Darling, you're wonderful, but you can't keep showering me with expensive presents."

"Why not?" She jabbed him in the ribs. "You're mine now."

———

Hannah convened a team meeting to update everyone on the interview with Kingsley Melton, and Bunny reported a conversation with Ivy Podmore's lawyer.

"Ivy was in poor health for years before her death and she suffered from dementia." Bunny sighed. "The fun of changing her mind about who should inherit kept her alive. The solicitor confirmed that Ivy talked about bequeathing her estate to Logan Prentice, but said a new will would never have stood up. She was too far gone. The charities which were deprived of bequests could have challenged the will in court."

"So that part of Melton's story is accurate?"

Bunny shrugged. "For what it's worth."

Hannah turned to the rest of the team. "If you're wondering, there are two reasons why it's worth devoting precious time and resources to checking up on his story. One, our job is to look at cold cases. We'd be failing in our duty if we ignored the allegation that Ivy was murdered, even if the chances of making a charge stick are vanishingly small. Two, we need to get a full picture of Kingsley Melton. I'm convinced that he knows more than he's prepared to admit."

Maggie said, "But you don't think Melton might be Vee?"

"Ramona's secret lover?" Les pulled a face. "If he's as repellent as Bunny makes out, no chance."

"This was more than twenty years ago," Maggie said. "What if there's more to him than meets the eye?"

"Trust me," Bunny said. "You'd have to be desperate to fancy such an oddball. A bloke who surrounds himself with stuffed birds, dolls' heads, and dead moths."

"Is he really that strange?" Maggie asked. "The family sold antiques; no wonder they filled the house with curiosities. You wouldn't judge a farmer by the fact that he works with cows and pigs."

"My uncle was a farmer, and he never kept animals in his sitting room. I'm telling you, Melton is weird. That rockery in his garden. Who knows what's lying underneath it?"

There was a moment's silence.

Les turned to Hannah. "Is it worth talking to Reece-Taylor?"

"About what?" Bunny said. "She's having a fling with a good-looking lad who knows how to fix computers. A match made in heaven. It could only be better if he was an electrician or a plumber."

Hannah said, "Melton has put us on notice about a possible threat to a woman's life. If we ignore it, and then the worst happens…"

Les made a throat-slitting gesture.

"Exactly."

"You're worried about her history of sudden cardiac arrest?" Maggie said. "Even though she survived?"

"Sounds to me as if she's lucky to be alive," Hannah said.

"Intent on having a short life and a merry one?"

"It might not be difficult to contrive a situation that killed her, while looking like a genuine accident."

"You think she's already changed her will in favour of Prentice?"

"All I know is this. We can't sit back and do nothing."

————

Hannah was in the kitchen area of Divisional HQ, pouring herself a cup of tea, when Maggie Eyre bustled up to her, flourishing a sheaf of printouts.

"Five minutes of your time, ma'am?"

Her eyes were shining, her excitement palpable. Hannah recognised the signs. Maggie had dug something up.

"Sure, let's talk over a cuppa."

They walked down to her office, and Maggie said, "Kingsley Melton intrigues me. He sounds like damaged goods."

"Bunny's right, he's an oddity. That doesn't mean that he buried Ramona Smith in his back garden. Against my better judgement, there were moments during the interview when I almost felt sorry for him."

"I couldn't resist the urge to check him out." Maggie laid the printouts down on the desk. "Old reports from local newspapers, related bits and pieces, going back forty-five years. This was a week before Melton's tenth birthday."

Hannah glanced at the documents. *Bowness Tragedy* was one of the headlines.

"An inquest into the death of Vesper Melton?"

"Our man's sister, yes. Bonny young girl, as far as you can tell from a grainy photograph."

Hannah peered more closely. "Drowned in the back garden of the family bungalow?"

"Yes, she fell into the ornamental pool."

"There isn't an ornamental pool." Hannah thought for a moment. "Just a rockery."

They looked at each other.

"After the child died, I don't suppose the Meltons couldn't bear to keep looking at the pond."

Maggie nodded. "A constant reminder of the tragedy."

"So they filled it in. Perhaps the rock garden was their idea of a memorial. Not that Melton looks after it. What happened? How did his sister fall in?"

"Not clear," Maggie said. "It was a summer afternoon. The parents were inside, talking to another antiques dealer."

"So the kids were left to their own devices?"

"Yes. Her brother found her in the water. He called for help, but it was too late. The little girl was dead. It's not clear exactly how the accident happened but there was no evidence of a struggle or that she'd been pushed in. Kingsley said he was in a corner of the garden, absorbed in a comic. He was terrified of water and always kept his distance from the pool. He didn't hear the splash. The coroner went to some lengths to make clear that no blame attached to him, but that sounds like kindness. God knows what the parents made of it."

Hannah looked up.

"And then, only the other day, Kingsley Melton witnesses someone dying in the water at the Crooked Shore?"

"Yes," Maggie said. "History repeating itself."

"But not in quite the same way," Hannah murmured. "Darren

Lace took his own life, no question. Kingsley watched him die. Makes you wonder if that's exactly what he did with his own sister."

———

"Tell me about Ben Kind," Kit Gleadall said. "Did he become fixated with the idea that Gerald Lace had killed Ramona Smith? Obsessed?"

He'd asked Hannah to give him an update. A fan whirred in the corner of the cubbyhole he used as an office, but the air was dry and so was her throat. She took a swig of water.

"Ben was persistent," Hannah said, "but not to the point of obsession. He was imaginative and shrewd."

"Like his son, then."

She ignored this. "People say that police work isn't cerebral. Detecting crimes is a team effort, but Ben preached the value of letting your imagination roam if there's a tricky problem to be solved. Running around like headless chickens gets us nowhere. We need to use our brains."

"I suppose bureaucracy didn't suit him?"

"He believed in results, not targets. Ninety percent of the time, he got those results. And not through breaking rules or being insensitive. He was a forceful man who knew his own mind, but never a bully." She drank some more water. "As for Lace, nobody is right all the time."

"Including juries," Gleadall said. "You think he may have been mistaken?"

"Most detectives in Ben's shoes would have formed the same opinion as him."

"But?"

She was forced to smile. Gleadall was shrewd as well as persistent. He and Ben Kind would probably have got on well.

"But knowing your own mind is one thing. Cutting off your nose to spite your face is something else."

She remembered that Ben had cut himself off from his two children after leaving home to make a new life with his mistress. His ex-wife had been resentful and difficult, but shouldn't he have tried harder to keep in touch with Daniel and Louise? The truth was, his pride had got in the way.

If only she'd seen more of Ben after his retirement instead of being preoccupied with the demands of the job while Ben was going downhill, drowning the sorrows of his failing second marriage. Alex Samaras had consoled him. She'd become his friend. Another reason to feel lacking when measured against her...

"We're all human," Gleadall said.

"Yes. The jury's verdict infuriated him. He thought justice had been denied. The evidence was strong enough to convict, even though it was only circumstantial. All the same, on the rare occasions he mentioned the case in later years, it was obvious he had regrets. I wonder if he began to have second thoughts. If he was afraid he'd become as blinkered as...well, as some of the detectives he didn't have a high regard for."

"That's why cold case reviews are so important," Gleadall said. "They give us a second chance to secure justice."

"I appreciate your support, sir."

"The press conference bought us some time, but I am—we are—still under pressure. Especially from Midge Van Beek." He coughed. "I don't know whether you know, but Midge is my ex-wife. One of two exes, actually. And I'm separated from my current wife. So when you say that we all make mistakes, I'm a prime example."

She kept her mouth shut.

"Three times I got it wrong." His tone was reflective. He might almost have been talking to himself. "Marrying career women suited me fine. Trouble was, none of them wanted children."

Perhaps he wasn't talking to himself at all. She was acutely conscious of his scrutiny. After a moment he gave a rueful shake of the head.

"Investigating a case more than two decades on is a tough gig, especially when your team is so small. Don't worry, I'm not expecting miracles. Far less an arrest. But you'll understand why I'm so desperate for us to be seen to be doing whatever we can." His smile was grim. "If Midge can find a way to crucify Cumbria Constabulary, and better still, me, she'll be over the moon."

"Understood." She gave him a concise update. "So the inquiry is in danger of expanding. Melton wants us to investigate another murder in the past and forestall one in the present. Meanwhile, Maggie Eyre has discovered something about Melton's past."

She told him about Vesper's death.

"You think he pushed his sister into the pond? Sibling rivalry?"

"Pure speculation on my part. At this distance of time, nothing can be proved. The reports of the incident are vague about what actually happened. Perhaps what he said was vague. But the crucial point is that he was just short of the age of criminal responsibility."

"So he might be very calculating?"

Hannah spread her arms. "Or very ruthless or very opportunistic or very mixed-up. Or even just very unlucky."

"Best guess?"

"One lesson Ben Kind drummed into me," she said. "Don't guess out loud."

"Fair enough. Time to give your imagination free rein?"

"I don't mean to be evasive, sir."

"Of course not." He looked at her intently. "Please, Hannah.

Call me Kit. When it's just you and me, no need to stand on ceremony."

She returned his gaze. "What I need to know is that if my enquiries lead me to step outside the narrow remit of this investigation, I have your backing."

"Absolutely." A wolfish grin. "You can have that in black and white if you like."

"That would give me some comfort."

He scribbled a note on a pad. "You'll receive an email within five minutes of leaving this office."

She got to her feet. "Thanks, I appreciate it."

Putting down his pen, he said. "I suppose it's too much to hope that you'll tell me what you have in mind?"

She smiled. "I'm not sure yet."

He grinned at her and for a fleeting instant she thought he was about to ask her for a drink. To her relief, he buttoned his lip. As she left the room, she heaved a sigh of relief. Life was complicated enough without getting personally involved with the Police and Crime Commissioner. Even if he did want a child.

———

"Must you go?" Tory asked.

"I promised I'd call on him after he finished work." Logan was pulling on a short-sleeved shirt. She was still in her bikini. Early evening and it still felt as though they were on the Riviera. "He's desperate to get his laptop up and running again, and I hate letting customers down."

She ruffled his hair as he finished dressing. "I suppose that's an acceptable excuse. I'm glad you take your responsibilities seriously. When will you be back?"

"You never know with an upgrade on this scale. He has a

lot of files he needs transferred to his new system. Might be as late as half ten. Don't worry about cooking for me. This client is based in Kendal, so I can pick up some fish and chips in town before I come back."

"I'll make do with a snack." She patted her stomach. "Need to lose a few pounds."

"You shouldn't worry about your weight."

"I need to keep healthy. I don't want to drop dead on you."

She kissed him, long and hard.

"You're insatiable," he said as they parted.

"Aren't you a lucky boy?"

"Very."

As he closed the door of the flat behind him and walked over to the van, he reflected that it was true. Finally his luck was turning. You should never count your chickens, but it looked as though Tory would transfer the money to wipe out the outstanding bills and pay for the first stage of Ingrid's treatment by the end of the week. The bank account was set up. Those long years of frustration and underachievement would soon be behind him.

He watched the gates open in front of him. A metaphor for the opportunities awaiting him. He was young and handsome, and soon he would be rich. The world lay at his feet.

Yet as the van jolted over the pot-holes of Strandbeck Lane, a tremor of uncertainty rippled through him. So much could still go awry. Not that he was worried about Kingsley Melton. The more that jealous old blancmange made a nuisance of himself, the more he'd infuriate Tory.

She was implacable. A woman who knew what she wanted and made sure she got it. Probably that was how she'd survived the cardiac arrest. He admired her determination, but at the same time, it unsettled him.

Part of him yearned to do what he usually did, and take the easy way out. How tempting to stay here in the lap of luxury. Tory offered the prospect of unlimited money and sex; what more could a red-blooded man want? He'd told her the truth when he said he preferred older women. In his experience they were less self-absorbed and more eager to please than girls of his own generation. Tory was a soft touch in more ways than one, but her folds of flesh didn't put him off. He liked to have his hands full.

Being a kept man had plenty of attractions. Already, though, he'd glimpsed warning signs. She'd already talked about buying him a piano and making him a monthly allowance. The more he demurred, the more she insisted. But he wasn't a gigolo or a stud. Or like a collector's item, like those horrible dead moths that Melton kept in a glass drawer.

No. As he reached the junction with the coastal lane, near to the Crooked Shore, he reminded himself of the old legend. It would be a mistake to outstay his welcome. He must stick to the original plan.

———

Logan threaded his van through the maze of Ulverston's streets before squeezing down the alley next to the Vietnamese take-away. It was such a tight fit that he'd never bothered to get the dented wing repaired; even if he could afford to splash the cash, it would be a waste of money, given how often he scraped his paintwork against the brick wall. Thank God his days of scrimping and saving were almost at an end. Leaving the van on the patch of asphalt at the back of the building, he unlocked the steel door leading to the staircase to his bedsit. He bounced up the steps, two at a time.

At the top was a narrow landing. To the right was a small bathroom and a store cupboard overflowing with stuff belonging to the owner of the takeaway. On the left, the door to his bedsit stood ajar. Grinning, he kicked it open.

A woman was sitting up in his bed, her blonde hair tied in a ponytail. Her clothes were scattered over the threadbare carpet. At first glance, she looked twenty, although if you studied her closely you could see crows'-feet around the corners of her eyes. Not that Logan cared; he wasn't looking at her wrinkles.

"Hi, Goldilocks," he said. "Who's been sleeping in my bed?"

"What kept you?" she retorted.

"Three guesses."

"You need to watch yourself with old Misery." She narrowed her eyes and mimicked Kathy Bates in the Stephen King film. *"I'm your number one fan."*

He laughed. "You're so wicked, Sheena."

"All I'm saying is, make sure she doesn't start chopping off your body parts. At least not the ones I'm interested in."

"Tory is lonely, that's all. And she's our passport to a better life."

"Tory?" She pouted. "Of all the stupid things to call yourself. Anyway, I've decided to change my own name," she said. "I always hated being named after an eighties pop star."

"You can be whoever you want to be, gorgeous."

The woman pushed aside the duvet and beckoned him forward.

"Okay, you got yourself a deal. From now on, I'm Ingrid."

Chapter Twenty-One

The warmest night of the year. Hot and sticky in his winceyette pyjamas, Kingsley hardly slept. As dawn broke, he was contemplating spidery cracks in the ceiling. This small square room had always been his private domain. His parents' old bedroom next door was twice the size, but moving in there after Mamma's death would have seemed like sacrilege.

Birds chirruped outside his window and rays of sunlight filtered through gaps in the curtains. Another scorcher, he told himself. The experts were warning that the weather would break before the end of the day, but he found it hard to credit. Soon people would be swarming through the village and around the lake, licking their ice creams and teasing the swans. The outsiders were so noisy and carefree; he'd always envied them, as well as resenting the way they treated his home turf as their own.

What now? He mustn't rush into his next move. Fortunately, he was a patient man. Too patient for his own good; his instinctive reticence was a handicap that had held him back in life. Yet on the rare occasions when he acted on impulse, it never ended well.

Handling Tory and Prentice demanded the utmost care. He

dare not afford a misstep or forget that the clock was ticking. Soon Greengables would deny him access to the Manor. Time was so short. He dare not allow Tory to slip out of reach.

He hauled himself out of bed and got dressed, putting on his suit because it was a working day, despite the heat and the fact he had no work to do. Whatever the appalling Annabel thought, he prided himself on not letting his standards slide. Breakfast comprised cornflakes, toast, and marmalade, washed down with tea, same as every other morning. After he'd finished he poured himself another cuppa and carried it into the sitting room. When he pulled the curtains apart, the glare made him screw up his eyes.

Could he rely on Hannah Scarlett to mark Prentice's card? She'd shocked him to the core by producing that old witness statement like a rabbit out of a hat. A dirty trick, when he'd put the whole business out of his mind. After all, he'd neither committed an offence nor been given a caution relating to his involvement with Leila Smith.

If only he'd denied knowing the woman, just as he'd denied knowing her daughter. With hindsight he realised that if the police hadn't panicked him into a hasty admission, it would have been the word of a decent citizen against the so-called diary of a dead prostitute. Nobody could have proved anything. He preferred to occupy the moral high ground, and the thought of those two female detectives, especially the older, unpleasant one, judging his behaviour and finding it wanting, made him burn with humiliation.

And yet. All was not lost. As he contemplated the stuffed toucan, he urged himself to look on the bright side. Twenty-four hours after meeting the police, he was getting things into perspective. Hannah Scarlett was diligent; only a painstaking search could have dredged up that flimsy sheet of foolscap. Like a true play-by-the-book public servant, she'd refused to commit herself, but surely there was a chance that she'd follow up the threat that Prentice posed to Tory? What if, God forbid, the worst happened, and he harmed her? Hannah Scarlett wouldn't want to risk being found guilty of dereliction of duty.

Nobody liked to have a death on their conscience. He knew that better than anyone.

Overall, he decided that yesterday could have been worse. Considering the shock he'd suffered, he hadn't acquitted himself too badly in the interview. There was still everything to hope for. You had only to look out of the window. Even the weeds in his back garden were shimmering in the sunlight.

As for Hannah Scarlett, she wasn't quite as bright as she liked to think. She underestimated him. She still didn't have a clue about what he was capable of.

———

"You spoil me," Tory said.

Logan had brought her breakfast in bed. Gingerbread waffles with maple syrup and a cappuccino.

"You're worth it."

She smiled.

"What?" he asked.

"You really need to look after me until the money goes through," she said.

His face puckered with anxiety. "You're not feeling unwell?"

"Oh, don't look so panic-stricken. I've never been better."

"That's all right, then. Joking apart, the next few days are neither here nor there. I want to look after you forever."

"You're so sweet." She patted his cheek. "To tell you the truth, I really don't think I deserve you."

"Don't be silly," he said. "My life changed the day I met you."

"Seriously?"

"Of course!" He gestured towards the bedroom window. Outside stretched the grounds of the Manor with a screen of tall trees in the distance. "This is marvellous. I really feel I belong here. With you."

"I'm glad," she said. "But my conscience is pricking."

He peered at her. "What do you mean?"

"It's been so long since I've been with a man. In any meaningful way. In his last few years, Winston wasn't well and he became very...passive. He turned in on himself, and he left me to my own devices, if you catch my drift. With you, it's different. You're young and active..."

"And devoted," he interrupted. "Don't forget devoted."

"I've been indulging myself with you. Oh, yes, I'm helping you out financially, but there's more to a relationship than money."

"You bet!" he said fervently.

"I ought to make more of an effort to support you. Not just financially, but taking an interest in the things that turn you on."

"Nothing," he said, "turns me on more than you."

"You pay such lovely compliments. I could listen to them all day."

"Then why don't you?"

"No, I mean what I say. I mustn't be selfish. I thought..."

"Yes?"

"I might go to your next performance."

He stared at her. "I don't follow."

"Oh, come on, sweetheart. The Newbies. Your am dram group." She smiled sweetly. "I looked you up on the internet last night, while you were out."

"You what?"

"Don't look so shocked. I read about the production you've lined up for Cartmel in September. *Hobson's Choice*."

He pulled a face. "A play so old it's got whiskers."

"You're not in the cast. I checked the web page to see if I could find you."

"Heavens, no. That sort of stuff isn't my cup of tea."

"Such a pity."

He shook his head. "You wouldn't say that if you'd ever seen me on stage. To be honest, I'm no great shakes as an actor. It took me a long time to admit the truth, even to myself, but I'm better suited to being behind the scenes."

"With looks like yours? Sweetheart, you're far too modest, you're very convincing. I'm sure you'd be brilliant in the right role. You'd make a wonderful…whatshisname? Willie Mossop? Though I'd might be a teeny bit jealous of the leading lady."

He swallowed. "Really, there's no need…"

"Actually, she reminds me of someone."

"What do you mean?" he demanded.

She shook her head. "That actress, Sheena something? Her face seems so familiar. I've been racking my brains. The funny thing is, I'd never heard of the Newbies until I met you, but I'm sure I've seen her somewhere before."

"You can't have done."

"It's only a local group, you told me. She must come from this neck of the woods."

"I hardly know her," he said. "She only joined the group recently. I think she works in a bank or something."

"Pretty young woman."

"I've kept my distance," he said. "The men buzz around her, but she's a bit of a diva."

"I wish I could remember who she is."

"Don't waste your time worrying about it," he urged. "Lots

of young women look like that. They're all much of a muchness. You've confused her with someone else, it's easily done."

"I'm sure I'm right," she said indignantly. "I mean, I'm definitely not going senile."

"Sorry, sorry, I didn't mean…"

"The fact is, I do know her from somewhere, and it will annoy me until I get it straight in my mind."

"Please don't give her another thought." He dropped a kiss on her cheek. "There are so many better ways we can make the most of our time together."

She frowned. "You make it sound as though it's coming to an end."

"God, no. Absolutely not. On the contrary. I'm going to spend much more time with you, not less. I'm bored with the Newbies. Getting involved with them was fun for a while. A distraction. But I don't need to be distracted anymore, do I? Not now I have you."

She smiled. "You say the sweetest things."

"It's true," he said. "My enthusiasm for drama was just a fad. Playing the piano is different. At least if you're not much good, you can still entertain yourself and your nearest and dearest. As a matter of fact, I've already told the Newbies that I can't help out back stage with the new production."

"Pity," she said. "I was looking forward to cheering you on from the front row. What did you say to them?"

He mustered a grin and pushed the breakfast things out of the way before clambering into bed.

"Oh, I just explained that I had my hands full."

As he slid his arms around her, she closed her eyes and surrendered to the warmth of his embrace.

———

Hannah's meetings were normally booked by a member of the admin team, but Tory Reece-Taylor justified special treatment. This was a woman she needed to handle with kid gloves. Besides, she was bursting with curiosity about her.

She dialled the landline number Kingsley Melton had given her and went through to voicemail. Rather than leave a message, she tried the mobile.

"Yes?"

"Ms. Reece-Taylor?"

"Yes?"

"My name is Hannah Scarlett, and I'm a DCI with Cumbria Constabulary. I wonder if I could…"

"Wrong number."

Tory cut her off.

Oh, well, it was worth a try. The call had always been a long shot. She'd better think up a Plan B. Twenty minutes later, Hannah was ploughing through a lengthy email from HR about the process for recruiting candidates for a transfer to her team when her phone rang.

"Is that DCI Hannah Scarlett?"

A surge of excitement rippled through her. "Ms. Reece-Taylor?"

"Yes, sorry I hung up on you. I couldn't talk. It's all right now, I've popped outside into the garden."

"Apologies if I interrupted you. I didn't realise you had someone with you."

No reply. Well, it was worth a try, even if Tory hadn't risen to the bait.

"Anyway, thank you very much for calling back." Better lay it on with a trowel. "I'm extremely grateful."

"What can I do for you, DCI Scarlett?"

Crisp, business-like, giving nothing away.

"I wondered if it would be possible for us to have a short conversation. I'm happy to visit you at Strandbeck Manor."

A pause. "What is this about?"

"I'd rather not discuss it over the telephone, if you don't mind, Ms. Reece-Taylor. I promise not to take up much of your time."

"Very cloak and dagger. Surely you can give me a hint?"

"Sorry, I really don't mean to cause you any alarm. This is simply a matter of crime prevention."

Another pause. "I see."

"Would you be willing to spare me twenty minutes?"

Hannah heard the other woman breathing hard. She waited.

"Kingsley Melton has been pestering you, I suppose?" The woman's tone struck Hannah as surprisingly cool and collected. Amused rather than outraged. "Filling your head with his paranoid accusations."

"As I say, it's better if we talk in person."

"Let me think it over," Tory Reece-Taylor said. "If I fancy a chat, I'll phone you back."

"Please call my direct line." Hannah gave her the number. "If I'm not around, you'll be diverted to a member of my team. And Ms. Reece-Taylor, may I ask…?"

But the woman had rung off.

——

Logan Prentice clambered out of the lake, and Tory, sitting cross-legged on the grass, handed him a gaudily coloured beach towel.

"You remind me of Colin Firth in *Pride and Prejudice*," she said.

"Who?"

"Mr. Darcy. He dived into a lake to cool his ardour for the girl he fancied. Mind you, he was wearing a white shirt."

Logan pushed damp hair out of his baffled eyes. "Sorry, you've lost me."

"Ah, of course. Before your time. A famous television scene, from the good old days." She watched him towelling himself. "I keep forgetting, we come from different worlds. Different generations."

"We're not so different, you and me."

"You don't think?"

"No." He grinned. "We both want the lovely things in life."

"This was what I always wanted." She waved her hand vaguely to encompass the Manor and grounds. "The posh house, the long lawn, the sexy man at my beck and call. Yet somehow…"

"What?" He squinted at her. "You're not getting fed up with me?"

"I can't help thinking about poor Ingrid," she said. "Last night I even dreamed about her."

"It's going to be all right," he said. "Thanks to your generosity, she has every chance of…"

"Hey!" She clapped a hand to her forehead. "That's it, I've remembered. Thank God, I've not lost my marbles after all."

"Remembered what?"

"The photo of the actress from the Newbies, the pretty girl you called a diva. She reminds me of Ingrid."

He dropped the towel on to the grass. "Really?"

"Don't you see the likeness, now that I've mentioned it?"

He shrugged. "I suppose there might be a superficial resemblance. Not that I've noticed it myself."

"Take a peek at the photo of her on the website, it's really striking."

"No need," he said brusquely. "I know perfectly well what

Sheena looks like. And I can promise you, she's very different from poor Ingrid."

"But..."

"Please, let's not talk about it."

He started to walk back towards the Manor. Tory called after him. "Sweetheart, what's wrong? Did I put my foot in it? Did I say something to upset you?"

She got to her feet and followed him.

Chapter Twenty-Two

The phone call came out of the blue. Kingsley's heart skipped as Tory's name popped up on the screen.

So she had relented. Faith and persistence had earned its reward.

"Tory?" His throat was dry, making him croak like a pensioner.

"Hello, Kingsley." A pause. "Are you all right?"

She did care!

"Yes, yes." His heart was thumping. "How are you?"

"I wanted to say sorry. For being unkind to you."

Was he dreaming? He needed to pinch himself to be sure he wasn't making it up.

"That's...that's all right. Please, don't mention it."

"I thought you were jealous, but that was unfair. You've only ever wanted to look out for me, from the day we first met."

He squeezed the phone in his hand. "Yes, Tory, you know how much I care for you."

"Don't be cross with me, please. It's just that he swept me off my feet."

"Prentice?"

"Yes, he's young and good-looking, and I'm a naïve old cow."

"Of course you're not old," he said stoutly. This was incredible. At a stroke, his worries were over, his problems solved. "Such a plausible, smooth-talking devil, anyone could be taken in. I was conned myself, to begin with. Until I understood what he's really like."

"Manipulative and selfish. Yes, you were right."

He wanted to burst into song. "Thank God you've seen through him. No harm done. Have you sent him packing?"

A long pause. Kingsley guessed that she was summoning up the nerve to make a confession.

"No, that's the trouble."

"I don't understand."

She hesitated. "He's still here."

"What—in the room with you?"

"No, obviously not." The way she snapped back, for a moment he thought he'd tested her patience. "Sorry, didn't mean to bite your head off. I'm on edge, that's the reason why I sound abrupt. Logan moved in with me. I'm ringing from the summer house. He's inside the flat."

"Have you told him to go?"

"We quarrelled, and when I asked him to leave, he refused." Her voice trembled. "He flew into a temper and said some... cruel things. After a few minutes he calmed down and apologised, said he'd made a big mistake and it wouldn't happen again. But last night we had another row and he slapped me across the face."

"My God," Kingsley breathed. "How dare he! So dreadful for you."

For her to confide in him like this was thrilling, a breakthrough. Incontrovertible evidence of how much he meant to her. Tender loving care, that was what Tory needed. He could never lay a finger on a woman; someone who hit a member of the fair sex was a despicable coward.

"I was frightened," she admitted. "The slap stung, though he barely left a mark. Afterwards, he started sobbing and said he hadn't been able to control himself."

"Crocodile tears."

"I said we couldn't go on like this, and he swore he'd mend his ways. I don't believe him."

"You're right," Kingsley assured her. "Leopards never change their spots."

"You never said a truer word. What scares me is the violence. He doesn't look it, but he's a disturbed young man. I'm afraid of what he might do if he's provoked."

"You could dial 999."

"I don't trust them to help. Chances are, they'd chalk it off as a domestic, give Logan a talking-to, and then leave us to sort out our differences. It would make the situation a hundred times worse."

"Yes," he said bitterly. "The police are useless."

"Logan would be furious with me. I don't know how he'd react. He's so passionate and there is that streak of violence. You can't imagine what he's capable of."

"Believe me," Kingsley said grimly, "I've got a very good idea. Prentice is a menace. You must remember what I said…"

"Oh, yes," she interrupted. "You warned me. Don't rub it in, I simply can't bear it. What an idiot I've been! I don't know which way to turn."

"Thank God you called me," he said. "I need to come over to the Manor."

"Really? Are you sure?"

"Of course. I'm at home now. It won't take me long to get there."

She breathed hard into the phone. "What…what are you going to do?"

"Get him to understand the facts of life." This was a magnificent line; he was rising to the occasion. Cometh the hour, cometh the man. "He needs to realise that he's made a terrible mistake. Interfering between you and me."

For a few moments, she was silent.

"That's all very well, Kingsley, but how can you possibly make him see reason?"

"Don't forget," he said quickly. "I have a gun."

Another pause.

"God, yes. The Smith & Wesson."

He hadn't meant to mention the gun. The words had spilled out of him before he could stop himself, but her response made him feel a warm glow. Not only had she believed him that time he'd boasted about the gun, she'd been sufficiently impressed to remember the maker's name.

"Exactly."

"Not that I want you to harm him, obviously," she said. "Don't get the wrong idea, Kingsley. For Heaven's sake, we ought to be grown up about this. Anyway, it's only an antique firearm. I don't suppose it works anymore."

"It's in very good order," he said. "I tested it not long ago."

"What?"

"Just to check that it was working. I oiled it and gave it a good clean. While you were out shopping, and nobody else was around, I fired a couple of shots into those trees behind the lake."

"Here? You brought the gun to the Manor? You're joking!"

Her voice throbbed with astonishment. Her reaction thrilled him. People often wrote him off as a fuddy-duddy, a dull dog. It wasn't fair, and it wasn't true, either.

"Believe me, I couldn't be more serious. I keep it in my office. Locked safely away in a drawer, you can't be too careful. I don't want it going off by accident."

"So...are you saying the gun is loaded?"

"Well, yes."

"I had no idea."

He was tempted to say *I don't tell you everything* in a masterful tone, but the conversation was going so well that he bit his tongue. She was so mercurial, so quick to jump down your throat. It was easy to infuriate her without meaning to.

"The Manor is lonely, out of the way."

"Aren't you forgetting the security cameras?" she said.

"The technology is unreliable. Two of the cameras don't work. The main entrance is covered, and the car park and drive. Not the rest of the Manor, or the gardens."

"That's a disgrace," she murmured. "When I think of the service charge..."

"Yes, I'd kick up a fuss with Greengables, if I were you," he said. "Penny-pinching idiots. Anyway, I thought that if ever an intruder broke into the grounds, it might be handy to wave the Smith & Wesson at him."

"To scare him off?"

"Purely as a deterrent, yes." Another good line sprang to his lips. "I'm not exactly the Sundance Kid."

He chortled at his own wit.

"Maybe not, Kingsley," she said slowly. "All the same, you have hidden depths."

———

The phone rang.

"Chief Inspector Scarlett?"

Hannah gave Les the thumbs-up. "Speaking. Thanks so much for calling back, Mrs. Reece-Taylor."

"All right, I'm willing to meet you. Against my better judgement, mind."

"That's helpful, I appreciate it. I can arrange…"

"Not here at the Manor," Tory interrupted. "Too awkward."

"I understand."

"You said it's important, so I'm willing to drive over to Kendal. No time like the present. If I set off now, I can be with you in three quarters of an hour."

———

Kingsley didn't repeat his previous surreptitious approach to the Manor. No need. What a difference a day makes, he thought, as he leaned out of his car window to enter the code for opening the gates. No more creeping around the place for him. He'd explain to Tory that he'd had his fill of Greengables, a company that lacked decent values. Judging by her comment about the service charge, she'd be entirely sympathetic. After this week, he'd come here by her invitation, not as Annabel's minion. He'd find that empowering, he couldn't wait.

First things first. He had to clear Logan Prentice out of the way, and nothing would give him greater pleasure. As he drove into the car park, he felt a stab of disappointment. Prentice's battered old van was parked right next to Tory's BMW. Frankly, it was an impertinence. He was tempted to shunt the wretched rust-heap into the wall.

He'd hoped against hope that Tory had already given Prentice his marching orders. Realistically, he supposed, that was asking too much of her. She was bound to be frightened.

Prentice had no scruples, no moral compass. No sense of

shame. He'd killed one elderly woman for gain and got away scot-free. Now he was contemplating an even more heinous murder, of a woman in her prime.

A man like that must be dealt with. Someone needed to stand up for what was right. To take responsibility. It was a public duty. You couldn't sit on the fence, you couldn't shilly-shally.

Kingsley manoeuvred his Corsa into the space on the other side of Tory's car, so close that the wing mirrors were almost touching. It seemed symbolic. He strode towards the Manor, his feet crunching the gravel. More than ever before, he felt as though he owned the place.

The sky was overcast, the humidity oppressive. By the time he reached his office door, he was drenched in sweat. Nobody was in sight. He let himself in and unlocked the drawer. For fully thirty seconds he contemplated the Smith & Wesson in silence before picking it up and letting it nestle in his palm. He found its quiet solidity reassuring. One look at this and Logan Prentice would know who was the master now.

———

"She's late." Bunny Cohen mopped her brow. "God, it's so close. We could do with that thunderstorm we've been promised. Clear the air."

Hannah checked her watch. "Let's give her another ten minutes or so before we write her off. You know Kendal traffic."

Bunny peered at her. "What are you up to?"

Hannah raised her eyebrows.

"You've got that look on your face."

"What look?"

"Your I've-had-a-bright-idea look. Come on, I'm too long in the tooth to take no for an answer. There's nobody else around. You can't fool me." She added as an afterthought, "Ma'am."

"Glad to have a decent detective on the team," Hannah said coolly. "Even if she is disgracefully insubordinate."

"We've known each other a long time," Bunny said in a wheedling tone.

"The bright idea may be wrong."

"Don't be such a tease."

"All right," Hannah said. "I'm curious about something Kingsley Melton said to us. Without meaning to, he gave the game away."

"About what?"

"About what really happened to Ramona Smith."

Chapter Twenty-Three

Kingsley opened the cupboard in the empty room and listened intently. Not a sound from the other side of the thin wall. Were Tory and Prentice outside? He edged towards the window that looked out over the grounds and glimpsed Logan Prentice, sitting at the end of the jetty. He was in his swimming trunks and his hair was wet, as if he'd taken a dip in the lake. To look at him, you'd think he hadn't a care in the world. His arrogance took Kingsley's breath away.

No sign of Tory. She didn't seem to be in the summer house. Perhaps she was in her flat, keeping out of harm's way. That would make sense. He'd risk calling her mobile. Keeping his eyes on Prentice, he dialled her number but it went through to voicemail.

Hi, this is Tory. Thanks for your call. Leave your number after the beep and I'll get back to you.

Calm and in control as always, but did the recorded message disguise the reality? Had she refused to pick up because she was afraid that Prentice would come in and interrupt their conversation?

He ended the call. Another glance out of the window

confirmed that Prentice was still lazing beside the lake. He'd put on his dark glasses and was lying on his towel. Shameless, defiant. Well, he'd better make the most of it. His days in the sun were about to come to an abrupt end.

Kingsley picked up a small canvas bag from his office and dropped the Smith & Wesson into it before walking round to the front of the Manor. He rang Tory's doorbell. When no reply came, he knocked loudly.

Nothing.

He lifted the flap of the letterbox and hissed, "Tory! Are you there?"

Still no answer. His spine felt a chill.

What had Prentice done to her?

Walking out through the main door felt like walking into a wall of heat. He inched around the building. When he turned a corner and Prentice came into view, he was ready to duck back out of sight, but the young man was taking no notice. Perhaps he'd fallen asleep. Kingsley moved along the wall of the Manor until he came to the terrace outside Tory's flat. The glass doors to the flat were ajar.

His imagination went into overdrive. Would he find her crumpled body on the floor? Had Prentice scared her into suffering a second cardiac arrest and then left her to rot while he sunned himself? Such a callous beast, Kingsley would put nothing past him.

He sneaked through into the main living area and hissed Tory's name.

There was no sign of life.

Where could she be? Given that her car was outside, she couldn't have gone far. There were no shops within walking distance, and she never socialised with neighbours.

He prowled around the flat. Prentice had already made

himself at home, he thought grimly. His belongings were strewn all over the place. Trainers, T-shirts, a laptop and assorted computer gizmos, even a guitar.

In Tory's bedroom, he lingered. The bed wasn't made. Kingsley bit his lip. He clutched the solid shape inside the canvas bag. If that vile bastard Prentice had harmed a hair on her head…

Satisfied that she wasn't in the flat, alive or dead, he retraced his steps and looked out from the terrace. Prentice hadn't moved an inch.

What to do next? One option was to wait, but for what, and for how long? Or he might slink away to fight another day, as he'd done so often before; but that meant he never fought at all. During every life, a time came to stand up and be counted.

Tory had been crystal clear. She'd discovered Prentice's true nature and nailed her colours to the mast. She needed help; she needed him. He could not let her down.

Lines from Shakespeare, recalled from schooldays, sprang into his head.

> *There is a tide in the affairs of men.*
> *Which, taken at the flood, leads on to fortune;*
> *Omitted, all the voyage of their life*
> *Is bound in shallows and in miseries.*
> *On such a full sea are we now afloat,*
> *And we must take the current when it serves,*
> *Or lose our ventures.*

Kingsley drew a breath, squared his shoulders. Nothing for it but to confront Prentice. Force the truth out of him. At gunpoint if need be.

"All right," Bunny said. "Understood. Good to have a plan."

Hannah checked the time. "Tory Reece-Taylor is running very late. Looks like she's had a change of heart. If she does show up, I'll give you a call. In the meantime I'll carry on ploughing through the old files. See if I can spot any promising leads."

"Good luck with that."

Hannah already read several of the original witness statements, those from Nadine Clarke, Ravi Thakor, and Ramona's colleagues at Guido's, the last people other than Gerald Lace who admitted having seen her alive. The additional background information was useful, but she hadn't picked up anything fresh.

Time to see what the Laces had to say for themselves.

First, Shirley Lace. The wife of Ramona's lover, the woman who had pursued a crusade for twenty years, maintaining that her husband was innocent of murder.

Hannah had only been reading for a couple of minutes when a sentence snagged her attention.

Surely not?

All at once, her throat felt parched. Her hands were actually shaking. It was as if she'd been studying a neat sample of embroidery the wrong way round, so that it seemed like an aimless tangle of threads. Now she'd got it right. She could see the pattern.

Was this how Nadine Bosman felt when she saw the light? When everything suddenly looks different?

She took a gulp of water to steady her nerves.

A single thought coursed through her mind.

This changes everything.

Chapter Twenty-Four

Kingsley was twenty yards short of the lake when Prentice spotted him. The young man levered himself into a sitting position and cocked his head on one side.

"Well, well, well. Look what blew in on the breeze." Whipping off his dark glasses, he considered Kingsley's appearance. Marks and Spencer suit, natty silk tie, laced black shoes. "Aren't you hot in your office gear? Not that I'm inviting you to strip off, love. Don't get the wrong idea. Those days have gone."

As Kingsley approached him, Prentice noticed the canvas bag.

"Brought your shopping? Don't tell me, it's not a little gift to celebrate the fact I've moved into the Manor?"

"Where is she?" Kingsley demanded.

Prentice sniggered. "Who?"

"Don't bandy words with me," he said, rather magnificently. "You know perfectly well who I mean."

"Oh, Tory?" Prentice pretended to scan the grounds. "Sorry, can't see her. Just as well, given that she'd spit feathers if she found you here after being warned off."

"You seem to forget, I work here."

"Yes, as our paid servant. In Tory's absence, I'm in charge. Time to get back into your hutch, little bunny."

"I'll ask you again. Where is she?"

Prentice shrugged his bare shoulders. "Inside, I expect. Taking a shower, perhaps. No peeking, love. And no re-enacting *Psycho*, either. You always did have an uncanny resemblance to a geriatric Norman Bates. You and that ugly old mother of yours."

The heat was sweltering. Kingsley tightened his grip on the handle of the canvas bag. Sticks and stones might break his bones, but words could never hurt him.

"Tory isn't in the flat. I've made a thorough search."

"Naughty. That's trespassing. Invasion of privacy. We can't have hired hands getting above their station." Prentice sniggered. "I'd better get on to Greengables and given them a piece of my mind."

Kingsley stood firm. "Tory wants you out of here. She told me."

Prentice laughed and gave him a V-sign.

Sweat was running off Kingsley's skin. "I'll give you sixty seconds to get moving. Pack your things and clear off."

"You can't be serious. Surely even you can't be so deluded? You know perfectly well that Tory is sick to death of you."

"Death?" Kingsley swallowed hard. "What have you done with her? If you've harmed a hair on her head, I'll…"

"You'll what?" Prentice stretched his arms in a luxuriant gesture, taunting Kingsley with the suppleness of his physique. "She only let you shag her out of pity. Like giving spare change to charity. She told me you were useless. Couldn't even get it up, I gather. That rang a bell, I must say. Remember? You poor limp little fellow."

Kingsley swung his right fist, but Prentice swayed out of reach.

"Fisticuffs, seriously?" Prentice stepped up on to the jetty. "Forget it, you sad eunuch. You're boxing out of your league."

"Is she dead? Another cardiac arrest? Engineered to look like death by natural causes, so that you can cash in? Just the way you murdered Ivy Podmore?"

"I didn't cash in on Ivy's death." Prentice's eyes narrowed. "You must know, she lied to me, the mad old bat."

Kingsley smirked. "Serves you right."

"Made me glad I killed her," Prentice said casually. "Served *her* right."

There was a long silence, broken only by the cry of a seagull. Despite everything that had happened, Kingsley couldn't quite believe this was happening. The sheer insolence of it. Prentice believed he was above the law. He was so utterly selfish. The normal rules didn't apply to him.

"You admit it?"

Kingsley's voice was hoarse with emotion. Vindication at long last. Mamma had been right. So had he. The doctor, the care home manager, the police, all those smug doubting Thomases had got it wrong. This man was a self-confessed murderer.

Prentice roared with laughter and went through a panto-mime of looking around the deserted grounds. "For your ears only, Kingsley. Privileged information. Obviously, I'll deny it if you tell anyone else. Nobody will believe you, trust me. Now why don't you just fuck off out of here?"

"You haven't told me what you've done with Tory."

"I haven't done anything with her."

"You slapped her, you bastard." Kingsley felt like spitting. "What else?"

Prentice screwed up his face as if he'd lifted a stone and found something unpleasant beneath it.

"Slapped her? You're crazy."

Kingsley had caught him out in a lie. He had Tory's word for what had happened.

"You don't fool me. I know that you're violent. You hit a defenceless woman."

Prentice snorted with exasperation. "Have it your own way. I couldn't care less."

He shrugged, a feudal lord dismissing a serf.

Kingsley glanced up to the heavens. A large black cloud had appeared, as if to match his mood. He reached into his canvas bag and pulled out the Smith & Wesson.

"Answer me. Where is Tory? Have you killed her too?"

Prentice took a step back on to the jetty. "What's that?"

"You've got eyes, haven't you?" This was more like it. Kingsley felt like preening. Merely to feel the weight of the gun in his hand gave him an indescribable sense of superiority and power. "Trust me, it still works. Now, where is she?"

Prentice seemed to be in a trance. Hypnotised by the Smith & Wesson.

"She can't be far," he said slowly. "In or around the flat. We can look for her together if you like."

"You're lying, as usual. She's not there." Kingsley's grip on the gun tightened. "Have you hidden her body?"

"Put the gun down," Prentice said. "Stop waving it about. You're not safe."

"No," Kingsley said. "I'm not safe at all. Neither are you. Now quit stalling and tell me about Tory."

"You talk like an ancient B-movie." It never took Prentice long to recover his poise, Kingsley thought. "I reckon you've finally flipped."

"I was never saner," Kingsley said. "Never more serious. I'll count to three."

Prentice stood on the edge of the jetty. The two men were facing each other, six feet apart.

"One," Kingsley said.

"You're not going to use the gun, so put it back in the bag," Prentice said.

"You always underestimated me," Kingsley said. "You're so arrogant. Fatally arrogant. You've killed Tory and now you're playing for time. Two."

"You're deluded," Prentice said. "You don't need Tory, you need psychiatric help."

"You're a self-confessed killer," Kingsley said. "I won't take any lessons from you. Three."

"Why don't…"

Prentice crouched, and Kingsley realised he was about to launch himself forward and try to seize the Smith & Wesson. Kingsley lifted the gun and squeezed the trigger. A warning shot into the trees to scare him into submission.

Prentice screamed and fell backwards, collapsing in a writhing heap on the jetty.

Kingsley had missed his aim. The warning shot had been so wild that it had smacked Prentice in the middle of the chest.

As he watched in speechless horror, the writhing stopped.

Chapter Twenty-Five

"Sorry I'm so late," Tory Reece-Taylor said. "My car's playing up so I decided to come by taxi, and the cabbie was delayed."

"Not a problem. Thanks for coming in."

Hannah had recovered her composure following that moment of revelation five minutes earlier. Her head was buzzing as she tried to make sense of the implications. As soon as this interview was over, she must decide what to do, but first things first.

She, Bunny, and Tory were in a meeting room. A small, inadequate fan was working overtime and three cups of coffee and a jug of milk stood on a tray on the table. Bunny had a notebook and pen on her lap, but the plan was to strive for informality. Hannah passed Tory her drink.

"So, Chief Inspector, what can I do for you?"

Hannah stirred milk into her own coffee as she wondered what made this woman tick.

Tory was as chic as an Italian film star. What lay behind the glamorous, well-preserved façade, the thick, lustrous blonde hair, almost flawless skin, enviably straight nose, full lips, and strong, even teeth? Nothing but the best for Tory Reece-Taylor.

The gold bracelets and taupe handbag must have cost a fortune. Not to mention the sky-blue dress, which emphasised her well-shaped legs and slim hips and flattered her figure. Easy to understand why any man might fall for her. Let alone Melton.

"As you know, Mr. Kingsley Melton is concerned for your well-being."

Tory sipped her drink. "He thinks Logan Prentice is after my money. He's afraid that I'll make Logan my heir, giving him a reason to scare me to death. A few years ago I suffered a sudden cardiac arrest."

"It's not our job to interfere in people's personal lives, but your medical history means you are at risk. When such a serious allegation is made, we're obliged to make you aware."

"Thanks." Tory sighed. "I've slept with both of them. Rotten choices, but it's a free country; I please myself. I felt sorry for Kingsley, and he made himself useful around the Manor. I never dreamed he'd become so jealous. He detests Logan, and for all his faults, I've discovered that Kingsley is right about one thing. Logan is on the make."

"Really?"

"Yes." Tory contemplated elegant turquoise fingernails. "Logan told me he had a sister, Ingrid. She'd moved to the United States, but suffered severe medical problems. One kidney lost to cancer, the other malfunctioning. Long story short, she was in urgent need of pioneering medical treatment which wasn't covered by insurance. I didn't understand the details, it was all gobbledygook to me. Coming back to Britain wasn't an option; she wasn't fit enough to travel. The leading specialist was ready and willing to operate, and Ingrid was excited because the surgeon was confident of success. But he and his team needed paying. It was a matter of life and death."

"Mr. Prentice wanted you to give money?"

"Goodness me, no. Give him credit for a smidgeon of subtlety. Logan created the circumstances where I became anxious to help. He didn't ask for a penny. I was the one who offered. Even then, he turned me down flat several times. I had to beg him to agree there was no alternative."

"In the end, he swallowed his pride?"

"Correct."

"How much money was he talking about?"

Tory named a figure that took Hannah's breath away.

"You were willing to spend that much?"

Tory nodded.

Hannah drained her cup. "Extraordinarily generous of you, Ms. Reece Taylor."

"A lot of money, yes, but it wouldn't clean me out. I've got the flat at the Manor, and these days my lifestyle isn't especially lavish. Logan is a hunk, and I wanted to be generous. The money wasn't going to him, but into a special bank account set up on behalf of his sister. I found that reassuring, as he intended. So, yes, I was gullible. A love-struck fool." She gave a rueful smile. "I don't mind admitting, it was out of character. My late husband once complained that I didn't have an unselfish bone in my body. For Logan, I was willing to make an exception. More fool me."

"Did you do any—due diligence, so to speak?"

Tory finished her coffee, and Bunny Cohen took the tray out of the room.

"I thought I'd checked out his story. There's a fund-raising website which I pored over, and I talked to Ingrid over the internet three or four times. She was lying in bed in some tiny cubicle in a Chicago hospital. Or so I thought. A pretty young woman, dreadfully frail. Winsome. I also spoke to the specialist."

"Or again, so you thought?"

"Yes, on reflection, I suppose I was in conversation with a pre-recorded message from Logan himself, American accent and all. He and Ingrid put on a convincing double act, and I fell for it." She sighed. "Ingrid isn't his sister. Her name is Sheena and she's a bank clerk from Grange. I presume she master-minded the fancy footwork with the account, while he did a few conjuring tricks with technology."

"How did you find this out?"

"Logan went out last night, supposedly to fix a client's computer, and I decided to do a bit of cyberstalking. Amateur dramatics is one of his hobbies, and when I looked up his group's website, I recognised their star performer. Ingrid, wearing a low-cut top instead of a hospital gown. It dawned on me that they'd rigged the whole thing up with the help of theatre props and computer wizardry. When it comes to IT, I'm easy to bamboo-zle. Mind you, he's getting careless. When he came home, he reeked of cheap perfume."

"Have you transferred the money?"

"Not a penny, thank goodness." Tory's smile was grim. "Perhaps deep down, I never quite believed all the passionate professions of eternal devotion."

Tory Reece-Taylor was a formidable woman, Hannah thought. Impossible not to admire her *sangfroid*. Admitting frailty was never easy, but her manner didn't hint at anger. Whatever her private feelings, she had a gift for hiding them. Of all her strengths, that was probably the most valuable.

The door opened and Bunny came back in.

———

Vesper, Vesper.

As he stared, blank-eyed, at Logan Prentice's crumpled,

bleeding body, Kingsley's mind slid back in time. Daniel Kind was right.

History repeats itself, but never in quite the same way.

His enemy was dead, and he was responsible. Long ago he'd watched Vesper die too.

Ah, lovely little Vesper, everyone's pet. From the moment of her birth, she'd been the apple of their parents' eye. That cute snub nose, the charming freckles, the auburn curls.

How Kingsley had hated her.

Prior to her intrusion into his life, everything had been perfect. He was just old enough to understand how much she'd cost him. No longer was he the centre of the parents' universe. He was the older one, demoted to second place. She was young, innocent, helpless. While their parents ran the shop, he was expected to keep her happy and entertained. She was mischievous, forever throwing her doll out of her pram and wailing until he picked it up so she could repeat the trick again and again until she got bored. If ever he pinched her, to remind her of his superior status, she screamed and told tales about him.

It was all so horribly unfair. She had only herself to blame.

———

Hannah leaned across the table. "Have you challenged Logan Prentice?"

"Not directly." Tory's smile was thin. "He'd only come up with some elaborate explanation of why I'd got it wrong. I can't be bothered with all that. I've spent too much of my life listening to men telling lies."

"And indirectly?"

"When I asked him about Sheena, he became amusingly evasive. I suppose he's shagging her too."

"Has Mr. Prentice done anything to jeopardise your health or well-being?"

A sardonic grin. "On the contrary. Ever since I said I'd transfer the money to the trust account, he couldn't have been more caring. No sense in killing the golden goose before the cash is in the bank."

Hannah had anticipated Tory's strength, but the woman's candour was breathtaking. At least so far.

"What do you propose to do?"

Tory pursed her lips. "I was just racking my brains when you rang."

"In view of what you've told us about Mr. Prentice, I could ask one of my colleagues to speak to him."

"You'll appreciate, Chief Inspector, that I haven't actually made a complaint about him. As a matter of fact, I've been frank with you, and I wonder if you could be equally frank with me?"

Her smile was disarming, her eyes watchful as a hawk's.

"What did you want to know?"

"Last week I saw you on television, giving an interview. You're in charge of cold cases, aren't you? I was puzzled about why you'd been talking to Kingsley Melton. I don't mean to be rude, but you do seem to be trespassing outside your bailiwick. Surely you have your hands full with the enquiry you were talking about—some old murder, wasn't it? It's good of you to show such an interest, but I'm not clear why my private life should concern such a senior officer."

"You're absolutely correct." Hannah was ready for this question. "In the normal course of events, I wouldn't become involved, but Mr. Melton particularly wanted to speak to me."

Tory raised her eyebrows. "You felt sorry for him?"

"We can't turn a blind eye to serious allegations."

"Kingsley told me that two years ago, the police weren't interested in what he had to say."

"They found no evidence to substantiate what he said." Hannah felt as if she were fencing with an accomplished duellist. "Given the possibility that you might be at risk, I decided it was right to speak to you."

Tory gave a brisk nod of satisfaction, as if Hannah had passed a test. "Because from your point of view, the previous incident is now a cold case?"

"Indeed."

"Good of you to take such an interest." Tory picked up her handbag. "Of course, I'll be on my guard, but when I tell Logan that I'm not paying up, he'll be off, quicker than you can say fraudster. Now, if you'll excuse me, I'd better look out for a cab. Good luck with your other enquiry."

She stood up, but the two detectives remained seated.

"About that other enquiry," Hannah said. "I wonder if you can help."

Tory consulted her watch. It looked expensive, possibly a Patek Philippe.

"I'm afraid I really ought to go."

"As you've gathered, we're investigating what happened to Ramona Smith, who vanished from Bowness twenty-one years ago."

"Yes, but…"

"We don't have much to go on. However, Ramona's fingerprints are on file. They were collected from her home as a matter of routine at the time of the original enquiry."

Hannah sat back in her chair and waited for her words to sink in.

Tory said, "Sorry, you've lost me."

"There's always been a strong presumption that Ramona is

dead," Hannah murmured. "Murdered. A ton of circumstantial evidence pointed that way. A man was even tried for the crime, but acquitted."

"So?"

"So my job, leading a cold case review, is to start from a blank sheet of paper."

"Meaning?"

"Meaning that I believe Ramona Smith is still alive."

Chapter Twenty-Six

"Ramona Smith's appearance couldn't be more different from yours," Hannah said. "But she was your height and general build."

Tory's face was a mask. Another advantage of cosmetic surgery. She had a lifetime's experience of hiding her feelings. Of hiding all sorts of blemishes.

Hannah gestured towards the chair she'd vacated. After a rare moment of indecision, Tory sat down again.

"Ramona would also be the same age as you, Ms. Reece-Taylor."

"So are a lot of people."

"True."

Hannah had very little evidence to support her hunch that Tory and Ramona were one and the same, let alone proof. Hence her determination to check Tory's prints. If they didn't match, she'd feel stupid and incompetent, but it wouldn't be the first time, and she'd get over it. Besides, she was convinced that by freeing up her imagination, she'd stumbled upon the truth.

Her theory explained so much that was otherwise coincidental. What had drawn this woman from the south of England to the spot where Ramona had disappeared? And to Kingsley

Melton, one of Leila Smith's clients? Like Ramona, Tory had a vigorous sex life but no interest in commitment. Tiny pointers, at best. But to boast that she loved coming back from the dead…

Tory's composed manner struck Hannah as remarkable but overdone. If she wasn't Ramona, surely she'd be more aggrieved by the outrageous suggestion that she'd faked her own death?

Tory cleared her throat. "I'm not sure what you expect me to say."

"That's up to you."

"Are you suggesting that I am Ramona Smith?"

"Do you deny it?"

"Really, this is ridiculous." Faint spots of colour appeared in her cheeks. "You've invited me here under false pretences."

"Not at all. You kindly volunteered to come to Kendal. This afternoon, you've confirmed that Logan Prentice's behaviour towards you is a cause of concern. While you are here, I'm simply taking the opportunity to ask you about Ramona Smith."

Tory folded her arms. In the silence, Hannah could almost hear the woman's brain shifting through the gears.

"It crossed my mind that there might be a reason you were so willing to meet the detective leading the cold case review. I suppose you hoped to assure yourself that we didn't suspect you of being Ramona Smith."

Tory took a breath. "I've never heard such nonsense."

No ranting, no raving. Her heart simply wasn't in it, Hannah thought. She was giving herself room to manoeuvre, taking care to avoid the lie outright. Like a gambler accustomed to playing for high stakes, she was smart enough to know when she was beaten. She'd have checked her legal position and discovered that she risked being charged with perverting the course of justice. When in a hole, don't keep digging.

Tory's relentlessness had enabled her to deceive everyone. Even Ben Kind. The only surprise was that it had taken her so long to see through Prentice, to recognise that he too was a practised liar. Perhaps for once she had been blinded by desire. For more than two decades, she'd ridden her luck. Today it had run out, and she knew it.

"Kingsley Melton said you love coming back from the dead. A favourite line of yours, isn't it? You've made two comebacks, haven't you? Once when you were resuscitated after the cardiac arrest. And once twenty-one years ago, when you left home to begin a new life under a new identity."

Tory's glance raked across Bunny Cohen. "You took my coffee cup away."

"Yes."

"Don't tell me you're going to check the fingerprints to see if they are a match for this Ramona Smith?"

Her tone was contemptuous, as if she were calling out a cheat.

"Will they match?" Hannah said.

———

Kingsley could see Vesper now, prancing around the back garden in Bowness that fateful afternoon. She'd taken up ballet lessons and proudly announced that when she grew up, she was going to be a ballerina. As far as he could tell, she had two left feet.

The parents were inside the bungalow, haggling with a fellow dealer who was selling up his stock. Their business discussions always took an age. Mamma had instructed Kingsley to look after his little sister. He'd nodded dutifully. In recent months, he'd adopted the line of least resistance and pretended to care about her well-being. Vesper knew he loathed her, but the parents fell for it, and fooling them was all he cared about.

He'd made himself comfortable in his father's old deckchair, next to the hydrangeas, and tried to concentrate on the excitement of *Biggles Hits the Trail*. Tomorrow he was due to return the book to the library, and he was desperate to get to the end of the story, but Vesper's squeals of excitement kept breaking his concentration.

He looked up and called, "Don't go near the pond!"

"Shut up!"

"It's dangerous."

"Stop bossing me about!"

With a noisy groan of exasperation, he clambered to his feet and beckoned her towards him, like a football referee about to send a player off the field of play.

"You're only a little kid; it's not safe."

"And you're a cowardy custard!"

She skipped around on the paving slabs that edged the pond. Her version of a pirouette.

He took a couple of paces towards her.

"Get away from the edge!"

"I'm learning to swim. Not nesh, like you. You're a scaredy cat! You're terrified of getting wet!"

He couldn't help retaliating. "And you're useless at ballet!"

Vesper stuck her small pink tongue out at him and spun around faster. But the slabs were uneven and her foot got caught, tripping her up. She fell backwards into the pond.

The strange thing was that it happened so quickly, she didn't have time to scream. There was just a loud splash as she hit the water.

Shock paralysed him. He glanced over his shoulder, half-expecting to see Mamma in hysterics, bellowing at his father to do something.

But the grown-ups were still in the front room, arguing about money.

He advanced to the edge of the pond. Vesper had cracked her head on a stone. There was a horrid gash on the side of her head, not quite concealed by her curls. The water wasn't really deep, but she was facedown and motionless. It looked as if the blow had knocked her out. Kingsley couldn't be sure if she was alive or not.

He turned in confusion. Should he run back to the house and raise the alarm? If Vesper were fished out, she'd be sure to make a terrible fuss. She'd tell a pack of lies and blame him for her accident. The grown-ups were sure to take her side.

Looking back over his shoulder, he saw her again. The little girl who had stolen his parents' love. She'd brought disaster on herself through sheer pig-headedness and stupidity. Really, he said to himself, she'd got what she deserved.

If anyone deserved to be taught a lesson, it was Vesper Melton.

He stopped in his tracks. No, he wouldn't raise the alarm just yet. Why shouldn't he bide his time? Let her learn how it felt to suffer.

Slowly, he returned to the deckchair and picked up his book. His thoughts were in rather a muddle, so it was easiest just to carry on reading. One more chapter, it wouldn't take that long.

———

Tory gave an ostentatious yawn. "I don't intend to discuss this."

"This is an informal conversation."

Hannah nodded to Bunny, who tossed her pen aside.

"DC Cohen won't take notes."

Tory heaved a sigh. What calculations were going through her head?

"All right. If you'd like me to listen to whatever you have to say, I'm not in a desperate rush to get back home. My lover is planning to kill me for my money. And a nutcase who thinks we're a match made in heaven is stalking me. Any fairy story you can spin will be welcome light relief."

Hannah and Bunny looked at each other. When they'd planned this meeting, Bunny had suggested keeping schtum until the fingerprints confirmed that Tory was Ramona Smith. Hannah, conscious of Tory's medical history, preferred to lay her cards on the table. A chat at this stage, when her speculations were unproven, was less stressful than an interview under caution once they'd uncovered evidence establishing Tory's true identity.

"All right, Ms. Reece-Taylor. Of course I may be wrong about the details. Feel free to put me right."

Tory leaned back in her chair. "I'm all ears."

"Very well." Hannah gave a wry smile as she echoed Kingsley Melton. "Are you sitting comfortably? Then I'll begin."

———

The glassy eyes of Logan Prentice's corpse stared at Kingsley in disbelief. He'd made the same mistake as Vesper, failing to comprehend what a meek person was capable of.

I'm their nemesis.

The thought comforted Kingsley as he stood on the jetty, contemplating his victim. With a start, he realised he was still clutching the Smith & Wesson as if his life depended on it.

How surreal this scene would seem to an onlooker. A dead body and a man with a gun, in a sunlit English country garden. How truly...

An ugly rattling noise in the distance broke into his reverie. A car coming down the drive! The Manor stood between the drive and the jetty. Nobody could see him at the moment, but he began to tremble.

Who was it?

The noise grew louder. He took a few steps forward, his movements erratic, as if he were a ramshackle mechanical toy. The answer came to him like a thunderclap. Fiona Hudson had come to inspect the flat they let out. Her gimcrack repair of the Passat's dodgy exhaust pipe must have failed. At least the hellish racket warned him of her impending arrival.

Sweat crawled down his face. His head was throbbing. Fiona and Molly owned a flat commanding a view of the lake. If she looked out of the living room window, she'd see him with Prentice's body.

He must do something, but his mind was a hopeless whirl.

The gun, he had to get rid of the gun.

Prentice's body he could drop into the lake. He wasn't sure if a watery grave was the safest resting place for his enemy, but he was short of options. Once he'd dodged the immediate threat, he could work out a plan.

The gun must go. He'd throw it as far as he could, so that it finished up in the muddy depths of the lake.

To lose the Smith & Wesson was a sacrifice, but what choice did he have?

Like a cricketer in the outfield, he wound himself up to hurl the gun. Releasing it with a tremendous effort, he stumbled forward and caught his foot on Logan Prentice's outstretched leg. Tripping headfirst, he plunged into the cold water.

He was too shocked to scream.

Just like Vesper was his last conscious thought.

Chapter Twenty-Seven

"The original investigation into Ramona Smith's disappearance established several facts," Hannah said. "Her home life was unhappy. Both her parents were heavy drinkers and they split up when she was seven. Her mother supplemented her income with part-time sex work. Ramona was bright, but lacked qualifications. She drifted from job to job and from affair to affair. The difference was that men used her mother, but Ramona used men."

"Sounds like she had her head screwed on."

"Yes, she was intelligent but never settled to anything. Her lovers were older and married and plied her with gifts. My guess is that she wasn't starry-eyed about any of them. She doesn't seem to have been interested in having children or settling down to a quiet family life."

"Perhaps," Tory said, "she discovered that she couldn't have children."

"You think so?"

"No idea, Chief Inspector. Carry on."

"Some of the men became besotted. She was charismatic, even if not a conventional beauty."

"I saw her photograph on the news," Tory said drily. "Ramona Smith wasn't a beauty of any kind."

"You do her a disservice," Hannah said. "Yes, she'd broken her nose; yes; her hair was mousy and nondescript; yes; her teeth were poor."

"Flat-chested, too, wasn't she?"

Hannah considered Tory's voluptuous figure. "All these things can be fixed."

"If you have the money."

"Precisely. I bet Ramona built up quite a nest egg of cash, thanks to the presents she received from her various admirers. She strikes me as quite shameless, making out that she was deep in debt, when actually she was saving for a rainy day. Or rather, the day when she could escape from here. In Bowness, her horizons were limited. I imagine she felt desperate to get away from the life she knew, especially when one of her exes, Gerry Lace, continued to pester her."

"Leave such a beautiful part of the world, simply because she'd split up with a man?" Tory said coolly. "Hardly the mark of a strong character."

"People who grow up here often take Cumbria for granted. Some folk need a bit of distance, time, and space, to appreciate the Lakes to the full."

Tory shook her head, like a chess player disappointed by an opponent's unworthiness, "Why be so elaborate? If she was footloose and fancy-free, why not simply sling her hook?"

"My guess is that for years, she'd dreamed of starting afresh, somewhere else in Britain. Maybe she longed to travel far and wide. She and her mother were never close. Much as she enjoyed walking the fells and cycling along the country lanes, there was nothing to keep her in the Lakes, other than her grandmother. Unfortunately, the old lady succumbed to dementia."

"If she cared that much for the grandmother, would she abandon her?"

Hannah's spine prickled. She'd gambled on the woman finding herself unable to resist the urge to engage, to try out lines of defence. She didn't mind revealing what was in her mind if it improved her chances of teasing out the truth.

"You're right. The old lady was still alive when Ramona disappeared. But dementia is a terrible curse. Personalities change out of all recognition. My guess is that Ramona found it too upsetting. She couldn't bear it anymore."

"As you say, you're guessing."

"The grandmother had become a stranger to her and didn't have long to live. Besides, it was easier to make a complete getaway while she was still alive."

"What makes you say that?"

"It's speculation, of course."

Tory gave her a measuring stare. "Evidently."

"Ramona was a fit woman and a keen cyclist. But she left her old bike behind her, so it seemed she couldn't have cycled anywhere. As a long shot, this morning I called Ravi Thakor."

Tory's face was a blank. If she knew the name, she wasn't admitting it.

"When I first spoke to him, he mentioned buying her a bicycle. Turns out it was a flashy parting gift, a different make from her old bike. Nobody else knew it existed. I wonder if she kept it at her grandma's house, in Bardsea, together with some money and a few essentials that she could take with her when she was ready for her getaway. An impromptu hair-dye, a few other changes to her appearance, and she wouldn't look much like the Ramona Smith everyone was familiar with."

"Long shots," Tory murmured. "Guesswork."

"In cold case policing, there's no avoiding them. By road

it's twenty-five miles from Bardsea to the mainline station at Oxenholme. From there you can catch a train to anywhere you fancy. London Euston is an obvious choice. She could have picked up the first train in the morning. A long ride in the dark takes a good two hours, but a fit cyclist in her early thirties could manage it easily enough."

"I'll take your word for it," Tory said. "I prefer to travel by BMW."

"I'm sure you do," Hannah said. "Nothing but the best, these days. Actually, I'm curious as to the real reason why you travelled here by taxi."

Tory's eyes narrowed. "You are so cynical, Chief Inspector."

"It comes with the job. Once we accept that Ramona is still alive, a lot of pieces fall into place. To vanish off the face of the earth, she must have made preparations over a long period of time. Her disappearance wasn't a whim or a panic move, she didn't flee on the spur of the moment. No, she had a plan, and she laid the groundwork by creating a false identity."

"If you're to be believed, Chief Inspector, this uneducated working class woman from Bowness was clever enough to out-fox everyone, including the mighty Cumbria Constabulary. Is that likely?"

"I don't underestimate Ramona. That's what she traded on; it's where the original investigation went wrong. I suppose she felt she'd been underestimated all her life. Taken for granted. Badly treated, especially by men. Gerald Lace, for instance. Another woman, someone she knew, had already accused Lace of attempted rape. Beneath the charming façade, he was unstable, volatile. Violent."

There was a long silence. Tory was as immobile as a statue.

"In those days," Hannah said, "there was a well-known method popularised by a thriller called *The Day of the Jackal*. The trick was to scout around graveyards and find the name of a dead child who was born at much the same time as yourself. Step two, apply for a copy of the deceased's birth certificate. Step three, use that as proof of identity when applying for a passport. Hey, presto! You became someone else. And that's exactly what Ramona did."

"Oh, yes?"

"Her new name was Victoria. Or Vee for short. She gave Vee a sort of life as an imaginary friend, someone she mentioned to other people whenever the opportunity arose, but who never showed her face. After Ramona, alias Victoria, made good her escape, she used an alternative short form of the name. She became Toria. Or Tory."

———

The name hung in the air. Tory hunched her shoulders.

"I have a wild idea," Hannah said, "that Ramona might have wanted to hit back at her father, Jimmy, by seeking out a comfortable, materialistic lifestyle. He was a rabid trade unionist."

Tory's lip curled. "A bully and a bigot, you mean? The sort who says *Never kiss a Tory*?"

Emboldened, Hannah said, "Choosing that name was a small retaliatory poke. Not like the elaborate revenge she took on Gerry Lace. Who must have hurt her very, very badly to justify such extreme measures."

"You said yourself, the man was a rapist."

"Never charged, let alone convicted."

"That's what's wrong with society, isn't it? Playing by the rules gets you nowhere. Brutal men walk free. Female victims who go to court are treated like criminals. There's no justice."

"Whatever Lace did to Ramona must have been serious. Only that explains her behaviour. My guess is that he raped her."

Tory's face was blank. "He sounds the type."

"Whatever happened, she decided that it wasn't enough to get away from the area and start a new life. He deserved to be punished. Nadine Bosman had been let down by the system when she made a complaint. Ramona decided to exact a different form of justice."

No response.

"I've read the transcripts of the police interviews with Lace. He admitted that he found her intoxicating. Tried to make out he was so smitten that he couldn't possibly have done her any harm. At one point he said he'd have left his wife for her. Shirley Lace, the woman who sacrificed everything for him."

"If you say so."

"The way I picture it, Ramona told Lace she was willing to see him again and proposed a tryst on the Crooked Shore. For her purposes, it was ideal. Isolated and not far from the grandmother's cottage at Bardsea. Walkable on a fine night, with little danger of being seen."

Tory yawned. "Would anyone in their right mind take the risk of going to a lonely spot with a violent rapist?"

"Ramona was an exceptional woman."

"Exceptionally stupid, by the sound of it."

"Ruthless, certainly. And well-prepared. She caught Lace off guard and knocked him out. Then she nicked herself with a pen-knife and daubed her own blood on her anorak. She hid the rucksack nearby and the anorak at Birkrigg Common, only a short detour from her route to Bardsea. She'd packed a bag of essentials and kept it at her grandmother's cottage, to take with her on the bike and train the next morning. Everything she did was designed to conjure up the scenario of a violent and desperate sex killer who tried to cover up his crime."

"Well, well," Tory said, "you've certainly brought something fresh to your cold case, Chief Inspector. If only an exotic imagination."

Bunny could contain herself no longer. "Perhaps this case needed looking at from a woman's point of view. The victim's perspective, not the man's."

Tory winced. "Feminist policing, is that the vogue?"

Hannah said, "On recovering consciousness, Lace must have felt bemused as well as shocked. When he heard about Ramona's disappearance, I suppose he didn't know what to make of it. When he was questioned, his instinct was to lie. He bullied his family into backing him up, a fatal mistake. What happened between him and Ramona on the Crooked Shore was bizarre. When he belatedly told the truth, his credibility was in bits. In court, the case for the defence was that Vee was a man and responsible for killing Ramona. A red herring, but more credible than Lace's story, which made little sense. Why would Ramona attack him, as he suggested, especially if she'd proposed they get together again?"

"From what I've heard," Tory said, "Lace got away with it by the skin of his teeth. Anyhow, none of this is my concern."

"Ramona didn't care about what happened to Gerry Lace, whether he was sentenced to life imprisonment or walked out of court a free man, but with his good name in tatters."

"Good name?" Tory's voice was edged with scorn. "A rapist?"

"Ramona, or Victoria as she became, didn't lift a finger to save him. One authenticated call, that's all it would have taken, to confirm that she was still alive and that Lace was innocent of her murder. It wouldn't have hurt her. But no, she preferred to let him sweat."

Tory shrugged. "Frankly, I sympathise."

"She strikes me as extraordinarily ruthless." Hannah paused. "It wasn't simply a question of hurting Gerald Lace. What about his wife and children? Their lives were also ruined."

"Shirley Lace, was that her name? Don't tell me she didn't know what sort of a man she'd married. And she turned a blind eye. Did she worry about the harm he did? I don't think so. Ask that Nadine woman you mentioned. As for the children, the parents should have taken better care of them. What happened to the son wasn't Ramona Smith's responsibility."

Hannah pursed her lips. "With her stash of money, Ramona made a new life in the south of England. Changed her appearance over time. Hair, nose, teeth, boobs. For twenty years or more, everything went well. She married a rich older man who let her do as she pleased. Even after her heart stopped, she made a wonderful recovery. For the second time, she came back from the dead."

"You've never suffered a cardiac arrest," Tory murmured, "so even a person with your vivid way of thinking will find it hard to understand the experience. It changes you, and I'm not just talking about the number of pills you're forced to take to reduce the risk of a recurrence. To this day, for instance, I still have unpredictable lapses of memory."

How many times, Hannah wondered, had Tory rehearsed for a moment like this, when her secret came out? Claiming memory loss as part of her strategy of self-defence. Another move in the game.

"After her husband died, she was ready to return to her roots. She had no ties, she'd survived her own near-death experience."

"Why come back to Cumbria, when according to you, she'd gone to such extraordinary lengths to get away?"

"However desperate she was to taste the good life , it must have been a wrench to leave such a lovely place. Where she used to cycle around the valleys and walk the fells."

Tory's lip curled. "She could have satisfied her curiosity on a day trip or a mini-break."

"It wasn't simply curiosity that drove her, I think. Or even just the pull of the familiar. She'd spent half her life in the Lakes. In a kind of way she still belonged here."

"But why choose Strandbeck and the Crooked Shore, of all places?"

"I suppose it was symbolic, moving to the place where she'd begun her new life. No need to worry about the old wives' tale, that strangers who outstay their welcome suffer misfortune. She wasn't a stranger." Hannah paused. "There is one thing that puzzles me."

"Only one?" Tory said coolly.

"Kingsley Melton lived in Bowness, just like the Smiths. He knew Ramona's mother; he was one of her clients..."

"Is that so?"

Tory's calm was remarkable. Hard not to admire, even if there was something monstrous about it. Hannah wasn't sure she'd met anyone quite like this woman.

"He claims his path never crossed with Ramona's. Presumably, he's afraid of being suspected of her murder, but I find his denial hard to believe, don't you?"

Tory shrugged. "Who knows? Perhaps Ramona caught him visiting the house just after her mother was first diagnosed with cancer. Perhaps she took out her anger and disgust on him."

"You think so?"

"From what you tell me, she could be quite a devil when she was in a foul temper. Maybe she scared him off coming back again. Gave him the fright of his life. Threatened to tell his mother."

Hannah considered. "Yes, that sounds plausible."

"One thing about poor Kingsley. He's easy to humiliate. Easy to bend to your will."

"Interesting that he didn't recognise Ramona when she came back to Strandbeck. A tribute to the success of her makeover."

"If you say so."

"I wonder if she was testing him—and herself. Perhaps it explains why she took their relationship further."

"What do you mean?"

"If she could sleep with him and he still failed to recognise her, she didn't have much to fear from anyone else."

"Risky, surely?"

"Not for a born risk-taker."

When Tory said nothing, Hannah asked, "Did that amuse you? His name is unusual. You must have realised who he was when you booked your appointment to view the Manor."

Tory gave her a quizzical look. "Kingsley is an unlikely Romeo, but I have a macabre sense of humour. I get bored very easily, you know. So horribly bored."

"I understand."

"I wonder if you do. I'm fortunate. Through my own efforts, I've got everything I ever dreamed of. Or so I thought until I discovered the truth about Logan." She shook her head. "Don't tell a soul, but somehow it's never seemed quite enough. Every now and then I wake up in a cold sweat. Not because I'm afraid my heart is going to give out on me again..."

Her voice dwindled to nothing.

"Then why?" Hannah asked gently.

"Because I can never figure out an answer to the question that haunts me. *Is this all there is?*"

Nobody spoke for a few moments, then Tory cleared her throat. "Forgive me, Chief Inspector. That was rather self-indulgent. Thanks for sharing your theories. Intriguing if fanciful. I can't say I like the sound of Ramona, and I definitely wouldn't want her life. I'd rather be dead in a ditch. And now, if you'll excuse me, I really must be going."

Chapter Twenty-Eight

"Guilty as charged," Bunny Cohen said. "Congratulations, you played a blinder."

Hannah smiled. Her emotions were stretched and her thoughts whirling. She still had urgent work to do, but was in desperate need of a few moments' reflection. A few splashes of rain marked the window. The storm was coming.

"Don't you want to see whether the fingerprints match?"

"Nah, if ever someone could see that the game is up, it's Tory Reece-Taylor. Or Ramona, should we call her? Talk about nerves of steel. She hardly flinched. Mind you, after twenty-one years of looking over her shoulder, she'd had plenty of time to practise her answers."

"I doubt she's ever looked over her shoulder." Hannah said. "She's utterly focused on getting what she wants. Nothing else matters. The end justifies the means."

"What do you think… Hello, Maggie, you'll never guess what…"

Maggie Eyre had burst in on them. "Sorry to interrupt, but you'll want to hear this."

"Go on," Hannah said.

"Breaking news. There's been a major incident at Strandbeck Manor."

———

"What could be more romantic?" Louise asked down the telephone. "A boat trip on a beautiful lake with two gorgeous women."

Sitting outside Tarn Cottage, sipping a lemonade well-earned after a couple of hours of nonstop writing, Daniel grinned. His sister was incorrigible.

"A boat trip for two. Not one with my sister in tow."

"You can't have everything," she said. "Anyway, I wasn't going to miss out. I've never sailed on Crummock Water."

"Is it really such a good idea? With a storm warning?"

"It's a very good idea. This is the Lake District. Rain is part of the deal. Part of the fun. And if you're worried that it won't dampen your baser urges, I'll make sure you behave yourself with Alex."

"I swear I've no intention of misbehaving. How many times do I have to remind you, I'm not in the market for a new relationship?"

"You can't fool me," Louise said. "All isn't well between you and Hannah. What's up; is work getting in the way? You can't go on like this forever, you know."

"Look, you called when I was in the middle of a synopsis," Daniel said. "I can't talk any more now."

"You always were a rotten liar," Louise said gleefully. "Especially when I got the better of you in an argument. See you later."

———

"Quite a day," Les Bryant said.

Hannah had brought the team together again. Events were racing forward; there was so much she was desperate to do, but she owed it to people to make sure they were up to speed. After rattling through a summary of her conversation with Tory Reece-Taylor, she'd reported that colleagues in the southwest of the county were investigating at Strandbeck Manor. A horrified woman who owned one of the flats had made a shocking discovery in the grounds.

"Yes," she said bleakly. "While Ramona was stonewalling us, her two lovers were fighting to the death at Strandbeck."

"So Melton turned sharp-shooter." Bunny whistled. "I knew he was crazy, but I didn't see that coming."

"Do they think," Maggie said slowly, "he killed Prentice and then took his own life?"

"Too soon to say," Hannah said. "That's the working presumption, but maybe his death was accidental. Perhaps they had a fight, and the gun went off and he fell in at the same time. As a child, he was afraid of water. We know that from the reports of his sister's death. Maybe he never learned to swim."

"Where did he get hold of a gun?"

"He dealt in antiques, don't forget. There are legal loopholes. Question is, what part did Ramona play in this mayhem?"

"How can she be involved?" Bunny asked. "Surely you and I have given her the perfect alibi."

"Yeah, very convenient. Remember her MO with Gerald Lace. Setting the scene to incriminate him, then making herself scarce."

"She couldn't control what happened after that."

"No, but she didn't need to. She deliberately caused enough mayhem to wreck Lace's life. Whatever happened. Whether he was tried for her murder or not. Whether he was found guilty or not."

"You think she set up a confrontation between Prentice and Melton?" Maggie asked. "Stage management?"

"I wouldn't bet against it. When she realised Prentice was cheating on her, in more ways than one, she probably said to herself: *it's him or me*. Don't forget, he might have tried to kill her if she'd handed over her money. Once she found out the truth, he was in big trouble."

"How would she know that Melton was going to show up and shoot Prentice?"

"If she knew Melton owned a gun, maybe she suspected he'd use it if provoked. Having lit the blue touch-paper, she made herself scarce and waited for an explosion."

"There was no guarantee that either man would harm the other."

"No, but perhaps she was content just to leave it to Fate. She's reckless, it's her hallmark."

"We may never know for sure," Les muttered.

"We can do our best to find answers," Hannah said. "She said her car was playing up. I've already sent a message to make sure it's checked. Apparently, it's an electric BMW, less than a year old. Chances of it going wrong so soon? What if she sneaked out of the grounds and called for a taxi to pick her up on the main road? If her car was still in the car park, Melton would assume she was still on site. If he couldn't find her..."

Bunny shivered. "You offered to go to the Manor, but she insisted on coming here."

Hannah nodded. "I thought I was so smart. But the truth is, she used us."

Les groaned. "The old, old story. Never trust a helpful suspect."

"It's only me," Alex Samaras said.

She'd wandered round the side of Tarn Cottage, as Louise had done on Sunday. A large bag was slung over her shoulders. Even in sailing gear, a black short-sleeved rash vest and shorts, she looked ridiculously attractive.

Daniel had finished writing and was lounging on the paved area behind the cottage with a paperback thriller, making the most of the weather while he had the chance. The clouds overhead were ominous and a moment earlier he'd felt a splash of rain.

He scrambled to his feet and Alex kissed him on the cheek.

"Fantastic to see you again. I've brought the dinghy on a trailer. Louise came round to my place."

"And Louise?"

"Waiting in the van."

"She tells me you're dead set on going to Crummock Water."

"Dead set is right." Alex smiled. "Believe me, I'm really excited about taking the two of you there."

"You don't think one of the lakes closer…?"

"Too busy." She laughed. "We don't want Joe Public getting in the way."

"Well…"

"Trust me, Crummock Water is perfect. You're not getting cold feet, are you?"

"I just thought that it will be getting dark by the time we get there, and if it's pelting down…"

She shook her head. "Don't worry. I've planned this carefully. You'd be surprised."

"I get the impression you're full of surprises."

Standing very close to him, she laughed again. There was a strange gleam in her big doleful eyes. He hoped she wasn't going to embrace him. This felt all wrong.

"You never said a truer word," she said.

With a single right-handed blow to his neck, she knocked him to the ground.

In the moment before he lost consciousness, he saw a strange look in her eyes. It was nothing to do with desire, everything to do with hate.

Chapter Twenty-Nine

"There's something else," Hannah said. "I think it could be important."

Her tone commanded everyone's attention.

"I've been reading the witness statements for myself. Just before Tory arrived, I read what Shirley Lace had to say. A name caught my eye."

"Whose name?" Bunny asked.

"She referred to their two children. The son, Darren Jason Lace, who blew his father's alibi and took his own life at Strandbeck. And the daughter, Sandi."

Maggie nodded. "You wanted us to trace her to see if she could cast any light on her father's involvement with Ramona. We've made progress. Turns out she married a Greek and went to live abroad, but she came back to Britain some time ago. Last heard of in London."

"Let me update you," Hannah said. "Sandi was a young girl's nickname. Short for Alexandra. Shirley's statement refers to her as Alexandra Rowan Lace. In later years, Sandi called herself Alexandra Rowan, probably to distance herself from the scandal about her father. She became an actor. After she married, she became known as Alex Samaras. She's alive and well and living in Grasmere."

———

Daniel began to come round as Alex Samaras dragged him, slowly and painfully, round the side of Tarn Cottage. She'd gagged and bound him with conspicuous efficiency. Tight ropes cut into his wrists and ankles. His mouth was sealed with duct tape. He could see and breathe and hear, but that was all. His neck hurt and his head throbbed. Groggy and distressed, he struggled to understand what was happening to him.

His scalp scraped against the rough ground as she hauled him along. An unmarked white van was parked in the space on the other side of the gate. Attached to the rear was a trailer bearing a large grey dinghy.

Impossible to utter a yelp of protest or pain, far less shriek for help. Not that the loudest scream would do any good. There were no neighbours, nothing but the running beck and the trees and the birds and wildlife. He'd always loved the seclusion of his cottage, but now the loneliness of Tarn Fold left him at Alex Samaras' mercy. She could do as she pleased.

What was she playing at? That blow she'd struck...

They'd talked about Alex practising martial arts. What had she said that first evening?

You don't want to mess with me.

———

Les Bryant gave Hannah a hard stare, like a barrister cross-examining a nervy witness.

"You're worried."

"Yes. I'm still processing what this means, but…"

"But?"

"Alex Samaras has befriended Daniel Kind and his sister Louise." She paused to allow the implications to sink in.

"The children of Ben Kind," Les muttered. "The detective who arrested Gerald Lace, the man blamed for Lace's suicide."

"Yes."

"And by extension for ruining the rest of Shirley Lace's life, and even for Darren's suicide."

"That's right."

"The last people she'd want to chum up with," Maggie said. "Or so you'd think."

"There's more," Hannah said. "She came back to the Lakes a few years back and worked in a pub in Oxenholme. Guess who she got to know?"

Maggie stared. "Ben Kind was living in Oxenholme at the time of his death."

"She chatted him up," Hannah said. "She's very pretty, and I bet Ben was easily hooked. Marriage on the rocks and a nice young girl taking an interest in him… Daniel told me about meeting her. Something she said to him takes on a sinister note once you know who she is."

"Surely you don't suppose..?" Bunny began.

"She wasn't working in the bar the night Ben was run over. What she told Daniel was that everyone deserved justice."

There was a shocked silence.

Maggie said, "But she never got involved with Shirley's campaign to clear Gerald Lace's name. On the contrary. She fell out with both her mother and her brother."

"She didn't go to their funerals, either," Hannah said. "Jade Hughes told me she never met her. I presumed that Sandi was desperate to forget the past."

"But?"

"I'm beginning to wonder if the truth is just the opposite. Suppose Sandi was hell-bent on vengeance and thought Shirley and Darren were far too soft."

"Let's assume she killed Ben and got away with it," Les said slowly. "That should have satisfied her thirst for revenge. Why did the obsession began to eat away at her again?"

"Daniel's book about murder has been widely publicised," Hannah said. "And she's been following his career ever since Ben told her about the son he lost touch with. With his kids both settled here, coming back to the Lake District gave her the chance to get close to them. What happened to her father wrecked Darren's life and may have done her untold damage."

"There was a lot of mental instability in that family," Maggie said. "Both parents and Darren."

"What if Alex is the most disturbed of the lot?" Bunny said.

"Despite the rift with her mother and brother," Hannah said, "it's possible that their deaths were the last straw. If she's so bitter and twisted, visiting Ben's perceived sins on his offspring must seem tempting."

"You said she was an actor."

"Yeah, she's been putting on quite a performance. She even saved Louise's life."

Les stared. "How come?"

Hannah told the story. "When you look at it, the coincidence of her moving to the village where Louise lives, and just happening to be on the spot when Louise fell into the Rothay is hard to swallow."

"You think it was a setup?" Bunny asked. "That actually Alex was stalking Louise?"

"It explains a good deal. If she tossed a stick into the river to encourage the dog to jump in...or maybe she just took advantage of a lucky chance to worm her way into Louise's affections. Knowing Louise's taste for the dramatic, I'd guess she was so grateful to her rescuer, she exaggerated the danger she was in. She'd probably have got out of the water unaided, who knows? The upshot was that Alex disarmed any suspicion and inveigled her way into the Kinds' lives."

"Pretending to be Daniel's greatest fan?" Bunny said.

Hannah gritted her teeth. "Too right."

"What do you think she's got in mind?" Maggie asked.

"No idea, but I want to find out."

"We have no evidence that she's committed any offence."

"True."

Hannah had wrestled with conflicting emotions ever since she'd discovered Alex Samaras's identity. What if she poked her nose in and proved to have misjudged the woman's motives? Was she guilty of wishful thinking, was she jealous because Daniel had taken a fancy to a younger woman? What if Alex, having lost her father, mother, and brother, was simply reaching out to Louise and Daniel because she'd known Ben and felt some sort of strange connection with them? A shared sense of grieving or loss. Or even just because she'd discovered they were delightful people?

Get this wrong, and Hannah had no doubt about the consequences. She would destroy her relationship with Daniel.

"Listen." Les got to his feet. "Suppose you're right."

"Go on."

"If she ran over Ben Kind, then Louise and Daniel are in danger."

"That's right," Bunny said.

"No time to waste," Les said. "We need to talk to this woman and find out what game she's playing."

"I won't ask if you're both comfy," Alex Samaras said. "I can see that you're not."

She'd heaved Daniel into a black nylon body bag before shoving him into the back of the van. Louise was there, gagged and bound and bagged. Her only movement was in the eyes. They flickered with terror and pain.

"How are your heads? Swimming, I hope, but not so much that you can't take things in. You need to understand what's happening to you. I've been practising for days on end, trying to get just the right amount of force to stun you both without killing you outright. That would be far too easy. A real anticlimax."

With a gleeful smile, she climbed into the van and began to mimic Louise. "But we thought you were our friend! Why are you doing this to us?"

The accuracy of the impersonation was uncanny, its cruelty grotesque. Alex Samaras really could act, Daniel thought. She'd hoodwinked them both.

"Simple, Louise." Alex reverted to her usual voice. "My father was Gerald Lace, and your father murdered him, just as surely as if he'd put a bullet through his brain. He might as well have killed the rest of us while he was at it. I'm not saying it was a perfect family, but we got by. Ben Kind destroyed all that. My mum lost the plot and so did my pathetic brother. They wasted their lives, dreaming of justice. But there isn't proper justice in this country. To get anything done, you have to take the law in your own hands."

"You mean you ran my father over?" Now Alex deepened her voice to become Daniel, her performance a cruel parody of his television persona, enthusiastic and inquiring.

"Well done, Daniel! The wannabe detective strikes again. If

not for me, you and he would've reunited. He might have found some happiness, and that would never do. Aren't I the naughty one? A real party-pooper!"

She laughed and resumed her squealy imitation of his sister. "But you saved my life!"

"Well, Louise, that night I was sorely tempted to let you drown. Not that it would have worked. You'd have saved yourself. Anyway, I didn't want to be denied the chance to enjoy myself in your company. Flirting madly with both of you. I'm surprised you managed to keep your hands off. If I'd given you any more encouragement…but no, I had to focus. Keep my eye on the big prize."

"The big prize?" Louise's voice again.

While she talked, Daniel was trying to wriggle free of his bonds, but she'd done too good a job. There was no escape.

"Promised to take you sailing on Crummock Water, didn't I? Just as I took a vow years ago, to make your father suffer for what he'd done. I always keep my word."

"Tell us more!" Now she was Daniel, eager for information.

"When Ben Kind heard my old van revving up behind him that night, he glanced over his shoulder. Saw me behind the wheel. For a few seconds he relaxed, until he saw I was bearing down on him. That look of betrayal…I'll never forget it as long as I live."

She became Louise again. "That's horrid! And why take it out on us?"

"Killing you two was an afterthought, to be honest, but I'm grateful for getting a second chance. Aren't I lucky? The one mistake I made with your father was not giving myself the opportunity to make him understand why he had to die. This time it's different. Working out my plan has kept me going. Made me feel alive again, which really doesn't happen as much as it should. How will I cope after tonight, when there's nothing more to look forward to? I suppose it will be like mowing your father down, feeling his body flailing under my wheels. A memory to cherish, to replay in my mind, again and again."

As Daniel, she mimicked a theatrical flash of enlightenment during a televised interview with a fellow expert. "What you're saying puts a whole new complexion on things! You're going to shove us in the dinghy, weight us down, sail us out into the lake, and then push us over the side?"

"Brilliant deduction!" Alex stamped on his ankle. "You'll be a huge loss to the ranks of amateur sleuthing, not to mention academe, telly, and publishing. Thanks for inscribing those books, incidentally. Each time I look at them, I'll remember you both, just as I last saw you. The sickness in your stomachs, the horror in your eyes, as you slide into that ice-cold water, one after the other, knowing your fate in advance, wondering precisely how long it will take you to die."

Chapter Thirty

"No answer from Louise or Daniel, home landline numbers or mobiles," Hannah said, putting down her phone. "I've texted warning messages, sent emails, all the obvious stuff. No response."

"Is that so unusual?" Bunny asked. "Two busy people…"

"She's on sabbatical, and he works from home."

Les cupped his ear. There was a steady beat of rain against the window. "If they ignored the forecast and went walking the fells, they're going to get sodden."

"We've nothing to go on except supposition," Hannah said. "But Ben was a smart guy who knew how to look after himself. I never understood how he managed to drop his guard so far that someone could run him over, even if he'd had a couple of drinks. To be honest, I'm worried sick."

"Me too," Les said. "We'd best go hunting for Daniel and Louise. And this woman Samaras."

———

"Time to go," Alex told her captives.

Daniel could hear the rain outside. The heavens were

opening. If only he could move, if only he could do something to save the two of them.

Alex kicked him. "It won't be a pleasant trip, but make the most of it. You won't have another. Crummock Water isn't my favourite lake for sailing, but I've found the perfect spot for launching you on your last boat ride together. The light will be fading by the time we get there, you won't have much chance to enjoy your last view of the Lakes."

She stamped on his ankle. "This weather is a nuisance, but I'm a glass-half-full girl. Even less risk of prying eyes in the middle of a downpour. You can't make an omelette without breaking an egg, and you can't hope to drown two people without getting wet."

In his dazed state, Daniel asked himself why she kept talking. A means of nerving herself to the double murder? Or did it simply give her a kick to prolong their agony?

Louise was staring straight at him. He thought he could read her mind.

I'm so sorry. This is my fault. I got it all wrong.

"Are you ready?" Alex jumped out of the back of the van and seized hold of the doors. "Let's hit the road."

———

"You drive," Hannah told Maggie as they dashed through the storm towards the car park. "I'll keep trying to make contact with one or other of them."

Les and Bunny had set off for Grasmere. Hannah and Maggie were heading for Tarn Cottage. In terms of miles, it wasn't far from Kendal, but given the way the rain was bouncing off the tarmac and blurring their vision, the last leg of their journey through Brackdale's twisting lanes would be tortuous.

"Did Daniel mention anything that might give us a clue about what he's up to? Or this Alex Samaras?"

Hannah trawled through her memory. "She's a fitness fanatic. Climbing, sailing. Louise wants them to go on a boat trip together."

"Outdoor pursuits," Maggie grunted as they jumped into the car. "Same as her father and brother."

"Yeah, I should have thought on."

"We could never have foreseen this. Nobody suggested Sandi was a threat. Or even that she was bothered about getting justice for her father."

They strapped themselves in. Outside the rain was redoubling in intensity.

Hannah said grimly, "Perhaps she has her own ideas about what constitutes justice."

———

The van's interior was dark. The driver's compartment was separate, and Daniel couldn't see Alex Samaras. Louise had shut her eyes. She suffered from mild claustrophobia and lying here, trussed up and helpless, must be the worst kind of torment. How he wished he could squeeze her hand and whisper words of comfort. But even if he were able to speak, what could he say?

Alex put the van into gear and it jolted forward as she shifted vehicle and trailer in the confined space outside the gate to the cottage. He guessed that she'd scouted out a lonely section of the northern lakes where she felt she could offload the bodies with little or no risk of being seen.

A vague memory rose to the surface of his brain, a murder case he'd read about years ago. A Yorkshireman had killed his wife and driven her to Crummock Water one night to dispose of her corpse. He botched the job and was soon found out. No doubt Alex had studied the case while working out how to kill two victims and get away with it.

If she cared about getting away with it. Everything about her frightened him. The scariest thing was her intensity. She'd murdered their father and never paid a price. Not even that had been enough to slake her thirst for vengeance.

The van jerked as Alex slammed on the brakes. She embarked on a stop-start manoeuvre, trying to turn round. Outside, the rain was lashing down.

A loud bang. Daniel guessed that Alex had clipped the side of the pack horse bridge. The van stalled and his head smacked against the floor again. Tears of pain and misery stung his eyes.

The engine revved. The van began to move. He felt it picking up speed.

———

Maggie was a nerveless driver. She'd learned how to handle vehicles on the family farm. The rain was torrential, and the slashing windscreen wipers could barely cope, but her concentration was intense, their progress rapid. The lanes were narrow, the bends tight, but there wasn't a shortcut that she didn't know.

Hannah's heart was thumping. Still no joy on the phone.

"Pick up," she muttered under her breath, dialling Daniel's number yet again. But he didn't.

Thankfully, Brackdale wasn't far from the town. They reached the valley in record time. Steep crags concealed it from the outside world. There was no through road. Daniel had chosen to make his home here at a time when he was desperate to escape the rat race. He'd wanted nothing but solitude.

They raced through the small village, past church and

pub, and over a cattle grid, squeezing along the lane between tall hedgerows and deep ditches. Ahead of them were long-abandoned quarry workings.

"Look!"

Maggie's sharp eyes had picked up the shape of a large vehicle through the murk. It was coming towards them from the direction of Tarn Fold.

"A van with a trailer," Hannah said. "I reckon that's her."

Their headlights were on full beam. The van gathered speed. Time for the blue light and siren.

———

Daniel heard the siren just as he realised Alex was putting her foot down. Driving in the Lakes was testing at the best of times. In bad weather, the narrow lanes were a death trap.

What was happening, was she trying to get them all killed?

It was his last conscious thought.

———

"She's coming straight at us," Maggie said.

"She'll cut us in half!" Hannah cried. "Get out of her way!"

Maggie wrenched the steering wheel and the car swung wildly as the van roared towards them.

Tory Reece-Taylor's words leapt into Hannah's head.

I'd rather be dead in a ditch.

She closed her eyes.

Chapter Thirty-One

"Another fine mess you got me into," Daniel said.

He and Hannah were sitting next to Louise's bed in the hospital, and she'd just opened her eyes. Seventy-two hours after the crash, she was recovering from her injuries.

As arranged, she'd turned up at Alex's rented cottage, tucked away behind the trees on the outskirts of Grasmere. Alex knocked her out with a blow to the side of the head, and she'd cracked her temple against a stone wall. The buffeting she'd received when Alex's van had come off the road and ploughed through a hedge hadn't helped.

The paramedics who were first on the scene had worried about possible brain damage, but Hannah and Daniel had just spent ten minutes with a doctor and nurse, and the prognosis was optimistic. Louise remained extremely weak, but she was no longer confused, and the scans revealed nothing terrifying. Her face was badly cut and bruised, but the gory wounds would heal.

"Sorry." Her croaky voice was scarcely recognisable.

He took her hand. "No problem. The medics reckon you'll be running around and causing mayhem in no time."

A weary attempt at a smile.

"Might take…a day or two." Her bloodshot eyes took in the plaster on his head and the bruising of his cheek and jaw. "How are you?"

"Where there's no sense, there's no feeling," Hannah said. "He's been checked over thoroughly. You were both knocked around, so the medics haven't taken any chances. He was kept in overnight for observation, but then released."

"What…happened?"

"Hannah came to the rescue," Daniel said. "She figured out that Alex was the Laces' daughter, thank God. Maggie drove her to Brackdale. We'd already had one narrow escape when Alex clipped the pack horse bridge and nearly ended up in the beck. Not easy to drive with a trailer when you're losing the plot and a downpour has made the road surfaces slippery. She saw the police car heading towards her and panicked. Seems she was trying to crash into Maggie and Hannah, but she slewed off the lane instead."

"Same as us," Hannah said. "We finished up in a ditch on the other side of the lane."

"How are you?" Louise asked.

"Fine. I managed to fracture a couple of ribs, but Maggie saved us from much worse. Smart woman, she scrambled free without a scratch. Then she helped me on to my feet and we found the van had crashed into a tree. The back doors had broken open, so pulling the pair of you was easy."

"Alex wanted to go out in a blaze of glory," Daniel said. "Luckily, she came off worst."

"Is she dead?"

"In a coma. Because she's young and fit, there's an outside chance she may pull through. What shape she'll be in afterwards is anyone's guess."

"I liked her," Louise said in a small voice.

"So did Dad." He squeezed her hand. "And she killed him."

A choked sob. "Oh, God. The hit and run…"

"She fooled everyone," Hannah said. "Nobody's to blame but her."

"I messed up," Louise said. "I should never…"

"Stop it," Daniel said. "No point in harking back. We all need to look to the future."

Hannah shot him a glance.

"Speaking of which…," she said.

"Oh, yes." He cleared his throat. "Actually, Hannah and I have got some news. We wanted you to be the first to know."

AFTERWARDS, CONTINUED

"All right, you win," Tory Reece-Taylor said. "Let me explain why Ramona Smith had to die."

She and Hannah were sitting in an interview room at Divisional HQ. Tory's lawyer, the most expensive and formidable criminal law solicitor in the county, was at her side. Hannah was accompanied by Bunny Cohen.

Tory had offered to make a voluntary statement. Cumbria Constabulary's legal advisers reckoned it was a smart move, designed to focus on damage limitation. In her designer dress, she looked as elegant as ever. Her face gave nothing away. If the deaths of Kingsley Melton and Logan Prentice preyed on her conscience, Hannah saw no sign of it. There was no likelihood of proving that she'd stage-managed the double tragedy at Strandbeck Manor.

"You must understand the turmoil Ramona was in. Her life was in pieces."

Hannah nodded. Tory insisted on speaking about Ramona as if she were a completely different person. Someone who was gone forever. A coping mechanism, or something more profound? She couldn't guess the answer.

"Ramona was never close to her mother," Tory said, "but watching her eaten away by cancer until there was almost nothing left was appalling. Her beloved grandmother's mind disintegrated, making her an utterly different person. Her whole life was going wrong. She'd always dreamed of escape. Not from the Lakes so much as from her dreary existence. When Gerry Lace refused to take no for an answer, and forced himself on her in that grubby storeroom, it was the last straw. Life no longer seemed worth living. But she wasn't weak, like Lace; she would never abandon hope."

There was a long pause. "And so?" Hannah prompted.

"And so the vague idea she'd cherished for years needed to become a reality. She must get away, start all over again, somewhere different."

"I understand. However, to do what she did..."

"It seemed like the only way. So that nobody would go after her. Not Thakor, not Lace, not...well, you get the picture. People had to believe she was dead."

"But to frame Lace for a murder he didn't commit..."

Tory's eyes were glazed, her mind apparently far away. "I don't expect Nadine Bosman was his first victim, and I'm absolutely certain Ramona wouldn't have been the last. His outbursts of rage were terrible. His wife was almost as bad, because she knew what he was like, and didn't care, as long as he stayed with her. The next woman he attacked would probably have wound up dead. But Ramona knew that if she complained to the police, she'd be made to feel that she was the criminal. She had to die, there was no choice."

Another silence.

"An idea came to her. For once, she could do something worthwhile. In dying, she could save other women from suffering at Lace's hands." Tory gave a rueful smile. "Ramona wasn't given to altruism. Just like me. It took many years for me to choose to do something selfless, to help someone else survive. That didn't end well either, did it?"

"We can talk about the deaths at Strandbeck Manor shortly," Hannah said. "See if you can help us to understand exactly what happened there on the day you came to see us."

"An inexplicable and dreadful mystery," Tory said calmly. "As for Ramona Smith, she has no grave. No headstone, no epitaph. Trust me, though, she is dead."

"Is that so?"

"Oh, yes. I am someone else entirely. And trust me on this as well. Whatever you and your colleagues do, Chief Inspector, one thing is certain. I will survive."

AUTHOR'S NOTE

As in previous Lake District Mysteries, I've made a few changes to Cumbrian topography to avoid confusion between the real world and its fictional counterpart. Strandbeck and the Crooked Shore don't exist, and the characters, events, organisations, and businesses which play a part in the story are fictitious. As regards Cumbria Constabulary, my version of that body and the people who work for it, portrays an imaginary equivalent of the real force; Hannah and her colleagues do not represent real life people in comparable roles. Similarly, although I read about a number of actual cases while planning the book and thinking about the psychological makeup of characters such as Logan Prentice, the crimes in this story are not intended as fictionalisations of real life murders.

When researching the story, I was helped by a number of people, including fellow novelist Zosia Wand, who took me on a tour of Hoad Hill and the surrounding area, while Helen May, David Whiteley, and family kindly shared their local knowledge with me. Michael Fowler, a crime novelist and former police officer, made helpful suggestions about the police investigation in the story. The inspiration for Strandbeck Manor and its setting came from a trip to North Wales and a tour of a similar estate conducted by Nora Bartley, from whom I also gained information about the practical effects of a sudden cardiac arrest. Merseyside Police and Crime Commissioner Jane Kennedy gave me invaluable insight into the nature of the role of PCC. In writing about suicide, I tried to keep in mind guidelines from the Society of Authors and the Samaritans. As always, I'm grateful to all those who have made editorial comments on the manuscript, my agent, and my publishers.

A special thank you to my readers. A great deal has happened in my writing career since I wrote the last Lake District Mystery, *The Dungeon House*, but amid all the excitement surrounding my other projects, I have been heartened by reaction from people who enjoy this series. The number of times people attending my events have asked when the eighth Lake District book is coming out, and the volume of emails I've received from all over the world asking what is next for Hannah and Daniel, indicates an interest in and an enthusiasm for the stories that is very precious. I'm indebted to everyone who has encouraged me to return to the Lakes, and I hope that this latest instalment keeps them wanting more.

Martin Edwards
www.martinedwardsbooks.com

If you've enjoyed *The Girl They All Forgot*,
read on for an excerpt from

the second book in another great series by
award-winning author Martin Edwards
available from

Epilogue

The man was dying. He knew it, and so did Rachel Savernake.

"You've discovered the truth, haven't you?" His voice was scratchy.

"Yes."

His hands trembled. "It was the perfect crime."

"Is there such a thing?" she asked.

He sighed, a long, low wheeze of surrender. "We thought so."

"Time is short." Leaning closer, she felt his sour breath on her cheeks. "Tell me what happened at Mortmain Hall."

Chapter 1

The ghost climbed out of a hackney carriage.

His head twitched from side to side as he checked to see if anyone was following him. Rachel Savernake was sure he'd failed to spot her. She stood deep in the shadows, on the opposite side of Westminster Bridge Road. A veil masked her face. Like the phantom, she was dressed in black from head to toe. During the half hour she'd waited for him to arrive, not one passer-by had given her a second glance. Women in mourning were a familiar sight outside the private station of the London Necropolis Company. This was the terminus for the funeral train.

With exaggerated care, the ghost pulled down the brim of his felt hat. During his years away, he'd grown a bushy moustache and beard. His left hand clutched a battered suitcase. As he limped towards the tall station building, Rachel stifled a groan.

The ghost's lameness gave him away. Gilbert Payne was still an amateur in deception.

Dodging between a double-decker bus and an ancient hearse, Rachel crossed to the station entrance. A curving road ran beneath a granite archway, affording access to the mortuary chambers. The building was fronted with red brick and warm terracotta; the white-glazed walls of the underpass were decorated with bay trees and palms. Behind the facade lurked a spindly pseudo-chimney which vented air to the morgues. Here coffined corpses became railway freight.

Ignoring the electric lift, she took long, athletic strides up the wrought-iron staircase. At the top she found herself beneath the glass roof of the first-class platform. The open doorway to the *chapelle ardente* revealed an oak catafalque, beige Wilton carpet, and walls treated in green and bronze. She considered the private waiting rooms. The first door bore a card with a name in neat script: *Mrs Cecilia Payne deceased*. It stood ajar, and Rachel glimpsed chairs upholstered in morocco, light oak panelling, and a shining parquet floor. Watercolour landscapes adorned the wall, as if this was a merchant's villa in Richmond. A tang of polish sharpened the air.

The ghost was nowhere to be seen.

A screen divided the platform. Behind it was the circulating area for third-class passengers. They had their own station entrance, so that those who paid for the privilege of a first-class funeral need not travel cheek-by-jowl with the grieving poor. The Necropolis Company prided itself on sensitivity to the feelings of the bereaved.

The ticket collector gave a discreet cough. He'd sprung out of his office like a bewhiskered jack-in-the-box. She thrust a small oblong of white card into his nicotine-stained hand.

"The express is waiting, ma'am." So it was, resplendent in olive-green livery, and belching steam, impatient as a starving dragon. "I'm afraid the hearse vans are already loaded."

While preparing for her journey, Rachel had learned that parties of first-class passengers were permitted to watch the coffin containing their loved one being loaded onto the funeral train. She marvelled at the entrepreneurs' ingenuity. They had transformed a moment of misery into a bonus for the privileged few.

"My fault for being late." She gave a nod of dismissal. "Thank you."

On the door of the nearest first-class compartment, a hand-written card matched the one outside the waiting room. A shadow was visible through the window. The ghost had taken his seat. Now he was trapped, as surely as if he'd locked himself in purgatory.

The air thickened with smoke and the smell of burning coal. The only person on the platform was a stout porter, shepherding an old lady into a third-class compartment at the end of the train. He spotted Rachel and broke into an unwise trot, puffing and grunting like an ancient locomotive destined for the breaker's yard.

"Just made it in time, ma'am," he wheezed. "We depart at eleven forty, sharp. Which party would you belong to?"

"The late Mrs Payne's." She thrust into his grimy paw a tip so extravagant that it risked making his heart stop. Her raised hand stifled his gasp of gratitude. "May I ask how many of our group are making the journey?"

He was sweating like a stoker. Rachel doubted his discomfiture was solely due to unaccustomed exercise. "I...well, ma'am, there seems to have been some confusion."

"Really?" She waited, confident that two gold sovereigns trumped any bribe paid to secure his silence.

"We expected six, ma'am, but only three gentlemen turned up. The pair who came early insisted they wouldn't travel in the compartment reserved for the...um, nearest and dearest. Most irregular. That's why the Company asks for bookings in advance. We don't want any mix-ups to spoil such a solemn occasion. Luckily, we only have one first-class funeral today."

A loyal servant, he didn't mention that the slump in trade and rising unemployment had meant business was much less brisk in the aftermath of the Wall Street Crash.

"You managed to accommodate those two gentlemen elsewhere?"

A knobbly thumb jerked towards the compartment beyond the one allocated for mourners of the late Mrs Payne. "Right next door."

"Can you tell me anything about them?"

The porter mopped his brow. "I'm sorry, ma'am. We really need to…"

"Please forgive me. I can't explain why this is so important to me," she said, leaning closer so that he could inhale her perfume. "Personal reasons. You do understand?"

He peered through her veil. Something in her expression made him quail.

"Well, I'm… I'm sure you have good cause to ask. Quarrels happen in the best families, don't they? One chap's a cockney, dressed as a vicar. Surprised me, that did. I thought…"

"He didn't seem quite like an ordinary vicar?" Rachel suggested.

"Funny thing," the porter said. "I never saw a reverend gentleman with a tattoo on his hand in all my days. Takes all sorts, I suppose, but…"

"And his companion?"

The porter frowned. "Big fellow. Beefy. Mitts like coal shovels."

"Intimidating?"

"I really can't say any more, ma'am." He took another look at Rachel, and breathed out noisily. "Let's just say they tried to look posh, but forgot to shine their shoes. Funerals are funny; people aren't their normal selves. Why say they didn't want to disturb the rest of the party, when it turns out there's only one…?"

"Perhaps they just wanted to be considerate."

He flinched at her sarcasm. "Now, really, ma'am, please, I must ask you to board. We can't delay…"

"Of course not." Her smile lacked humour. "Thank you so much for your assistance."

He lumbered towards the compartment bearing the name of the late Mrs Payne, and opened the door. Ignoring his helping hand, Rachel jumped inside.

The compartment smelled of leather and tobacco. Seated at the far end, suitcase by his side, the ghost was gazing out of the window, lost in thought. One month short of his fortieth birthday, he seemed ten years older. Exile in northwest Africa's international zone had browned his cheeks and fattened his frame, but she doubted it was the sybaritic life that had aged him. The real cause was the never-ending dread of a knife thrust between his shoulder blades.

The porter slammed the door shut, knocking the ghost out of his reverie. Perched on the edge of the seat, Rachel gave a nod of greeting.

"Good morning," she said.

The ghost gave an anxious grunt. Her casual friendliness was all the more disturbing because her presence in the compartment was inexplicable. When he spoke, his voice trembled.

"Good…good morning."

"How pleasant to meet you," she said, "albeit in such sad circumstances."

A whistle sounded, and with a disconcerting jolt, the train began its journey to the cemetery. The ghost shuddered. Rachel pictured the cogwheels of his brain spinning. *Who was she? What, if anything, should he say?*

"My name," he said, "is—"

"You don't need to introduce yourself," Rachel said. "You're not really a ghost. You're Gilbert Payne, the missing publisher. Welcome back from the dead."

As the train rumbled down the track, the man rocked back and forth on his seat. The beard and moustache were fig leaves for naked vulnerability. His eyelids flickered under her scrutiny. She guessed his despair, but she hadn't followed him in order to sympathise. Long before his disappearance, he'd been notorious for recklessness. People found it easy to believe that it had cost him his life. He gulped, and she wondered if he was about to be sick.

"You…you are mistaken, madam," he muttered. "My name is Bertram Jones."

Rachel lifted her veil. His bloodshot eyes widened as he took in her youth, her beauty, and the chill of her smile.

"Not Bertram Jones, the old drinking chum of Gilbert Payne, who has lived in Tangier these past four years?"

"That's right!" He was as hapless as a man tumbling into a ravine, clutching at stubs of vegetation in the hope of salvation. "It's true…there is a…vague likeness between the two of us. A similarity in the cheekbones, perhaps. Poor Gilbert joked about it more than once before…"

"Before he feigned death by drowning, fled from London, and sailed under cover of darkness for the Continent?" Rachel asked. "Before he made his way in search of the esoteric delights of Tangier?"

The ghost slumped back in his seat, as if she'd thrust a hatpin into his heart.

"Long before he heard the tragic news of the death of the mother he'd adored?" She was relentless. "The woman who worshipped him, whose heart finally gave way without her knowing that her only child was still alive?"

"It's a lie, a cruel lie!" He stared at her. "In God's name, who are you?"

The train was picking up speed. Rachel was in no hurry. They were not at risk of being disturbed. The funeral express made no stops along the way.

"My name doesn't matter."

"What…" His voice was hoarse and barely audible. "What do you want with me?"

She pursed her lips. "I'm offering to save you from being murdered."

ABOUT THE AUTHOR

Martin Edwards received the CWA Diamond Dagger, the highest honour in UK crime writing, in 2020. He has been described by Otto Penzler as "the best living practitioner of the classic detective story" and by the British Library as "the leading expert on classic crime." He is the author of twenty-one novels, including *Gallows Court* and *Mortmain Hall*. He also conceived and edited *Howdunit*, an award-winning masterclass in crime writing by members of the legendary Detection Club, ranging from Agatha Christie to Ann Cleeves. He has received the Edgar, Agatha, and Poirot Awards, two H.R.F. Keating Awards, two Macavity Awards, the CWA Margery Allingham Short Story Prize, the CWA Short Story Dagger, and the CWA Dagger in the Library. He has been nominated for CWA Gold Daggers three times and once for the Historical Dagger; he has also been short-listed for the Theakston's Prize for Best Crime Novel of the Year for *The Coffin Trail*. As consultant to the British

Library's Crime Classics series (published by Poisoned Pen Press in the U.S.), archivist for the CWA and Detection Club, and well-known blogger, he has been responsible for the rediscovery of many long-forgotten Golden Age authors and novels. A former chair of the CWA, he has been president of the Detection Club since 2015. His novels include the Harry Devlin series (the first of which, *All the Lonely People*, was nominated for the CWA John Creasey Memorial Dagger) and the Lake District Mysteries. He has published nine nonfiction books and seventy short stories and edited more than forty anthologies of crime writing, which have yielded many award-winning stories.